GLACIER WORLD

An Earl Armstrong Novel
by
Fredrick Cooper

ISBN: 978-0988198388

Cover photography by Ron Niebrugge, Niebrugge Images, LLC, Seward, Alaska

This book is available in both print and eBook versions from most online retailers.

Printed in the United States of America

In Memory of:
Charles "Charlie" Nelson, Sr.
(Alaskan Native)
Craig, Alaska

AUTHOR'S NOTE

For readers who are familiar with the present-day areas of Icy Strait and Chatham Strait, including the Native community of Hoonah, and my own people, the Shoalwater Bay Tribe, you will note that I have taken literary license with places and names. As a Native American author, I always try to maintain my sincere respect for all Native people and their culture.

The setting for this novel resulted from my many years of exploring and fishing in Southeast Alaska and growing up in Ketchikan. I loved to hear the legends and stories told by my uncle, Charlie Nelson, from Craig, who was an avid outdoorsman and commercial fisherman. He taught me about Native culture and a deep respect for the environment that ultimately impacted my career path.

I owe my gratitude to my steadfast editors, Kyra Hearn and Julia Smit, for their many reviews and for keeping me focused my characters and storytelling. My thanks also to Gary Corbin and Leigh Goodison for their well appreciated critiques of this manuscript.

CHAPTER 1

Southeast Alaska

Eddie Jackson had trained himself to be methodical and carefully plan his work, like a skilled surgeon, scrubbed and ready to commence a surgical procedure he had performed a hundred times. After all, they had something in common. They both used very sharp implements in their professions. Neatly laid out beside Eddie on a soft, well-tanned piece of deer hide were his tools—bone-handled carving knives in a multitude of shapes and sizes, chisels, an adze, and a small stone hammer. He had lovingly crafted each of these tools himself. While yet inanimate and plain, his subject, a small block of cedar lumber which lay before him, would soon come to life. Or as any apprentice carver soon learned, its spirit would be revealed as his adze, chisels and knives did their work. Apprentice carvers were also taught to respect what they were about to create. Preparation involved much more than simply sketching out a design. It started with purification of the person's body by spending several hours in a sweat lodge and smudging with the smoke of a white sage stick.

To the side of his carving bench, a similar block of wood now revealed six salmon leaping head to tail in a never ending circle. Each salmon seemed as alive as its relatives in the rushing waters of the streams that entered the bay nearby. He was as proud of that finished carving as a metallurgist would be that had designed a coat of arms for a Scottish clan or a stone mason whose job it was to complete an alter depicting the Virgin Mary. Finishing the carving also marked a special day in the life of Eddie Jackson. It was his 250th day of sobriety. Leaving his tribe's small reservation on the coast of Washington to come to Alaska and train under a master carver had been the most important decision in his life. Jobs were few in his home community and he had attempted various dead end jobs after being discharged from the Marines only to be let go for being drunk and failing to report to work. With no brothers or sisters, he had to care for his terminally ill mother and, because of his love for cheap whiskey, he failed at that task as well.

The native community of Hoonah, Alaska was his new home, at least that is, until he finished his apprenticeship. Learning the art of carving Native American crafts such as canoes, totems and ceremonial masks suited him. It filled the void in his mind left over from too many years fighting in Iraq. He found contentment as he spent long hours carving away wood to produce his next project. Eddie was a quiet person, a quick learner and soon became quite skilled in his new occupation. Although he was a member of a different tribe, he saw that his culture was similar to the Tlingit's that resided in Hoonah. He had become accepted, if not out of respect for his work, then for his naturally friendly smile.

His work had been noticed by others as well. A construction supervisor on a large project not far from Hoonah had showed up one day looking for a carver who could handle some work at their project site. It was a chance to earn some good money and practice his new profession. So he volunteered for the project. Three days a week, the construction company would send a boat to pick him up for the ten mile trip to the project site. Some residents of Hoonah resented the fact that he had gotten the job because most of the project's employees were Asian and too few local able-bodied men had been hired. He was often quizzed about what was happening at the construction site, usually in the cafe where he had his breakfast. He was unable to tell them because that was one of the conditions of his hire—not to talk about his work. His supervisor said public information about the project was tightly controlled. There was also lots of site security.

As much as Eddie Jackson loved the special assignment and good pay, the security at the project bothered him. It was like he was being watched constantly. He was restricted to his own work area and never got an opportunity to see any other part of the site. Everything needed for the construction arrived by ship or barge. There were no roads. A small air strip was only used to fly in and out the top brass. Most of the workers lived in dormitories, called a man camp, right at the construction site. The warehouses used to store newly arrived equipment were strictly off-limits, except for the one time his supervisor had a small job for him in one of them. The blocks of cedar wood on his carving bench were the result of that special assignment. He had been assigned to cut them from the ends of large timbers which he assumed were being used in the construction. Once the blocks were removed, he was instructed to place them in a dumpster which was emptied daily at a place where construction debris was burned. What Eddie found odd was why he had to cut off the ends of the timbers in the first place. Each end bore a brand of the supplier, a mill that Eddie actually knew about. It belonged to the Shoalwater Corporation, a tribally owned company not far from Eddie's own reservation. One of Eddie's buddies, Leon Pence, had told him about the guy who managed the company. His name was Earl Armstrong, a forester and member of the Shoalwater Indian Tribe, and mighty proud of his high quality timber products. Eddie felt it was a shame to waste chunks of beautiful straight grain and expensive cedar wood. So when the security people were not watching him, he placed a few of pieces in his backpack to take back to Hoonah. No one kept count of the pieces that were supposed to be destroyed so he felt they would not be missed. Then one day when Eddie was being ferried home, one of the security men had picked up his backpack to hand it to him as he climbed over the rail onto the dock. The man felt how heavy the pack was and took a peek inside. He stared at Eddie with a questioning look in his eyes. When Eddie didn't say anything, the man shrugged his shoulders and didn't ask.

The next time he reported to the construction site he was escorted to his earlier job rather than finish the work of cutting the ends off the Shoalwater Corporation timbers. Later that morning he sensed he was being watched again. A person he hadn't seen before stood several hundred feet away talking to a security guard. The man smoked a cigar and seemed to be staring at him.

Eddie Jackson picked up one of his chisels and began to carve. But the feeling of peace and contentment that usually accompanied working with wood didn't come. Perhaps he shouldn't have taken the blocks of cedar. And who was the man who had become interested in him?

CHAPTER 2

Olympic National Park, Washington

In the stillness of the early morning hours, something woke Earl Armstrong. Maybe it was the discomfort of the hard surface beneath his body and having to roll over once more. Or maybe it was the stiffness in his legs and the hint of a cramp creeping up his left calf. He took few seconds to move his legs and recall where he was. Then remembering their tent was pitched on the eastern slope of Mount Olympus, Earl groaned and rolled on his side. A noise had disturbed his light sleep—from somewhere close by. He raised a hand and touched the inside of the nylon tent. It wasn't shaking in a gale and hadn't blown down—a good sign. Earl pushed the top of his down-filled sleeping bag away while reaching down to rub his sore calf. He heard the sound again—a scratching on the bare rock outside the tent. His first thought was a predator close by. A gentle brush of crisp early morning air on his face wiped away the last vestiges of sleep and put his body on alert. The tent fly was open. Turning his head, he noticed that his son Bernie was awake and watching something through the opening. There was more scratching. Peering through the partially open tent fly Earl could see the slick surface of Camp Pan glistening under the light of a waning moon. The starry sky was yielding to the approaching dawn.

Somewhere to his left would be the bundled form of Leon Pence sleeping on the open ground. Leon had guided them to this lonely yet breathtaking location on the slopes of one of the most remote mountain ranges in North America.

Earl heard Bernie exhale as something moved just a few feet from them. He caught a brief glimpse too. A small, dark form scurried from under a ledge and perched on a boulder just a few feet away—one of the bold little marmots that had entertained them while they ate their dinner the evening before.

Earl rolled onto his stomach and adjusted the tent flap to share the opening with Bernie. A sliver of light was beginning to appear along the eastern horizon. Earl and Bernie lay side by side watching the dawn chase away the chilly dark of the night. Minute by minute the ridgeline of the Olympic Mountains became silhouetted like a gigantic shadow box stretching to the ends of the earth. The marmot stood motionless on his rock, also watching the band of light silently overtake the blackness with purple, then red and orange tinges of the dawn.

"It's gorgeous beyond belief isn't it, Son?"

"Yeah. Thanks for bringing me," replied Bernie.

"Scenes like this make it well worth the challenge and a few sore muscles." Earl rubbed his calf muscles more intently. "And you've done pretty well for your first backcountry trek. I've been watching you. Leon thinks so too. He was hesitant when I said I wanted to bring you. Said it is a dangerous trek. One careless step and one of us could be hurt or killed."

"Leon knows his stuff. He wouldn't let anything happen to us."

"Well, to a degree. We do what he says and pay attention to our safety equipment. But things happen. Like the ocean—mountains are unforgiving."

Earl had convinced Leon Pence to guide them on a seven-day trek in Olympic National Park. Leon Pence was a full-blood Indian and a member of the coastal Quileute Tribe. The Olympics were part of Leon's ancestral lands and he was very familiar with its wilderness trails. A few years younger than Earl, Leon kept his body at a high level of fitness. Tall for a Native American, he had broad shoulders and well-muscled arms and legs. He ran three to five miles every day. Leon wore his hair in a ponytail tied with a piece of rawhide and practiced many of the traditional ways including frequent use of a sweat lodge.

Leon had become a good friend to Earl after saving the lives of his entire family several years ago. They had been kidnapped on the Washington coast by a madman seeking a valuable Tlingit Indian artifact that was hidden in a location that only Earl had known about. It had taken a long time for the trauma of that incident to dissipate, and Leon had been there to help.

Earl Armstrong's ancestry was also Native American on his mother's side. His mother was a Lower Chehalis Band descendent. He had met Sally while attending the University of Washington's school of forestry. Sally had been finishing her doctorate degree in medical science. Earl and Sally truly loved the outdoors, and the Washington coast offered endless opportunities for hiking, camping, and kayaking.

Bernie, their second child, had recently celebrated his fifteenth birthday. Earl told him the backpacking trip in the Olympics was a birthday present, but as much as Bernie enjoyed the trek, he hadn't been fooled. He knew his dad really wanted to make this trip for himself. Earl was always trying to prove he could do challenging things such as whitewater and sea kayaking or long, arduous hikes. It was his Indian blood—he told everyone with a grin. But his own family never believed him. Earl simply thrived on adventure. So when he got the bug to set off on another quest, Bernie and the rest of the family knew that there would never be a dull moment. Earl also had a knack for finding trouble and on more than one occasion it started with finding a dead body. From that aspect, this trip had been uneventful—they had not even stumbled across a dead animal. It was the hike itself that presented the physical challenges and real danger.

Earl had proposed to Leon a difficult hike, and the Olympic National Park offered several options—all with incredible scenery. The challenge to their climbing skills as alpine novices was exhilarating, too. Each morning Leon reviewed what lay ahead while they sipped a cup of camp coffee or instant hot chocolate. Each evening they chatted about their day's adventures while pitching their tent among patches of snow on slate-grey rock and watching the mountain ridges become awash in purple and red hues from the setting sun.

After each evening's meal, Leon told stories of the early mountain men of the Olympics. Bernie was impressed with the adventures of Herb Crisler, an adventurer and wildlife photographer, who the *Seattle Times* had challenged back in the 1930s to survive in the Olympic wilderness for thirty days with just what he carried on his back. Crisler succeeded, but only by catching and eating marmots and what berries he could find.

Earl chose the same difficult route as Crisler—the Bailey Range Traverse.

The hardest part of the Baily Range was behind them and Leon figured they would reach the overlook for the Blue Glacier sometime today. From there the Hoh River Trail was an easy downward hike through one of the most beautiful rainforests in the Pacific Northwest. In a few days, all this would be just a memory of what had been a terrific birthday gift for Bernie.

Earl's and Bernie's faces were bathed in last orange twilight before the sunrise when Bernie finally broke the magic of the moment.

"I like Leon. He's shown us some beautiful country and taught me a lot about trekking in a wilderness. You sure have to carry the right equipment and know how to use it. Otherwise a person can be in real trouble."

"Yup, you sure can. But being away from others has its rewards too, like now—watching this sunrise with Mr. Marmot. Not many people get to witness what we are seeing. It's good for one's sanity too, which is something you'll get to appreciate as you get older. Some jobs can be pretty stressful."

"I'm going to be my own boss. Maybe invent things that help other people, like robotics. I read a magazine article about engineers inventing a driverless car. Then there are robotic submarines and robots used in manufacturing. I could...."

"Okay. I get the message. You're getting turned on to robots."

"Dad, I am already. I belong to the school robotics club."

"You do?"

"Yeah, we're finishing building a robotics submarine. There's a competition we can enter with it."

"Ah, that's good, so you'll learn that all jobs, even if on your own, have deadlines. And deadlines to finish a task can be stressful."

"Is that why you wanted us to go camping in such a remote location—to get away?"

"Just worked out that way," Earl replied. "A few weeks before our trip, the Tribal Council informed me they needed a major timber sale in order to begin exporting lumber to Japan which would generate more profit. It's something I've never done before so it was stressful. It got shipped and it's now out of my hands. But you know, I haven't thought about my work in six days and I'm not going to until we are home. Like Mr. Marmot out there sitting on his rock, we need to enjoy these moments and stop worrying about the things that can make our lives complex."

Earl and Bernie's shared moment was interrupted by their tent shaking and Leon's deep, gravelly voice. "Hey you two. Quit jabbering and roll out of those bags. Got a long day ahead of us."

***

By midmorning, the three climbers were well into the seventh day of their trek. The Bailey Range Traverse was not a highly technical route but was considered to be physically demanding. Nor was the route considered a well-defined trail, for it was not much more than a mountain goat path connecting a series of major peaks—all over seven thousand feet.

The climbers had spent most of the first six days of their trip scrambling over steep rocky slopes rather than trekking across alpine meadows—from the terrifying start on the rocky spine of the Cat Walk with drops hundreds of feet on both sides of the narrow trail, to the numerous steep side slopes. One slip on the gravel could send a hiker carrying a forty-pound pack tumbling, resulting in a broken arm or leg or even death. The three climbed through broad snowfields so encrusted with ice they had to use their ice axes and wear their crampons. And then there was Crisler's Ladder, a thirty-foot vertical cliff climb using roots and clefts in the rocks for handholds.

The sun had begun its own steady climb over the crest of Hurricane Ridge into a cloudless sky, warming the three climbers. They had trekked across yet another snowfield and were approaching the Hoh Glacier.

They traveled in single file with the boy's father normally in the last position. Leon, who had made the trek several times before, usually took the lead. As a safety precaution for the young boy, they roped themselves together whenever traversing a difficult area. One lay just ahead of them—the ascent to Blizzard Pass from under the Hoh Glacier. Below the glacier was another steep side slope to cross, just above a cliff that dropped into a basin with a blue-green lake. With their course of travel obvious, Earl took the lead position for a change. He was not quite a neophyte to leading difficult hikes. One was the Third Beach Trail along the Pacific Ocean beaches. But rock scrambling and side slope areas had taken a toll on his leg muscles.

When Earl and Leon were deciding on their route, Earl had agreed to the longer route for trekking the Bailey. They could have dropped down into the Elwha Valley or the Queets River drainage to shorten their trip, but the weather for early October had remained sunny and dry, and this might be his only opportunity to experience it. They could have included a climb to the top of Mount Olympus, considered a rite of passage for beginning climbers, but Mount Olympus was not on Earl's bucket list. He and Leon had selected a route to skirt around the flanks of the group of peaks that made up this famous feature of the Pacific Northwest. Blizzard Pass, which he could now see up ahead, would be their last challenge. It was the highest point of the trek before their final descent.

Wildlife viewing was one of the pleasures of wilderness backpacking in the Olympics. On their third day, while hiking from Mount Carrie to Stephen Peak, they had seen a herd of mountain goats from a distance. The shaggy white beasts had been grazing in a meadow and ran up a near vertical ridge at the sound of their approach. A young coyote attempted to steal Bernie's breakfast one morning. A black bear had ambled close to their camp one evening before being startled by their yells. Bears were not a serious problem in the Olympics because of the rigid rules for all backcountry hikers to use bear-proof containers for their food. Mountain goats were another story. They craved the salt residue left behind by hikers urinating along the trails and were known to become aggressive and charge unwary hikers.

Up ahead of Bernie, Earl stopped to take in the beauty of the azure lake and a stand of timber in the valley hundreds of feet below them. One of the three peaks of Mount Olympus rose gracefully above it with its snowfields glistening against a deep blue sky. The ground around them was a stark contrast of barren hard rock and gravel scree with pockets of wildflowers adding splashes of vivid color. Below the trail, the steep slope gave way to a nearly sheer cliff that dropped hundreds of feet into the valley. Earl was attempting to remove a small camera from his shirt pocket when he heard a frantic yell behind him.

"Dad!" Bernie screamed. "Watch out! There's a mountain goat coming your way."

Earl looked first at Bernie then turned to look up the trail when he heard the sound of rolling rocks. A huge, hairy white object with two short horns was hurtling towards him. Before Earl could dive out of the way, it butted him in the stomach, lifting him off his feet. Earl hit the ground on his side, sliding off the trail. He grabbed for rocks and tufts of vegetation, trying to stop his slide toward the precipice. The rope tied to Bernie raked across the slope like a slow-motion pendulum. Loose scree pummeled his body and face as he grabbed for the rope. His downward momentum stopped with a jerk but he continued to slip towards the precipice.

With a jerk, Earl looked above him trying to see what happened to Bernie. On the trail above him, he saw Bernie and Leon lying on the ground. Somehow they had avoided the charging goat. He heard Leon yell.

"Don't get up. Roll onto your back. Plant your feet on the rocks at the edge of the trail."

The rope jerked again and Earl slipped several more inches. He pumped up and down with his legs trying to find a foothold to stop his slide only to slip further while scraping his elbows and knees on the rock.

Looking up, he could see Leon scramble to reach over Bernie and grab the section of rope tied to him. Bernie was flat on his back. Leon wrapped the rope around his right arm, taking the strain with gloved hands. His feet slid towards the edge of the trail as he took the full weight of Earl and his forty-pound pack.

"Bernie," Leon shouted. "Get my ice axe and jam it into the rocks as hard as you can."

With the strain from the rope gone, Bernie rolled onto his stomach. He pulled the tool out of the loops on Leon's pack. Earl heard the thuds as the ice axe pounded into a crack in the rocks.

"Okay, Earl. Now get on your feet and use the rope to climb. I'll do a slow belay on this end."

Leon's arms had to be burning from the tightened rope, but Earl saw he was no longer sliding. He struggled to get his legs turned and then pushed himself upright. Once on his feet, he glanced over his shoulder. The edge of the cliff where the slope fell away looked like an abyss into space. He gulped, averted his eyes, and climbed upward towards Leon, Bernie, and the edge of the trail. Beads of sweat formed on Earl's forehead and streamed down his cheeks mixed with the dirt and blood from abrasions on his face. He grunted and struggled upwards step by step. When Earl was just a few feet away, he heard Leon give another command. "He's just below us, Bernie. Reach over and grab the top of his pack. We'll lift together."

Earl made a slight grin when he saw Bernie's face. He was on his belly and reaching down to grab the strap on the top his backpack. Together, Leon and Bernie pulled him back onto the trail. Leon fell back against the uphill slope, unwinding the rope from his reddening arm. There were signs of pain in his eyes, but neither Earl nor Bernie took notice. They were gripping each other tightly. Leon rolled next to them and the three men remained motionless for several minutes. Finally, Earl struggled into a sitting position and peered down at the edge of the cliff. He was shaking.

"You know, I didn't have time to be scared. I am now. I should have kept my eyes on the trail. That was my responsibility as the lead person. I put all of us in danger."

"That's why we rope up," Leon replied. "There's a chance to survive."

"Well, next time we encounter a mountain goat the size of a Mack Truck or a grizzly bear, I want you in the lead, Leon. That was too much excitement for me."

"I'd rather be face-to-face with an insurgent carrying an AK-47 than meet a grizzly bear on this narrow trail." Leon said. He found his water bottle, took a swallow and then dampened his handkerchief.

"Are there grizzlies in the Olympics?" Bernie asked.

"Nope, just little black fellas," Leon grimaced as he placed the handkerchief over the rope burns on his arm.

"Don't know why I said grizzly," Earl said. "If we were in the Rocky Mountains or Alaska, they'd be a threat. There are some big brown bear in Alaska. Even Leon would have a real challenge with one of them."

"You are a funny guy. Yeah, that would be quite a ruckus."

The three laughed again.

"In any event," Earl said. "I'll be more than happy to let Leon lead us out of here. It's been a great trip until now and our last day can still be enjoyable.

But I've had enough of this view and am looking forward to the rainforest with some tall trees and flat ground on all sides of me. How about you, Bernie?"

"I'm glad you're safe, Dad. I was really scared when you were pushed off the trail. I've learned an important lesson about wilderness survival—you have to watch out for each other. It was just a little bit more than I expected."

"Well, this was one lesson I wasn't expecting to offer," Earl shuddered a bit as he glanced over the cliff.

For the rest of the day, until the trio was safely in the Hoh River Valley, Earl's senses were wired to every rolling rock and the ever changing spirit winds of Mount Olympus. Winds that were already setting something sinister in motion and more chilling that Earl could imagine.

CHAPTER 3

Icy Strait, Alaska

He had done it hundreds of times—on calm days when the water surface of Icy Strait was like a mirror reflecting the snow-capped peaks of the Chilkat Range or in fog so thick it streamed from his face and soaked the front of his jacket. Then there were unpleasant days, like today, when the windblown salt spray made his eyes sting and the chop was so bad his teeth hurt with every slam of his boat into an oncoming wave.

Icy Strait was the gateway to Glacier Bay National Park and ran east-west some thirty miles. Six miles directly across from Glacier Bay was the Tlingit village of Hoonah, where Erasmus Hunt had started his crossing, home of the Hunt family for five generations. He was one of the Hunt brothers, and for some damn reason his mother had named him Erasmus, thankfully shortened to Raz by the residents of the village. He and his younger brother, Pete, fished during the short summer season and ran trap lines in the winter. Their father, uncles, and grandfathers had done the same before them. Trapping mink, martins, and foxes provided a nice income during the months when they could not find other work. If a man didn't fish, he worked at the restored cannery that the village corporation operated as a tourist attraction, or whatever he could find in pick-up work—boat or fishing net repair, or possibly logging, if he were lucky enough to get hired on. But these were seasonal jobs, and once the cruise ships left and the fishing season was over, there were too few jobs remaining to go around, just some government positions.

With a lousy fishing season now over, Raz Hunt desperately needed money. He decided to start trapping a bit early, well before the first snow. He had cleaned up and boiled his traps, and two sacks of them sat tucked into the bow of his small aluminum skiff.

The monotonous pounding of the skiff during the crossing let Raz ponder his conversation with his brother earlier that morning. Raz had finished readying the skiff and had walked up to the café to meet Pete. Inside, his brother sat drinking coffee dressed in his going-to-town clothes.

"Hey, Raz!" Pete had said as he raised his coffee cup when his older brother entered.

Raz rubbed his rough, scarred hands together to warm them while he walked over to the table. He threw his well-worn jacket over a chair and sat down without so much as a good morning, then poured a cup of coffee for himself from a carafe already on the table. Raz had a habit of seldom shaving, and his long

hair protruded in all directions from under a dirty
Mariners baseball cap. Out of habit he rubbed his left
temple with his fingers, tracing the line of a scar from
an old accident. The scar pulling up the corner of his
left eyelid caused a perpetual menacing look.

"What's eating you this morning?" Pete had
asked.

"You see that article in the *Juneau Empire* on
that damn Glacier World?" Raz had answered. "Word
is they're tightening up the access to the inlet by
adding more security patrols. We're not supposed to
be doing no trapping or nothing around that place.
Damn, where are our sovereign rights these days?"

"The state legislature passed a law giving them
full, private access. I guess they can enforce their
rights,"

Nearly the opposite in appearance from his
older brother, as well as most of the other Hoonah
men, Pete kept his black hair short, and due to the
insistence of his wife, shaved daily. Despite a slightly
misshaped nose from a fight with Raz, he had a
handsome face with a strong chin, high cheekbones
and a pleasant smile.

His brother had a few inches on him as well
as a few pounds. Raz thought he might still be able to
take him in a fight but wasn't sure. He drank too
much.

"I don't give a hoot!" Raz had stammered.
"We got rights too, and we were here first. That's our
homelands where we got hunting, fishing, and

trapping rights." Raz stirred a couple of packs of sugar into his cup of coffee. He let his eyes wander over his brother from head to foot, taking in the long sleeve dress shirt and pressed grey slacks Pete was wearing. "You're not dressed for a day in the woods. This your way of showing me you're chickening out? You afraid one of those pretty blue patrol boats will run us over and sink our skiff or something?"

Pete avoided looking at him and sprinkled pepper on the fried eggs Flo had just set in front of him. "Sorry I didn't let you know earlier, but Liz woke up last night with some abdominal pain. She's worried about the baby. I gotta take her in to her doctor's office in Juneau. We'll be back late this afternoon." Raz saw the pleading in his brother's eyes when he looked up. "Can you move things back a day?"

"Hell, I've got the boat all gassed up and loaded," replied Raz, raising his voice in frustration. "When things go south, you're always hiding behind somebody. Like when Mom and Dad died..." Raz paused when he noticed several men in the café look their way then resume their conversations. He lowered his voice. "Damn it, with the temperature dropping there could be a foot of snow in the next few days. I wanna get those damn traps set."

Pete gave him that helpless little brother look as he replied. "Yeah, but I've got to go into Juneau. Liz is in a panic."

Raz took a sip of his coffee and, shaking his head just slightly, replied in a calmer voice. "Well, I know Liz can be concerned about a thing like that being it's her first one."

"Really sorry I can't be with you."

"Well, I'm going without you. I need the money." Raz finished his coffee and stood up. He had still been fuming as he put on his jacket and stomped towards the door. "At least you can pay for my damn coffee."

A drifting log dead ahead of the skiff caught Raz's attention, tearing his thoughts away from his brother. He jerked the tiller over to avoid hitting it. He let out a sigh and resigned himself to Pete's decision that his new family came first before him. He gazed at the rocky shoreline just off to his right. It was a stretch of Icy Strait that the locals referred to as Home Shore. In the lee of the shore, the wind chop subsided and he was able to increase his speed as he entered Excursion Inlet. Up ahead on the east side of the inlet was an enormous tourism complex under construction on the site of an old fish processing plant. It infuriated the elder Hunt that the construction of yet another tourist resort near Glacier Bay National Park would not be such a great deal for the economy and definitely not for him or others from his village. From the tone of several Juneau newspaper articles, it seemed like everyone else in southeastern Alaska welcomed the construction project. There would be lots of jobs and more cruise ships when it was completed—so the state economists said—but the construction jobs they predicted had mostly been filled with imported laborers.

The Juneau newspaper referred to the place as Glacier World. Raz laughed aloud at the thought. There were no real glaciers in Excursion Inlet—the nearest one was over seventy miles away at the far end of Glacier Bay.

As Raz got closer to the complex, he stared at the tall building near its center—five stories, all clad in reflective green glass. It didn't fit. According to the newspapers, the resort would not supply accommodations or restaurants. Visitors would have everything provided onboard their cruise ship, which would moor at a huge new dock that stretched from one end of the complex to the other.

A container barge and a large ocean trawler were docked next to the old cannery. He could see that a huge dock had been constructed along with several new warehouses at the south end of the complex. Raz hated large fishing vessels, too. They hauled in everything off the bottom of the gulf, wasting much of what they scooped up.

Facing the rest of the new dock was a long row of buildings resembling a Klondike boomtown from the Alaskan gold rush era of the 1800s. There was storefront after storefront. Some were gussied up to resemble saloons. Others bore signs like mercantile, assay office, and mining supplies. The line of buildings went on and on. At the far end, a water park was under construction that was supposed to be bigger than the one at Sea World in Southern California. There had been a picture of it in the newspaper.

Raz opened up the throttle on his outboard motor and hugged the western shore of the inlet. He watched for one of the sleek, blue-hulled patrol boats to come out to intercept him, but they remained tied to the dock. The security guards had to have seen him.

He had been furious the day he first learned that Excursion Inlet would be off limits for trapping as well as hunting and fishing. It didn't take more than a couple of shots of whiskey for him to begin ranting about Glacier World and the special privileges the state legislature handed out to the resort owners. He told Pete and anyone else who would listen that those sons of bitches developing the resort were not stopping him from setting his traps. That he would shoot the bastards if anyone touched his traps or prevented him from beaching his boat at the end of the bay. He always carried a rifle or a shotgun because of the risk of a run-in with a brown bear or a wolverine, and, by God, he would blow a few holes in the hull of one of the resort's pretty blue patrol boats if they tried to stop him.

The editor of the Juneau newspaper had recently interviewed the new operations manager about the restrictions and the progress of construction. Raz would never forget the manager's name and the face that had stared at him from the front page of the newspaper. The eyes and the shape of Raul bin Rahman's mouth reminded Raz of the cunning face of a wolf. He had met men like Rahman before. He had once dealt with a Russian fur buyer who had those eyes. The Russian man had lied, tricked him into selling some fur pelts at a lower price and accepting some crappy Chinese-made fishing line as part of the trade, then laughed when Raz left his store.

Raul bin Rahman came from Singapore and represented a Singaporean company called Global Resorts International. Rahman proudly proclaimed to the newspaper reporter that the park was one of several that GRI was developing worldwide and the park here in Alaska would entertain over 150,000 Southeast Asian tourists each year. The Arctic and Alaska held wide appeal for international tourists, according to Rahman, and the park would offer everything in one destination resort. Rahman was excited to describe its most curious feature: a transportation system using driverless golf carts that wound through a labyrinth of large-diameter tunnels. The series of tunnels complete with strategically placed plexiglass viewing windows, led to observation platforms in huge open enclosures filled with all of the major wildlife of Alaska. The animals would be the star attraction of Glacier World. The resort, when it opened early next summer, would offer visitors choices from whale watching to glacier tours into the national park just next door, but according to Rahman, the chance to see wild animals up close in a natural setting was what visitors wanted to experience.

The elder Hunt scoffed at the idea that the tunnels with their big windows were supposed to put the tourists right next some of the deadliest mammals of North America—the huge Alaskan brown bears, Arctic wolves, and smaller mammals that were almost as deadly, such as wolverines and otters.

Raz wondered why the resort manager was so intent on exhibiting land otters. To the unfamiliar, otters excited people with their playfulness, but the local natives like Raz knew better. An otter in the wild would just as soon maul you as play with you. Raz hated land otters—they played with his traps so that he wouldn't catch anything. Sometimes they stole his traps or dragged them into thick brush where they were hard to locate.

The thought of an exhibit of land otters somewhere in this complex sent a shudder down his spine. Not only did he hate them for messing around with his traps, but, like many of the Tlingit, he had grown up with stories about land otters—the Kushtaka, or land otter people. They could change form at will, sometimes appearing to look like a deceased friend, family member, or other ghostly figure. They could move from place to place in an instant. Many believed, including Raz, that they were telepathic and tried to trick you—wanting to bring you harm or even death. They were evil, and not the lithe, playful, furry critters that many people took them to be.

Raz still vividly recalled a story told during the winter potlatch by an old man who had narrowly escaped being killed by the Kushtaka when he was a boy. His parents and siblings had drowned when their canoe overturned on Icy Strait, but the boy was rescued by several men who he later learned were actually Kushtaka. Their canoe traveled southward for days and was getting farther and farther from his home when it finally arrived at a large village—a place called the Bay of Death. There were many land otters living there, but there were also people. At first, no one would talk to the boy. They appeared to be slaves to the land otters. Then one day an old woman approached the boy. He was surprised when he recognized her as an aunt who had supposedly drowned many years before.

"You must leave this place, my nephew," she whispered to him with tears in her eyes. "The ravens have told me that my oldest brother and another man from our village have been searching for you. Come see me this evening and I will take you to them. I can no longer leave, as the Kushtaka took my soul. I am now a land otter." Then she shape-shifted into an otter, chirped, and scampered away into a hole under a large cedar tree.

As his aunt instructed, the boy came to her den late that night and waited. Soon she appeared and again looked like his aunt. "You must not stay here, or the land otter people will steal your soul and make you a slave or worse—tear you to pieces with their sharp claws and teeth." After seeing that all of the land otters were sleeping, she led him down to the canoes where his uncle and the other man from his village were waiting. The boy thanked his aunt and bid her farewell.

For two days, they paddled northward without stopping. On the third day, they saw a canoe of land otters giving chase. As they neared their village, the canoe of land otters closed in and several leapt on the back of the man seated behind the boy. They snarled, hissed, bit, and scratched him with such ferocity that he fell into the ocean. Then the land otters turned on the young boy and began scratching at his back, head, and face. Fearing the same fate, the boy and his uncle fought back. The uncle used his shaman stick to push them back. When men from the village saw them, they immediately set out in canoes to drive the land otters away. Though the boy lived, he had lost his sight and bore terrible scars on his face and body.

Raz pictured the old blind man with the ravaged body as he sped up the inlet towards a stream and tide flats at the far end of Excursion Inlet.

The dark green forest, touched with an early frost and reflecting in the glassy, gray surface of the water, gave the inlet a serene setting. While shrouded in low-hanging clouds, rugged, snow-covered mountains ringed the inlet. On the easterly side, several peaks of the Chilkat Range rose over five thousand feet. There were hanging valleys, sheer granite cliffs, and ice fields—places no one in their right mind would venture. It was true wilderness with no roads or easy access.

A group of black scoters and marbled murrelets repeatedly dove and bobbed back to the surface in front of Raz's skiff—the small diver ducks easily avoiding the bow as it cut through the frigid water. Near the mouth of the river, Raz could see the light frost on the beach and marsh grass. Below the beach the rusty brown, slick kelp and bone-white, barnacle-covered rocks of a broad tide flat were being quickly inundated by the rising tide.

He turned his boat toward the shoreline short of the river mouth where the water would remain deeper. Here the exposed beach was narrow and rocky and jutted up to a low bank, beyond which was a secondary-growth forest of alder and spruce. Raz shut off the engine and let the boat drift into the shallows. The silence of the place engulfed him. When the metal hull scrunched on the barnacle-covered rocks, he carefully stepped over the side and pulled a long line with him to tie to a branch of a tree that had fallen onto the beach. He grabbed one of his sacks of traps, stuffed it into a backpack, then picked up his shotgun and started to trek up the beach towards the flats. The brown kelp popped quietly as the small heads were crushed under his knee-high black rubber boots.

A blaze on a tree trunk among the thick line of trees above the bank caught his eye and he smiled as he turned towards it. The mark was old, made by his father years ago. It marked the path to the family trap line along a small stream that lay hidden in the forest. Raz looked around him, took a moment to sling the shotgun over his shoulder, and then, grabbing several roots with his free hands, climbed up the low bank. At the top of the bank, he was careful not to grab the yellow, woody branches of devil's club plants that partially blocked his route. The branches, covered with nasty thorns, left painful wounds.

The silence of the inlet was replaced by the welcoming sounds in the forest beyond the beach. In the deep woods, two ravens repeatedly called to each other as if they were announcing his arrival. A squirrel chattered from a nest above his head. A belted kingfisher chirped as it flew from its hidden perch and swooped over the water, only to land on a protruding dead tree further up the beach. Raz shifted the knapsack into a comfortable position and struck out for the family trap line. It followed a creek that entered the river at the end of the bay and began a small waterfall about a mile or so up. He planned to set out twenty traps where there were signs of small mammal crossings.

As he approached the stream and his first trap location, Raz noticed that the woods around him had turned dead quiet. The friendly sounds were gone and an uneasy feeling crept up his spine. The dense Alaskan forest always made him uncomfortable with its thick undergrowth, moss covered tree stumps and lack of sunlight. But today was different. The silence could mean there was a bear or other predator close by, maybe along the stream. He let the uneasy feeling pass and was approaching his first trap location when he heard a distinct sound, like a lone bird chirping. It was coming from an area of thick brush just beyond the creek. The single chirp changed to an angry cough which was joined by several more sources. An even louder caterwaul scream came from farther up the stream to his left.

Raz's uneasiness changed to panic as he recognized the sounds—land otters.

The sounds grew louder and louder in his ears—'hah, hiss, hah.'

He quickly shucked his knapsack, turned, and fled back the way he came. The beach and his boat—there he would be safe. The angry sounds followed him as if unseen forms gave chase, grabbing at his clothes. Branches of devil's club slapped at his arms and legs like creatures trying to entrap him. He stumbled in the black muck of a patch of skunk cabbage, dropping his shotgun. One of his boots was sucked off as he struggled to rise. Ahead of him through an opening in the trees, he saw the bay and the hull of a boat—only to realize it was not his own. This boat was icy blue in color. Startled, he tripped on a root and took a tumble down the bank onto the beach. Raz felt a sharp pain above his right eye as he lost consciousness. The last things he remembered were the salty taste of the kelp against his face and the chill of the rising tidewater that soaked into his clothes.

***

Hours later, Raz Hunt opened his left eye. There was total darkness. Instead of barnacled rock and decaying kelp, the surface under his body was smooth and hard. The smell of damp concrete penetrated his nostrils. Struggling to a sitting position, he heard the same chilling sounds—the snarling and hissing noises of the land otters—only different this time. It seemed to come from all around him. They were there, waiting. He could smell their presence.

Ignoring the aches in his limbs, Raz leapt up and turned in a circle, trying to determine which way to run. He saw a small red light not far away. It offered a glimmer of safety. He plunged through the ring of creatures and ran towards it—only to run smack into a glass wall. Stunned, he staggered backward and stared at the light.

As he stared at the red glow, it became brighter, revealing a man's face just inches from his own. The facial features shone red except for the eye sockets, which were like black pits. The face did not move, but brightened and darkened with the intensity of the glowing end of the cigarette.

"Help me!" Raz hollered as he pounded on the thick glass.

There was no movement or response from the man beyond the glass. Raz screamed as something hit his back, dug its sharp claws into his jacket and flannel shirt—biting the back of his neck and head. Raz twisted his body, trying to shake the creature off as several more attached themselves to his legs, shredding his pants and flesh. A large, dark form jumped onto Raz's chest, tearing at his throat with its razor sharp teeth. He grabbed it with his hands, ripping it away and flinging it against the glass wall. Raz touched the front of his shirt. It was wet and warm. His hands were slick with his own blood that spewed from the bites to his neck.

Raz turned once more to face the glass surface and pleaded to the red glowing face beyond. His voice faltered as he recognized the face—he had seen it before on the front page of the Juneau newspaper. A pair of metallic sunglasses were pulled down over the ice-cold eyes.

The grim face turned away and faded into the darkness.

Raz pounded a bloody hand on the glass and croaked again, "Help me!"

He struggled vainly to detach the squirming dark forms as he slipped to his knees. Then, as if a switch had been thrown, the crazed land otters withdrew and went silent as Erasmus Hunt slumped to the floor of the enclosure. The concrete floor, slick with his blood, was warm and peaceful against his ravaged body.

CHAPTER 4

Gulf of Alaska

For the offshore waters south of Kodiak Island, the marine forecast reported a high pressure area moving slowly eastward over the Gulf of Alaska for the next twenty-four hours, fog forming after midnight and dissipating near noon, calm winds, and three- to five-foot seas.

James Baker, the captain of the *Northern Explorer*, was pleased with this report, except for the fog. His container ship was crossing an area of the gulf that was heavily fished by long-line ocean trawlers, and he was concerned about running into one of their mile-long nets. But with long- and short-range radar and AIS reception, there should not be any difficulty with navigation or maintaining their planned course and speed.

The *Northern Explorer* was just one of thousands of large cargo ships plying the seas. In fact there were over forty thousand such ships, plus numerous seagoing barges loaded with stacks of shipping containers. Baker was proud of his merchant ship. It was owned by an international expeditor that used the latest technology for supply chain management, documentation, and brokerage. His ship was fast and dependable for on-time delivery regardless of the weather it encountered. The onboard computers tracked every one of the three hundred containers loaded onto his ship and where each was destined to be off-loaded. This technology was referred to as MATTS, or Marine Asset Tag Tracking System. Each container was equipped with a miniature sensor the size of a deck of cards that included a radio transceiver and a GPS tracking unit. Captain Baker could locate any container on his ship whether it was below deck or stacked above deck, and identify the cargo, the shipper, and if the container had been tampered with during their journey.

It was the *Northern Explorer's* third day out of Tacoma on Puget Sound and the first port of call was Busan, South Korea. He had reviewed the manifest prior to departure and was aware that many of the containers onboard held silicon wafers for semiconductor fabrication. Others contained high-value export lumber products.

Captain Baker had elected to take this particular watch as it was his first officer's birthday, and the crew had thrown him a small party after dinner. At half past two in the morning, the navigation officer asked him to come over to his station. There were two large displays in front of him, plus various forms of communication, including ship-to-shore and ship-to-ship radios and satellite phone.

The man removed his headphones and pointed at one of the displays. "Captain, I'm having a problem with the short-range radar. A few minutes ago it was working fine and I had five vessels within a five-mile radius and another vessel about a mile off to our port. Now I have nothing."

"How about the long-range radar?" The captain asked. "Will it pick them up?"

The officer checked the other system. "No, sir. Same problem just happened with it."

"Increase your range and see if you can detect the deep-sea buoy off the southeast tip of Kodiak Island."

The officer made some adjustments and the green glow of the distance rings narrowed until the radar screen indicated a range of one hundred miles. No objects appeared.

"Huh! We have nothing at all detected by our radar, but we do have some AIS observed traffic."

"So the AIS receiver unit is still working," said Baker. "Okay, shut down the radar and reboot. I'll inform the helmsman to use caution and keep a close eye on the AIS locations. Then I'll wake up the first officer and have him post some bow, stern, and midship watchmen."

"Yes, sir," replied the officer. "I'll work on this problem and let you know as soon as they come back up. It's kind of weird since we just had a thorough system check and calibration before leaving Tacoma."

Captain Baker shook his head as he walked back to his station next to the helmsman. This was a bad situation. He looked at the navigation display monitor. It clearly showed AIS signals for the six vessels reported by the navigation officer. Five were some distance off and had names displayed on the screen. The sixth one, which was less than one mile from their position, displayed only a number. The captain leaned closer in an attempt to read the MMSI number and touched the screen to expand the information in order to show its speed, heading, and hailing sign. The signal went dark.

"That's strange," the captain stated. "We just lost contact with the AIS signal for the closest ship." He grabbed the microphone for the ship's intercom. "Mike, I need a bow, midship, and stern watch immediately. We have a vessel within a mile, and both radar and AIS have lost contact. We're trying to reboot the instruments. I'm altering our course and reducing our speed until we have more information. Have your watchmen be in continual contact with the bridge. Now get to it." He turned to the helmsmen. "Reduce speed to six knots and turn ten degrees to port away from the last location of that AIS observed vessel."

Within five minutes the watchmen were at their stations. But with the thick fog, their visibility was less than two hundred feet. It was the stern watch that first made a report. "Cap'n, I can't see a blasted thing back here but I think I can hear a boat getting closer."

"Please confirm. There's a boat closing on our stern?"

"Yes, sir," the man answered. "Sounds like a fast boat, maybe with an outboard motor?" The stern watch used his binoculars to scan for the boat. "Whoa! I've got a visual. It's a big inflatable, sir. It's heading directly at us."

"What are they doing? Are they trying to hail us? Do they need some assistance?"

The stern watchman ignored the captain's questions. "Sir, I don't like the looks of this. I've made a few trips through the Suez and around the Horn of Africa and been chased by Somali pirates more than once. This is like a déjà vu or something."

"Pirates?" The captain said. "There have been some recent reports of piracy in the North Pacific. I should have..."

"Call the Coast Guard, Cap'n!" The watchman yelled into his radio. "We're about to be boarded."

The captain grabbed his VHF radio microphone and immediately put out a call to the Coast Guard. There was no response. He increased the gain and tried again. All he heard were a lot of squeals emitting from the speaker. He ran to the navigation officer's desk and picked up the SAT phone. When it booted, the display indicated "No Service."

"How the hell do both our VHF and satellite communications go down simultaneously? Has to be some type of jamming system."

He asked the navigation officer to try the single side band radio next, but before he could place the call, two masked men burst through the starboard door to the bridge. The men pointed automatic weapons at the crew and ordered everyone away from their stations.

One man smashed the ship's radios with the butt of his weapon, while the other picked up the intercom. "All crew members are to report to the dining area immediately."

Once everyone assembled in the ship's dining lounge, the intruders ordered the crew to place hoods over their heads and lie on the floor, where their hands were zip-tied behind their backs. Several of the boarders searched the ship and made reports back to their leader.

The leader counted the number of men lying on the floor and spoke again. "Someone is missing. Where is he? You have ten seconds to answer or the captain will be shot. One...two...three...four..."

"Wait!" One of the ship's crew cried out. "Maybe it's Smith. He was on bow watch. He... he's not here."

"Smith? If you're present, speak now!" the leader ordered. No one answered. He turned to one of his men. "Find this Smith. The rest of you carry out your assignments."

Captain Baker and the entire crew of the *Northern Explorer* were ordered to remain on the floor and be silent. All they could do was listen to the sounds of the ship. Baker heard the engines slow and begin to idle. Then he heard metal-on-metal noises from somewhere forward, but as far as he could tell, none of his ship's cranes or machinery were being operated. How many men boarded the ship or what are they after? If they are pirates, are they going to take possession of my ship?

Almost three hours later, the crewmembers around Baker were becoming restless and starting to move around on the floor. No one spoke or stopped them. The mechanical sounds had ceased.

The captain whispered to a man lying next to him. "Pull off my damned hood!"

The man squirmed around, got his hands on the hood over the captain's head, and pulled. Captain Baker glanced around the room then sat up. There was no one present except his men.

"They're gone!" The captain shouted. "Everyone get up, and someone find a knife to cut us loose." Within minutes he and the crew were free of the bindings on their wrists and feet. "Anyone hurt?"

A member of the crew reported. "Otis Nelson's got a nasty cut on his head. He wouldn't leave his post in the engine room and tried to take one of the guys out with a wrench."

"Okay, clean him up and get some antiseptic on his wound. We'll try to reach the Coast Guard to get him taken off for proper medical attention. Right now, let's take back control of our ship. They had weapons so be careful."

Captain Baker, followed by the first officer, ran for the bridge. They discovered it empty, their ship drifting. A few minutes later, the helmsman appeared carrying a baseball bat. He hesitated, then leaned it in a corner next to the door.

"We don't think any of them are still on board, sir," said the helmsman, breathing heavily.

"Okay, then take your station and get us underway," the captain ordered. He turned to the first officer. "Mike, see if you can find a way to raise the Coast Guard or any damn vessel near us. Then check the MATTS computer to see if they tampered with any of our cargo containers." He picked up the intercom mike and ordered the entire crew to conduct a thorough search for any of the boarders or evidence of what they might have been doing while onboard his ship. An hour later, he had everyone report to the bridge. While the communications systems were still not functional, the radar was working again, along with the GPS navigation system. His crew reported that nothing on the ship had been touched. According to the MATTS data logger, all of the cargo containers were accounted for and secure. The pirates had appeared out of nowhere and apparently had not taken anything or done anything to the ship. The radar and AIS systems were running again and still showed the same five fishing vessels. But the sixth vessel, whatever it was, had vanished.

CHAPTER 5

Hoonah, Alaska

Pete Hunt shucked off his jacket and took his usual seat near the big window of the only café in the small Native town of Hoonah. From the window, one could see across the harbor all the way to the rugged Fairweather Range and watch the boats entering and leaving the marina. He looked at his watch and pulled out his cell phone for the fourth time since waking up at five that morning. His brother's number was the last one called, and he punched it again. Moments later he got Raz's very unsociable recorded greeting. He didn't bother to leave a message. Pete waved a hand at Flo Whiting to bring his usual order of eggs over easy and a first cup of coffee.

Pete had spent his entire life in Hoonah. Like many other Native residents, going to college had not been an option. Families struggled to make a living in a harsh land, depending on seasonal blue-collar jobs and government subsidies. Many young men accepted this fact or they became alcoholics like his brother Raz. Some even committed suicide. What made things worse for Pete and Raz was losing their parents and being left to care for themselves.

Two years ago, Pete had begun taking a few natural resource courses at the community college in Juneau. While Raz had drawn himself inward, Pete was more outgoing and worked hard to improve his social skills. He wanted a better education and started studying to be a guide. His dream was to one day apply for a park ranger position at Glacier Bay National Park. Pete had married his high school girlfriend, and their first child would be born in a few months. Looking out for his brother and taking care of his wife, and soon a child, tied him to Hoonah whether he liked it or not.

Pete added some milk to his steaming black coffee, stirred it for a moment, and thought about his brother. He had been trying to reach Raz for three days, ever since returning from Juneau. Pete hadn't liked leaving his brother to lay out the trap line by himself for the first time, and Raz had expressed his displeasure when he walked out that morning. Raz could be bullheaded and even threatening to him and other people—always lashing out spontaneously without rationalizing a situation—but Pete knew different. Raz was like a kid trying to find his way in the world—change frightened him, and he covered up his fear by making preposterous statements and claims.

The café was busy, and a half dozen or so men had walked in since Pete arrived. They nodded his way but didn't come over even though there were two empty chairs across from him. Since getting back from Juneau, he had asked each one of them whether or not they had seen his older brother anywhere, but no one had seen Raz or his boat, or really cared, for that matter.

At first, Pete hadn't been that concerned. His brother was known for binge drinking and disappearing, sleeping it off at his house or somewhere in town and not showing up for days. Then there were the weather conditions. There had been rain and four-foot seas out in Icy Strait for two days. Four-footers didn't make it impossible to cross in a skiff, but a wise person generally didn't try and just waited a day or two. Raz had the good sense not to try it and could have found a place to hold over in Excursion Inlet or at the fish camp that the family used on Pleasant Island.

There were other possible reasons for his brother being missing that nagged at him. Raz could have had mechanical problems with the boat's outboard motor or he could have suffered an accident in the woods while setting his traps. Another possibility crossed his mind. Maybe Raz had been crazy enough to go ashore at Glacier World, cause some trouble and get detained or arrested. It was not something he wanted to think about. Glacier World had suffered a spate of deadly accidents. If Raz didn't show up by late morning, Pete was going to have to contact the Alaska State Troopers to see if they would investigate.

The door to the café banged open again as a young girl entered. She lingered near the door for a few seconds, as though she were checking on who was present and who was not. She glanced at Flo, who had her back to the door and was taking several breakfast plates from the pass through window to the kitchen, then saw Pete, smiled, and turned towards his table. She wore an oversized army jacket embroidered with bright flower designs and a pair of laddered jeans. Her long black hair fell past her shoulders and was parted to fall partially over her left eye. The hair was streaked with red and yellow coloring, matching her red sneakers with bright yellow laces. Despite her casual appearance, she moved with a dancer's grace, and when she sat down across from Pete, she sat up straight, not slouching like a typical teenager.

Pete set his coffee cup down, put his elbows on the table, and crossed his arms. He smiled back as he shook his head. "Morning, Brook! You trying to make a fashion statement around here?"

"It's Brooklyn!" the girl replied. "Why do you insist on calling me Brook? That's a stream, not a person."

Pete chuckled. "I don't know. It just seems more appropriate. More feminine, like your mother over there."

Brooklyn glanced at her mother, who was wearing a well-worn yellow pinafore dress and dirty white apron, and rolled her eyes like a typical seventeen-year-old. She was a pretty girl, with a round face and small mouth that always seemed to bear a smile like her mother's—unlike most of the native Hoonah females, who almost never smiled. Then there were her eyes, which had a sparkle. She had a darker complexion than her mother, who was one of the few Caucasians living in a town that was largely Alaskan Native. It was no secret that Flo Whiting had fallen in love with a young Native man who had left her after she got pregnant. She was raising Brooklyn as a single parent in a tough town with little prospect for the future, something Pete had a lot of respect for.

Flo brought over a bowl of hot cereal and a glass of orange juice and set them in front of the girl without lingering to talk. There were plenty of customers needing attention.

"Mom works too hard," Brooklyn stated in a firm voice as she pushed her hair back with both hands. "I wish she could have an easier job than working in this place. I've tried to convince her to learn how to use a computer but she won't even try. She says they're for young people like me." She took a sip of her orange juice. "How's Liz doing?"

"She's doing all right," Pete answered, unfolding his arms and leaning back in his chair to stretch. "The doc in Juneau said that the baby is just getting more active and kicks a lot, which is normal. He told her to drink herbal tea before going to bed to relax her, and then the baby would relax. She's too tense about things."

The girl removed her fingerless gloves and slipped out of her jacket. Underneath, she wore an oversized maroon sweatshirt with a hood. The word BRAVES announced the Hoonah high school basketball team. Basketball was the primary competitive sport in Southeast Alaska. Around her neck dangled a large silver pendent in a Native American design depicting an eagle feather along with a small turquoise stone. Pete admired the representation of her roots, living in a small Native village in spite of the fact she had no clan like himself. He and his brother belonged to the raven clan—one of the three principal Tlingit clans in his town. Brooklyn poured a small amount of the remaining milk Pete had used for his coffee onto her bowl of cereal and picked up a spoon, studying it for a moment like it was a science class specimen.

"Did Raz show up last night?" she asked finally.

"No. He didn't." Pete shook his head. His face clearly showed how worried he was. "And I appreciate your concern. No one else in town seems to care."

"Well, he's not exactly the friendliest guy in the world. He sure scared me when I was a little kid."

"Yeah. For a long time I tried to cover for him, but no one listens to a younger brother. His reputation as a troublemaker and bad-mouthing people kind of put him on the outs around here. It's just too small a community. But he's the only brother

I've got and with Mom and Dad drowned in a boat accident, he's my only living relative."

"A boat accident?" asked Brooklyn. "You never told me about that."

"I guess it's been eight or ten years now since they disappeared coming back from our family's fish camp. That tragedy hit Raz pretty hard. He's convinced the Kushtaka took them."

"I don't believe in those old Tlingit legends," the girl answered firmly. She blew on a spoonful of hot cereal.

Pete didn't pursue her statement, and Flo's delivery of his own breakfast gave him an opportunity to change the subject. "I heard you've been helping Lewis Teebottom with some project over at the job training center."

"Uh huh," Brooklyn replied. Her eyes sparkled even more. "Mr. Tee has got to be the weirdest guy in Hoonah, but he's a great teacher and an absolute genius with computers. You know, he is having a team of high school students building an ROV—that's a robotic underwater vehicle. It has two cameras and a robotic arm that can pick up things. We tried it out down at the docks last week. We even had to develop, with Mr. Tee's help of course, the computer programs to control it."

"Hey," said Pete, nodding his head slowly, "that's pretty cool. Lewis is doing something this community has needed for a long time—showing you kids there's a future."

"I guess so. We're entering a competition in Juneau early next summer. It's the Ranger Class MATE competition."

"Mate?" asked Pete. "Never heard of it."

"MATE stands for Marine Advanced Technical Education. There are regional events all over the country where college and high school teams have to demonstrate technical, science, and math skills with their ROVs. Mr. Tee decided to start a robotics team here in Hoonah and thinks we have a chance to win the state competition. If we do, we get to go to the Pacific Northwest Regional competition in Anchorage. Teams will have to compete by operating their ROVs under ice."

"You're part of this robotics team?"

"Officially, I'm an alternate and help with the computer programming. Mr. Tee has another interesting project that me and a couple of other students help with. It's a fisheries research project that gathers data using nanosats."

"Nanosats? What the heck are they?" He took another bite of his fried eggs.

"They're super small satellites—not much bigger than a Rubik's Cube. NASA has a program that allows scientists to put them in one of their rockets instead of ballast and then they get released at low altitudes. Hundreds can be launched at one time. They only last a few months before being pulled back into the upper atmosphere and burning up, but they are a neat way to study the Earth. Mr. Tee worked with this professor at the University of Alaska while getting his master's in computer science and helped write a NOAA grant to use nanosats to study fishing activities in the Gulf of Alaska."

"Wow, I'm impressed. ROVs and nanosats— I had no idea all this was happening with you kids here in Hoonah, My brother and I never had such learning opportunity." replied Pete.

"The NOAA grant is pretty boring stuff and really quite straightforward. Using the nanosats, we gather data on AIS transmissions from the fishing boats and monitor their movement. Mr. Tee is having us make graphical plots for thousands of—"

Pete's raised a hand as his attention was drawn to the café window facing the bay. One of the state's thirty-two-foot patrol boats was moving fast and coming in close to the shore. It turned broadside and slowed its speed as if it were going to go around the breakwater and enter the harbor. "Just a second, Brooklyn. I've got an uneasy feeling about this," Pete said.

Brooklyn looked out the window and spotted the boat too. "Oh my God!" she exclaimed. "They're towing Raz's skiff!"

Pete's cell phone rang, and he quickly pulled it out of his pocket. "Hello? Yeah, this is Pete Hunt." Brooklyn could see the worried frown grow on Pete's face as he listened. "Okay," Pete said, "I'll be there in a minute." He looked at Brooklyn as he jumped up and grabbed his coat. "That was the state troopers.

They asked me to meet them at the transient dock as soon as I can."

Pete's anxiety had his heart pounding as he leapt down the steps of the café and ran towards the boat basin. Brooklyn ran right behind him, not wanting to miss what was going on. In a few minutes, half of the town would be down at the basin.

By the time Pete reached the patrol boat tied up at the transient dock, a crowd of fishermen and other curious folks from the docks had already gathered, turning to stare at him like a flock of sparrows on a wire. Yellow ribbon stretched between two pilings to keep people at a distance. Pete glanced back toward the shore to see another dozen or so people coming down the ramp from the parking lot and another twenty or so standing or sitting along the top of the breakwater. Pete walked up to two troopers standing on the dock. They were still wearing their life jackets, and the smell of the forest on their clothes and the bay mud on their boots told him where they had been before they even said anything.

Pete ducked under the yellow tape and stood near the bow of the aluminum vessel. There was an all-terrain vehicle tied down in the open cargo area in front of a small pilothouse.

"Pete Hunt?" one of the troopers said. "I'm Dave Williams. I'm afraid I have some bad news. We got a report late last night from the security office over at Glacier World concerning a boat that was beached up near the end of Excursion Inlet. They sent one of their patrol boats over to check it out since the area is closed to public entry. They contacted us and reported seeing what appeared to be a man's body on the bank near the boat. We were asked to come in and investigate and we arrived at daylight this morning. Identification on the body was for Erasmus Hunt."

"My brother is dead? What happened?"

"Did you know that he was going into a restricted area?" asked Williams. "Excursion Inlet has this exclusion zone—no hunting or fishing, and is totally closed to the general public."

"Yeah," answered Pete, stumbling for the right words. "I...I knew he was going there. I meant...I mean...I was supposed to go with him to set up a trap line. It's been a traditional trapping location for our family for generations. But I had to take my wife into Juneau to see her doctor."

Pete watched Williams unbuckle his life jacket, pat several of the pockets of his vest, and then take out a cell phone. It was like watching the man move in slow motion. Pete exhaled a deep breath and glanced at the crowd of people gathered at both ends of the dock. All friends and people he'd known his entire life now just a wall of nameless faces standing there watching him, no one uttering a word. He picked out Brooklyn, who was staring at the patrol boat's cargo area. He slowly turned his head, following her gaze. On the deck of the boat behind the muddy ATV were two black body bags.

"Mr. Hunt. I need you to take a look at a few pictures," said Williams trying to get his attention. "Mr. Hunt?"

Pete stared at the body bags. The trooper's voice faded and when he refocused on the officer, it was as if he had experienced a loud concussion. He saw the man's lips moving but couldn't hear him speak.

"Mr. Hunt," Williams said again more loudly. "I'm sure you have a lot of questions, but until we can conduct an investigation there are not many answers we can provide." Williams held up the cell phone for Pete to look at a photographic image. "Can you identify the person in this photo?" He moved closer to Pete and spoke more quietly. "I don't want to uncover the body right now—too many onlookers. Ah...I'm sorry if the image is disturbing to you. He was in pretty bad shape."

Pete looked at the image, closed his eyes and shook his head. "That's Raz. He has an old scar above his left eye. I did that when I accidentally hit him with a gaff hook when we were kids. Geez, what happened to him? He's all scratched up."

"We're not sure. We backtracked from the beach near his boat and found a sack of traps and a shotgun. It was loaded but with no round in the chamber. We found one of his boots stuck in some mud. Apparently, he was running and didn't stop to retrieve it. As to the condition of the body, it had too many bites and scratches for us to count. The cause is unknown, as we did not find any animal tracks. So, we have to leave that to the coroner to try to determine."

Someone standing next to Brooklyn heard the officer's description and whispered loud enough for a number of other people to hear. "Kushtaka...the land otter people got him." There were murmurs in the crowd and the words spread up the dock like a fast-moving flame.

Pete paid no attention to the murmuring in the crowd. He took a moment to rub the back of his neck and sighed. "But I'm still confused," he said. "You had me identify one body but it looks like you have two bodies on board."

"Sure do," replied Williams. "Got another body from the same place—Glacier World. A contractor was killed by a couple of wolves in one of their predator exhibits. I'm afraid he looks a lot worse than your brother. Picking up bodies over at Glacier World is starting to worry me."

Pete's knees felt weak, and with Williams's assistance, he sat down on the edge of the dock. The image of Raz shook him to the core. He stared at his hands and then at the boat, feeling helpless and lost.

Even the impending birth of his baby boy couldn't replace the loss of his brother.

***

That same day, just two blocks from the Senate office
building in Juneau, Senator William "Mac"
MacDonald sat at a table in a restaurant noted for fine
dining. It was his favorite place to enjoy a quiet lunch
away from the tourist hangouts farther down on
Front Street and Marine Way. There were two cruise
ships docked—the last for the season and, to Mac,
the streets of downtown Juneau were as crowded with
tourists as the salmon in the local streams during
spawning. He ordered a Bijou cocktail and waited for
one of his key reelection campaign supporters to join
him. Mac was pleased with how the campaign was
proceeding even though he was experiencing more
opposition than the last three times he ran for state
office. His inner circle of supporters included some
powerful business owners, several gold mine
executives, and the president of the Alaska Native
Brotherhood. Jobs for Southeast Alaska were the
number one priority in his platform, which proved to
be popular among those with money, though it did
result in a vocal opposition among environmental
advocates. Tony Walsh, the editor for the *Juneau
Empire*, was still sitting on the fence and had not yet
endorsed any candidate, and Mac needed that
endorsement. To help influence Walsh's decision,
Mac's campaign advisor suggested he come out
stronger in his support for Glacier World.
Construction of the park had been underway for two
years and was a $500 million investment by Global
Resorts International. Senator MacDonald used his

political persuasion to get the state legislature to offer GRI some very lucrative incentives to build the park. These included allowing an exclusion zone and fast-tracking much of the permitting process, which had angered environmental groups and fishermen.

To kick off this new strategy for supporting Glacier World development, Mac needed to know more about it. His lunch guest today was the new general manager, Raul bin Rahman. He'd met Mr. Rahman only once, at a fundraiser nearly two years ago. The man had written a $10,000 check for his campaign and asked how else he might extend the appreciation of GRI for his assistance. Mac jumped at the offer, and a month later he was the owner of a new thirty-five-foot Beneteau sailboat, which he guessed had cost GRI nearly $200,000. He sailed the boat to Juneau from Seattle and didn't give it a second thought that it had not cost him anything except to register it in Alaska. He was not a particularly adept sailor, but he loved that boat.

Mac saw Rahman enter the restaurant, and he stood to welcome the man.

"Mr. Rahman, it is indeed a pleasure to see you again. How are things at Glacier World? Is this fine fall weather helping to finish the construction?"

"Yes, we are very busy," said Rahman with a gracious smile. "The park is within a few months of receiving its very first cruise ship. GRI is quite excited that day is finally arriving."

"That's wonderful news," said Mac. "Please, take a chair. What do you want to drink?" Mac waved to his waiter to come over to the table.

"I drink Dewar's Scotch, if they have it. Thank you." Rahman removed his light jacket. He was wearing a Club Monaco denim shirt with a scarf tucked inside the collar. Mac knew that Rahman was a native of Malaysia, and it was obvious from his darker skin, round eyes, and short stature. Rahman kept his carefully groomed black hair slightly long, and he had a mustache. But his eyebrows were his most striking facial feature. Their fullness and black color added darkness to his eyes. While his outward mannerisms were friendly, his eyes were just the opposite and very unsettling.

Mac tried not to focus on the man's eyes. While they waited for Rahman's drink to arrive, he started with his questions. "What do you find is most exciting about Glacier World as you wrap up the construction?"

Rahman smiled and took a sip of his drink before answering. "Well, first you must come and see for yourself. We are planning a special pre-opening day for citizens of Juneau. If you can come, there would be an opportunity to say a few words at a special ceremony. We have invited the mayor and, of course, the press. I think your friend Tony Walsh plans to attend."

"That would be an honor," replied Mac. "I'll pass that invitation on to my campaign manager and he can talk to your PR people. As a matter of fact, I might bring my wife. She gets pretty excited when she sees one of Alaska's fiercer predators."

Rahman chuckled. "She will definitely have that chance. The park will be getting a delivery soon of a Kodiak brown bear and two polar bears. The Kodiak is a very fine specimen despite the fact that he is a man-eater. My general curator assures me these bears can be accommodated and will be key attractions. Can you imagine riding in an aerial gondola across a river and over an open meadow full of such predators? That's what our Tundra Sky Ride has to offer. There will be many more exhibits where visitors can be quite close to the wildlife. Then there's our replica of a gold rush town, complete with theatrical drama of Alaska's early gold rush era."

"Marvelous!" said Mac. "I can't wait to take your Sky Ride and tour the rest of the park. Let's order and then you can tell me more about Glacier World. It does sound fascinating."

Rahman smiled once more, but like his eyes, it was cold.

CHAPTER 6

Aberdeen, Washington

The deafening noise of the crowd in the bleachers on the far side of the swimming pool was affecting Bernie Armstrong's concentration. He tapped furiously on a laptop keyboard while sitting on a folding chair, surrounded by five other students from his high school in South Bend. The four boys and one girl wore red T-shirts identifying them as the South Bend Sea Lions. All of them had worried looks on their faces as they kept glancing toward another group of students positioned at the Mission Station on the far side of the pool. The other team wore bright blue T-shirts with the words "Aberdeen Aquanauts" stenciled on the front. The two teams were competing in the regional level Marine Advanced Technical Education competition, known as MATE. To compete, each high school team built their own remote operated underwater vehicle. An ROV had to perform a series of underwater maneuvers and tasks within a fifteen-minute time period. The Aquanauts had just completed the fourth task out of five with their ROV. The task was a particularly difficult one that involved picking up five different types of tools off the floor of the pool and placing them in a simulated box made of PVC pipe. None of the other teams in the competition had been able to recover all five tools. The Sea Lions were up next and would be the last team to compete.

Bernie and his team sorely wanted to beat the Aquanauts and, based on their score up to this final event, had a chance. But right now, there was a problem with the computer program controlling the main camera on their submersible. If the camera did not work properly, one of his teammates would not be able to maneuver their ROV through the different underwater challenges or locate the objects.

"Hurry up, Armstrong," said one of the boys on Bernie's team. "The Aquanauts are almost finished."

"I'm almost done, Tommy," replied Bernie as he tapped the enter key to save the revised program. "There. Someone watch the camera. Tommy, use your controls to turn the camera above the manipulator arm to the left. "

Tommy went to the control panel and tilted one of the joysticks. Next to him on their assigned repair table, a hum came from a tiny servomotor mounted on a rectangular frame of PVC tubing. All sorts of devices were mounted to the frame, including a ballast tank, a small pump, the underwater camera, two thrusters, a temperature sensor, an attitude adjustment controller, and a small robotic manipulator arm that could rotate and pick up objects. Once the ROV was lowered into the water, Tommy, as the team's operations engineer, would take control. Bernie was the software engineer. Each of the others had specific roles to help with maintenance, safety, and data monitoring.

"It's working!" shouted Tommy. "We're ready to go."

Bernie relaxed and let his team finish getting the ROV ready to launch. He avoided watching how the other team was doing by looking for his dad in the bleacher area. He picked out his father halfway up in the stands and gave him a thumbs-up and a grin. A loud groan rose from the Aberdeen spectators, drawing his attention to the scoreboard. In their excitement about getting a perfect run on the tool retrieval, the Aberdeen team had failed a safety inspection. For the last task, the team had switched members, and the new member forgot to put on a life vest. Several of Bernie's teammates cheered. The door was open for the South Bend Sea Lions to win the competition, but they would have to receive a near-perfect score.

Minutes later, Earl Armstrong smiled as he watched Bernie and his team move their ROV to the judge's area, referred to as the Mission Station. The team and their ROV had to be inspection before getting approval to lower the ROV into the pool. He checked his notes. Bernie's team had a perfect score on their technical presentation, while the Aquanauts had scored ninety-five points. The opponents had just lost another two points on their safety score. The Sea Lions could win this event if they did well on all of the technical missions and didn't make any dumb mistakes.

Up to this point, Earl's mind had been elsewhere. An earlier phone conversation with his tribe's business manager left him concerned and finding it difficult to keep his attention on his son's competition. His job as a tribal forester had its easy days and rough days. He spent a lot of time outdoors appraising timber and arranging for timber sales, but the management and administration responsibilities and long hours were difficult at times. Instead of one boss to please, he had six who were all members of the Tribal Council. They looked upon his job of putting together profitable timber sales as highly important to the tribe's annual budget. They needed more funds for expanding the health clinic and housing improvements on the reservation.

Earl was now forty-four years old, and meeting the Tribal Council's expectations for his job was mentally and sometimes physically tiring. He had just spent ten long, grueling days supervising a logging operation for another shipment of logs to an overseas customer. It was the third shipment of some of the best, premium-quality logs the tribe's timber operations had ever produced. The first two had shipped from the Port of Aberdeen to Asian buyers several months ago, and now he had to spend the next few days overseeing preparation and loading of a third sale of high-value logs into cargo containers for shipment. It was the second part of an order being shipped to the same specialty mill in Japan.

The cell phone in his shirt pocket vibrated, and Earl took it out to check the caller ID. The caller was Leon Pence. Earl frowned. He had only talked to Leon two or three times since their Olympics trek nearly nine months ago. He felt obligated to answer Leon's call, but with the noisy crowd around him, he first made his way down from the bleachers and out into a hallway near the main exit. Leon had already left a message. "Call me. Urgent."

Earl punched the return call key and Leon answered immediately. "Thanks for the call, Earl. This is kind of an odd request but if you have a moment to listen, I think it is important to you as well as to me."

"I'm listening, Leon."

"Okay. One of the women living here in LaPush got hold of me this morning. She has a son who is learning woodcarving and went up to Alaska a year ago to apprentice under a master totem pole carver. Apparently, he was killed in an accident last week. She was pretty distraught as she talked to me. His name is Eddie Jackson. We served together in Afghanistan while we were in the Marines. He and I spent some time commercial fishing with my dad's boat after getting out, and then he took a job in Forks because his father was seriously ill. Eddie had a difficult transition back to civilian life on the reservation and has had an alcohol problem. Then he got this idea that doing something culturally might help him stop drinking, get his personal respect back and build a new life. He was getting pretty good at carving canoe paddles and such, but he wanted to carve large totems."

"Okay, Leon. I know there has to be a reason for you telling me about this guy, but what's up?"

"Well, the law enforcement officer who contacted her said it was some sort of workplace death—an accident. She wants me to go up, check into things, and then arrange to send Eddie's body back home."

"Why do I have a feeling there's more to this? You didn't call me just to say you are headed for Alaska, did you?"

"Correct. I'm hoping you can explain something to me." Leon paused as if he was looking for something, and Earl could hear a few beeps as Leon searched his phone. "Ah, here it is. Eddie sent his mother pictures of the carving projects that he was working on. He was pleased with his work, and she was proud of him, so she showed some of the photos to me. One of his last projects caught my attention. It was a cedar carving of a crest with a leaping salmon design around the circumference. I recognized the crest, Earl. It was the imprinted brand for your tribe's Shoalwater Corporation. Would someone with your tribe have commissioned Eddie Jackson to do this?"

"Someone with the Shoalwater Corporation?" Earl answered with confusion in his voice. "I haven't heard about it."

"Well I checked your tribe's website and it sure looks identical. If he did not have a commission from you or someone else at Shoalwater, why did he take on such a project?"

Earl frowned and thought for a moment. "You said he used a piece of wood with my tribe's brand? We only use the branding to identify our premium cedar products, and I'm pretty sure we don't sell in the Alaskan market. How would Eddie have gotten ahold of some our wood in the first place?"

"I do not know, Earl. But your brand is clearly stamped, not redrawn, on a piece of cedar that he used to carve a really nice plaque. Hang on. I am going to send you a text message with the picture attached. See if you recognize it."

A few seconds later Earl was looking at the picture of Eddie's carving project. "Huh, looks like our brand, alright. We stamp it near the end of each log or piece of lumber that we market since most of it is high-value wood and we want to identify the point of origin." In the background there was a cheer along with a lot of clapping from the pool. Earl shook his head, realizing that he may have just missed the end of Bernie's team competing with their ROV. The winner had probably just been announced.

"Ah… Leon, I'm kind of missing out on an important event involving Bernie and need to get back to watching him compete. I have to agree with you that something strange has occurred. Let me look into this with my lumber broker and get back to you. He handled my recent prime timber shipments that went to Korea and Japan. I need to call him and find out whether the shipments arrived. They should have gotten there by now. What worries me is that the Japanese account payment is approaching sixty days overdue, and the tribe hasn't been paid on its letter of credit. I'm about to send the second part of their order."

"Okay, let me know, Earl," said Leon. "I have decided to fly up as soon as I can and take care of things for Eddie's mother. If some of your lumber is missing, you might want to join me."

"I just don't know how my premium cedar would end up in Alaska. So where in Alaska are you headed?" Earl asked.

"Hoonah. It is in Southeast Alaska—a small Native town west of Juneau."

"That's interesting."

"How come?" Leon answered.

"Juneau is where my grandfather was raised and where he met my grandmother. It would be interesting to visit the place where he grew up and worked his entire career after World War II—maybe bring Bernie along."

"Was your grandfather in the military? Alaska was a pretty important campaign in the war with Japan."

"He didn't get drafted because of an injury when he was younger but he had some interesting stories to tell. He was a pretty modest guy but I considered him a war hero."

"Really?" responded Leon. "You need to tell me about him sometime. Anyway, talk to Sally about coming along with me, alright?"

"Okay," replied Earl. "I'll call you tomorrow." He hung up. The noise from the pool area was over. Darn, I've missed the announcement of the winner. Might as well call Ron.

Earl scrolled through his cell phone contact list for the number of the office of R.A. Pike, his tribe's lumber broker in Portland. The company had been in the brokerage and freight forwarding business for nearly fifty years and had assisted Earl ever since he started as the tribe's forester twenty years ago. Ron Pike always seemed to be a step ahead of market fluctuations in lumber prices and had good connections in the Asian and European markets, which was why Earl had started exporting premium lumber. Asian clients were very particular about product quality but were willing to pay a good price. Earl's first sale to South Korea had done well, and the tribe made considerably more money than selling in the domestic market. His second sale to a customer in Japan was just as important. He had personally overseen loading twenty containers. If he couldn't deliver lumber to a key overseas customer, he could lose his job.

"Good morning, Ron. It's Earl Armstrong."

"Hey, Earl!" replied Ron. "How have you been?"

"Fine, Ron. Has your office received any word on our latest shipment to Japan? The last thing I heard was from our tribal financial officer. There has not been any receipt of payment or action on the letter of credit."

"I…I don't think so," answered Ron. "Why?"

"Seriously, I need an update right away. Check your computer records. Make some calls. Do whatever you have to, but get back to me right away. I have to know if my shipment made it to Japan."

"What do you mean, like it didn't arrive? You know something I don't know?" Ron asked. "You sound concerned about something."

"I'm quite concerned," replied Earl. "Just make the calls and get right back to me. And one more thing—has any of our premium cedar been purchased by someone located in Alaska, say in the last six months?"

"Alaska? Don't think so, at least not at the wholesale level. Could be someone purchased Shoalwater Corporation product domestically for use on a project up there. You know, like a big general contractor?"

That possibility hadn't crossed Earl's mind and he relaxed slightly. "Yeah, I guess that's possible. But get back to me on this, okay?"

"Sure, but give me a couple of days. The transiting department at the Japanese port is a bureaucracy unto itself and takes its sweet time updating records even in this age of global computer networks."

At that moment Bernie rushed out into the hallway searching for Earl, beaming from ear to ear.

***

The only time the town of Hoonah, Alaska, experienced so much as a traffic snarl was during the Fourth of July parade when everything with two or more wheels was on the road. At midnight on an early summer evening, when even a new moon was shielded by light rain clouds, it was easy to see any vehicles traveling through town. As strange as it was, no one noticed a black Chevy Suburban come in via the Airport Road, make a right turn just past the post office, and then pull over at the east end of Huna Court. The vehicle's headlights turned off, and five minutes later two men climbed out and walked up the south side of the street. A dog barked once further up. One of the men checked a map on his cell phone and pointed to a large house with an old cabin just behind it. The two men looked for lights in any of the houses close by, then slipped between two houses and crept up to the cabin. A shoulder shove and the door pushed in. Force wasn't needed as it wasn't even locked. Within five minutes, the men slipped back out the door, each carrying a stuffed pillowcase. In another fifteen minutes, the Suburban had retraced its route, driven by the harbor and back up the road towards the airport.

CHAPTER 7

Excursion Inlet, Alaska

The noise of the jet's engines echoed off the steep forested slope of the Chilkat Range above the airstrip. The airstrip for the Glacier World theme park had been built many years ago when the site was a fish processing plant and had been recently improved to handle private jets. The plane turned at the far end and slowly taxied back to where Raul bin Rahman waited. The sleek jet was a Citation X—the fastest civilian aircraft in the world—and it had flown in from Japan after a brief stop in Anchorage to go through US Customs. Aboard were six men from Singapore and all GRI shareholders.

Construction at the park was nearly complete, and stocking the various enclosures with wildlife had just begun. Rahman was satisfied with the progress and despite several unanticipated setbacks felt certain he could keep the project on schedule for its opening and the arrival of the first cruise ship.

The architectural design company from Montreal had done a marvelous job with the design of the park's attractions. His favorites were the Journey to the Arctic Aquarium with its beluga whales and walrus, and the Brown Bear River Loop with its waterfalls where visitors could enjoy watching huge brown bears and black bears fishing for salmon and even get a glimpse inside a bear den. Getting his hands on a couple of beluga whales, a few walrus, and a really big male Kodiak bear had cost a lot of money, both in paying a black market hunter and bribing government officials.

A VIP tour to see the nearly finished park attractions and its recent acquisitions had been arranged for the six men before they settled into their suites on the top floor of the office tower. Three electric carts were lined up next to Rahman, with several of his best guides ready to whisk them into the park. The computer tech guys were still testing the auto drive system in the tunnels, so he had arranged for drivers.

That evening they would enjoy an Alaskan seafood and wild game dinner prepared by a world-class chef in a private dining room, and several of the prettiest female staff would be joining them. As was traditional with Asian business men, pleasure always preceded serious business. That would commence the next morning, and what was to be discussed had Rahman a lot more on edge than the details of being a host and managing the park's construction and budget. These six men were all multi-billionaires and exerted considerable power.

But powerful men had weaknesses, and Rahman had files on each of his visitors. He would let them enjoy their visit and satisfy their curiosity about what he had accomplished with the millions of dollars they had invested. Beyond that, he ignored their management concerns and ran operations as he saw fit.

***

At 10:00 a.m. sharp the next morning, Rahman began his report to the investors. It started with the latest details on the construction. Most of the men were duly impressed by what they had seen on the tour and conveyed looks of satisfaction from an enjoyable evening. He easily fielded several questions about some of the park's features, the predators that were on display, and the water theatre complex still under construction. One of the investors expressed disappointment in not being able to view any glaciers or humpback whales, to which Rahman answered that he must return when the park was fully operational. It took Rahman another hour to discuss the financial reports and to summarize the risks that had risen with startup and the importance of maintaining secrecy of some operations. However, he knew the investors' visit to Glacier World just before its grand opening was no coincidence. There had to be something else they were saving for their questions.

Mr. Lee, a large man and one of the bigger investors, took off his glasses and flipped them around in the stubby fingers of his right hand. "Mr.

Rahman, we all know you are doing a fine job with bringing this theme park on line. It will be a stellar attraction worldwide for GRI. The security force here is more than three times that of any other GRI facility and we understand why such measures have been taken. Yet, on several occasions in the last year, there have been serious security breaches. Some of us have discussed this matter and are extremely concerned."

Rahman didn't immediately respond. He glanced out the window where in the distance at the airfield he could see the gleaming white body of the Citation X. He checked his watch then spoke to the group while focusing on Mr. Lee. "Gentlemen, you each have a full written report and copies of the latest financial statements. In addition to what I have presented, these can be studied at your leisure. Your plane is scheduled to leave for Paris in two hours and an excellent lunch has been prepared for your enjoyment before departure. I'll inform Mr. Lee of the details as to his concern in my private office and he can report back to you later." Then without waiting for any further comments, he turned and walked out of the conference.

Lee sat puzzled for a moment, then rose and quickly followed Rahman into a large office that adjoined the conference room. Rahman's new head of security, Nigel Fishman, was already in the office. He closed the door and stood by it.

"Mr. Rahman," sputtered Lee. "I don't understand why we must have this conversation in private. I must insist you answer the question in front of all of the investors. And not taking any further questions. This is outrageous."

Rahman ignored Lee's statement. "How did you hear of the security breaches?" he demanded. "This information was not included in any of my reports." He moved to a small bar and filled two glasses from a stoppered decanter.

"I...I have my sources," Lee replied. "As major investors, we have a right to know. Your reports leave out a number of details regarding security as well as major expenditures that were not part of the original plans. Your animal acquisition costs far exceed the budget. You spent a huge sum on building a lodge somewhere. Your security measures have attracted public attention. You...you are acting too much like a...like a lone wolf." Lee made a weak grin with his choice of words.

Rahman was not smiling as he approached Lee and handed him one of the glasses. He walked over to his desk and set down his own glass. He continued to ignore Mr. Lee turning his back on him and facing the huge window that looked out over the park and the waters in Excursion Inlet. A ship was undocking near his warehouses. The reflection of his face in the window pane was blank and cold. Finally responded to Lee with carefully chosen words. "Each of you gave me full authority to do what was required. I am taking all of the risks. You and the other investors stand to make huge profits from what I have built here at Glacier World." He turned and pointed a finger at Lee. "Isn't that what you wanted along with the bragging rights associated with being an owner of an international theme park?"

Lee nodded. Beads of sweat formed on his forehead. He took a sip of his drink. "Yes, the financial returns should meet our expectations but they are considerably slower than projected...but you have not...answered our concerns...about... security risks." Lee touched his forehead with his left hand and felt the drops of perspiration. His lips felt numb and he was having difficulty speaking. "You...you...have not...informed us...about..."

Lee's drink slipped from his hand and dropped onto the carpeted floor, breaking and spilling its contents. Lee looked down at it in surprise. His legs weakened. He slumped to his knees and then collapsed on his face onto the carpet.

Rahman looked over Fishman. "Mr. Lee seems to have fainted. Have Hayden and Cheng carry him to more appropriate accommodations where he can recover," he said. "Then I have an assignment for you." Rahman went over and patted Lee's pockets. He removed a cell phone and handed it to Fishman. "We have an informant among our staff. Find this person and deal with it."

***

Two hours later, Lee stirred and woke to the roaring sound of the jet engines coming to full speed. He was groggy and slowly opened his eyes, squinting in the bright light coming through the small window near his right shoulder. His eyes grew wide as he watched the Citation jet start its takeoff, roll down the runway, and become smaller as it lifted off. He jerked his head up hitting it hard on the concrete edge of the opening. Reacting, he fell backwards onto a damp, hard surface. In the light from the opening he could see he was in a small room. A foul smell hit him like a bucket of cold water, causing him to recoil against a rough wall. His hands and his clothes were covered in animal dung.

There was a mechanical hissing noise that drew his attention to the far wall. A door slid to one side revealing a dimly lit passageway. Lee hesitated, then scrambled to his feet and rushed towards the opening then suddenly stop as the light in the passageway disappeared.

Something had moved into the other end of the passageway and was coming towards him.

Lee slowly backed away from the door as a huge dark form with piercing eyes uttered a low growl and slowly lumbered into the room. He turned and ran back to the small opening, seeking to escape, but it was too small for his bulky body. The men working at the dock were too far away to hear Lee's muffled screams inside the thick walls of the animal den.

CHAPTER 8

South Bend, Washington

Monday morning after the competition in Aberdeen, Earl decided to break the news to his wife about Leon's anticipated trip to Alaska, his decision to go along, and his desire to take Bernie with him.

Sally was awake before him, and he could hear her in the kitchen making coffee and laying out some cereals and breakfast dishes. He dressed and passed by Bernie's room on his way downstairs. Earl noticed that Bernie was still sleeping, and his ribbon medal for winning the robotics competition in Aberdeen hung on a bedpost close to his head. Earl smiled. The next bedroom door was open and the bed made. His daughter Christine, two years older than Bernie, was taking a summer science class and was already up and gone. The Marine Science Center in Seattle was sponsoring a course at the Grays Harbor Community College on exoskeleton structure of small marine life. Earl smiled again and shook his head. Christine was like her mother is so many ways—smart and driven. It was two weeks since her high school graduation, where she had graduated at the top of her class. Just last week, she had received a letter from the

University of Washington offering her a full scholarship. That night, Christine had announced to him and Sally that she wanted to become a doctor like her mother.

Entering the kitchen, Earl slipped up behind Sally and gave her a kiss on the neck.

"Christine already left for her summer class?" He asked walking over to the coffee pot and grabbing a cup from the cupboard above it.

"Oh yes," replied Sally. "She was out of here thirty minutes ago. She took your old Volvo, in case you wanted to drive it today."

"That girl is so much like you, Sally," said Earl. "I don't know where you two get all that drive and energy. I need a good half hour to sit and have a cup of coffee and figure out my day." He sat down in a chair in the breakfast nook and looked out the window at the Willapa River. The house Sally and Earl had purchased nearly twenty years ago was situated on the hill above the town's main street. The house was nearly one hundred years old and had been built by the owner of one of the early lumber mills in South Bend. Earl and Sally had remodeled it several times, but one thing they would never change was the great view of the river and the bay.

Earl poured some cereal into a bowl. Sally set the milk on the table and sat down with her cup of coffee. "Now don't get started on your reasons why Christine is just like me. She's your daughter too, and she has your genes as well. She's going to be just like both of us. And right now she's still walking a foot off the ground because of the letter about her scholarship."

"Hmm," said Earl, picking up the milk and pouring some on his Raisin Bran. "I guess I should be paying more attention to her growing up lately. All of a sudden she's no longer my little girl and becoming a young lady."

"Yes, you should," said Sally. "In fact, you haven't paid much attention to any of us these last several weeks."

"Okay." Earl threw up his arms in defeat. "How about you? Are you going to be late again getting home today?"

Sally Armstrong was part of the senior medical staff at the community hospital. The two of them had met while attending UW in Seattle, where Earl graduated with a degree in forest management and Sally with her doctorate in neurology from the medical school.

"Can't say." Sally took a quick bite of buttered toast. "I have a staff meeting this morning. The workload will depend on what the emergency room had to handle over the weekend and the new patient admittance schedule."

"Just thinking about supper tonight. How about if you pull one of your lasagnas out of the freezer? I'll put it in the oven and make a salad?"

"Sounds fine. You going into the office, or do you have to go to the tribal offices in Tokeland?

That's why I asked about the car. Christine should be home around noon."

"It's the office today—at least I think so. No call or message on my cell phone so far about having to meet anyone at the tribal offices." Sally started to get up to put her coffee cup in the dishwasher. "Before you go, there's something I need to tell you. It's about Leon Pence."

"Leon?" She hesitated, then put down her coffee cup and waited for Earl to say more. She watched his face. He had a look that she couldn't read, and she knew her husband. Something was on his mind. "What's going on?"

"Leon called me while I was watching Bernie at the robotics competition. Apparently a friend of his was killed up in Alaska. He's going up to check on things and arrange to bring the body home. He wants me to go with him. I haven't taken any time off, and my big log delivery is finished. I said yes—that I would go. I'd like to take Bernie along. Christine has her class and Bernie doesn't have anything planned for the summer. And, like you mentioned a few minutes ago, I can pay some attention to my son."

"He would be thrilled, I imagine," answered Sally. "You do need some days with less stress. As your in-house doctor, I've been noticing some signs lately."

Earl chuckled. "Yeah, this one was a rough assignment. I had a lot of pressure to get the shipment out on time."

"Well, I think it is a fine thing to do," remarked Sally. "We owe Leon more than we can ever repay. One can never do enough for someone who saves your life and your children's too."

"That's how I feel, Sally. It's why I had to say yes. There's also the matter of... " Earl hesitated. Do I tell her about the Eddie Jackson finding some of my lumber in Alaska? That Leon thinks I have something to look into as well?

"The matter of what?"

"Oh, I was just wondering about leaving you to help Christine with her plans to move to Seattle. We were going to go up and look at apartments."

"I think the two of us can do that by ourselves. We'll have fun without you and Bernie making weird comments about what a girl wants in a place to live. Go ahead and break the news to Bernie when he gets up. I've got to leave for the hospital. Doc Adams insists on starting his meetings on time."

"Yeah, I know," said Earl. Sally gave him a kiss on his forehead. "Don't forget to find the lasagna and set it out."

Earl finished his cereal and poured himself another cup of coffee. He washed out the pot and put dishes in the dishwasher, then sat back down to make a call to Leon to ask about travel arrangements so he could get airline tickets for himself and Bernie. He felt good about the decision and was glad that Sally was okay with it. There was no answer on Leon's cell phone. He left a message and sat for a moment trying to decide what to do. He wanted to get the flight arranged since Leon had said he wanted to go up to Juneau in the next couple of days. Earl decided to call the tribal police at LaPush and see if they knew where to find Leon. LaPush was a small place. He found the telephone number on their website.

A man answered the telephone. "Officer Perkins, can I help you?"

"Oscar? This is Earl Armstrong. How are you?"

"Well, Earl. How the heck you doing? What's it been—five years—since we seen each other?"

"Yeah, I guess so. The kids sure have grown up. Sally's fine too." Earl paused to take a sip of his coffee. "Can you locate Leon Pence for me? It's pretty important that I talk to him this morning. He wants me to go up to Alaska with him to help in the matter of Eddie Jackson's death."

"Leon? Yeah, we can track him down," replied Oscar. "Damn shame about Eddie. He was an alright guy. We are planning an honor ceremony for him when Leon brings his body back—being a veteran and all."

"That's a great thing to do. I remember attending the one for Leon's brother several years ago. Eddie's mother must be proud." Earl paused for a second and had another thought on how to locate Leon. "Say, maybe Mrs. Jackson would know. Leon is supposed to be making these arrangements for her."

"Ida Jackson? Eddie's mother?" Oscar replied with a puzzled voice. "You must have heard wrong, Earl. Ida Jackson died five years ago."

Earl was stunned. "But Leon said he talked to her. She gave him some pictures and asked for his help."

"I do not know about that," replied Oscar. "She died of heart failure a year after her husband died of cancer."

Earl didn't say anything for a minute and stared out the kitchen window. *What is going on? This isn't like Leon for him to lie to me about something.*

"Earl? You still there?" asked Oscar.

"Yeah. I'm just trying to figure something out. Well, if you locate Leon, have him call me. Okay?"

"Sure will. Take care, Earl."

CHAPTER 9

Juneau, Alaska

The Alaska Airlines flight carrying Earl, Bernie, and Leon landed in Juneau just before noon. Leon had arranged ahead for a chartered floatplane to take them the short distance across Chatham Strait to Hoonah later that afternoon. He wanted time in Juneau to meet with the Alaska state police to review their report on Eddie Jackson's accident and interview the state trooper who had conducted the investigation.

Earl had not approached Leon as to why he had lied about Eddie Jackson's mother. When the time was right, Leon would tell him. It was Leon's problem—not his. For now, Earl was glad to have a few hours in Juneau to show Bernie his grandparents' home. His grandfather had built a small house a few blocks north of downtown, not far from the Governor's Mansion. A young couple currently owned the house, and Earl enjoyed chatting with them and telling them a little bit of the history and what stories he knew about its first occupants. Bernie was in awe of the stories, tales of the days when Alaska was a territory after World War II, and fascinated by a city surrounded by mountains.

Walking back to the waterfront, all of these exciting and new things were outdone by a poster he saw in the window of a bookstore.

"Hey, Dad, look!" Bernie exclaimed. "There's going to be a MATE competition at the high school in two weeks. Are we going to still be here?"

"I don't think so, Son," Earl answered. "We're flying out to another town. We've got reservations to fly home in a week. I guess if we are still here, we might be able to do that. But didn't you have enough excitement winning the regional competition in Aberdeen?"

"Yeah, that was pretty great. But I'd love to watch what happens at this event. Teams will be operating their ROVs under simulated ice. That means relying totally on your onboard underwater cameras."

"I guess that would be interesting," Earl said as he tugged Bernie away from the poster. "It's time to meet up with Leon and then catch our flight. You're going to enjoy the floatplane. It's an opportunity to see just how rugged this country really is." Earl pointed up towards Mount Roberts, which was almost four thousand feet in elevation. A tram ascended from the cruise ship docks. "See those mountains up above? I'm going to ask Leon if he can get the pilot to make a loop up there so we can see the ice fields on the other side."

"Do you think there are hiking trails into the mountains where we're going?"

"I don't know, Bernie. I've never been to Hoonah. It's a lot smaller than Juneau—maybe only a couple hundred residents. Hiking is another matter, too. Hoonah is located on Chichagof Island, which has a large number of grizzlies. I mean lots of them." Earl winced at the thought of taking a hike and stumbling upon a bear. He still remembered running into a mountain goat in the Olympics and almost falling off a cliff. That feeling of nothing below him but empty space returned, sending a shiver up his spine.

Their walk through town took them past the Frontier Bar where a drinking crowd spilled out onto the sidewalk. Leon saw them approaching the bar from across the street and started across to meet them. They were a rough looking bunch, and he feared a confrontation as Earl pushed his way through. Leon's assumption proved to be right. Bernie bumped the arm of one of the men talking loudly with several buddies watching auto racing on one of the bar's TVs, spilling some of his beer. The man turned around to curse at Bernie, grabbing his arm in one of his meaty hands. "Hey, kid! Watch where you're going."

Earl stopped and stared at the man who wore a short-sleeve uniform shirt over huge muscled arms. He was bald except for a short beard and was at least a head taller than Earl.

Not known for his bravado, Earl suddenly became angry that the man had ahold of his son.

"Hey, bud. Ease off. He didn't mean to spill your beer."

The beefy man let go of Bernie and stuck a finger in Earl's chest. "What? Are you threatening me little man?" The man yelled in Earl's face and raised his arm to throw a punch at Earl.

"I ought to..."

Leon stepped forward and caught the man's wrist before he could strike Earl. He held it for a few seconds, looking directly into the man's shocked eyes. Then he bent the arm back and flipped him over onto his back on the sidewalk. The rest of the man's beer spilled on his chest.

"If you want to throw some punches, try me," Leon snarled as he stepped in front of Earl. He watched the shocked man struggle to regain an upright position. One of his buddies reached out to assist him.

"Easy, Hayden!" said a wiry young Asian man as he restrained his buddy. "I think it's time to get back to the supply boat. We're gonna be late."

The man called Hayden threw off his buddy's hand and stared, red-faced, at Leon. He was about to launch himself then backed off and snarled. "Maybe next time—just you and me." He threw his empty beer bottle onto the sidewalk, turned, and stomped off towards the docks. His buddy followed. Bernie watched in disbelief. Earl noticed the shock on Bernie's. He was a little amazed himself. Leon had taken the guy with one hand.

Bernie finally spoke. "Wow! That was great. But you know that was kind of weird about those guys in uniform? There was a logo on their shirts with the words 'Glacier World Security.' Have you ever heard of it?"

"Nope, I haven't," Earl replied. "If they work for a company or private lodge around here, it won't be on my bucket list, that's for sure."

The restaurant they picked was just above an old seaplane base now used by floatplanes for short flights over the ice fields. Earl had learned from a man on their flight from Seattle that the restaurant served great king crab legs. They were lucky and got a table next to the windows overlooking the harbor.

"What do you think of Alaska?" Leon asked Bernie as they reached their table.

"It's fantastic!" Bernie replied, putting aside the confrontation with the Glacier World man. "Mountains and snow everywhere you look. When I'm twenty-one, I'm going to come to Alaska and find a job."

Earl and Leon both laughed and looked at each other, realizing that they would have each said the same thing when they were teenagers.

"We'll see about that," said Earl. "First, you'll need to finish college. But I won't deny saying Alaska offers a lot of opportunity for a young man that wants to make something of himself. My grandfather did it and retired as a regional director for Alaska Fish and Game."

"Knowing you, Earl, I can see quite a lot of him in you."

Earl laughed at Leon's remark. "Well, the apple usually doesn't fall very far from the tree."

"Apple tree?" Bernie said. "What does an apple tree have to do with our family?"

Now both Leon and Earl laughed as Bernie stared at them, totally not understanding what his dad had meant.

So Earl explained. "It's just a saying. People tend to be a lot like their parents or grandparents."

They took a minute to check the menu and order two Alaskan Amber beers. Then Earl got to what was on his mind while Bernie studied his menu between watching the floatplanes land and take off. "So, Leon, did you learn anything about Eddie Jackson's accident?"

Leon shook his head. "It's more what I didn't learn."

"Really?" Earl responded. He laid down his menu to listen expectantly to Leon.

"Yeah, the written report and lack of answers to my questions did not give me a good feeling about the matter. The report included two statements by eyewitnesses to his accident, but both men were part of a construction team that returned to Singapore two days after the accident. Their work visas had apparently expired, and they left before being interviewed. Also, the accident scene was supposedly on a vessel that also departed the next day. The body had been removed and kept in a walk-in cooler on the dock. When I talked to the investigator, he said there wasn't much else to put in his report. The coroner here in Juneau concluded that the injuries and cause of death was clearly due to the body being badly crushed. He could not find any sign of foul play or other injury that might suggest any other cause of death."

"Huh. Sounds like it was just a freak accident."

"Yes, but the circumstances are kind of odd. First, Eddie was hired to work on a special park construction crew as a woodworker. For a couple of days, he was given a job assignment in one of the warehouses. There was no record of him working on a ship or a barge. If so, what was he doing on a vessel? The coroner's report did state that there was no blood-alcohol reading but the smell of alcohol was on his clothing. That conflicts with statements of people who knew him in Hoonah—that Eddie had quit drinking. So the accident could not be definitely pinned on alcohol."

"Then I guess you want to look into the matter some more. That why we're going to Hoonah?"

"Yup."

Before Earl could pursue Leon's plans further, the waitress returned with their drinks. Bernie had finished choosing and was watching another float plane land and taxi to the dock just below them.

Farther out in the channel, a large grey fishing boat headed towards a fuel dock.

Leon ran his left hand back over his ponytail and glanced back at his menu. He ordered an open-faced crab sandwich. Earl ordered a bowl of chowder, and Bernie chose the bucket of steamed clams. The restaurant had run out of crab legs.

After the waitress left to place their order, Leon elaborated on what he was thinking they should do next. "At least the state police said my paperwork is all in order. I can take custody of Eddie's remains. There is a funeral home here in Juneau that contracts with the state for situations like this. I just need to make a call to them to have the body airfreighted to Seattle. I want to get that done as soon as we finish lunch. We should still go out to Hoonah and take a look at where Eddie was living and try talk to some friends he may have made after coming up here. And then there is the matter of your missing lumber."

Leon went silent again and watched the fishing boat tie up to the fuel dock, thinking about what Frank, Eddie's mentor in Hoonah, had told him on the phone shortly after Eddie's death. Earl noticed Leon's silence and didn't press him further but wondered if there was something Leon was not telling him.

CHAPTER 10

Hoonah, Alaska

The short flight over to Hoonah from Juneau was nothing short of amazing for Bernie. After a circle above the Juneau Ice Fields and Mendenhall Glacier, as requested by Leon, the floatplane flew at a low altitude and followed the inside passage over a lighthouse, numerous small islets, and boats traveling in various directions. The pilot pointed to several humpback whales, but they dove before Bernie got a glimpse. Once they left Juneau, there were no roads. To get anywhere else, you had to take either a plane or a boat.

As they approached Hoonah, Bernie could make out the rugged snow-capped peaks of a high mountain range several miles distant beyond the broad expanse of open water. It was the Fairweather Range—a major source of the large glaciers in Glacier Bay National Park, one of the largest parks in the United States but with probably the fewest visitors because of its remoteness. There were two small communities just outside the boundaries of the park: Hoonah—an Alaskan Native village—and Gustavus, near the park's headquarters. The latter had several guest lodges and a small golf course frequented by golf addicts living in Juneau, which had no course of its own.

To Bernie's disappointment, the floatplane had wheels and landed on a runway a few miles out of town rather than on the water. Leon arranged for the town taxi to pick them up. There was a sign painted on the cab's doors that read "New York City Cab Company." How a Checker cab from New York ended up in a small Alaskan town no one seemed to know. Despite its rusted-out fenders and a lot of rattles, the old cab got them into town and dropped them off at a small bed-and-breakfast across the street from the café.

Hoonah, in addition to being an Alaskan Native settlement and one of the villages of the Tlingit Indians, was a fishing community. Between the city dock and a boat basin, upwards of 120 boats could be moored. The principal store was a trading company that stocked everything from groceries and beer to hardware. The town's main street extended from the boat basin to a former cannery site that the village corporation converted into an attraction for tourists disgorged from the cruise ships that docked at the facility several times a week during the summer.

As they arrived at the bed-and-breakfast and were collecting their luggage, Bernie's attention was drawn to a pretty girl with multi-colored hair sitting on the steps of the café. She seemed out of place, and his first thought was she might be visiting from back

East or maybe Seattle. She smiled as she watched Bernie, Earl, and Leon get out of the cab and enter the manager's office for the B&B.

"Bernie," called Earl. "Bernie!"

The boy jerked his gaze away from the girl on the steps. "Yeah, Dad. I'm coming."

"After we get our things into our rooms, Leon and I have to find the places where Eddie Jackson lived and worked. We want to talk to some of the people here in Hoonah that he may have known. If you want to wander around, that's okay, go ahead. Just be back in two hours and we'll have dinner in that café across the street."

Bernie glanced back across the street at the café. The girl on the steps was gone. He took his knapsack to their room and then decided to take his dad's suggestion. He checked out the harbor first, walking a short distance out onto the high breakwater that enclosed it. Most of the boats were fairly large and appeared to be working vessels equipped for what he guessed to be salmon fishing. Just across the entrance channel to the basin was a small rocky island with a few trees. There were also some crosses that he guessed were graves or some type of memorial.

Up the hill from the boat basin were several large buildings, so he walked in their direction next. One of the buildings was a community center. On the front of the building were three large animal paintings in Native American motif. They were colorful, and he wasn't sure what they were or why they were there.

He noticed the same girl he had seen when they arrived in Hoonah walking towards the center. However, this time it wasn't the girl that held his attention, but what she was carrying. He knew what it was and picked up his pace, heading for the main door to the building. He dashed up the wood steps and opened the door for her.

"Hi!" he said, trying not to show that he was breathing hard as he held one the double doors open. "Is that what I think it is?"

"I dunno what you think," the girl replied, "but thanks for holding the door. I didn't want to set it down. It's pretty delicate."

Bernie made a quick decision to follow her inside. "Excuse me, but I'm pretty sure that is an ROV."

"Yup, it's just one of the basic ROV kits, but we've added a lot of accessories," the girl responded. "You know something about ROVs?"

"Yeah, sure do. Back home, my buddies and I built one and competed with it."

"Where's home?"

"South Bend, Washington. Ah….it's about a hundred miles from Seattle, on the coast. South Bend is a small town kind of like here."

"That's cool," she said as she carefully set the ROV on a small table just inside the entry door. She took off her fatigue jacket and hung it next to some other jackets. Then she stuck out a hand. "My name's

Brooklyn. I saw you arrive in town earlier. Hmm, you said you competed in an ROV event?"

Bernie hesitated in accepting a handshake from a girl. Then, to avoid being embarrassed, took her hand. It was warm and soft. "Yeah, uh…two times. This year my team won the regional competition. That was just last week. Ah…my name is Bernie, Bernie Armstrong."

"Nice to meet you, Bernie. You can let go of my hand now. I think we've been introduced."

"Oh! Sorry," He blushed and withdrew his hand quickly as if he had just touched a hot stove.

"You going to be around town this evening? I'd like to see you again."

"See me? This evening? Yeah, I guess so…I mean we're staying in Hoonah for a few days. My dad and his friend have some business to attend to. Sure! But—"

Brooklyn smiled and quickly responded. "Now it's my turn to apologize. Our ROV team will be meeting here this evening to work on preparations for the Southeast Alaska regional competition in Juneau. It would be fantastic if you could come and tell us about your competition. We've never competed before."

"Wow, I saw a poster about that competition this afternoon. Sure! I mean… I'll have to ask my dad. I guess I could tell you about our event and my team's ROV. It was pretty exciting being a winner, and we beat a pretty good team from Aberdeen. They won the event last year. Just before the competition, we installed a 3D Robotics Attitude and Heading Reference System. It gave us better control for positioning our ROV."

"Wow, you had an AHRS on your ROV? I've read about them. I need to ask Mr. Tee if we have time to upgrade. It might be just the edge we need to beat the other ROVs for operating under ice."

"It's pretty superior to anything available unless you spend a lot of money. I'd be happy to explain it. Ah…that is if your team understands a little bit about programming and…"

"Not a problem with my team. Then it's set. We're meeting right here around 7:00 p.m. Now I have to hurry. I'm meeting with Mr. Tee. He's our computer mentor and the person that got a bunch of us interested in ROVs. You'll meet him this evening. He might look somewhat dorky, but he's really smart and has taught me a lot about computers and computer programming, that's for sure."

"My dad always says not to judge people until you really get to know something about them." He stepped back towards the front door and then stopped. "Can I ask you something? What are the animal figures painted on the outside wall of this building?"

"Oh, those are our clan symbols. Not mine, unfortunately, but the village's—the raven, wolf, and bear."

"Why do you say not mine? This is your town, isn't it?"

The girl smiled and her blue eyes sparkled. "My mom came up here from Seattle when she was young. She fell in love with one of the young Hoonah guys who ran off when she got pregnant. Since a person's clan symbol comes from your mother, I guess that makes me a non-raven or a non-wolf or non-bear. I'm a nothing clan."

Bernie nodded, understanding what she meant. "Do you know why she named you Brooklyn?"

"Mom said the guy was such a sweet talker, he could have sold her the Brooklyn Bridge. All she got was me. So, when I was born she decided to name me Brooklyn. Someday I'm going to go see that bridge."

"I like it—your name I mean," Bernie blushed as he took another step backward towards the door. Not knowing what else to say, he made a small hand wave. "So, see you later." He turned and bumped his forehead on the door.

Brooklyn made a small wave by twiddling her fingers and then hid a big smile with her hand.

Outside, Bernie walked quickly towards the B&B to meet his dad and Leon, his face red with embarrassment. He thought about Brooklyn—how smart she was and how her eyes sparkled with laughter. He had never met a girl like her before, and he had made a fool of himself in front of her. Maybe he could make a better impression tonight.

***

Earl and Leon left the B&B at the same time as Bernie and walked into the older part of the settlement. They were looking for the carving shed and the master carver who had been teaching Eddie Jackson. Just a short distance from the bayfront, they found the place used by the woodcarvers. There were several buildings—one was just a roofed-over pole structure open on all sides, used to carve long totem poles and canoes. Next to a brightly painted canoe, a large cedar log was in the process of being carved into a totem. There was a second building used as a lumber drying shed, and another building that was used for making masks, paddles, and other craft items for selling to tourists in the gift store at the cannery dock.

Earl quizzed Leon as they stopped to admire the canoe. "What do you expect to learn that you didn't already learn from the state troopers?"

"I do not know. Maybe what kind of man he became? Something I can tell his family that would give them comfort. Something to remember him by other than being a drunkard and pitying himself."

"I see what you mean. You're accepting the facts surrounding his death, however slim they are, and focusing on making him into someone who can be remembered for his better qualities. That's a fine thing to do, Leon."

"I guess that is all I can do under the circumstances," he answered. "Then we will focus on your problem—finding your missing logs."

"I don't even know where to begin to look. My broker swears the shipment made it to its destination which certainly wasn't Alaska. Ron said the shipping manifest and computer records all agree. Each and every container was tracked in a database used for international shipments. The records also agree with those kept by Lloyds of London, who insured my cargo. Only one problem—under the policy provisions, they won't honor any insurance claim unless I can prove otherwise."

"Then we will find them or at least how they got here. If we can prove that your logs were here in Southeast Alaska, they will have to pay up on your insurance policy."

"Yeah, in a region that has more timber than perhaps anywhere else in the world, except maybe the Amazon jungle. We need somewhere to start. Proving that Eddie Jackson's death was not an accident sounds like an easier problem."

"Hey, you might have something there. Maybe I am approaching this all wrong. Maybe I should assume Eddie was killed and look at the evidence that way."

"Well, let's find this master carver and see what he knows. The owner of the B&B said his name is Frank. Maybe Frank chatted with Eddie while working side by side on their carving projects. They may have talked about something that doesn't fit with what the troopers learned."

"I hope so," replied Leon as they entered the third building, which was just one large room.

Cedar shavings and chips covered the floor, giving off a pleasant aromatic odor. Earl liked the smell. It reminded him of the cedar mills back home.

The old carver sat working on a beautiful carving of a moon mask when Leon and Earl found him. His gnarled hands showed signs of arthritis, yet his strokes with a paintbrush were steady and smooth as he added red color next to black acrylic paint on the face of the mask. The two men patiently watched him work, not wanting to disturb his concentration. Finally, he cleaned his brush, laid it carefully among several others, and then looked up at Earl and Leon.

"Friends of Eddie?"

The old carver brushed aside some thin strands of long white hair and looked them over.

Leon spoke first. "I am Leon Pence. I spoke to you by phone after hearing about Eddie's death. I met with the state troopers in Juneau earlier today. They could not tell me much. We are trying to learn about what he was—"

Leon didn't get to finish his question before Frank spoke. "Well, I liked his work for one thing. His objects expressed originality rather than being copies of what other carvers make. He was going to be a good carver. He was part of a team working on that totem out there in the shed."

Earl started to ask a question. "Unfortunately, he died under strange circumstances that are not—"

"We never know when our time has come, young man," the old carver said. His sad eyes seemed to look right into Earl's skull. "It is not right that a man of his talent does not have the opportunity to carve his own totem to be remembered by before he passes over to the other shore."

"I think we would agree on that. Ah, we were told he was carving a—"

"Son, making a clan symbol and having it displayed before your people is a great honor to a carver. I teach this to all of my apprentices. We begin a project by cleansing ourselves in a sweat lodge and then seeking a Shaman's blessing of the wood. What we produce has a soul and becomes a part of our lives. Eddie embraced these principles—maybe because of his past problems with the liquor."

"We…we believe he had completed a representation of a particular clan symbol. Did you assist him with that?" Earl's question was the first one they had been able to fully express.

Instead of answering directly, the old carver turned his head slightly to look across the room at another worktable. Something lay on the table covered with an old wool blanket. Earl and Leon followed his gaze. They both knew what lay beneath it.

The master carver continued to stare across the room. "Eddie seemed to know he had to do this project as part of his healing. There was something about the source of the wood—said it came from a place near his homeland. He brought several pieces back from his job across the strait. He told me they insisted the scraps be destroyed but he couldn't do that. So he began with the cleansing and having a blessing of the wood. He would stare at the piece for long periods, touching it and turning it. Then he began to carve."

"Frank, I believe the clan symbol is that of my tribe. May we see it?" Earl asked.

"Of course! Why didn't you ask sooner?"

Earl and Leon walked over to the bench and carefully pulled the blanket to one side. What lay underneath was a remarkable carving—the very same one in the picture that Leon had received. There were six salmon carved in relief around the edge of the circular object. They were beautifully painted and seemed to leap right off the carving. In the center was the Shoalwater brand—an eagle sitting on a post with its wings spread, ready to take flight.

CHAPTER 11

Hoonah, Alaska

The telephone call from Ron Pike was unexpected. Earl sat in the café with Leon, having a Coke and talking with several residents of Hoonah who were acquainted with Eddie Jackson. He saw a message in his voicemail, excused himself, and walked across the street to their room to return the call and see if Bernie had showed up so they could have dinner. He could tell by the tone of Ron's message that something was wrong. Earl was right about his suspicion, as Ron got straight to the problem.

"Got a report from Japan in response to my inquiry," said Ron. "Your containers were off-loaded from the ship and held up in the customs yard. It took three days for an official to inspect the cargo against the manifest."

"Yes?"

"There's a bit of a problem. The container identification numbers check out and seals in place, but when they opened them, ten of them were empty."

"That's not possible. I personally watched both the loading process and the US Customs official in

Aberdeen place a seal on each of the OFI cargo containers. Something must be messed up in the records."

"I've got a copy right here. Let me look at it again." Ron took a few seconds to flip through the documents that had been forwarded to him through the freight forwarder's office in Japan. "The entry for each of the flagged containers states 'No Contents.' They are red flagged to be checked for possible theft while in the transit yard. We're going to have to do the same thing on this end before they were loaded on the ship. I don't know what else to tell you, Earl. This doesn't look good."

"Well, I appreciate the information. It rather confirms what I already know, which really stinks. I need you to keep on this, Ron. Check out where those OFI containers were every step of the way."

"Wait a second, Earl. Did your say they your containers were from OFI, Overseas Freightways International? "

"Absolutely, I arranged for them myself."

"All twenty of them?"

"Yup."

Ron took another look at the manifest from Japan. "It says here that the ten empty containers were supplied by World Freight Limited. The ID numbers match, but the container company doesn't. I'm definitely going to look into this."

"Okay, Ron. We both have some work to do on this." He hung up and looked again at Eddie

Jackson's beautiful wood carving, which now lay on the small desk next to him. "How the heck did you get here?"

***

Bernie arrived early at the community center. He was in the main lobby, wondering where Brooklyn's team was going to meet, when he heard a man's voice coming from a partly open door to his right. Bernie decided to ask him.

At the doorway, his eyes got wide with his first look at the room's interior. It reminded him of pictures of a NASA control room. There were two long rows of desktop computers, some with two or three monitors. Several moving displays had blinking red and green dots on a grid. Others showed overlapping arcs with in an assortment of colors. On the far side of the room, there was a larger console with a man seated in front of it. The console held a half dozen monitors. The man was concentrating on what was on the monitors and tapping on a keyboard. He wore earphones, and his head nodded rhythmically. The man had long jet-black hair that stuck out in every direction. His round face was unshaven. He looked rather peculiar to Bernie. The man was short with a stocky body and no neck to speak of. His wild hair made his head appear much larger than an average person's.

Bernie hesitated to enter the room and approach the man. His question about where to find the ROV team seemed insignificant among such complex equipment. He was about to turn around when the man suddenly stopped working, pulled off his headset, and stared directly at Bernie.

"Are you one of the three outlanders here in our village to find out about Eddie Jackson?" the man bellowed.

Bernie stood frozen with the man's words.

"Come on in, young man. You might find this room interesting. I bet you're the ROV champ that Brooklyn told me about. Your name's what? Bernie Armstrong?"

"Ah…yes, sir," Bernie replied as he discovered he could still move his feet. He cautiously approached the man while looking around the room.

"Welcome! My name is Lewis Teebottom. But everyone calls me Lewis, or Mr. Tee to the young folk. Take your pick." The man swung his chair around and stood up to shake hands.

Bernie was surprised to notice Mr. Tee was shorter than he was. The man wore denim jeans and a dirty Star Wars T-shirt imprinted with the words "Fly closer Hans! That's no Moon!"

He waved one of his arms towards the numerous racks of electronic components around the room like he was directing an orchestra. "By the look on your face, I suppose you're surprised to see such stuff outside of a NASA control center. We're not

NASA, but our work is pretty close to theirs in retrospect."

Still puzzled, Bernie took a closer look at the banks of electronic displays and noticed that all of them had labels above them. A set of monitors close to him was labeled NS 101-129. He had no idea what it meant, but he nodded anyway.

Mr. Tee laughed as he recognized the boy's bewilderment. "It's satellite monitoring equipment, my boy. We're monitoring over fifty very small satellites, called nanosats, which circle Earth in low orbit, gathering data on a fishing fleet in the Gulf of Alaska as well as any other vessels in the area. This is a research project for the University of Alaska, and like I said, we're not NASA, but we are funded by NOAA, and NASA launched them for us. The purpose is to better understand the migration of various species of bottom fish like halibut and cod. The data we collect on vessel movement is interfaced with catch records kept by our monitors onboard ten of the fishing boats. Several of our brightest high school students are assisting me with the data development and mapping. You've met one of them."

Bernie understood why several consoles along one wall were set up as computer workstations. Some of the monitors were dark, while others showed a series of loops and squiggly colored lines overlaying a grid of longitude and latitude lines.

The sound of voices and the building's main doors opening and banging shut interrupted Lewis's explanation. Five young people following Brooklyn surged into the room, their laughter and carrying on diminishing to just a few jabs at one another and some whispers. The gang fell silent, and all eyes were on Bernie as Brooklyn spoke.

"Hi, Mr. Tee. I see you've met our celebrity guest speaker for this evening." She turned to her friends. "Hey, team, this is Bernie Armstrong from the Lower 48. He won a regional MATE competition. With his advice, we are going to win the Alaska state competition."

The gang cheered, and Bernie swallowed hard as he offered a weak smile. What had he walked into? He kept smiling as the group pressed forward to greet him and shake his hand. They were not much different from his own team back home—same age, same eagerness to learn and work together—except for Lewis Teebottom and these kids being Alaskan Native. While he had felt a bit uneasy meeting Mr. Tee, the friendliness of this small group his own age melted away his uneasiness with the Native culture and the strange environment of this small Alaskan community.

Bernie spent the next hour and a half talking about his own experience competing in a MATE competition and the preparation and hours of practicing that his team had done. He told them about how important it was for each team member to have a specific duty and to practice it. A lot of high school teams that competed had not done enough practicing. He was surprised to find that they were all interested in being the software engineer, as Bernie had been for his team. Obviously they had all learned well under Lewis Teebottom's tutelage.

Mr. Tee listened to Bernie's entire talk rather than returning to his work station. He even had questions of his own, although Bernie felt he already knew the answers and only asked the questions for the benefit of the group. Even so, Bernie was very impressed and could see why Brooklyn and the others loved the odd little man.

When Bernie finished, the group finally gathered around the ROV and examined a newly installed manipulator arm with its claw for picking up things. They were discussing possible names for the ROV and their team when the door to the center opened. Leon and Earl entered. Bernie looked up and invited them to join the group. He did the introductions and was pleased he could remember each of the kids' names. He pointed out each of the boys and paused ever so slightly with the introduction of Brooklyn. "And this is Brooklyn." He beamed proudly as he introduced them to his dad. "This is my father, Earl Armstrong, and his friend, Leon Pence."

Mr. Tee did not wait to be introduced, stepping forward to greet Earl and Leon. "Hi, I'm Lewis Teebottom." He shook hands with Earl and then Leon. "Kind of figured you two would get around to finding me sooner or later. Let's let these young people figure out what to name their ROV while we talk in my office." Lewis led the way to a small office, where he cleared stacks of books and reams of computer printouts off of a couple of well-used folding chairs.

"So, you want to know about Eddie Jackson?"

Earl and Leon both nodded.

"Well, first of all, I was shocked to learn about Eddie's death, and I'm glad you're here to look into it. If you haven't discovered it already, there's something fishy about the whole thing. In addition to the mystery, something weird happened a few days ago. Eddie lived in a cabin that I own, and it was ransacked. That was when I knew for sure something was not right. We never have break-ins like that around here. No one even locks their doors."

"How well did you know Eddie?" asked Leon. "Were you friends? Did he tell you about working at Glacier World?"

"Just about everybody in town knew that, because they haven't been hiring local people. Some guys in town might have been a little jealous about Eddie getting hired, but he got the job because he was a woodworker, wasn't local, and all our other carvers were busy. Eddie also needed the money. I can't call us friends, but we chatted occasionally about stuff."

"Did he ever mention what they were having him work on, like on the dock?" asked Leon.

"No, he avoided saying anything about his employers or what he was doing day to day. In fact, I think he mentioned that he wasn't supposed to speak about it, which I found interesting. A couple of weeks after he started work at Glacier World, I noticed a change in Eddie's mood. He seemed disturbed about something and wouldn't respond to light chitchat."

"So what was your impression of him overall?" asked Earl. "Were you aware he was an alcoholic?"

"This is a small town. He told me once that he had been a heavy drinker, but as far as I know, he never drank after he got here. We've got plenty of hard-case drinkers, but Eddie didn't join them. I'd say he loved his time in Hoonah. He did mention his friends and family down in Washington quite a bit, that he wasn't going to let them down. He would be somebody someday."

Earl nodded quite a few times listening to Lewis. What he said fit everything they knew so far and supported their conclusion that things had been going well for Eddie and alcohol was no longer a problem in his life. They had to rule out alcohol as a cause of his accident. Eddie had everything going for him.

Earl brought up his timber problem, which increasingly seemed to be connected to Eddie. He described how he, as a forester, had put together a valuable timber sale that had been shipped to Japan but had never arrived.

Lewis frowned when Earl told him about his containers showing up in Japan marked "No Contents," and that it simply was not possible given the fact that they were sealed before shipment and still sealed upon arrival at the customs yard in Japan.

"Just a second," Lewis said, interrupting Earl. "Tell me again the name of the shipper and either the date these containers left Aberdeen or arrived in Japan."

"The company is OFI, and I'm pretty sure the containers arrived around the first of last month."

"Okay," Lewis said, interrupting Earl again. "Hold your story right there. Let's see if we can find the records ourselves, and whether or not there is something else they didn't tell you."

"You can access OFI's records?" asked Leon, who had been listening while he studied Lewis. He was very impressed with his knowledge.

"Not officially, of course," Lewis replied as he turned to a small laptop on his desk.

Lewis took a small black notebook out of the back pocket of his trousers and set it next to his keyboard, then started tapping away on the keys. There were a number of beeps and odd sounds to which he shook his head and tapped quickly on the keyboard with his stubby fingers. He smiled and scrolled through a few screens, then he paused and clicked another key at the top of the keyboard. A large monitor behind him came to life, and Leon and Earl could see what he was looking at on his laptop, lines of data across the screen.

"Okay, I'm in OFI's database. It's not very sophisticated, so let's find your records." A few seconds later, Lewis's rapid scrolling stopped and they could see a record of the twenty containers for the Shoalwater Corporation. He clicked the cursor over each of the lines and columns of entered data, then stopped. Lewis shook his head as he spoke. "As I thought, I'm not the only person who has hacked into this database. Some of the key information has been altered."

"What?" Earl said. "You're saying the shipping records have been altered? Who would do that? Maybe it was someone outside of OFI that changed the records. But why?"

"If it was, that shouldn't be too hard to determine if they didn't cover their tracks well," Lewis answered. He took a moment to jot down some information in his notebook and then started hammering away again on the keyboard, all the while shaking his head and smiling. "They went through a group in China that is well known for corporate hacking. The IP address is as plain as if they had handed us their business card. Then again, these guys don't care and figure they're pretty immune to being caught." Lewis took a drink from a can of Coke that was sitting next to his console, and then belched as he started tapping the keyboard again. "What I want to do is see if I can follow the trail further and find out who really wanted the shipment information changed. To do so, I've got to hack the hackers."

Earl and Leon were hopeless in trying to follow the code and lines of data on the screen. Lewis obviously knew what he was looking for, and seconds later the screen stopped scrolling again. It displayed a copy of an electronic financial transaction. At the top of it was a name—GRI, Global Resorts International, Singapore.

Lewis relaxed and sat back in his chair and pointed to the line of text. "I don't suppose either of you recognize that name, but probably everyone living here in Hoonah sure does. GRI is the owner of Glacier World."

Earl was shocked. "You mean that big theme park under construction somehow stole my cargo of premium lumber? Why would they do that? If they wanted good timber for something they are building over there, they could just contact us and we would gladly sell them all they wanted."

"I think it is bigger than that," commented Leon as he studied the data still visible on Lewis's monitor. "Only ten of the twenty containers in your shipment are reported as empty. The other ten checked out. If you look further down the ship's manifest, there are ten containers for other shippers also reported as empty of their cargo. Based on what they were supposed to contain, whoever emptied them made off with a pretty valuable haul—military hardware, tractor parts, and sportswear."

Lewis examined the data then wrote down some more numbers in his notebook. "Guys, if someone over at Glacier World or GRI is behind this, there's one way to find out for sure."

"What are you referring to?" Earl asked.

"You're going to have to access their computers." Lewis leaned back in his chair. "I can't do that from here. They have too many security protocols. The only possible way the records can be accessed is to get inside Glacier World."

Earl looked at Leon, who was nodding in agreement. Earl wasn't sure of the idea and decided to shift back to their original objective—finding out about Eddie Jackson's death.

"I think we should sleep on that idea. Lewis, you said you could show us where Eddie lived. Leon and I would like to do that. We met with Frank and know what Eddie was did, but maybe there's something at his residence that can tell us more about the last couple weeks of his life while he was working over in Glacier World."

"Let's do it," replied Lewis, jumping up from his chair. "I've got my car right outside. We could walk, but with my short legs, I prefer to ride." He turned to Brooklyn and her friends. "Can you guys close up the building and get Bernie back to the B&B?"

"Sure, Mr. Tee," replied Brooklyn.

Earl and Leon rode up to the cabin with Lewis. It was not what they had expected. The place was an old log cabin and might have fallen over if it weren't for some poles supporting one side. The cabin door was broken, and Lewis hadn't fixed it. Inside they found the place a mess with clothing and other contents of drawers all strewn about. Still, Leon and Earl prowled around looking for anything that would tell them more about Eddie's job at Glacier World. Leon discovered some pay stubs along with some unopened mail next to a coffee pot in the kitchen area. While Leon was examining the dates on the pay stubs, Earl picked up a framed picture from among some clothes and other objects strewn about the floor. It showed three men wearing desert military fatigues. The man in the center was Leon. Earl assumed one of the other men was Eddie Jackson, but he wondered who the third man was. The three men were all Native American and appeared to be close friends. Did the picture have something to do with Leon lying? Earl placed the picture on a bureau that was absent its drawers. He turned towards Leon, but his friend showed no sign of seeing Earl examine the photograph.

CHAPTER 12

Hoonah, Alaska

The following morning, Earl and Leon sat at a table in the café, sipping their cups of black coffee. It was early, and they had let Bernie sleep in. Both men had slept little, thinking about everything they had learned over the last twenty-four hours from the state police, Frank, and then Lewis Teebottom. Lewis was a great help in closing the loop, and now both Earl and Leon had come to the same conclusion. Glacier World was somehow behind both of their situations—Eddie Jackson's death and Earl's missing lumber. Were Eddie being murdered and his residence being ransacked a cover-up? If so why? What could be so important at a tourist attraction? Was Lewis correct in his suggestion that they had to break into Glacier World's computers?

The bacon and eggs breakfast plate order for Earl arrived. He attacked it. For some reason he was quite hungry and could think of no other reason than being in Alaska. The weather was a lot cooler than at home, but most of all, it was invigorating.

Leon had ordered French toast, and the order Flo Whiting set in front of him was huge.

"What are we going to do now?" Earl asked. "From what we've learned, not many people around here know what's going on over at this Glacier World theme park or whatever the place is. It's supposed to be off-limits—at least until it opens for tourist business."

Leon poured some huckleberry syrup on the French toast before answering. "Well, since we cannot just walk in and talk to those folks, there is only one thing we can do."

"What's that?" Earl asked. "Other than taking our rather fantastic story to the state police, I'm at a loss at what to do."

"We do what I was taught while in the Marines." Leon scooped up a forkful of hash browns. "Do a recon mission."

"Okay. Just how would we do that?" Earl asked, taking a swallow of his coffee.

"According to Lewis, GRI requested their building plans not be made public. With no plans and no recent aerial photos of the area, we need to find out what it looks like today and observe what is going on. We find a high point and take our own photographs and observations."

"You mean charter another plane and do a fly over?" Earl asked.

"Nope. On the west side of the inlet there is a high ridge—not quite a mountain range, but high enough. We could look right down on the place. The only problem is there are not any roads. It is in the national park and a remote area. We have to hike up from the far side through national park lands."

"Take another hike in a national park? Not the same result as the last hike, I hope," said Earl. He thought about it for a minute, took a bite of his eggs and another swallow of coffee then nodded his head. "Sounds plausible. Take a little hike and take a few photographs that we can study, then decide what to do next."

Earl finished off his hearty breakfast and looked for Flo for a refill of his coffee cup. Leon ate his French toast as he thought through how they could perform a recon.

"Actually, I am thinking we should plan on several days. Has to be more than a day hike. We have got to find some proper camping gear plus someone who has a rifle they can loan us. It is serious bear country. One of the guys I talked to yesterday said there is a man here in Hoonah whose brother was killed late last year over in Excursion Inlet. His name is Pete Hunt. He and his brother had a fish camp on an island not far from there, so he is probably well equipped to camp out under any conditions. We would have to find a location to set up our camp at an elevation of several thousand feet, quite possibly in a snow field. No fire and no lights—it would have to be total blackout to avoid being observed. We cannot take a chance of being seen, and that means at night as well as during the day."

"So, what can I do? I'm coming along, right?" Earl asked.

"There is plenty for you to do. I am sure part of your training and work as a forester is mapping, right? I want you to draw us a detailed map of every inch of Glacier World. If we get the chance to go there, and we probably will, we need to be able to find our way around even at night."

Earl shoved his empty plate aside and took a sip of his refilled cup of coffee. "I like it, Leon. Let's do it."

***

For the next several days, Leon and Earl worked on arrangements for their trip to the top of Excursion Ridge. They would be camping at three thousand feet in a saddle between two mountain peaks, which would put them less than a half mile from the Glacier World complex. They would be able to easily observe any activities going on among the buildings or along the dock, as well as at an airfield just south of the resort.

Leon began by asking where to find Pete Hunt. He found him helping some friends on a fishing boat at the marina. They were putting a new seine net on the boat using a large power block suspended in the boat's rigging. He watched them work for a few minutes from the finger float before starting a conversation.

"That power block must make hauling in a net full of fish a lot easier," he remarked.

A tall, slender young man responded with a slight laugh in his voice. "Yeah, if only the net was full of salmon. It was a lousy season this year."

"One of you guys named Pete Hunt?" Leon asked. "I was told he might be down here somewhere."

"That would be me," the slender man answered. "You're one of those curious strangers in town everyone's been talking about. Right?"

"Name is Leon Pence. I am a friend of Eddie Jackson, the guy who was killed in an accident working at Glacier World."

"Huh, too many accidents associated with Glacier World, if you ask me," responded Pete.

"I am," said Leon. "When you get a chance I would like to talk to you about Eddie and this place called Glacier World. Can I buy you lunch up at the café?"

"I didn't know Jackson, and most of us here in Hoonah don't have many good things to say about Glacier World, but that's an offer I sure will accept. These guys aren't paying me a damn thing for helping them out." The other two guys on the boat laughed. "See what I mean?" said Pete. He pulled off his work gloves, jumped off the boat onto the dock, and approached Leon.

"The least I can do is shake hands with my lunch ticket," said Pete as he stuck out a hand.

"Pleased to meet you, Leon Pence. Let's go see what Flo Whiting has got for lunch specials."

Pete and Leon walked up to the café. They chatted about the uncertainties of making a living at commercial fishing as they walked. It was still early, and the café's lunch crowd had not yet arrived. Flo Whiting was taking a coffee break before the noon crowd arrived, sitting at a back table with Brooklyn as they walked through the door.

"Morning Flo. Morning Brooklyn," Pete said with a big smile as he hung his jacket on the back of his chair. "You two been introduced to Leon Pence?"

"I met Brooklyn at the center last night," said Leon, nodding in recognition to her. "Pleasure to meet you, Flo. You serve a man-sized meal. Glad I brought a big appetite with me from the Lower 48."

"Well then it's a good thing you two got here early," replied Flo with a smile as she shook hands with Leon. "The special today is meat loaf, and it goes quickly with the hungry eaters here in Hoonah."

Leon and Pete both chuckled and responded at the same time. "Sounds good to me." They sat down at the table near the big window, Flo right behind them with two cups of coffee.

"I hear you and Eddie Jackson were friends," said Flo as she set a cup of fresh black coffee in front of each of them along with a pitcher of milk for Pete. "You take milk or cream, Mr. Pence?"

"Take mine black, Flo, and call me Leon, okay?"

"Alright," she replied. "You belong to the same tribe as Eddie?"

"Yeah, the Quileute Tribe, down in Washington State," said Leon. "Did you know Eddie?"

"Chatted with him quite a bit," Flo answered. "He would come in late most mornings for a cup of coffee and dry toast. Eddie liked to talk when other folks were not around. He sure could smile. I don't think I ever saw him without a grin on his face. You noticed because he was missing a couple of teeth."

"Yeah, that was Eddie," replied Leon. "You could not help but like him because he was always grinning. Did he tell you any of his dumb Indian jokes?"

"Oh yeah, I think I must've heard the same ones two or three times."

"Eddie and I served together in Afghanistan. After a couple of blast concussions his memory cells got a little rattled. But you know? I miss hearing him tell his silly stories."

"I guess I do too," said Flo. "I keep expecting him to walk through that door." A couple of new customers walked in and took a table near where Brooklyn sat. "We'll have to continue this conversation another time. I've got some customers. Your meat loaf plate lunch should be ready in a few minutes." Flo headed over to the two guys that had just walked in. "Hello, Danny, Joe. You guys want the special today, or do you want to see a menu?"

Pete's eyes followed Flo as she walked away. "Wouldn't be the same without Flo, either. She's kind of a fixture around here now—her and Brooklyn. My brother was too, but in a different kind of way."

"How is that?" asked Leon. "Do you mind talking about him?"

"Not at all," Pete replied. "I think about him almost every day. Kind of keeps him alive in a way. He was an ornery kind of guy. He would open his mouth and say something that would tick off everyone around him. But you got immune to it. Now that he's gone, you miss hearing him be a loud mouth."

"I talked to Dave Williams with the state troopers a few days ago. They told me you were his brother. Dave mentioned a few things about your brother's death. Excuse me for asking, but did he really die from being mauled by some type of predator?"

"Yeah, the coroner's report alluded to the fact that he suffered some trauma from a blow to the head, but it could have been from a fall. He died from loss of blood due to his throat being ripped out. There were a lot of bites and scratches all over his body from some kind of small animal. The coroner couldn't make a positive identification—maybe a wolverine or land otter—at least according to the superstitious folks around town. I don't know what to make of it and neither did Dave Williams. Neither he nor his deputy could find any kind of animal tracks near the body. The other odd thing was no blood except on his clothes. Of course it could have been washed away by the rain or tidewater."

"You do not sound convinced," said Leon. Flo interrupted the conversation, bringing over lunch.

"Enjoy the meat loaf, guys," she said. "No seconds though. It's popular around here."

"Thanks, Flo." replied Leon. He took a quick bite. "Hmmm…just like my mother used to make." The two men ate silently for a few minutes, enjoying the hot meal. Leon could see that Pete was thinking about what he had said.

"I wasn't convinced by either the coroner's report or Dave Williams," Pete finally said as he put down his fork and took a sip of his coffee. "The facts don't add up—no blood and no animal tracks. Yes, Raz could have been trying to reach the safety of his boat. But why did he drop his gun and not try to shoot some critter? The whole thing could have been staged."

"Dave Williams never mentioned that possibility to me," replied Leon as he finished off his piece of meat loaf.

"That's because he's not allowed to speculate and has to go by the facts. His problem was those Glacier World security—apparently they were no help at all and kept telling him that their patrols had reported a bunch of land otters were hanging around the mouth of the river for several days before they saw Raz's body on the beach."

"Pete, I have to confess something." Leon glanced around to see if anyone was focused on their conversation. "I want to do a little investigation into how Eddie Jackson died over at Glacier World. To do that, I want to observe the place with a friend of mine, then maybe sneak in and look around. Maybe find an employee or two who would be willing to talk to me. I need your help."

"Interesting idea," said Pete. "Just how do you plan on doing that?"

"I want to hike up the back side of the ridge opposite the place and set up an observation post for a couple of days. That means locating some camping gear and a guide to take my friend Earl Armstrong and I up there."

"You just found your guide. Count me in for whatever you need. For my brother's sake." Pete reached over with his right hand to shake on it.

Leon smiled. "I sure appreciate being able to count on your help."

Old Frank, the wood carver, came through the front door. Leon's expression changed when he saw him, and he pushed back from their table. "Excuse me Pete, but I have to speak to Frank about something important. I owe you a bunch of lunches, now." Leon rose and started to walk over to where Frank had taken a seat at another table.

"No you won't," replied Pete. "I'm doing this for Raz."

***

Later that afternoon, Leon walked over to the wood carving sheds, thinking about old Frank. He could swear the guy was a psychic. Maybe it was the look on his face as he had approached Frank in the café, or maybe it was the call he had made to Frank several weeks ago while he was still at home, but Frank seemed to know that at some point Leon needed to see him and have a serious chat. Whatever the reason, Frank had told him to come on over later without Leon even asking.

Leon's thoughts drifted as he walked up to the carving sheds. His body shook as he experienced flashbacks to his time in Afghanistan, along with memories of Eddie and his brother, both now dead. He needed more than a chat with Frank. He was messed up again and needed to seriously talk to somebody about Eddie.

When he arrived at the shed, Frank had a surprise for him. Behind the shed, Frank had a sweat lodge prepared with a fire started. The animal-hide-covered structure was filled with steam. Leon just shook his head. Frank truly was reading his mind. He had prepared the perfect place for the two of them to sit and deal with the bad spirits that had been gnawing on his soul for weeks.

After spending several hours with Frank in the sweat lodge, Leon felt good. In fact, he felt better than he had in weeks. He was ready to share the details of his plan to observe and investigate Glacier World with Earl and Lewis, but he still owed Earl an explanation for lying to him about Ida Jackson. Maybe he could muster enough courage to do that while they were camped out on the ridge.

***

Pete Hunt was the perfect addition to their team. He had everything they would need, had climbed Excursion Ridge several times, and knew the park ranger who would have to be notified about their backcountry hike. In fact, using a guided trip made the perfect cover for what they were planning. Pete would take care of the national park arrangements and arrange for a boat to take them across Icy Strait.

Meanwhile, Leon and Earl met Lewis Teebottom at his office to study available aerial photos and set up a communication link for any emergency. Lewis had a couple of extra satellite phones for use by his NOAA grant monitors assigned to the fishing boats out in the Gulf of Alaska. Lewis also had another good surprise for them. He spent some of his time off photographing wildlife and let them have his Canon camera with a 400 mm super telephoto lens and a tripod. Pete Hunt had a spotting scope which he said would come in handy for their observations.

Pete warned that they were very likely to encounter snow. On the higher elevations of the ridge, the snow cover had not melted off and often didn't even by late summer. This would add to their problem of stealth, since they would need to camouflage themselves against a white background. Pete's wife, Liz, was enlisted to make each of them slipover jackets and pants out of white bed sheets. By the time all of their gear was assembled and ready to be loaded onto the boat, they figured there were over two hundred pounds of equipment and supplies. Pete generously offered to make several trips up the ridge from a friend's home in Gustavus, which would be their starting point, while Leon and Earl set up their base camp and began their observations.

They all had dinner together at the café before leaving. Pete and Liz were invited along with Lewis. To everyone, the risk that Earl and Leon were taking made for a somber gathering. The deaths of Eddie and Raz were a subject they found impossible to avoid. They were still mystified about Eddie's accident and the peculiar circumstances surrounding Raz's death. Had there been a cover-up in both instances? The people at Glacier World had shown little cooperation with the state troopers. This and the strict enforcement of the exclusion zone around Glacier World meant that spying on the place was dangerous.

From the start of their planning, Earl had been adamant that Bernie had to stay in Hoonah. Bernie sulked for a day. When Earl presented his concerns to Pete and asked for advice on what to do with Bernie, Pete immediately offered his home. Liz would take care of him. Lewis offered to look after Bernie during daytime hours when he could be at the center and perhaps assist with the work on tracking fishing vessels out in the gulf. When Bernie was informed about the offer to work on the NOAA grant, it more than offset his desire to accompany his dad. He was the happiest person at the dinner and spent the whole evening chatting quietly with Brooklyn.

CHAPTER 13

Gustavus, Alaska

The next morning when they checked the weather forecast, a light rain was predicted for the Hoonah and Gustavus areas. It would be clear by late evening so they did not rush to cross over to the north side of Icy Strait, planning to spend the night at the home of Pete's friend. Their ascent of Expedition Ridge would start the following morning. With little more than game trails to follow, the trek would be difficult. The first mile involved cross-country hiking through large patches of muskeg. Pete had told them it was like thawed tundra and they had to be careful when crossing it. Once they cleared the timber-covered slopes, they would probably be in snowfields. Leon always carried a compass and had brought it with him to Alaska, but having Pete guide them to the top of the ridge was more reassuring, as Pete could pick the easiest route.

Leon was the first person to step outside early the next morning to check the weather. It had cleared just as predicted with a rosy-pink sky casting a glow on the forested mountains. They would climb that day and start their reconnaissance of Glacier World the next.

The first part of their journey was simple. Pete's friend drove them to the end of the road, but from there they had to first cross a fast-flowing stream at the bottom of a small canyon, then climb up the other side before reaching a mile-wide stretch of muskeg.

When they reached the muskeg, Earl noticed that at least the terrain made it easy to see where you were headed. There was not much brush, and the trees were widely spaced. The problem was the ground. It was either spongy grass growing over a peat bog or small ponds that were too deep to wade, with no solid bottom. They ended up meandering across the muskeg terrain rather than following a straight line.

Both Leon and Earl took this part of the trek in stride. It turned out not to be difficult—just frustrating—and gave them time to think about what lay ahead once they reached the top. They withheld their feelings of anticipation, and the only conversation between them during the first part of the climb dealt with adjusting loads and a few jokes about what heavy items they may have packed and would not need. Once in a while, one of them made a wisecrack about what they may have left behind, but there was not too much concern about that, as they could always radio Lewis to see that whatever they needed got to Gustavus for one of Pete's return trips.

It took the three men over three hours to reach the first of last winter's snow. With the rain the day before, the snow was wet and affected their progress. It also caused their pants and shoes to become soaked. As they got closer to the top of the ridge, the snow was deeper and firmer, holding their weight. Pete was the first to enter the small bowl-shaped saddle between the two peaks that they had selected as their vantage point.

"There's good shelter for setting up your tent next to that overhanging rock on the south side," said Pete.

Earl dropped his pack and started walking off towards the east side of the bowl, curious to see what the theme park looked like.

Leon hollered at him. "Hold on, Earl. Taking a look is okay but wait until we have picked the best spot. We are here to observe—not to be observed."

"Sorry!" Earl answered as he stopped and turned. "You're right, of course. That was stupid of me. I could have messed up all of our planning."

"Watch where you walk around in the snow as well," said Leon as he pointed to Earl's tracks across the deeper snow in the saddle. "If they have a plane and it flies this way, our tracks will stand out like a road sign. Try using the rocky ground where the snow has melted off."

"Another mistake," replied Earl. "Maybe we can wipe them out or if a wind comes up they will get covered up."

"That is okay, Earl. It is not quite like our lives depend on it. At least, I hope not."

It took an hour to set up their camp and give Pete a bit of rest before he headed back down. He had less than four hours until it was dark, and they figured that with an empty pack and a downhill journey he should make it down in time. Pete would spend the night at his friend's cabin and head back up the next morning. They said their goodbyes, and Pete headed back to the west. "At least you'll have a hot meal and a glass of scotch waiting for you, Pete," commented Earl as he rested against his pack.

"Yeah!" Pete answered. "I'm planning on it. Those thoughts will keep me going. You guys enjoy your cold chicken, and be sure to keep your food stowed in those bear drums. I noticed several bear caves on the way up, and you wouldn't want extra guests showing up for dinner."

Earl and Leon chuckled at Pete's remarks, but when he disappeared over the crest of the bowl, there wasn't much more to joke about. Without a rifle, they would be helpless if they were discovered by a hungry brown bear that could be a worse problem than the security men guarding Glacier World just three thousand feet below them.

CHAPTER 14

Glacier World

The interior of Warehouse No. 2 next to the docks at the south end of the theme park bustled with activity. Raul Rahman and Nigel Fishman, head of security, watched intently as twenty men unloaded the shipping containers that had been taken off the *Northern Explorer*. Once offloaded, the contents were moved into Warehouse No. 1 for inventory. The empty containers were either stored outside or moved to a paint shop, where they were repainted in the colors and logos of other shipping companies. The operations center provided the foreman in the paint shop with a list of the exact specifications of containers that would be needed for the next cargo extraction mission. An electronics technician worked alone carefully removing the MATTS units from each container and carrying them to a workbench where they could be reprogrammed.

"Impressive, Mr. Rahman," Fishman commented. He was a big man, tall enough to be a forward on a professional basketball team, and well-muscled like a wrestler. He had a long dossier listing corporate security positions—several in high risk locations, especially Africa and the Middle East. He had spent six years early in his career with the Israeli intelligence involved in rooting out Palestinian smuggling operations in the West Bank. When Rahman personally selected him for his current position, Fishman figured it for a laid-back job with a fat paycheck. Once he was handed his duties, he knew it would be the most demanding assignment of his career, with a boss who was nothing short of ruthless.

"Yes, our operations are running more efficiently," replied Rahman. "We've cut our transit time from when cargo is received and shipped back out from 240 hours to 72 hours. A significant amount of the savings has been in taking less time to match our latest inventory to buyer's requests. As our list of clients improves and we learn more about what they want, we will do even better."

"You're filling special orders?" asked Fishman.

"Certainly, but within reason, of course. Certain American-made products are very much in demand, especially in North Korea and Southeast Asia. Our software developers have devised a search routine to scan the databases of the freight forwarding companies handling US exports for specific products. GRI has a perfectly legal export subsidiary headquartered in Shanghai, which has accounts with most of these trans-Pacific shippers. It gives us a gateway to hack into other records."

"Pretty ingenious."

"With today's technology, it's simple, really," Rahman said. "Once we identify where and when the requested product is going to be shipped and its specific carrier, we record the owner and contents of the cargo containers along with their serial numbers. Our extraction team already knows ahead of time exactly where the containers have been placed by row and level on board the ship. Just like the shippers, we use the GPS units in each of the containers to locate the ones we want to take off."

Rahman watched a crew off-load another container and pull the loaded trailer away with a tractor. A second tractor and trailer were already moving into position for the next container.

"Won't the shippers or the Coast Guard catch on to what is happening to their containers?" asked Fishman. "For instance, they could place other GPS units in them and easily track the containers to this location."

"I've given that possibility some consideration. While we scan the containers for other electronic security devices, changes will inevitably be necessary. With the infrastructure we now have in place, I think we could shift our focus to onshore locations. Intermodal facilities where shipping containers are stored and transferred to ships have extensive security, but the trucking operations to move containers to major export and import locations are all too vulnerable."

"Then our own ships and barges will continue to bring them here for processing?"

"Yes," replied Rahman. "To that end, I want to emphasize the importance of monitoring the off-duty activities of the employees involved with the ship and warehouse operations. These people should not associate or fraternize in any way with the employees of the park. They have their own work schedule, separate housing and recreational facilities. Nearly all of them are here on work visas arranged through my government contacts and most of them do not even speak English. Part of your job is to ensure this separation is maintained. This operation cannot have leaks. It is projected to generate millions of dollars in profits for GRI—far more profit than Glacier World."

CHAPTER 15

Excursion Ridge

The rain during the night had been expected, but it was not the sound of the driving rain on the tent that disturbed their sleep. It was the fierce wind whipping their small shelter, even though they had set up camp next to an overhanging rock ledge. Earl stretched in his sleeping bag and tried to undo the stiffness in his back and legs. Unzipping the tent fly, he peered out. The wind was calm but everything was grey and wet. There was a dense mist in the air preventing him from seeing more than a few feet. Then he realized they were actually immersed in a low cloud.

"Kind of messes up our observation plans," mumbled Earl as he turned his head to see if Leon was awake.

"I took a look a few hours ago. Chance for a few more winks," murmured Leon. He rolled on his side with his back to Earl, who frowned at Leon's response.

"Well there must be something we can do," said Earl. "I'll start with making coffee." He sat up and began getting dressed. He put on two pairs of dry socks and his leather boots, still damp from the hike up the mountain the day before. He muttered about the dampness, which Leon didn't seem to hear. "Maybe the cloud cover will make it easier to move around without being seen. Maybe we can find a lower observation point and get warmer at the same time. This blasted dampness creeps right up your spine." Again there was no response from Leon. Earl put on his jacket along with his white slipover camouflage shirt and crawled out of the tent. "I'll see if I can make us a pot of coffee on that little propane stove. Then we'll see if we can still salvage part of this miserable day."

He pulled out the stove Pete had loaned them, heated some water, and made two cups of coffee. "Coffee is ready, Leon," he said as he looked back at the tent. Leon had not emerged. He carried the cups over and pulled back the flap. Leon was in his sleeping bag, shaking like he had a chill.

"You okay?" Earl asked. Leon didn't seem to notice him. "Hey! Leon!" Earl hollered.

Leon looked up at him. His eyes were wide open, staring at the misty figure of Earl. Then he blinked several times and he struggled to sit up, still shaking. "Yeah, give me in a minute."

They sat together, sipping their coffee and not talking for several minutes. Earl found a couple of breakfast bars for them to eat.

Leon was silent for a long time before finally speaking. "There is something I have to tell you. I lied to you about Eddie Jackson, but it is more than that."

"I know about Eddie Jackson's mother being dead," replied Earl. "Oscar Perkins told me when I tried to reach you before our trip."

"Eddie sent the photos to me. In fact, I talked to him quite often. When I did not get him to answer a call after a week, I contacted Frank and he informed me about Eddie's death."

"But why did you lie to me?" Earl asked.

"I could not do this trip alone. I needed your support, Earl. Besides, it was not all a lie. Eddie told me about finding the Shoalwater Corporation lumber, but let me start at the beginning. Eddie Jackson and I have been friends from childhood. When we finished high school, we both enlisted in the Marines. We wanted to be in Special Forces, but Eddie did not qualify. He was a fearless fighter, maybe because he was a little guy, but he had poor vision. So he took medical training while I went the Special Forces route. When the war in Afghanistan started we both ended up at the same base, Bagram Air Base near Kandahar. I was assigned to a patrol unit and he was assigned to a medevac helicopter unit. There was another Indian in my squad. His name was Ronnie Running Horse. He was a Rosebud Sioux. Everyone called him Horse—maybe because of his name or maybe because he was a big man. The three of us were always together when we had free time at the base—playing tag football, telling stories, and joking around. We were like three brothers. Then our base commander got orders to increase the number of patrols, plus incorporate some Afghan troops into our squads. They were a hindrance since they were not from the same tribal region, so we just took them along in case we encountered any serious enemy fire and needed more firepower.

"On one particular January patrol, we were dropped on a mountain to do recon and we got socked in pretty thick with clouds—like now—and had a hard time finding our extraction point. I was leading the patrol and got turned around. We walked right into a bunch of Taliban fighters. I should have used my compass, but instead I relied on my intuition.

"It got bad. The Taliban surrounded us and we were outnumbered. Neither the Taliban fighters nor us could see well in the mist, but there was so much shooting we started taking casualties. The Afghan guys ran out of ammo and one was killed. Horse was firing our RPG and the Taliban zeroed in on him. He got wounded but didn't stop fighting back. We had called for an air evacuation, but with the low cloud cover it was nearly four hours before they could get to us. By then we had three guys dead and two wounded. I got shot in my shoulder. Then a grenade exploded near Horse. As I crawled over to him I got shot again in my right leg. One of my best friends was dead.

"The clouds finally began to lift, and the helicopter gunship laid down rapid fire on the Taliban positions, then landed about one hundred meters from us. Eddie had volunteered for that rescue mission when he found out it was my unit. He was the first man out of the helicopter and got me and everyone else aboard.

"I owed Eddie my life that terrible day, but it did not end there. I was sent to Germany, then back to the States for my recovery. When I was discharged, I was suffering from PTSD, because I felt responsible for Horse and three other men getting killed. When Eddie got out and came home to LaPush, he helped get me through that period too.

"Well, you know the rest of the story about Eddie. When he was killed, it triggered all my old problems, yet I knew I just had to take care of things and bring his body home. It happened again this morning when we woke up in this damn cloud."

Leon sipped his cup of coffee. It was cold. He looked at Earl. "Thanks for coming along, Earl, but I am not sure I can do this. I do not want to put another friend in danger because of something I am afraid to do myself."

"You don't need to worry about that, and I can't believe you would be afraid, Leon," replied Earl. "Thanks for telling me .From now on consider me as taking the place of Eddie. We came here because of him, and we'll finish the job together. Okay?"

"I appreciate your offer. I really do." He gave a weak smile and extended a hand to Earl, who took it and then reached over and patted Leon on the back.

"You're a good leader, Leon. I trust your judgement. Let's get to work."

They took their time securing their tiny camp and began scouting the ridge crest facing east, where they should have been able to see the park complex on the far shore of the inlet. Earl's tracks in the deep snow had indeed been covered by the wind during the night.

They selected several observation points that could be easily reached from their camp, but the question of how good they would be once there was visibility would have to wait. Taking advantage of the low visibility, they decided to try to get closer and make their way down the side of the ridge. They avoided patches of snow and remained in the trees and brush as much as possible. If the clouds suddenly lifted, they would be exposed if they used the more open areas of muskeg. They were about five hundred feet from the bottom when they could finally see the surface of the water in Excursion Inlet.

Emerging from a dense grove of spruce trees, they approached a rock ledge. Leon motioned to Earl that they had come down far enough. "This spot ought to be good," stated Leon as he slipped off his pack. He looked around and selected a location where there would be brush behind them and a flat rock surface to set up their camera tripod and spotting scope. Earl took out his drawing pad and some pencils. His job was to take photos, draw sketches of the park's layout, and make notes while Leon observed what was happening below them. A few sounds periodically carried across the inlet—mainly larger equipment noise. Otherwise, the only sounds were the wind in the trees behind them and the squawks of a few seagulls on the near shoreline. Their conversation became almost a whisper for fear it would carry down to the shoreline and out onto the water surface of the inlet.

They shared a package of cookies and drank coffee from a thermos while waiting to see if the clouds would lift. Earl welcomed the hot coffee. An hour later, they could finally make out the dock and buildings across the inlet. They were astounded at what they saw laid out below them. It was like looking back in time at an early Alaskan gold mining town. A long dock stretched into the inlet, with a promenade and several rows of low wooden buildings behind it. Beyond the buildings were a rolling meadow, a meandering stream, and several structures that appeared to be observation towers. But the most striking building was in the center of the complex—a five story, all-glass building that resembled a child's stack of toy blocks. Its glazing gave the structure a metallic sheen, as though it were made of gold. A similar, but smaller, glass-clad structure anchored the north end of the complex. It looked like an outdoor amphitheater with huge glass canopies. Earl and Leon took several minutes to marvel at the immensity and detail of the park, then got to work.

Leon noticed considerable activity of both men and equipment at several locations. With the aid of his spotting scope, he could see several vehicles that looked like oversized golf carts moving along the waterfront. There was occasional movement of similar vehicles farther back in the park and next to a large ship moored near a group of warehouses at the south end of the complex.

A small patrol boat pulled away from the dock near the ship and moved up the center of the inlet. It left a wake that made an arc pointing directly at their position. Leon motioned to Earl to stay down and not to move while he kept the scope tracking with the patrol boat. There were two men on the back deck and another at the helm. Each wore dark blue trousers with a light blue shirt and dark blue jacket and cap. He could make out the features of the men on the deck. They appeared to be Asian and were smoking cigarettes. Neither of the men bothered to look up at the ridge. The patrol boat continued to the center of the channel and then changed direction towards the head of the inlet. Earl stayed low as Leon had requested and suddenly realized that he had been holding his breath.

"All clear," said Leon.

Earl exhaled.

Leon went back to studying the unloading and loading activity on the dock that involved the strange-looking ship, while Earl began to snap pictures of the immediate waterfront buildings and make notes. There were dozens of buildings that reminded Earl of a trip to Disneyland with his family. The buildings were modern construction with carefully detailed

fronts to give the appearance of a town from the late
1800s. Yet on the rooftops, he could see mechanical
heating equipment carefully hidden from view. There
were general merchandise stores, several saloons, a
bakery, a hotel, a bank, and several cafés. Farther
down the dock was another group of storefronts with
signs identifying them as an assay office, a livery
stable, and a stage station. Earl made sketches of the
dock, the promenade, and each group of buildings
noting where there were alleys or streets that led
farther into the complex.

After taking a break to eat a sandwich and
drink some water, Earl resumed his photographing
and map sketching, and Leon scoped the promenade
for further activity that might tell him more about the
place. A lone man wearing a blue uniform caught his
attention. He had stepped out of one of the
storefronts that had a sign identifying it as the stage
station. The man unplugged a cable connected to a
dark blue, rubber-tired vehicle similar to a golf cart,
got behind the steering wheel, and sped away only to
make a sharp right turn and disappear into an opening
marked with an overhead sign that read "Mine
Entrance." He did not reappear behind the buildings,
which puzzled Leon. He turned his attention to the
open areas beyond the buildings to examine the odd-
looking towers.

One of the towers was off to the far right
next to a series of small waterfalls on a stream. It
flowed out of a lake that lay to the east of an airstrip.

They had not seen any planes, but Leon made a mental note to watch that airstrip and whatever used it during their observation time. He noticed some movement at the river tower and watched two men dump a container of something over a balcony into the stream below. Whatever it was they had dumped into the stream drifted down through a cascade and over a waterfall. Leon saw several bears that had been lying down in high grass next to the waterfall get up, lunge at the objects, and carry them in their mouths over to the shoreline. They were brown bears and he guessed the objects had to be salmon carcasses. The first bear to carry a salmon to the shore was maybe twice the size of the others. Based on Leon's knowledge of Alaskan brown bears, it had to be a Kodiak bear. He recalled that Kodiaks were not native to Southeast Alaska and must have been brought in.

He shifted the field of the spotting scope from the feeding bears back to the tower and saw the two men load their container into the back of one of the electric vehicles, climb in, and drive away. It disappeared from view by entering a dark opening in the building facing the promenade. Leon changed his field of view again and scanned a broader area, looking for where the vehicle had gone. After a few minutes, he saw it appear next to another tower in a small valley near the middle of the meadow. The two men took another container out of the back of their cart and dumped it over a rock ledge next to the tower. This time, he witnessed several silvery grey creatures leap on whatever the two men had dumped. Leon nodded as he realized what they were—timber wolves, and apparently quite hungry, given how they fought over whatever had been tossed to them. He looked for the men and their cart. They had disappeared.

Switching his view to the far left, Leon grinned in satisfaction as he once again saw the lone blue-clothed man who had disappeared while driving the electric vehicle. He had stopped his cart at the north end of the promenade next to the glass-canopied building with the water pools. The building was shaped like an amphitheater with row upon row of seating. There was something very large swimming in one of the pools.

"Dolphins!" Leon said quietly, but loud enough that Earl heard him and looked to see what he was observing.

Earl focused his telephoto lens. "Looks like something right out of Sea World. They've built an open-air marine amphitheater for people to watch dolphins perform. I bet they have orca or something else in there too."

"Yeah!" answered Leon. "Probably have them in that larger pool. But what intrigues me is the blue man down by the entrance talking to a couple of guys in hard hats. He appeared out of nowhere in that vehicle. A few minutes ago he drove into that mine entrance in front of us."

"So what are you saying, Leon? That there's a tunnel under that row of buildings?"

"Not one tunnel, there is a whole network of tunnels," Leon answered as he watched the blue man get back into his cart and drive into a dark hole behind the amphitheater. "Have to get back to our camp. Pete will be there soon, and with the weather clearing up, I do not want us to be spotted. That patrol boat should be making its way back any time now. They might see us climbing, if they bother to even look up."

The climb back to the summit took them over an hour, and Pete was already in camp. He had a pot of hot water heating on a small propane stove, and as soon as Pete saw them, he made Earl and Leon each a cup of fresh coffee and added an ounce of Baileys to each cup. Anything hot would have been welcome, but what he offered them was terrific. Pete planned to stay with them overnight and had brought everything to make a big pot of venison stew with carrots and potatoes.

Unable to use any lights, the three men retired early. Their tent was crowded that night, but they figured they might be warmer.

"Being on top of a mountain and seeing the moon and stars reminds me of a story I learned as a kid," Pete mentioned. "You guys care to listen to it?"

"Is this a legend?" asked Earl. "Or is it one of those dark and dreary around-the-campfire type stories?"

Pete laughed. "It's a legend. Every Tlingit storyteller will tell it differently, but this is the way I remember it. One day Raven decided people should have more light in the world. For as many years as people in a village on the Nass River could remember, nights were always very dark, but in the lodge of an old man, Raven had hidden several bundles high amongst the log beams.

"One day, a baby boy was born to the old man's daughter, and he took care of the boy in his lodge. The baby saw Raven fly in through the smoke hole and peck at one of the bundles. The baby pointed to them and cried, as he wanted to play with one of them. Finally, the old man relented and gave one of the bundles to the child, who rolled it around on the floor of the lodge. The thongs holding the bundle closed loosened, and its contents spilled out. They were tiny pins of light which drifted up and out of the smoke hole of the lodge to become the stars we see today. The baby cried again and was given a second bag, which he played with for a while before again losing the contents. The light drifted up through the smoke hole, where it became the moon."

Pete paused in his storytelling, and then laughed along with Leon. Earl was snoring. With the laughter, he stirred.

"What?" said Earl. "What happened after Raven wanted more light?"

CHAPTER 16

Hoonah, Alaska

The following morning, Bernie Armstrong strolled down to the Hoonah harbor and was looking longingly at a yacht called the *Nordic Quest* moored at the transient dock when he heard someone call his name. He turned to see Brooklyn waving as she walked towards where he stood on the breakwater.

She wore a pair of rubber boots that came nearly to her knees and were almost the same reddish-orange color as the streaks in her hair. Other than the boots, Bernie thought she looked a little sharper today, wearing a heavy woolen sweater in place of her colorful army jacket.

"Hi, Bernie. How are things this morning? Have you heard from your dad and his friend on their camping trip in the national park?"

"Nope, they won't call unless there is a problem. I'm guessing they'll be gone for a few more days. Hey, it sure was neat working with you on Mr. Tee's fisheries project yesterday. I'd love to help some more but maybe not today. I didn't sleep well last night and decided to take a walk to clear my head. Liz's baby fussed all night."

Brooklyn smiled. "Well, put yourself in Liz's place. She probably slept less than you having to take care of a fussy baby. Would you want to be her?"

"No thanks. She's a nice lady and I don't envy her. That little guy is a handful."

"Did she make her famous huckleberry scones for breakfast?"

"Sure did!" Bernie responded. "They were fantastic."

"So I saw you watching the boats in the harbor. Since Mr. Tee is busy today, how would you like to take a boat ride? Johnny, one of Mom's boyfriends, is the skipper of a whale watching boat."

"Really?"

"Yeah! He does whale watching trips over to Point Adolphus for the tourists who visit the old cannery. There's a cruise ship due in later this morning so he has a trip or two planned."

"Wow! That would be great," Bernie said as he looked towards the entrance of the bay, half expecting to see a huge cruise ship already approaching. "Can you arrange for me to go out with him?"

"Of course! I'm going along. Johnny likes to have me do the dialogue and describe to the tourists all about the humpback whales. That way he can concentrate on staying out of the way of the whales and provide the best viewing and picture taking. Besides, he admitted to me on one of my early trips that I know a heck of a lot more about humpbacks than he does."

"Okay. I've got to go back and tell Liz. Where and when do you want to meet?"

Brooklyn looked at her Mickey Mouse wristwatch and made a funny face, thinking for a few seconds. "Ah, let's see. The cruise ship is due in at ten thirty, and the tourists have a salmon buffet at noon. Johnny likes to be ready to take his first group out an hour later. That way he can make two round trips before the cruise ship has to depart." Brooklyn pointed down at a boat with a white hull and blue trim in a slip just beyond the transient dock. The boat had a lot of windows and a top deck with railings. "That's Johnny's boat—the *Huna Spirit*. Be down on the dock by eleven thirty and we'll ride over to the cannery with him."

***

The diesel engine on Johnny's boat was throbbing steadily as Bernie reached the slip. Brooklyn and Johnny were chatting in the pilothouse, but noticing Bernie's approach, Brooklyn waved for him to climb aboard. She was wearing a life jacket and offered Bernie one as he entered the cabin. "Hi, Bernie. Meet Johnny, one of the best skippers in all of Icy Strait."

"Glad to meet you, Bernie," Johnny said. "I hear you're a celebrity visiting the fine village of

Hoonah—some kind of robotic champion. Well, welcome aboard the *Huna Spirit*."

Bernie's ears turned red as he realized Brooklyn had been talking about him. He stammered again, not sure what to say. "Ah...thanks for letting me come along." Bernie answered. "I'm really excited about a chance to see some humpbacks. We have gray whales pass the Washington coast where I live, but they're just traveling and not nearly as exciting to watch as the humpback whales are up here in Alaska. I've seen a couple of programs about your whales on the Discovery Channel."

"Yeah, and a lot of that filming was done right here in Icy Strait. In fact, Johnny had a film crew from Animal Kingdom on board his boat last year."

"Wow! Wish I could have been on that trip."

"Oh, you'll see lots of whales today, I'm sure," replied Johnny. He looked at Brooklyn and nodded towards the bow of the boat. "Okay, now that I have a crew aboard, let's get underway."

Bernie watched Brooklyn nimbly scramble along the side of the boat, releasing the bow dock line as Johnny pulled in the stern line. Then Johnny deftly reversed his boat out of the slip and between several other large fishing boats. He did a quick turn and slowly motored out of the harbor. Once they cleared the breakwater and the no wake zone, he increased his speed, and in a few minutes they were approaching a huge white cruise ship anchored just off the old fish cannery. It had been renovated into a major tourist attraction. A cruise ship was anchored just offshore and busy unloading over fifteen hundred tourists using several launches to shuttle back and forth to the cannery dock. Two other whale-watching boats were already tied to the dock, with long lines of people waiting to board. While they approached, Brooklyn gave Bernie instructions on how to use a dock line to secure the stern while she handled the bowline. Johnny brought the boat in smartly, and the two of them made their ties. Brooklyn smiled and gave Bernie a thumbs up for how well he did on his first attempt.

For the next two hours, Johnny guided his boat, now loaded to capacity with thirty people, around the nearshore waters next to Point Adolphus. Bernie had a forward seat next to the wheel with a great view. Brooklyn stood next to him and used the boat's PA system to explain to everyone about the humpback whales. The boat crowd cheered whenever one of the humpbacks breached high out of the water, and they stared in awe when five or six whales performed a bubble-netting act right alongside the boat. Bernie was wide-eyed as the whales broke the surface with their mouths wide open to swallow thousands of herring that the whales had pushed into a tight ball as they swam in a circle. They dove to create a curtain of bubbles, then came up through the mass of herring.

Bernie noticed that there were quite a few other boats also enjoying the feeding whales. In addition to the three whale-watching boats with their cruise ship guests, there were four private cruisers and two sailboats. Several of the cruisers and one of the sailboats moved around quite a lot rather than drifting as the *Huna Spirit* had been doing. Bernie was a bit alarmed at how close they got to the whales, particularly next to two small calves that played on the surface rather than diving with the adults.

"Johnny, are they allowed to get so close to the whales?" Bernie asked.

Johnny glanced at the other boats and his face clearly showed his disgust. "Disrupting their natural behavior is illegal under the Marine Mammals Protection Act. Besides, there's no need to use your boat engine to get up close. With so many whales around, they end up coming close to us if we just drift. Sometimes I have to back away, mainly for the safety of the people aboard. You don't want to be in the middle of a group of whales that are bubble netting when they come to the surface. It could capsize this boat or damage it. If a whale was to just hit our rudder, we would be in trouble."

"So why do people ignore the guidelines?" said Bernie.

"I don't know. Just plain stupidity, I guess. Then there are people like on that fancy sailboat over there."

Bernie read the name on the stern of the sailboat. "The *Glacier Gal*?"

"Yeah," said Johnny. "Belongs to a guy by the name of MacDonald. He's the state senator for the Juneau Borough. He got the state legislature to approve the building of that damn destination resort up in Excursion Inlet. It wasn't long after the project got approved that he sailed that boat up from Puget Sound. The guy thinks this is his own personal playground or something. Doesn't give a damn about anyone else's rights, the wildlife, or nothing—just like the people building the resort. A few weeks ago, they netted a bunch of dolphins and some orca just outside the national park. Got them in holding pens over there, I hear."

"Can they do that?" Bernie asked as he watched the *Glacier Gal* move in close to a baby humpback whose mother was feeding close by with some of the other adult whales.

"Bernie, if you've got lots of money, Senator MacDonald and the state legislature will let you do almost anything if it will create jobs or help the economy now that we're running out of oil in Alaska."

Bernie stared at the sailboat as it made a quick maneuver. A huge grey and white fluke suddenly struck the side of the boat, and it heeled over on its port side, exposing most of the bottom of the boat. Its keel had been sheared off. When it righted itself, the stern was partially under water. The marine radio just above Johnny's head blared with a call for help.

"Mayday, Mayday, Mayday, calling the Coast Guard," a frantic voice yelled over Johnny's VHF radio. "This is the *Glacier Gal*. We've been struck by a whale and are sinking."

It was followed by an immediate response. "This is Coast Guard Sector Juneau. What is your position *Glacier Gal*?"

"That idiot!" Johnny said shaking his head. "He provoked the mother of that calf by getting too close. Brooklyn, get on the PA and tell everyone to sit down. We're going to have to try to help rescue whoever is on that sailboat."

"Everyone, please take a seat," Brooklyn calmly announced over the PA speakers. "You folks on the top deck please hang on. Looks like we're going to be part of a sea rescue. There's a boat close by that is sinking and we have to assist."

Johnny increased the volume on the VHF radio so everyone on board could hear the conversation with the coast guard. "Any boats in the vicinity of Point Adolphus are requested to assist the sailboat *Glacier Gal* that is reported to be sinking. There are two people on board."

Johnny responded to the call. "This is the *Huna Spirit*. We have a visual on the *Glacier Gal* and are proceeding to its location." Johnny brought his boat about to run towards the sailboat. As the boat surged ahead, Bernie and Brooklyn clung to grab bars in the pilothouse. They were still several hundred yards from it when the bow raised slightly and then slid underwater. Moments later, its tall mast disappeared. Two people in orange life vests were in the water waving their arms. Within five minutes, Johnny and several of the tourists were pulling a man and a woman onto the *Huna Spirit*, which then turned to run back to the cannery dock. Shortly after they arrived, an Alaska State Trooper boat appeared to take the senator and his friend aboard.

The senator sat shivering with one of Johnny's blankets wrapped around him. "If any of you folks took pictures, send them to my office in Juneau, okay? My insurance company is going to need to see what that blasted whale did to my boat. I'll pay for some good pictures." A couple of tourists nodded.

"Huh!" snickered Brooklyn as she and Bernie watched the state trooper boat pull away from the cannery dock with the senator. "The guy didn't even offer a simple thank you for saving his life."

CHAPTER 17

Excursion Ridge

The weather improved just before sunset, and from their camp on Excursion Ridge, Earl enjoyed a spectacular Alaskan sunset that silhouetted the snow-white Fairweather Range on the western edge of Glacier Bay National Park. Earl and Leon now had a fully fixed-up camp, so Pete headed back down to Gustavus early in the afternoon. He planned to take the boat back to Hoonah and await their call to come back and help get them off the mountain.

Leon decided they should rest and try observing the theme park after dark by returning to their little forward observation post, as Leon had taken to calling it. Their dinner was simple—canned spaghetti heated over a small propane stove with bread and cheese. Huddled with their backs to the rock ledge, they drank hot chocolate and again discussed what they had discovered over the last day and a half.

"I am convinced there is a series of tunnels throughout the complex—one tunnel system to access various parts of the park and possibly a separate maintenance tunnel," said Leon. "We need to study how they use these tunnels over the next couple of days and try to map the entry points. It may help us move around the place undetected."

"What about entering through the back of one of the animal enclosures?" Earl asked. "One or two of the observation towers used by tourists to view the animals are pretty close to the outer wall."

"I do not cotton to that approach," replied Leon. "With the number of predators we have seen in the enclosures, gaining entry to the park from the east or south would be dangerous, if not fatal. But the north end needs further observation. The enclosures at that end appear to hold smaller animals."

"Small but maybe just as dangerous," said Earl. "I think that's where they have the wolverines."

"Let me take a look at your sketches," said Leon.

Earl took out his sketchpad and turned to the one he had done for the north end. He had drawn in the theatre complex and some of the animal enclosures. He used dotted lines to separate some of them as he wasn't sure of the barrier locations.

There was a small boat dock just north of the amphitheater. Leon pointed it out to Earl. "That far dock with the two blue-hulled boats might be our access point or maybe a pick up point for getting back out. Did you get some pictures of it?"

"I'm pretty sure I did. I've taken a couple hundred photos."

"Good, we will enlarge those of this area when we get back to Hoonah. What about the south end? I am curious about the warehouses. They are huge and there is a lot more activity than needed to support the operation of a theme park."

Earl found another one of his sketches showing the warehouses. "Maybe they're for storage of construction materials?"

"Why build new ones for that purpose? There are plenty of shipping containers to use for storage. Some of the buildings look older, possibly from the time when the site was an operating salmon cannery. But two of the warehouses look new and one has an large amount of mechanical equipment on the roof, like an industrial processing building."

"I don't know what it would be for. Maybe a waste incinerator?" replied Earl.

***

Long days had already begun in Southeast Alaska, and it was after ten o'clock before there was enough darkness for them to start back down the ridge. Reaching the spot where the park below them came into view, Earl was just as amazed as he had been on their first trip at what he saw. The mountain range that rose up behind the east side of the park reflected the multi-colored glow from all of the park's lighting.

"Geez! It looks like a small city or a movie set," exclaimed Earl.

"That is a pretty good description," Leon answered. "It is all fake, just like a movie set, except for the predators. They are real. They could be a problem for getting into the place. With patrol boats on the water side and predator enclosures on the back side, we do not have many options."

They settled and in a few minutes had their observation equipment set up. Earl used the camera with the telephoto lens, and Leon had his spotting scope. In front of them, the entire length of the park's dock was bathed in light. The gold mining town had multi-colored lights that resembled the Las Vegas Strip more than an early Alaskan town. At the far end of the dock, next to the freighter, they observed a lot more activity than during daytime observations. The deck was well lit, and a crane handled containers, swinging them from the dock onto the ship's deck. A string of containers waiting to be loaded stretched from one of the new warehouses to the ship. Leon and Earl watched this operation with interest.

"Seems odd that so much stuff is being shipped out rather than into a place like this," Earl commented.

"I have been thinking the same thing. The way those containers are being handled tells me they are full. They should be empty."

"And why are they working at night?" Earl asked. "The ship's been here all day. We saw almost no activity around it this morning."

Leon used the highest power on the spotting scope and focused on the open door to the large warehouse where the containers were being removed. "Sure is a lot of stuff stored in there. I can see two men standing just inside the main door with tablets in their hands and using radios to give directions. It is like they are directing what containers are to be brought out. Again, if the containers were empty, why would they care in what order they were handled?"

The crane on the ship carefully picked up a container off the dock and placed it on top of several others already loaded. The tractor with its empty trailer moved away and circled back to the warehouse, while another tractor moved into place to have its container picked up next.

"Yeah, I've heard there can be huge stacks of empty containers waiting at Alaskan ports to be loaded onto barges and hauled south to Seattle or Tacoma," Earl said. "It's almost like they don't want people noticing what they are doing. Maybe that's a reason for all of the security."

"Funny you should mention security, Earl. There are two patrol boats on duty tonight—one just below us and another farther out by the entrance to the inlet." The boat below them suddenly turned on a powerful spotlight that swung around, searching the water away from the dock and the shoreline. Then it raised the light into the tree-covered slope just below where they were hidden. "Keep your head down. I hope the lights cannot reach up this far."

The spotlight turned off, and Earl resumed scanning the main part of the park. "No activity along the rest of the dock. They sure have a lot of lights on, though, especially in that center building. Did you notice where their power comes from?"

"Yeah, there is a lake maybe a half mile or so on the far side of their airfield. I saw a road and a power line coming down from there. They probably have a small hydro plant where the stream leaves the lake."

"Take a look at that glass building," Earl said. "As I recall, there are five floors. All the lights are turned on for the fourth floor, but the other floors are mostly dark. There are just a few lighted windows on the first floor and the top floor. Can you see anybody in those areas with your spotting scope?"

Leon took a minute to readjust the focus of his scope and studied each floor of the building. "That is interesting. I think we have discovered another piece of the puzzle about this place. You should be able to see with the binoculars. Check out the windows on the fourth floor. What do you see?"

Earl set down his camera, propped his elbows on the big log in front of him, and used the binoculars to look at the fourth floor windows. "I can see right into the rooms. I couldn't do that this morning because the exterior glass was so damn reflective." The interior of the fourth floor was one big open area filled with cubicles. Each cubicle held a desk with two large computer monitors. Nearly all of the workstations were occupied by people engaged in computer tasks.

"Why are there so many people working at night in a theme park that isn't even open for business yet?"

"That struck me as strange as well," answered Leon. "The floor looks like it is set up as an operations center. Maybe a training exercise?" Leon tilted his scope to look at the floor below. "Look at the next floor down. There is another operations center. It is smaller with no activity."

"Huh. What's going on here, Leon?" Earl put down the binoculars and stared at the park. "We've got a bunch of guys busy loading containers on a ship, and we've got a bunch of other people engaged in computer work. Neither activity seems logical as part of a theme park that is about to open."

"I agree with you, Earl. Everything seems ready for opening the park. Yet they have forty or fifty people working overtime doing tasks unrelated to construction. "

"If GRI somehow grabbed some of my valuable timber and changed the records to hide their tracks, then like Lewis said, the answers might be right where we are looking—in those computers and the warehouses. We've got to get in there."

"I have to agree with you, but we have a couple of major problems. The place has a lot of security. It is going to be difficult to get into the park, let alone get into that building. The next problem is we would not know what to look for on their computers. We need to take Lewis with us."

"Take Lewis in there?" Earl said with a start. "I hadn't thought that far ahead. Accessing the GRI computer system from the inside would require special skills to hack into their computer data files. What if the software used by GRI is in Chinese or some other language?"

"We need a plan, Earl. We have to plan every possible step, and then have a backup plan in case something goes wrong. Most important, we need to plan a couple of ways to get out of there. If we miss a crucial piece of information about the place, we will be in a lot of trouble. The way I see it, we need Lewis, and it will be three times as hard getting him in and out of there."

"Three times as hard? What happened to twice as hard?" Earl started to stow his binoculars after noticing that Leon was putting away the spotting scope.

"Two times is getting *you* in there with me," responded Leon with a smile big enough that his teeth flashed in the light from the park promenade. He grabbed his pack and stuffed the scope inside. "We have seen enough for tonight."

They would have to climb back up twenty five hundred feet in almost total darkness.

CHAPTER 18

Hoonah, Alaska

It was several days later, when Earl and Leon finally finished with their reconnaissance of Glacier World and Pete Hunt had them safely on a boat back in Hoonah. They told Pete a few things about the park as the boat departed the Gustavus dock, and Pete was looking forward to hearing more of the details. Ever since his brother's death, Pete had a nagging suspicion that Glacier World was somehow responsible for his brother's death. Pete was not superstitious like a lot of the Hoonah residents. While Raz's body had borne the marks of being ravaged by wild animals, possibly land otters, he refused to believe it was the land otter people, the Kushtaka. He was even more suspicious when Earl told him there was a big otter enclosure at the park.

On their way back to Hoonah, Leon and Earl agreed they should meet with Lewis right away. As they were unloading their gear at the harbor, Earl gave Lewis's camera to Pete, who said he would return it to Lewis with a request to print the digital images for everyone to see. Pete said he would set up the meeting for Lewis's office at 6:00 p.m., which gave Earl a few hours to get a shower, change clothes, study all the notes and sketches he had made, and maybe have a chance to stretch out on his bed.

At the B&B, Earl noticed that Bernie was relieved to see him return safely. He was tired, smelled bad, and suffering from numerous mosquito bites. Earl felt a lot better after a hot shower, and he patiently listened to stories of Bernie's adventures while he found some clean clothes and put on his trademark forester's vest. Bernie told him about the rescue of Senator MacDonald, helping with Mr. Tee's NOAA grant project, and the time he had spent training Hoonah's ROV team for their competition. The conversation kept coming around to time Bernie spent with Brooklyn, and by the time he had heard everything, Earl detected a bit of teenage infatuation.

He got out his notebook and sketches and began making a large map of the park. Bernie was fascinated with all of the predator enclosures as Earl sketched them on his map. When he finished, he realized just how tired he was and wanted to get an hour or so of rest. That is, if Bernie would stop talking about predators and Brooklyn. So he got him to go see Flo at the cafe and arrange for some pizza and for someone to bring some beers and sodas. Both sounded wonderful to Earl after their days with only basic provisions up on the ridge.

Lewis was waiting for them at the center.

"Welcome back to Hoonah. Glad to see you aren't missing any arms or legs to a brown bear."

Earl laughed, but Pete and Leon were tired and only managed weak smiles. Lewis hustled around the office clearing stacks of papers and reports off of a table and two chairs. He grabbed an empty Coke can and tossed it in a trash basket. Hoonah didn't have a recycling program. Leon and Pete pulled the chairs together around the small conference table while Earl unrolled his map, taped it onto a whiteboard, and then joined the others at the table.

Leon began. "Well, we had a pretty successful mission. We saw some rather strange activities at Glacier World. There is a lot more going on there than just preparing the park for its opening. We observed the place for four days hidden atop Excursion Ridge without being detected."

"At least we think so, despite having to constantly keep out of sight of their patrol boats," Earl said with a slight grimace.

Leon nodded in agreement. "Yes. There is a whole lot of security over there. More than one would think necessary for a tourist facility."

"And they're well-armed, too," Earl added. "It was like they were more concerned about keeping trespassers away than protecting people from their predators."

"Yeah, I will describe their security in a minute. But it is the ship traffic that is the most puzzling. We watched two ships come into the dock, unload, then load, and depart within twelve hours. The first ship appeared to be an ordinary container ship, but the second ship was very, very interesting. We thought it might be one of those roll-on/roll-off container vessels, except from our vantage point, we could see the rigging was fake and the deck area had been equipped with retractable covers. With the covers in place, it looks like a deep ocean fishing trawler. It had a container crane carefully disguised as a net gantry and the trawler's stern ramp could be used to move containers quickly under the deck. We watched it unload nearly twenty containers and then load another twenty in a matter of hours."

Earl watched Lewis's reaction to this discovery. The man refused to believe what Leon described. "It's called a gallows," Lewis interjected. "What you are referring to as a net gantry, is the gallows. They're used to lift the towed net over the stern deck. Whowee, does this beat all. They're employing a trawler for piracy in the Gulf of Alaska. Did you get any of this ship?"

"I did." Earl answered. "Look at the image dates. They'll be ones dated two days ago."

Lewis opened the photo file on his computer and scanned to the end of the file. There were a half dozen pictures of the vessel being loaded.

"Geez, I have fisheries research monitors on a dozen trawlers out there in the gulf and never once imagined that the design has the potential for other uses."

"They are pretty clever about it," Leon said. "But the trawler is not all that is strange. On our last day on the ridge, we observed two men applying decals to the sides of recently painted container just minutes before they were loaded onto the vessel. It appears they have the capability to repaint empty containers and give them the identity of another shipper."

Pete chimed in. "Sounds like a pretty sophisticated operation—one that could only be undertaken from a remote location. How convenient to have a deep water port just a few miles from the Gulf of Alaska on a route routinely used by cruise ships, container ships, and sea-going tugs towing barges loaded with containers."

Earl paced back and forth shaking his head. "So they bring in stolen containers with valuable cargo under the guise of bringing in materials for the theme park, then ship it back out somewhere in other containers. So how do they do it? We don't know, but here's something else we learned." Earl stopped in front of his detailed map of Glacier World showing his added notations and names for each building and area. Bernie sat listening to his dad, fascinated with the description of this strange place.

"There is a five-story office tower in the center of the complex. We discovered that the fourth floor is some kind of huge computer center. It was full of tech people working at night. They have a small day shift working on the fourth floor and a much larger night shift working on the fifth floor. Why?"

Lewis looked at his watch. "I've got a possible answer. GRI has its headquarters in Singapore. That's eight hours different from Alaska. Could be they are tied in with another computer center in Singapore. We can check that out. Leon, you said you were going to describe the rest of the park. What's going on in the park itself?"

While Leon, with the aid of Earl's map, described the attractions and animal enclosures, Brooklyn arrived carrying several pizzas from the café and put them on the table. Everyone agreed the rest of the presentation could wait. They thanked Brooklyn for bringing over some of her mom's pizza, with a special thanks to Pete, who brought the beer.

After hearing their recap, and with every piece of pizza consumed, Lewis sat back with his third bottle of Alaskan Amber and launched into a series of questions for Leon and Earl. "Okay, now that we are pretty convinced that Glacier World serves as a cover for GRI's piracy operation, how are we going to get hard evidence that can be used in making an arrest and in a court of law? You've got some interesting photos, but they might not be enough for the FBI to get a search warrant. GRI could easily cover everything up. Do you think management will let any of us near their people or allow them to be interviewed? Do their employees even speak English? I've heard most of the construction laborers are from Southeast Asia. Do we alert the Coast Guard to try to track this mysterious trawler you saw at their dock?

Are they really breaking any international laws? If so, do we take our suspicions to the FBI or some international court? Come to think of it, if they conduct a major part of their operation offshore and in other countries, we might prevail in shutting down Glacier World, but this might only force them to move their operation elsewhere."

Pete nodded his head, acknowledging Lewis's questions without offering a response to any of them. He tried to sum things up from what he had heard the others say. "It sounds to me like there is a connection between the computer center and warehouse operation. Maybe it is like a big online marketplace—a black market Amazon or Alibaba. They inventory what they have stolen, then put it up on a site for international buyers and ship their orders on the next ship."

Earl picked up on Pete's idea. "So my timber was brought here, repackaged to get rid of the identifying marks, put up on Alibaba, and sold?"

"It makes sense from what we know, Earl," said Lewis. "You stated that they switched container markings. They probably altered the serial numbers and the MATTS data as well. All that new information on cargo and container identification goes to their computer center, where they hack into the shipper's databases and make the changes. The records for your containers show they can do that. Heck, for all we know, they put some of their containers back on pirated ships and no one even knows they are delivering illegal cargo."

Pete raised another question. "Could this be the reason both Eddie and my brother died? Could they have seen things they shouldn't have?"

"Possibly," said Leon. "We may never be able to prove that, but we can try to get some evidence that will send them to prison for high seas piracy." He walked over to Earl's map. "So, here is what I think we have to do." He pointed to the office tower in the center of Glacier World. "We get into this building, search their computers, and copy enough data that will make the authorities take action. I think you all know where this is leading. We will do something illegal and could be arrested. And we have to take Lewis with us. The operation cannot be done without him."

The room was silent for a minute.

Brooklyn, who had watched and listened since she arrived with the pizza, broke the silence. "Ah...I think I know how you can walk right into Glacier World."

"Walk right in?" Earl said with a puzzled look.

"Yes, I know what Brooklyn is thinking," Lewis responded. "Three days ago, while you two were spying on Glacier World, its manager and Senator MacDonald jointly announced on TV and in the Juneau newspaper that this coming Saturday would be an open house. Anyone in Juneau or the surrounding area is welcome to ride one of several shuttle vessels they will be operating from the Auke Bay Marina in Juneau and come see what Glacier World will be offering as an international tourist attraction."

There were a few murmurs, and a low whistle from Pete. Lewis lifted his little black notebook off his desk and stuck it in a pocket of his trousers, then opened a desk drawer and removed a WWII army flying cap. He pulled it over his head and ears, pushing down his wild hair so that it fell around his thick neck. "I'm in, gentlemen. We have three days to come up with a plan, and from what I have heard about Leon's background, it's going to be an interesting and well-planned mission. I just hope he can extract me in one piece."

***

For the next two days, Leon kept to himself except for their meals at the café. He told Earl he had a lot of thinking to do about their mission, but he couldn't get the conversation with the old woodcarver out of his mind. He decided that before they left to do reconnaissance of Glacier World, he would talk to Frank some more. Maybe a talk with Frank would help with closure about Eddie. While Leon had his own reason for wanting to go after the people at GRI, he didn't want the events of his past to jeopardize the safety of Earl and his new friends. It would be hard to prove that someone associated with Glacier World was behind Eddie's death. Nevertheless, he would try to learn the truth.

Earl wanted to be part of the team that went into Glacier World, and Leon readily agreed in spite of the risks. After all, the theft of his tribe's lumber had been a key issue in them knowing as much as they did.

Earl was no longer concerned about losing his job, but he was concerned what his wife would say about their idea. Leon had to agree with Earl about not telling Sally too much. The fact that they planned to take part in Glacier World's open house was enough. Earl also told him that he had called Ron Pike to file an insurance claim. More evidence that the lumber had been stolen would help support the claim. According to Pike, piracy was an unusual business liability, and there was an outside possibility of exclusion just as there was for acts of war.

Over the next two days, Leon roamed around Hoonah. He took the NYC taxi out to the Hoonah airport and then back to the marina, where he looked at every one of the smaller boats. He chatted with Johnny, who was cleaning up his whale watching boat after another day of taking tourists out. He spent several hours with Lewis behind a closed office door. He had coffee and another chat with Flo Whiting. Finally, on Thursday evening at dinner, Leon informed everyone that they should be at the community center that evening, and he would present his plan.

At the community center, Earl was the first person to ask. "How about it, Leon? Do you think we can pull it off?"

"Well, every mission leader has to think positive, and I think we have a pretty good chance. So let me lay it out before there are more questions." Leon tacked Earl's map of Glacier World on a wall along with a bunch of enlarged photos. "Our success will depend on speed and avoiding detection. We have several things in our favor—the first being the open house Glacier World has planned. It is not likely that GRI will have people working at the warehouse during the open house. If the warehouse folks are not working, the computer center staff may not be as well.

"Second, if we can access their tunnels, we should be able move quickly through the complex without being seen. We will use a four-man team— two to investigate the warehouses and take pictures, and two to get into the computer center. The computer center team will be Lewis and myself. The warehouse team will be Earl and Pete." Leon pointed to each location on the map, and the general course of the tunnels leading to them. "During the open house, each team needs to ride on the people movers, memorize the routes, and look for places where we can hide. There could be mechanical rooms or maintenance areas that are not accessed over on the weekend or when the staff has other duties. After each team has completed their assignment, we will rendezvous at a single point for extraction by water. Johnny has volunteered his boat, the *Huna* Spirit. It is fast and that is what we need. I have agreed to allow Brooklyn to be with him to handle radio communication and to act as a spotter. Each team will have a cell phone, but it will only be used for emergency communication in the event our situation changes or we have to use an alternative plan for extraction."

"You gonna have a helicopter swoop in and pick us up like Mission Impossible?" Pete asked.

Leon laughed. "No, we are not going to try to be superheroes. I am hoping they will not even see us leave. Besides, their airfield will have security, and it is too far from where we will be operating. We would be exposed while trying to reach it. The docks are our best bet. Even if they do see us, their patrol boats are not equipped with heavy weapons and only have the small arms carried by the security men on board. We just have to outrun them."

"Where on the docks are we supposed to meet?" Earl asked. "There's that small set of floats that they use for their whale watching and glacier tour trips."

"That is our pickup location, Earl. It is right next to a people mover station. We can pop out of the tunnel next to the aquarium, cross the promenade, and head down the ramp. But let me finish talking about our plan. There is a crucial step—as I said earlier, we have to slip away from all of the other

Juneau visitors, use a hiding spot in the tunnels that we select during our tours, and then wait until one or two a.m. to begin our work. To do that we need a diversion. Late Saturday afternoon, at the end of the open house, they have scheduled an assembly in the center of the gold rush town." Again, Leon pointed to a spot on the map. "It is near where the shuttle boats let people disembark. Senator MacDonald is supposed to appear and make a short speech—"

"Ha!" Pete interrupted Leon. "MacDonald doesn't need to make speeches. He gets votes by buying off people with all his corporate campaign contributions."

Lewis was quick to answer. "Nevertheless, Pete, the Juneau newspaper stated that MacDonald intends to take some credit publicly for bringing Glacier World to Southeast Alaska and the positive impact it will have on the economy."

"So we plan to make it a little warmer reception than Senator MacDonald had planned? That I'd like to see!" Pete quipped.

"I think we have it covered," said Leon. "While Earl and I were doing our reconnaissance, Brooklyn and Bernie were out with Johnny on a whale-watching trip. You all know what happened. They rescued MacDonald when a whale sank his expensive sailboat. He never offered a thank you to anyone for rescuing him, and Brooklyn will take issue with him—publicly pointing out what a fool he was and to try to create a disturbance. This should distract any security watching the nearby entrance to the tunnel system—the one called the Mine Entrance."

"And your other critical point is?" asked Pete.

Leon looked at Pete. He paused for a moment before he spoke. When he did, his voice was more serious than before. "It may be a bit tricky getting out of Glacier World. If something goes wrong and we cannot reach the boat, we will try to get out by a back door."

"Wait a minute. I don't recall seeing another entrance when we were on the ridge," Earl said, looking a little confused. "The back of the park is all fenced in with animal enclosures."

"I am not referring to a gate. I did not see one either, but there is a way." Leon pointed to the map again. "This observation tower is in the bear enclosure. I noticed some construction men working on a section of the perimeter wall just up from the tower, installing cameras or something on top of the wall. They had a couple of ladders and other construction equipment, which they leave behind each day. So, my alternate way out is to borrow their ladder and climb over the wall, then follow the stream up past the lake and come back down to the shore of the bay well outside the park's restricted zone to the south. There is an abandoned house and the remains of a dock, which can be our assembly point for pickup."

"Sounds pretty easy for a backup plan," said Lewis.

"We have to be careful," Leon continued. "This part of the wall is in the bear enclosure, and there is one hell of a big Kodiak bear in there. So, we drop off the tower, move fast to the wall, and get the hell out of there."

CHAPTER 19

Glacier World

Nigel Fishman did not like it one bit that the general public was going to have an opportunity to wander around Glacier World, but he kept his mouth shut and was tougher than usual on his security staff. Rahman had decided to shut down warehouse operations during the event, as well as switching the techs in the computer center to help control crowds at the different park venues. He planned to back up each of his regular security teams with other employees. They grumbled about going through security training during off hours, and Nigel worried how effective they would actually be in controlling the crowd of people from Juneau. He decided to hire a half dozen off-duty cops from Juneau to help with crowd control at the dock. That way, he could use his own men more effectively at critical places within the park. He had temporary fence and guard stations set up to keep visitors from wandering down towards the warehouses, and he added additional security posts along the road to the airfield and around the staff housing areas. He liked the idea of a short ceremony near closing time, which was set for 5:00 p.m., as it gave his people time to shut down the people movers and sweep the observation points and the rest of the park for stragglers. Essentially, everyone would be on the docks, the promenade, or in the shops and food stalls along it. Once he received reports that the park had been cleared, he could relax and have the extra help stand down.

On Friday morning, Rahman called a staff meeting to go over some additional details concerning the open house. He opened his talk with a stern comment. "I want all employees to be extremely courteous to the visitors and, Mr. Fishman, that applies to your staff and the additional people assigned to security as well. The training of new park staff has been completed, and they are ready to operate the people movers and man the observation towers, shops, and food stations. Nigel, your people will handle crowd control and keep visitors away from the warehouses. State Senator MacDonald will be making an appearance at the closing ceremony. Hopefully his speech will be short and won't create a scene. He is not well liked with some voters."

"I plan to personally be close by," responded Fishman.

"Good. Some of his constituents may try to disrupt this part of the ceremony. You will need to deal with them and quickly usher the troublemakers to the boats going back to Juneau. Senator MacDonald is a strong ally, and there is some important legislation pending that will reduce our state tax liability."

Rahman studied the faces of the core security staff present. None looked too thrilled with the prospect of having a huge throng of opening day visitors roaming the park, even though they would be handled in organized groups.

Fishman took the opportunity to ask, "Sir, some of the security, warehouse, and tech staff have been asking about some free time during and after the event. Since Sunday is their scheduled day off, they would like have a party in their housing area."

Rahman nodded, sensing that this might contribute to better cooperation and enthusiasm during the open house. "Okay," he answered. "I think that would be fine. Non-essential staff will be released at 8:00 p.m. or when you report to me that the entire park has been cleared of visitors."

Fishman and several of his men exchanged glances, and Rahman noticed there was a perceptible change in their attitude. He continued with his orders. "One more thing—we have a few areas of the park where construction is not substantially complete. This work will be put on hold until Monday following the open house. The marine amphitheater will not be open to the public, but the aquarium can be. Also, we will not be offering whale watching or glacier tours. And have the contractor personnel working on the perimeter wall stop their work today and remove or cover up any equipment so it is out of sight. I want a nice-looking setting for folks and the press to experience. Any further questions?"

"What about our scheduled patrols of the inlet?" asked a security officer who handled the crews for the park's patrol boats. "The *Predator* is not due back here until Monday. Do you want us to still maintain a schedule of two boats on the water at all times?"

Realizing where this was leading, and that the men assigned to patrol boats would miss the staff party, Rahman reluctantly agreed to a change. "Okay, one patrol boat will suffice with a shift change at 1:00 a.m., and the crew going on duty better be sober."

CHAPTER 20

Juneau, Alaska

The *Huna Spirit* transported everyone to Juneau who would be attending the Glacier World opening day. They booked rooms at the Klondike Motel, which was not far from the marina in Auke Bay where the shuttle boats would depart. There were seven people: Earl, Leon, Pete, and Lewis, along with Johnny, Brooklyn, and Bernie. Although Earl had initially disliked bringing Bernie, it was hard to leave him behind again with Liz and the baby. Earl finally agreed it might help avoid any suspicion. They intended to look like any other excited residents from Juneau anxious to take their first look at Glacier World.

After dinner at the same dockside restaurant they had gone to on their first day in Juneau, Earl asked Bernie to take a walk with him. As they passed the Frontier Bar, Earl noted that all was calm, with no drunks hanging around hassling tourists. They walked up the hill towards the Governor's Mansion and old state museum.

"Bernie, I wanted to spend a few minutes alone with you before we get involved in tomorrow's events. The visit to Glacier World should be a lot of fun, especially for you, and I want you to enjoy yourself—even to the point of overacting it a bit. But when the time comes for Brooklyn to do her little part disrupting the senator's speech, I want you safe and on one of the shuttle boats."

"Do I have to?" Bernie asked with a look of disappointment.

"Bernie, this is serious business, and you should know that I'm very nervous about you going with us at all. If Mom knew, she would shoot me for exposing you to possible danger."

"But what if the security people try to grab Brooklyn, what am I supposed to do?" asked Bernie.

"Nothing. You will be on the shuttle boat. Brooklyn can handle herself in most situations and probably all they will do is place her on a boat, even if it is by force. But no matter what happens, you have to get yourself back to our motel here in Juneau."

"No problem, Dad," replied Bernie. "Will you be coming here later?"

"Yes. It might be late Sunday, but we're coming back to Juneau. We're planning on meeting with the Alaska state police and the FBI to offer them our evidence to convince them about what we think is happening at Glacier World. We're hoping Lewis will find something."

Earl and Bernie had turned back down the hill, when Earl remembered a small ice cream shop close by the restaurant they had just left. "Let's go get

ourselves some ice cream before we meet the others
and head back to the motel."

    While walking, Earl pondered what he had
just told Bernie and what he had not told him. He was
definitely worried about what could go wrong. What
if one or all of them were captured? Did Leon have a
plan for that? What if they couldn't reach the second
pickup spot? What then? Leon had mentioned using a
back door, which meant exiting through the bear
enclosure. Earl did not relish running for the
perimeter wall, finding a ladder, and climbing over
with a bear or two challenging them. He tried to
remember what the terrain beyond the wall had
looked like from the vantage point on the ridge. It
was heavy forest. They would have to drop down,
orient themselves, and find their way in the dark
around the lake to Johnny's boat. Did Leon really
mean that the back door was over the mountains?
Earl shuddered with that thought. The scheme is
crazy. Someone could get injured or die. We could all
die.

CHAPTER 21

Glacier World

The group arrived from Juneau on the second shuttle boat to Glacier World. They were each given a glossy location map for the park and instructions on how to use the people mover to visit the animal enclosures, plus locations of other planned activity venues and the park's food stalls and restaurants.

Earl's own map was not all that bad, and surprisingly accurate. There were a few people mover stations they had not known about, including one inside the bear dens, near where they planned to hop over the wall, if necessary. The map also showed the Sky Ride route over Moose & Caribou Plateau and the Timber Wolf Valley area. They had not seen the Sky Ride in use from their high vantage point on the ridge.

Just as Leon had instructed during their planning time, everyone rode the people movers, first memorizing their routes and looking for possible hiding places. The whole group opted to see the predators before wandering around Gold Rush Town, then relax and snack on free hot dogs and ice cream sundaes. The group split up.

Earl had Bernie with him, and they followed the signs to board one of the underground trams that led to the bears. Earl was impressed with the design of the park's transportation system. The electric vehicles traveled in a prefabricated concrete vault that had been constructed in segments, much like the utilidors he knew were used in Arctic construction to prevent utilities from freezing. Several of the vehicles could be coupled together, and they were equipped with sensors so that they could be operated without a driver. Most of the system was underground, but there were a few sections aboveground that were equipped with windows. Riders got a bird's-eye view of the predator enclosures.

Leon and Pete also took one of the trams, and Leon quickly noticed that he had been correct to assume that there was a separate service tunnel that ran the length of the park, connecting the office tower and facilities on the extreme north end with the supply facilities on the south end. At several points, the two underground tunnel systems intersected one another.

Earl, with Bernie at his side, rode the tram route that started at the mine entrance in Gold Rush Town and looped through several smaller enclosures that held the wolves and two pairs of wolverines. The vehicle stopped briefly in the middle of Musk Ox Meadows, then continued to an observation tower near the river.

They got off and walked up to the top deck, where they glimpsed several large brown bears wandering along the shoreline and lying in the grass along the streambank. Checking around to see if anyone was watching him, Earl studied the perimeter wall, which was about a hundred yards from the east side of the tower. He could see where the ladders and construction materials had been in use several days earlier, now neatly stowed under a tarp next to the wall. He estimated the wall to be eight to ten feet high, constructed of concrete panels much like ones used for highway sound walls and patterned to appear like natural rock. Not far from the tower, Earl noticed several caves set into a small hill. While he watched, a bear emerged from one of the caves.

A few minutes later, another people mover arrived at the tower. A group of visitors got off, and Earl and Bernie boarded. Just after reentering the tunnel system, it slowed next to an underground viewing window looking into the bear dens, where a female bear and two cubs slept close to the heavy plate glass windows.

While Earl was checking out Bear River, Leon sought a way into the office tower. He discovered that the service tunnel went right under the building. There had to be an underground access. Near the intersection of the two tunnel systems, he saw a sign on a door that read "Employee Washroom and Lockers." Leon guessed that if there were lockers, there could be uniforms, perhaps even a few with name badges. It was possible that no one even bothered to secure their lockers due to the park's perimeter security. The room was definitely worth checking out.

Some yelling and people scattering along the promenade caught Leon's and Pete's attention. People were running their way and looking back towards one of the alleys next to a fake saloon storefront. A moment later, a wolf trotted out into the dock area. Right behind it were two of the animal keepers and two security guards. The wolf stopped in the middle of the promenade, unsure which way to run. One of the security men dropped to one knee and removed a canister from his belt. He rested the device on his knee and pointed it in the direction of the confused wolf. With a loud pop, a net flew out of the end of the canister and neatly dropped over the wolf. The animal keepers swarmed in on the entangled animal, and one of them used a syringe to inject it with a tranquilizer drug. The crowd watched curiously as the animal stopped struggling and was carried back into the alley to be returned to its enclosure.

Leon watched from the crowd of visitors, impressed with the efficiency of the capture operation. It could just have easily been a man they had snared.

"That was both exciting and very interesting," he remarked. "We need to remember about the net guns that the security guards carry."

"Yeah," replied Pete. "They've got all these dangerous predators here for people to gawk at. It's supposed to be exciting and fun, but it gives me the creeps knowing my brother died from predator wounds close to where I'm standing."

"That is okay, Pete," said Leon. "You do not have to like it. Come on, we need to explore some more and see what is behind these fake buildings. We could not see that area from the ridge."

The two men used the same alley where the wolf had appeared and checked out the beginning of the animal enclosures. There was plenty of signage pointing out paths to observations points to see the otters, musk ox, and even a polar bear enclosure with real icebergs. Overhead, the Sky Ride went back and forth, carrying carloads of people looking down onto wolves, bears, and other Alaskan wildlife.

Near the north end of the Sky Ride, they passed the land otter enclosure. Two of the park security guards watched the crowd from a refreshment stand close by. Leon noticed Pete stop short of the exhibit and turn pale, unable to move. He grabbed Pete's arm and steered him down another pathway. "Keep moving, Pete," he said. "We do not want to attract attention to us." He risked a quick glance back at the two security men. They were drinking sodas and watching people board the Sky Ride, not looking at Pete.

"We will split up," said Leon. "You focus on the layout of the park down by the warehouses, and not on your brother. I saw how you looked back there when you saw the otters."

"Yeah, maybe I am superstitious about those critters, like Raz was."

Leon put his arm on Pete's back as they kept walking. "Go check out the warehouses at the south end. I will see you at our rendezvous point."

Pete was glad to let Leon wander the animal area alone and strolled down to the south end. He found a bench where he could observe the dock area beyond the barrier to the warehouses and service buildings. About one hundred yards from the first warehouse, which Earl and Leon thought might be used for unloading containers, there was an exit from the service tunnel. During the time he sat there, Pete observed several vehicles exit the tunnel and park near a loading dock for one of the service buildings. An employee pushed some loaded racks onto a vehicle, and then it headed back into the tunnel. Pete surmised that the was some type of food preparation or supply building for vendors in the complex. He sat with his park map in his lap and pretended to study it while checking for security cameras and floodlights. It took his mind off the land otter pen.

There were plenty of floodlights along the dock, but no exterior cameras that he could see. There was one security station located close to the fence at the end of the promenade. Pete smiled, realizing that guards at that location would be looking away from the tunnel, making a blind spot based on the shack's orientation. He presumed that the service tunnel represented their best access to the warehouses, even though they had to cross one hundred yards of open space. Pete smiled to himself one more time while he glanced at his wristwatch. He stood up and stretched, then started walking back along the promenade through the crowd of Juneau families. They had all agreed to meet at the Lulu Belle Saloon for a late afternoon meal before the excitement commenced.

The fifth and sixth members of their little team strolled first towards the saloon in the middle of Gold Rush Town. They stopped and watched a theatrical drama featuring a couple of gold miners brawling over the favors of a dancehall girl until one shot the other to the cheers of the on-looking crowd. Then they browsed the shops.

Brooklyn and Lewis took a ride on the people mover up to the observation tower above Moose and Caribou Plateau. It offered a great view of the north end of the park. From there they saw the Journey to the Arctic Marine Amphitheater at the end of the cruise ship dock. They walked towards the aquarium next but didn't really focus on anything in the exhibits, using the walk as an opportunity to check out the dock ramp to the fishing and whale-watching boats. The tour boats and dock were quiet, with no one entering or leaving. They was a locked gate at the head of the ramp. They too had just enough time to grab some food before finding the rendezvous point.

They had to tell Leon about the problem with the locked gate.

At 3:30 p.m., the park PA system started making announcements about the opening day ceremony. Visitors were requested to gather on the promenade near the shuttle boat pier. There would be a gift for everyone who had attended. Hearing the announcement, the teams began to assemble near the mine entrance tunnel. Bernie and Brooklyn made their way through the gathering crowd to stand close to a temporary stage erected on the pier. Bernie could see the ramp to the shuttle boats but hung back, staying close to Brooklyn instead of proceeding to the boats as his dad had ordered.

Promptly at 4:00 p.m., a PR spokesperson for the park began speaking. "Welcome, everyone from Juneau. Did you enjoy your day at Glacier World?"

There was a rousing cheer from the gathered crowd.

"Great!" said the announcer. "In a few weeks, thousands of international visitors will be following in your footsteps and enjoying what Southeast Alaska has to offer as the ultimate vacation destination. Over one hundred fifty thousand visitors are expected to visit this park over the next year—most on their first visit to Alaska. There is one person who, for many years, has supported the vision of this park and helped it become a reality. He is here this afternoon to offer a few words of welcome and dedicate the park as an economic engine for the 2020s and your future. Please welcome your state senator, William MacDonald!"

There was scattered applause from the crowd.

MacDonald stepped forward and quickly mounted the steps of a small bandstand with his right arm waving to the crowd. "Good afternoon, folks. Welcome to this magnificent park located on the doorstep to Southeast Alaska. It is just fantastic what Global Resource International has been able to do with this old cannery site that has been part of our history for over one hundred years. I, for one, am truly thankful for the investment the folks at GRI have made and know it will—"

MacDonald's opening remarks were interrupted by a female voice shouting from the crowd. "Yeah, Senator, you're thankful for the money they put in your back pocket, and what about thanking the people who saved your life last week when your fancy boat hit a whale and sank?"

There was scattered laughter, and the Senator attempted a suitable response while searching the crowd for the heckler. "Ah, that was unfortunate. Hypothermia is a dangerous condition. I...I may have been slightly confused at the time, but I do appreciate the quick reaction of my rescuers from the fine town of Hoonah and the Alaska State Troopers."

"What about the whale? Are you going to thank it, too?" Brooklyn hollered. This time there was a lot of laughter from the people gathered along the waterfront.

"Yeah, senator," a man added to Brooklyn's remark. "What about those dolphins your friends here at the park captured and are holding to put on display for tourists?"

Brooklyn took the advantage before the senator could respond. "Is that part of your great economic plan, senator? Damn with the environment?"

Senator MacDonald spotted Brooklyn and pointed her out to several security people standing just below him. They quickly pushed through the crowd, grabbed her by both arms, and started dragging her towards the gangway to the shuttle boats. She faked some resistance so they had to partly carry her.

Bernie, who had been standing next to Brooklyn, followed and hit their arms with his fists. "Hey, leave her alone!" he hollered. He kicked one of them in a shin when the man refused to let go of Brooklyn. The man grabbed Bernie by the back of his jacket and pulled him along as they pushed through the crowd of onlookers.

Earl, along with many of the people in the crowd, could not see what was happening, but he did see the two security men next to the tunnel entrance become curious, leave their post, and walk closer to the crowd. He glanced at Leon, who nodded and, without hesitating, walked quickly into the entrance, followed by Pete and Lewis. Earl followed, taking one last glance hoping to see where Bernie was, then ducked into the tunnel with the others. They didn't slow down, but kept moving until they reached the intersection of the two tunnels. Leon tried the door to a mechanical room he had noticed earlier in the day. It was unlocked. The four men slipped inside and turned on the lights to check the room.

There were several electrical control panels in the center of the floor and a door marked "Pump Room" on the far wall. It was partly obscured by the electrical panels.

Again, the door was unlocked, but lockable from the inside or with a key. They turned out the lights and settled down for a long wait in the confines of the small room with the door locked. There was not enough room for them all to lay down on the floor, so they took turns.

About three hours later, they heard a door open and a beam of light showed below the door of their small room. Someone walked across the control room and tried the doorknob to their room, then walked away. The light when out.

CHAPTER 22

Glacier World

Brooklyn and Bernie showed no more resistance after they were hauled out of the crowd and over to the edge of the dock where several other security men were standing. One big man appeared to be the supervisor. Brooklyn saw a name badge on his chest that read N. Fishman. The man did not appear friendly as he spoke to her.

"What's your name?" he demanded.

"Brooklyn."

Someone close by in the crowd shouted for the security guys to let them go, that they were just children. Fishman looked at the man in the crowd and then down at Bernie. "What is your name and where are your parents?"

Bernie looked down at the shuttle boat next to the dock. There were maybe ten or twelve people already on board, ready to return to Juneau. He waved and a woman waved back. "My name is Bernie Armstrong and my parents are on that boat."

Fishman glanced at the boat as Bernie waved. "Alright. You two are banned from Glacier World for one year. I better not see either of you in the park or there will be trouble for your parents." He turned to one of his subordinates and gave an order. "Put them on that boat and make sure they do not get back off."

Brooklyn and Bernie stood at the rail of the shuttle boat while MacDonald finished his short speech and then was hustled off to an electric cart that took him and his wife out to the airstrip. People started walking down the ramp to the boats. Soon their boat was full and pulled away from the dock to return to Auke Bay. Brooklyn looked for Earl and the others and couldn't find them in the crowd. The next step was to meet up with Johnny in Juneau and be back to the pickup site at daylight. The abandoned dock would be much harder to reach than their first choice, which Brooklyn had discovered had a locked gate. It was going to be a very long night for everyone.

CHAPTER 23

Glacier World

The hours dragged on, and Earl found it hard to sleep. When it was finally time for the team to slip out of their hiding place, his body was stiff from the cramped conditions in the small room. Leon had them wait in the control room while he checked the service tunnel. A few minutes later, he returned and beckoned them to follow him. They walked several hundred feet to another door, close to where the service tunnel intersected with the main tunnel. It was the staff locker room that Leon had located while riding the people mover.

Leon used a small LED flashlight to search the lockers and quickly found four sets of coveralls and several security badges. He swiped one of the badges on the room's lock and found that it locked and unlocked the door. At least now they had an easier chance of getting into the office tower.

Minutes later the teams split up, with Earl and Pete going one way down the service tunnel that would take them to the warehouses, and Leon and Lewis going the other way towards the office tower. They agreed to meet in two hours at the tunnel that led to the Bear River observation tower and Leon's back door out of Glacier World.

**

Johnny was waiting on the transient dock in Auke Bay when the shuttle boat with Bernie and Brooklyn tied up. He'd spoken to Brooklyn by cell phone, and his boat was fueled and ready for their trip back to Excursion Inlet. Bernie wanted badly to go along, but Brooklyn was adamant that he couldn't go. There were things she knew from the talk she and Leon had had during the planning stage of the mission. Leon did not want to put both Earl and his son in danger, and had strong reservations even with Brooklyn's involvement. But Brooklyn, the smart girl that she was, had convinced Leon that two people in the pickup boat was advisable. There were any number of tasks—from handling lines to using the spotlight on the top of the cabin to keeping an eye out for the park's patrol boats—that required an extra person. Leon and Brooklyn had also worked out a third pickup location in advance, just in case the backup location became too dangerous.

With Bernie safely at the motel in Juneau, Brooklyn and Johnny headed west. Even at top speed, they had a two-hour trip. They ate some sandwiches that Johnny had picked up at the diner in Auke Bay and then Brooklyn curled up on one of the cushioned benches to try and get some sleep. The long night was just beginning.

***

The basement door to the office tower was locked, as Leon had expected it would be. However, the security badges from the uniforms they were wearing worked with the outer doors. Avoiding the elevators in case a security station monitored their operation, they used a stairway. Leon and Lewis climbed quickly to the fourth floor. By the time they reached it, Lewis was breathing hard.

"Can we hold here for a second?" Lewis asked. His heart beat rapidly, and his feet were heavy like he was wearing boots filled with concrete.

Leon was patient and took the opportunity to slightly open the door to the fourth floor. He checked for security cameras and an access to the computer area. There was a hallway and a large room with interior glass windows facing the elevators and stairway. Except for a single security light the room was dark and unoccupied. Leon could not see any security cameras in the hallway either. After giving Lewis another minute or two to catch his breath, they crept into the hallway and tried the door to the computer control room. Leon used his stolen security pass just in case there was an alarm on the door. There was none.

They chose what appeared to be a supervisor's office to access the computer system. Luckily, the computer was turned on, and they did not have to boot it. Lewis quickly cracked the password and was into the main system. Leon didn't ask how he did it. Hackers had a unique talent for those things.

Leon kept an eye on the hallway through the interior glass windows while Lewis started to work. He took out two high-capacity flash drives and his little black notebook, which he opened to a tabbed page with his previous notes regarding GRI.

Lewis's eyes gleamed in the glow of the monitor, and Leon noticed signs of pleasure. The anticipation of actually getting what they wanted was exciting to him, too. After a few minutes, the little man inserted one of the flash drives into a computer port, hit a key, and waited for the files to copy. Leon was getting anxious, and put a hand on Lewis' shoulder when he noticed a light come on over the elevator doors in the hallway.

Lewis dimmed the monitor as they slipped down behind the desk to wait. He could see the file transfer working on the monitor and hoped whoever was out there would not notice the activity on the screen. They could hear footsteps as the guard approached the main door, then saw the beam of a flashlight sweep through the room. Moments later, the elevator door opened and closed again, but Leon waited another two minutes before letting Lewis continue. Lewis inserted the second flash drive to download more files, then after several more tense minutes, he finally closed the programs he had accessed and turned off the monitor.

"I think I've got what we need," said Lewis almost at a whisper as he placed the devices in a pocket of his jeans.

Leon checked the hallway and motioned for Lewis to follow him. Moments later they were in the stairway and moving swiftly back down to the basement level and into the tunnel.

Back in the data center manager's office, Lewis's notebook lay next to the computer.

***

Earl and Pete had a longer walk in the service tunnel to reach the warehouses. Lighting in the tunnel was widely spaced, and they found themselves hurrying through the pools of dim light to seek the safety of the darker areas.

They heard one of the electric vehicles approaching from behind them. Pete saw a side door up ahead, and they rushed through it. Pete used his flashlight for a few seconds to survey the room. There were several refrigerators, bags stacked on pallets, and a second door.

"Over there!" Pete whispered as they heard the vehicle stop in the tunnel just outside the door.

The interior room was pitch black and smelled like spoiled meat, but they couldn't chance using their flashlights until the security vehicle moved on. A door opened. Through a crack under the door, lights flashed on and off without anyone approaching. Earl heard a rustling sound behind them, along with a low growl. Earl couldn't wait any longer to use his flashlight.

"This is not good!" he said as he searched the darkness with the beam. Two sets of predator eyes gleamed back at him. "Oh oh! Go back! Go back! We have to go back through that door right now."

He held the beam on the beady eyes as he and Pete moved, crashing through the door and quickly slamming it behind them just as something hit the other side. Earl's flashlight was still on, and he focused the beam on a sign on the door.

Pete said the sign. "Wolverine Den. Keep Closed. Whoa! That was close."

"Yeah, we were almost dinner for those critters." Earl responded.

They waited a full two minutes before opening the door to tunnel. The security men were gone. The remainder of the service tunnel was uneventful, and they reached the last entrance undetected. On the edge of the dock, a hundred yards to their right, was the guard station Pete had noted earlier. An overhead luminaire made it look like it stood on an island of yellow light. The dock in front of them was semi-dark but empty. The warehouses were still some distance to the left. That area was completely dark.

"What do you think?" Earl whispered to Pete.

"As good a time as any, I guess. Do we run or do we stroll?" Pete asked in return.

"Hey, that's a good idea. We're wearing these damn uniforms. Why not look like we belong here?" Earl took the lead, stepped out of the tunnel, and started walking towards the closest warehouse.

Pete followed, trying to look relaxed. Neither of them risked a glance towards the guard shack. No one hollered for them to stop.

They used an access door on the end of the closest warehouse. Inside, Earl turned on his flashlight and located a set of light switches. If any light spilled outside, they would just have to take that risk. They needed photographs. The dockside of the warehouse held row upon row of huge shipping containers stacked two high. On the other side were pallets of machinery, appliances, big screen TVs, and cartons too numerous and too many to identify. Some particular items that intrigued Earl were eight Harley-Davidson motorcycles still in their cartons. He snapped some pictures, including close-ups of the shipping labels with the serial numbers of the bikes. If anything in the place was traceable to the shipper and to the original buyer, Earl figured these ought to be.

They moved down the row of cargo, taking more pictures, then back along the other side taking pictures of the containers and their serial numbers.

Just before reaching the door they had used to enter the warehouse, Earl stopped.

"Wait a second, Pete. Do you hear something?" Earl flipped off the lights and peeked out the door. A vehicle was headed their way from the direction of the guard shack. "We may have company. Alert Leon. Then take off your coveralls. We'll stuff them in that garbage can by the door."

While Pete used his cell phone to alert Leon of their problem, Earl thought through their situation. The pictures he had just taken could be serious trouble. But if the only pictures in his camera were those taken earlier in the day when he was acting like any other visitor, they might bluff their way out. He removed the memory card from the camera and slipped it inside one of his shoes. He put his other card back in the camera.

"Let's try to slip away before they get here, Pete. If they stop us, we tell them we are errant tourists."

"Wandering around their warehouse in the middle of the night? I say we make a run for it. I don't relish the thought of becoming a meal for one of their predators," answered Pete. He opened the door just slightly to see where the men were. Two security guards stood next to their vehicle, about fifty feet from the building. Each of them had something that looked like a large flashlight in their hands. Pete opened the door just as the yard lights outside the warehouse came on.

"They must have called the guard shack and asked for the lights. Follow me!" Pete ran for the corner of the warehouse.

Earl wasn't sure what they would do or where they could go from there, but he ran after Pete. The two guards saw them immediately and started after them. One of the guards shouted something as Pete and Earl ran for the darkest area between two warehouses. Earl heard the pounding of footsteps and then a popping sound. He stumbled and went down hard, wrapped in a nearly invisible net.

Pete heard him fall and looked back. He saw Earl struggling to stand up. Then the guards were on top of him, and one of them whacked Earl on the head with a baton. Pete stopped and raised his hands.

Earl was dazed from the blow to his head and lay still as one of the guards removed the netting that covered his body. His right shoulder hurt from hitting the pavement. He tried to focus as he looked at his captors, and recognized the man that who had grabbed Pete and was leading him back towards their vehicle. It was Hayden, the burly man who had tried to pick a fight with him in front of the bar in Juneau.

CHAPTER 24

Glacier World

Nigel Fishman had gone to bed late but was pleased they were finished with the opening day. He hoped the park would be more manageable when cruise ships started to dock. Other than the disturbance during the closing ceremony, it had gone well. He had watched the faces and listened to the chitchat as people departed. Most of the visitors appeared to have a good time and enjoy the experience.

The disturbance itself nagged at him. He had witnessed many disturbances over the years, some of them turning violent. This one, while quite tame, seemed almost as if it had been planned. For what reason? The senator was not all that popular. Everyone knew that. So why pick this moment and place to heckle the senator? Rahman had chosen to issue his own carefully worded press releases. The heckling was clearly initiated by a young girl. He remembered her name being Brooklyn, an odd name. The boy wasn't likely her brother, because her skin was dark—probably Alaskan Native—and the boy was fair complexioned. But they clearly knew each other. Neither of the kids showed any fear of being apprehended or what might happen to them. If it had not been for the support of the crowd on the dock, he could have made them sweat a bit to find out what they were up to. He remembered the boy, Bernie Armstrong, being cooperative, perhaps a little too cooperative. Had they staged the disturbance to cover up something else?

Fishman finally fell asleep around midnight but was wakened three hours later by the buzzing of his cell phone. "Mr. Fishman? This is Hayden. I'm at Warehouse One and we just took two intruders into custody. I think you better get over here right away. One of them may have been taking pictures in the warehouse. His ID says his name is Armstrong, and his residence is in Washington State. The other guy's name is Hunt and is from Hoonah. He could be a relative of that guy who was killed by the otters a couple of months ago."

"One of them is named Armstrong?" replied Fishman. "One of the kids involved in the disturbance this afternoon was named Armstrong." Fishman's thoughts flashed back to just before he had fallen asleep. "It was a diversion. Damn it! I'll be there as soon as I can. I'm putting the whole park on alert and everyone on a search for any other intruders. Hangovers from a party be damned!" Fishman clicked off and called the main security office to get search teams going, then grabbed his clothes and his weapon.

***

Leon felt his cell phone vibrate in his shirt pocket. He answered without saying a word. Pete's message about being spotted and in trouble was disturbing, but not entirely unexpected.

"On my way to you right now!" replied Leon. His training as a Marine was to expect the worst to happen but to also help your buddies. He turned to Lewis. "We are using the back door to get out of here. Earl and Pete are in trouble and I am gonna get them. Go as quickly as you can to the beginning of the tunnel that leads to the bear area and wait for us there. If we do not show up in twenty minutes, go to the bear observation tower, use a ladder to get over the wall, and head for the pickup point. You have to get out of here with the data."

Leon turned and ran down the service tunnel in the direction of the warehouses. Another row of lights turned on somewhere, and the tunnel became well lit. Leon figured it was because the park's security was alerted. It would only be a matter of minutes until they would be searching everywhere. He kept running without regard to being seen or to his own safety.

One of the men stationed at the guard shack had moved to stand right outside the tunnel. He was watching what was happening near the warehouse, his back toward the tunnel. Leon crashed into him and used his right hand to land a heavy blow on the back of the man's neck. He slipped the man's pistol out of his holster before he hit the ground. Grabbing the guard's hat and putting it on, he slowed to a walk as he continued towards the warehouse.

Next to the security vehicle, Hayden had started questioning Earl and Pete. He took their IDs, Pete's phone, and Earl's camera. The other guard with Hayden turned to see Leon approaching, but in the dim light on the dock he assumed Leon was one of the other guards and turned back to watch Hayden examine the photos on the camera. Leon walked up behind him and hit him on the head with the pistol. The man grunted and fell to the pavement. Hayden turned to see Leon standing with the pistol leveled at him.

"Yes, I know how to use it," said Leon. "Move towards that door. Now!"

"You! I know you." Hayden pointed a finger at Leon but hesitated. He could see the pistol was cocked and there was a deadly serious look in Leon's eyes. Hayden laid the camera on a seat of the vehicle, turned slowly, and walked to the open warehouse door. Just inside he darted sidewise into the shadows, turned, and grabbed Leon's arm that held the pistol and slammed his right fist at Leon's left cheek. The blow only partially connected as Leon attempted to duck his head, but the force on his arm caused him to drop the pistol.

Leon kept his balance, wheeled around on his left foot, and landed his right foot square in the middle of Hayden's chest. Hayden hit the wall but bounced back. He snarled as he lowered his head to charge Leon, trying to wrap his arms around Leon's body. Leon chopped down on the back of Hayden's neck with both hands then brought a knee up under his chin. Hayden went down and didn't move.

Leon looked around for the pistol and saw it lying in the light coming through the door opening. He grabbed it and ran out to where Earl and Pete still stood next to the vehicle.

"Get in!" Leon jumped behind the wheel, started the vehicle, and turned towards the tunnel entrance even as Earl and Pete were scrambling to climb aboard. "We have maybe ten minutes to get out of here before there are security guys everywhere."

CHAPTER 25

Glacier World

Alone in the service tunnel, Lewis Teebottom felt panicky. He knew where he had to go and what to do if the rest of the group didn't make it to the assembly point. Whether he could accomplish this on his own, he seriously doubted. For one thing, he was deathly afraid of bears after being attacked by a brown bear when he was only six years old. It was one reason he wore his hair long—to hide the scars on his scalp. Even if he did manage to find a ladder and scale the perimeter wall, he was not very good at orienting himself in a forest. His feelings battled with the fact that his friends were depending on him as he cautiously approached the cross tunnel for the people mover loop to the bear enclosure. He stopped every few minutes to listen—hoping Leon would be back before the park security guards discovered him. The tunnels were well lit now and the only hiding place he could see was a door marked for the wolf dens. He definitely was not going to use that as a place to hide.

Lewis watched and waited in the shadows next to the door. He looked at his watch and saw that Leon had maybe another five minutes to find him.

The minutes went by and none of his friends came. Finally, as instructed by Leon, he started walking up the tunnel that led to the bear observation tower. He had no idea how far ahead it was. After several hundred yards, he heard something behind him. A pair of headlights appeared as a vehicle turned off the service tunnel and headed in his direction. He ran but it was gaining. Out of breath, he stopped and flattened himself against the side of the passageway with his hands raised. There was no way for him to escape.

The headlights of the electric vehicle blinded him. It stopped and a voice shouted, "Get in!"

Lewis was so scared he couldn't get his body to move like it was glued to the wall. "Leon? Earl?"

Four hands reached out and grabbed Lewis's arms, hauling him into the vehicle as Leon jammed the pedal to the floor and the vehicle tore on up the tunnel. Minutes later he slammed on the brakes at the observation tower station.

"Okay, we have to get over that wall. Then maybe we will have a chance."

The four men ran up the stairway to the observation deck and looked out towards the wall. The sky was already beginning to lighten. In the dim light it appeared the construction equipment was still stored next to the wall, and no bears in sight. Peering down, Earl realized that he had not planned on how to get down to the ground. Pete was right behind him and saw Earl start to climb over the railing.

"Wait, Earl!" Pete said. "There's a door at the bottom of the stairwell we just came up. Maybe it will let us out." They rushed down the stairs and found that Pete was correct. The door offered access to the enclosure but was locked. Leon used his key card and the door unlocked. Earl was the first person through and headed directly for the pile of construction equipment. Pulling the tarp aside, his spirits faded. The ladder was only six feet long.

"We need to find another way over the wall," he hollered as the others joined him.

They searched the rock wall in each direction looking for handholds or a way over. The wall continued its full height down the slope to the river. In the other direction, where it ran close to the bear dens, the forested slope of the hill was almost as high as the wall. Earl looked at the construction tools once more.

"We've got a chain saw here. Maybe I can drop a tree onto the wall and we can walk along its trunk, using the branches to drop down on the other side." Earl didn't wait for anyone to agree or disagree with his idea as he grabbed the saw and headed for the slope. Selecting a cedar tree about a foot in diameter that leaned slightly towards the wall, he set the choke, flipped the on switch, and prayed as he pulled the starter cord. It started on the first pull. Earl set the chain against the far side of the tree and revved the saw to full throttle. It began to cut. The noise was bound to carry all the way down to the dock, but maybe they could be over the wall before security arrived.

Pete hollered over the noise of the saw, "We've got company. Better hurry Earl! There's a bear coming up from the river."

There was a well-trod path from the river up to the bear dens next to the observation tower. Pete could see the back of the bear as it followed the path through a patch of brush that was nearly as tall as Pete. Branches snapped as it pushed its way through. Pete watched as the Kodak bear emerged from the brush, left the trail, and turned towards them, unafraid of the noisy chain saw. Pete glanced over at Earl and saw it was not a good situation. Earl was still trying to fell a tree, and there was no way he would get it done before the bear got to them. Lewis was watching the bear too and looking around for a way to retreat.

When the Kodiak was less than fifty feet away, it stopped and swayed from side to side, hesitating. Pete and Lewis watched as it looked away from the men, over towards the entrance to the dens. Another bear, the female with the cubs, had come out of the den. Despite her smaller size, she began making threatening moves of her own, but not at them. She didn't like the Kodiak being so close to her cubs. Looking at Pete and the others, then at the female bear, the Kodiak hesitated and backed away. The female bear pawed at the dirt in front of the den and held her ground. The Kodiak retreated. For the moment, there was a stalemate.

Earl twisted the saw in his cut to help clear it of sawdust. He pressed harder and gave the throttle everything he could. There was a loud crack and the tree started to fall. He kept cutting and seconds later the tree fell towards the wall. It landed perfectly. Earl walked up the trunk, cutting a few branches that blocked their way, then tossed the saw over the wall and swung down on one of the branches that dipped to the ground on the far side. Lewis was right behind him, then Pete, and finally Leon. A bullet smacked into the tree trunk right beside Leon's right foot and another whizzed by his head.

"Those are pistol shots. They are not very accurate at this range."

No sooner than saying those words, Pete let out a yell and grabbed his leg, but kept his balance and kept moving. Two more shots went wide. Leon glanced at the tower and saw two men as he dropped over the wall. They were staying put in the safety of the tower. Once on the ground, he went to Pete, who was pulling up a pant leg to examine his wound. The bullet had grazed his right calf, and a steady stream of blood flowed down his leg and was starting to soak his sock. Leon tore off a strip from the bottom of his shirt and bound the wound tightly. "Seen a lot worse, Pete. It should stop bleeding, but walking on it is going to be painful."

Pete grimaced but still had a sense of humor. He looked over at Earl, who was brushing sawdust out of his hair and eyes. "Good work, Earl. You ever think about entering one of those logger competitions down your way?"

"Nope! I'm afraid of heights. I would fail miserably in the tree-topping event."

His response raised a little chuckle from everyone. Their spirits lifted—after all that had happened to them inside the park, they appeared to be clear of it.

Leon took the lead and led the group towards the lake. They were in heavy timber, and his intent was to go around the lake on the far side, away from the power plant, and then double back to the shore of the inlet. They had been walking for maybe fifteen minutes when his phone buzzed—Brooklyn.

"Leon, wherever you guys are, don't come near the pickup point," Brooklyn shouted into the phone over the throaty engine noise on the *Huna Spirit*. "There are two patrol boats from the park headed this way. We can't stay here any longer."

Leon stopped walking and held up an arm for the others to hold up. "I understand, Brooklyn. You guys clear out and be careful. You remember what we talked about as a backup plan?"

"Yeah!" Brooklyn shouted over the whine of the engines as Johnny increased the throttle and headed the *Huna Spirit* away from the approaching patrol boats. "We pick you up at the Sisters. You'll be taking the old miner's trail over the Chilkats."

"That is right. Give us two days. We will try to be on the beach by sunset. Pete got shot in the leg but says he is okay. We need him to show us the trail." Leon turned to face Pete and the others. "Can you find the mountain trail and make it, Pete?"

"I'll manage. It's just a flesh wound."

Leon glanced at Pete's leg. His pant leg and shoes were soaked in blood.

"There's something I didn't tell you about the trail, Leon. There's an old miner's cabin just below the tree line on this side of the Chilkats. If we can find it, there might be some medical stuff to take care of this wound as well as some things to help us get over the snowfields and the glacier. Old Mike, who built that cabin near his gold mine, used the trail to go into Juneau for supplies. He died a couple of years ago. I remember reading about his passing in the Juneau newspaper. He was pretty well known in the area as an independent old cuss. Stayed in that cabin year round, so it could be pretty well stocked unless someone went up there and tore it apart looking for any gold he might have hidden."

"Any kind of cabin would be a welcome sight to me," Lewis added. "Never did like the woods that much, even though I've lived in Hoonah all my life. Always feel like there is a bear tracking me. Makes the hair on the back of my neck stand up like right now. Let's get moving and go find that cabin." Lewis didn't elaborate on why he had the sensation, but it was real, and it scared him to death.

**

Fishman's security men watched the place where the four men had gone over the perimeter wall of the bear enclosure. They remained within the safety of the observation tower, not daring to venture closer to the downed tree. Everyone else had been called into the park offices for a briefing after finishing a thorough search of the park. About an hour after the escape of the intruders, they noticed movement in the trees above the bear dens. One of them raised his pistol and watched. He swore to himself as he saw the big Kodiak brown bear walk out of the trees, put one of its huge front paws up on the downed tree trunk, then leap up and begin walking along it. It paused to sniff something on the trunk, then continued up to where the tree rested on the wall. It sniffed again, then disappeared over the other side.

The guard mumbled to his partner. "Will you look at that! That damn bear escaped. Rahman's not gonna be happy losing his prize Kodiak bear." He re-holstered his pistol.

"Yeah, I heard he paid a lot of money to a black market big game hunter for that bear," replied the other guard.

"That's not the only problem," said the first guard. "It's a man-eater. Killed two fishermen last year. That big game hunter was supposed to destroy that bear but instead he captured it alive and made some extra bucks selling it to Rahman, who figured there wouldn't be any problem 'cause of the park's security fences."

"Well, Rahman better not ask me to go after it. I don't even like the looks of that forest beyond the wall. I'd quit first."

CHAPTER 26

Glacier World

Rahman had not heard about the missing bear, but he was mad enough to kill somebody when he learned about the night's events. All he could think about was what the hell they were up to. He ordered a thorough search of the park.

Nigel Fishman entered the briefing room with a very concerned look on this face. It was his responsibility to have an explanation for his boss. Fishman knew his new job was at risk, and quite likely his remaining career in corporate security. What had seemed like an easy job just a few weeks before was now a nightmare. He slumped into a chair and made his report.

"So far we have been able to determine that there were four men," Fishman said, pouring himself a cup of coffee from a carafe on the conference table. "They probably came into the park with the rest of the visitors and were able to hide themselves in the tunnels during the disruption of the senator's speech at the ceremony. My conclusion is that the disturbance was deliberate and the two kids were part of the group. One of my men found a candy wrapper in a mechanical room just inside the people mover tunnel. I don't know how they learned about the tunnel system, but I have to say they were clever. The pump room door inside the mechanical control room is lockable, and during the check yesterday evening, it was assumed to have been locked all day. I agree that was a mistake, and it prevented the group from being discovered."

"So, who are they and what were they after?" Rahman asked.

"As to the who, we have names on the two that broke into Warehouse One." Fishman laid two driver's licenses on the table and slid them over to Rahman. "One of them is from Hoonah. His name is Pete Hunt, and is quite likely related to the man we placed in the otter pen last fall. He was mentioned in the newspaper article about the death."

"So, Hunt was not convinced it was an accident and was looking for evidence regarding his brother's death? He could not have found anything in the warehouse, but I'm sure he got an eyeful of what is in there."

"I don't think the dead brother was the purpose of them coming here, but probably was the reason a relative was part of the group. He was curious."

"Why do you think that? Because of the other guy?" asked Rahman as he examined the other license. "Armstrong. Why is that name familiar?"

"His son was one of the instigators of the disturbance. As you can see, he's from out of state. Right now, it's a mystery as to why he would be part of the group, but there has to be a reason. He had a camera and took a lot of pictures around the park and maybe inside the warehouse. Hayden didn't get the opportunity to examine everything before the two were rescued by one of their friends."

"Hmm." Rahman rubbed his chin and stared at the license. "Have our computer guys run a check on him. He's from some town on the Washington coast. What about the other two? You said there were four men?"

"No names yet, but Hayden recognized one of them. They fought at the warehouse when this guy surprised him and another guard while he was interrogating Armstrong and Hunt. This guy was definitely Indian. He had long black hair and dark skin. Hayden had a brief encounter with the guy in Juneau over a week ago. He was with Armstrong and his son."

There was a light rap on the conference room door. One of Fishman's men stood just outside holding up something for him to see. Fishman beckoned for him to enter. The man looked nervous as he handed him a small black notebook, along with two ID badges. He backed away while explaining in a quiet voice where the items had been found, like he was afraid to mention it to Rahman. After hearing what he said, Fishman sprang from his chair and struck the guard squarely on his jaw with his fist and drew his sidearm.

"You stupid fool!" Fishman raged. "You were supposed to check every room in the building, including the control centers! How the hell did they get in there?" He looked at the ID badges and realized they had been used just for that purpose. "Get out of my sight!" Fishman yelled at the guard.

Rahman was on his feet and livid as he asked Fishman what happened. The guard got to his feet and fled the room.

"They broke into the computer center."

"Which one did they get into?" Rahman demanded.

"They were on the fourth floor. The data center manager found this notebook next to his computer."

Rahman grabbed the notebook and thumbed through the pages of scribbles. There was a name with an address on the first page—Lewis Teebottom. The phone number and address were for Hoonah. He flipped to the last entry and saw several IP addresses, including one below the letters GRI. Rahman recognized the other company names written beside the addresses. He threw the notebook at Fishman and screamed, "Damn it! They hacked into our computer system. Get that manager up here right now. I want to know every damn file they saw and whether anything was copied."

CHAPTER 27

Chilkat Range, Alaska

The first two miles after climbing over the wall were relatively easy as the four men tried to put some distance between them and the park. The terrain, while heavily forested, was relatively flat. They went single file, with Leon in the lead, taking directions every ten minutes or so from Pete. They were able to avoid areas with muskeg, the terrain dotted with water lily-filled ponds. By chance, they came upon a well-used bear trail and followed it for a while.

All that changed when they encountered a canyon and a series of waterfalls. With cliffs in either direction, the best route was to climb up beside the waterfalls. The first one was easy—a height of maybe ten to fifteen feet. The final one was over thirty feet high and the rocks were wet, slick, and covered in moss. With the help of tree roots and vines, they slowly worked their way up the face of the rocks. Lewis and Earl were the last two up, and with his short legs, Lewis had difficulty climbing. They were attempting the last climb when Lewis slipped.

"Oh, oh," shouted Lewis as he fell against Earl, who was just below him. The two slid all the way down.

"You okay, Lewis?" asked Earl as he brushed dirt and moss off himself.

"Yeah, I think it's just my pride that hurts. I've been trying to keep up with you guys."

They started up again, and this time Earl stayed closer to Lewis and pushed him up when he needed help. After joining Leon and Pete at the top, Earl checked his jacket pockets.

"Damn, I lost the camera," said Earl. "I must have lost it when we fell."

"Leave it, Earl," Leon insisted. "They are going to be after us soon, if not already. We will be wasting time and it will be harder going back down than it was getting up here. You okay otherwise?"

"Yeah, I'm okay, I guess. Got a few skinned knuckles and probably a bruise or two. Give me a minute to wash my hands and get a drink from the stream."

It was midmorning and the four men still had not reached the tree line. They followed a stream in a canyon, with the terrain rising steeply on both sides. There was only one way to go. They struggled through thick brush and downed timber, crossing the stream several times before they found the trail Pete had been looking for. It led right to Old Mike's cabin and then on up the mountain. The group had covered maybe four miles—all of which had taken a toll on

Lewis as well as Pete. Lewis's physical condition was not even close to the others', and Pete endured a bad limp and obvious pain from his leg wound. The wound was still bleeding and needed proper bandaging—a problem that was solved upon arrival at the old cabin.

It had not been vandalized and looked just like the old miner had left it. The cabin was small and constructed of rough-cut logs. A single door faced a clearing where the brush was beginning to take over. They had to force their way through, which to their relief indicated no one had been using the cabin for some time. The door was in good shape and unlocked.

They found a medical kit and took care of Pete's injury before seeing what else there was that might aid in their trek over the top of the mountain range. Pete felt a lot better after taking several painkillers and relaxing on a small bunk while Leon and Earl explored the cabin. They found some canned goods, rope, and an old lever action .30-30 Winchester rifle that still functioned.

Lewis sat on a stump just outside the old cabin and nervously watched their back trail. Well below them he could see Excursion Inlet and the top of the green glass office tower in the middle of Glacier World. It was hard for him to imagine that just a few hours before, he had sat in a comfortable chair working at a computer in that building. Lewis pulled off his aviator flying helmet and ran his hand through his soaking wet hair. He patted a pocket of his jeans, then dug a hand in it and removed one of the flash drives he had used to store the copied data files. He turned it over and over, trying to imagine what evidence he might have captured.

Earl joined him and asked what he was thinking.

"Well, I'm glad I have these. I could have lost one or both of these in that fall."

"But you didn't," replied Earl. "Sorry I lost your camera though."

"That's okay. It's replaceable."

"We'll make it through, Lewis. You can do it. Then we can turn the data over to the authorities."

Lewis nodded in agreement, but his mind was on what he had done in that operations center. At the last minute, he had made a second copy. It renewed his spirits that they had got what they came for, but he couldn't shake a nervous feeling he had that they were being followed.

If he and Earl had been watching closely, they would have seen four men cross the dam towards their side of the lake and enter the trees below them. Somewhere between the two groups of men was the Kodiak.

CHAPTER 28

Glacier World

Fishman quickly organized himself and three other men to pursue the intruders. Hayden insisted on being part of the group, and while Fishman knew Hayden was better in a fight than the other men, he hoped the hatred he noticed in Hayden's eyes for the beating he took from Armstrong's friend wouldn't be a problem. Each man would carry a high caliber rifle along with a blanket, water, and food for themselves. He had no idea how long it would take to catch up with them, but he believed they had the advantage. His security people reported that one of the intruders had been shot after finding blood on the downed tree they had used to get over the wall. His patrol boats had chased away a boat that presumably had been their means of escape, which meant the intruders were somewhere in the wilderness above the park. He assigned six men to be stationed along the shoreline of the inlet in case the intruders doubled back, hoping to somehow escape by boat. Rahman's private aircraft, a four-seat Cessna, would make aerial reconnaissance flights and report any sightings to his team on the ground. Finding them would be an easy task.

While they would be better equipped to survive the Alaskan wilderness than the intruders, neither he nor any of his men from Glacier World had ventured beyond the park boundaries. Fishman had seen the area from the air several times. The country beyond the borders of the park and the lake was steep, and several cliffs limited the direction the intruders might have taken. If they attempted to climb to the snowfields above, they would be exposed and the plane would spot them.

Fishman and his three men left at midday and picked up their trail on the far side of the wall. All were confident they would soon discover the intruders and would deal with them. Only Fishman knew of one complication that also had to be dealt with. He was given the report about the Kodiak bear escaping—a report he kept to himself and had not passed on to either his men or Rahman.

***

Earl was satisfied to be the last man as the group trekked up the mountain, led by Leon. He still remembered his last and almost fatal attempt to lead when the mountain goat knocked him off the trail in the Olympic Mountains. He was never going to be that foolish again.

Pete walked just behind Leon and was doing much better after having his leg wound taken care of at the cabin, which now lay over a thousand feet below them. They still had some high brush and scattered scrub timber as cover, but they would soon reach the alpine zone and have no cover at all. They heard a plane circling, presumably searching for them, but cloud cover prevented it from flying low, and they had plenty of opportunity to duck down in the brush to avoid being seen.

Upon reaching a point where the old miner's trail entered the alpine zone, Leon motioned for a rest stop and for them to gather around for a talk. They were all dead tired and had been constantly on the go for over twelve hours. At some point they were going to have to really rest if they were going to make it over the mountains and down to the shoreline of Lynn Canal on the other side. It was time to tell the others where they were headed and what they faced up ahead.

"There are some things we have to talk about before we move on," said Leon as he looked at each of his companions.

Lewis lay flat on his back. Pete pulled out a small bottle of aspirin. They were long ago outdated, but taking several helped lessen the pain. For the last hour he had been limping again but hadn't complained. Earl sat slumped against a granite boulder, facing their rear, watching for anyone who may have picked up their trail. He had the rifle cradled in his arms.

"I reckon we covered about six miles since climbing over the wall. I know you are all tired, but we have a long way to go and I am afraid it is going to get tougher." Leon paused and took a swallow of water from a canteen they had scrounged in the abandoned cabin and then passed it over to Pete. "One of the things I learned in the Marines was that when planning a mission, always have two ways to get you and your team out. The second thing you need is speed. You all know our primary pickup point got compromised, and we ended up losing the advantage of getting away quickly when we were cut off. I did plan for something to go wrong, and while I regret Pete getting shot, we all made it out. Pete told me about the existence of this trail up over the Chilkats, and we owe him for finding both the trail and the cabin. But Pete has never been over the trail, so from this point on we have to rely on our own wits and each other.

"When I examined the aerial photos, I could see one hell of a lot of snow. There is also at least one glacier that we have to cross. It will be easy to lose the trail on both counts. So keep your eyes peeled for cairns or other trail markers that may have been made by the old-timer or previous trekkers. Johnny and Brooklyn will be waiting for us where we hit the beach. I figure we have at least ten miles to go. We have got some rope, some water, and a bit of food, along with an old rifle and a pistol off of one of the guards. We should survive. My cell phone battery is low, and there may not even be coverage for a good part of the way.

"One thing we need to keep doing is what Earl is doing now—we need to watch behind us. It is foolish to think they will not come after us. Hopefully it will take them a while to figure out what we did and to organize a team to pick up our trail—"

"Ah, you might be wrong on that," said Lewis, who suddenly sat straight up and was patting his pockets looking for something. "I think I left my little notebook in the office where we used one of their computers. I've got the flash drives but they now have my notebook. My name and phone number are in it."

"They've got Pete's and my driver's licenses too, Leon," Earl added. "They took them when we were captured outside the warehouse, and in our rush to get away, we forgot to retrieve them. I was pretty dazed from hitting the pavement hard when they lassoed me with that throw net or whatever it was."

"They clobbered you with a club, Earl," said Pete.

"They used a net gun to stop you," replied Leon. "It is a fairly common piece of equipment carried by law enforcement in some of the Asian countries. We have our Tasers and side arms here in the US, but Asians prefer batons and net guns as a more humane means of restraining someone who is trying to evade capture or is causing a disturbance. Our military has experimented with them, but, like a Taser, they only have a limited range and do not necessarily prevent the person being restrained from still being able to fire a weapon."

Lewis had searched all of his pockets again for his notebook while Leon and the others were talking, and finally spoke again. "I don't have it. Either I left it there or lost it somewhere during our escape."

"Do not worry about that now," replied Leon. "We have to assume they now know who at least two of us are. Maybe they will not figure out why we were there."

Lewis took off his hat and scratched at his wild hair. "If they decipher my notes and back check, they'll know what I looked at, I'm afraid. They are not going to be very pleased."

Earl tried to sum it up. "So we have some pissed-off, heavily armed modern day pirates on our trail. If we don't want to resort to throwing rocks at them, I say we get going. It just might be possible that we know something they don't. We know where we're going. I don't think any of us wants to get hauled back down there. That is, if they don't decide to just kill us here on the mountain. I say, let's get over that damn glacier and down to the boat. Maybe they'll have a thermos of hot coffee and doughnuts."

Lewis managed a laugh even though he was kicking himself about the notebook. As tired as they were, all four men struggled to their feet and started back up the trail. Earl continued to stay at the rear of their little column. He carried the rifle, and Leon kept the pistol tucked under his belt as he led them forward at a steady pace.

On the next little rise, they all caught sight of the snowfields, which appeared to go up for a long, long ways. There were no stretches of bare rock to make their trek easier. They were only five hundred yards into the crusty snow when their pants, shoes, and socks became soaked and their feet started to get cold.

Earl tried to put the misery of tired muscles and cold, wet feet aside by thinking of his wife, Sally, and daughter, Christine. He missed them and felt guilty for not telling Sally more before they departed on their secret mission, yet there was no way to explain what he had been about to do. But he could have chatted about what Sally had to contend with on her own. Christine was seventeen and turned on to boys and about to go to college away from home. Sally had her hands full dealing with the boyfriend thing, making arrangements for Christine to attend UW in Seattle come fall, plus her full-time job at the hospital. He knew he was a very lucky guy to have such a wonderful wife. Here he was, trudging up a mountain without proper equipment, almost no food or water, maybe going to be shot in the back at any moment by their pursuers, or fall down a crevasse in the glacier up ahead, or simply have his toes freeze. Could he make his situation any worse?

CHAPTER 29

Chilkat Range, Alaska

Several thousand feet below Earl and his friends, Nigel Fishman was more than frustrated with the slow progress his men were making in staying on their trail. Fishman had spent some time in African forests, and they were like a city park compared to the dense, forested mountainsides of Southeast Alaska. When the brush and downed trees weren't so thick as to be almost impenetrable, everything was rotting and covered in moss. There were pools of water in every direction. The closeness of the vegetation and limited sight distance was getting to him. For once in his life, he was actually afraid, knowing there was a huge Kodiak bear somewhere close by. If that bear charged him from the thick brush, he would have less than five seconds to try to bring it down. Even with the other men staying in sight of one another and him, he could feel the fear creep up his back and he kept glancing at their rear trail to see if they were being stalked.

By mid-afternoon they still had not found the trail of the men they were pursuing. Fishman leaned against a large tree to rest and checked his watch. He didn't relish the thought of spending the night in this damned forest, nor did he want to report back to Rahman that the intruders hadn't been found. If they were not found in the next few hours, he would have to make a tough decision. His planning was interrupted by hollering from Feng Lee, the man farthest away on his right. "Over here! I've found a trail with fresh footprints," the man shouted. "Damn, there's bear paw prints, too, and it's a big one."

Fishman called to Hayden and the other two men. They made their way over to where Feng squatted, examining the tracks. He was surprised with the condition of the trail—it was like a highway compared to what they had been plowing through for more than three hours.

Hayden pulled out a compass and pointed back down the trail. "I'd guess this trail leads down to the south end of the lake. According to their tracks, they went in the opposite direction. Look up there. Ain't nothing that way but steep mountains and a lot of damned snow."

"Yet that's where they have to be headed," said Fishman. "They probably know we are watching the shoreline. If there's a trail, then maybe there is a way over the mountains. Now that we know where they're going, we can make better time and catch them above the tree line where we can pick them off one at a time." Fishman looked down at the tracks in the mud once more. Some of the human footprints were overlain by the bear prints. They were longer than a man's foot, with deep indents from its claws. He pointed up the trail. "Hayden, you take the lead and keep your rifle at the ready. If a bear is using this trail, we don't want to surprise it."

Fishman and his men reached the abandoned cabin within another hour. Hayden, seemingly unconcerned with encountering a brown bear, had trotted on ahead and was waiting for them. The door to the cabin was open.

"They've been here, all right," remarked Hayden as the other three walked up to the cabin. "They used a first aid kit to take care of a wound. So one of them is hurt. That should slow them down some."

"Feng, scout around the cabin and see if you can pick up their trail," ordered Fishman.

"No need for that," Hayden answered. "Same trail continues on. I checked it out already, and that's the way they went. No bear tracks, so I guess it turned off in some other direction."

Fishman looked at his watch again. With only four hours of sleep the night before, he was tired. "Alright, we'll use the cabin for the night and head out at first light. If there's a stove in there, one of you guys get a fire started. Everyone's on their own for provisions. We'll all take two hour shifts standing watch, starting with Feng."

Feng Lee was a street fighter from the slums of Singapore. He was born into a lower class and knew he would never be rich. He served six years with the military, doing security duty for public buildings. He was a city man, and while he knew Glacier World was located in the wilds of Alaska, he didn't mind it much as long as he was inside its fences. Now he was outside the fence, and he was so nervous he could not focus on the simplest of tasks. It was not much more than an hour after full darkness when Feng had been relieved by one of the other men and he realized he had forgotten a rather important task.

Feng spoke to Alex Cheng, who had the next round of watch. "I've gotta go out to that outhouse, Alex. Can I borrow your flashlight?"

"Hey man!" Cheng answered. "You should have taken care of business like the rest of us before it got dark. You're crazy going out there now."

"I know, I know, but nature's call is pretty damn strong, and no one gave me the chance. I gotta go now!"

"Okay, but don't expect me to stand outside," said Cheng. "I ain't going out there."

Feng Lee took his rifle and crept outside. Cheng slammed the door behind him causing him to jump. He flashed the beam of light on the wall of trees and brush just beyond the cabin. He listened but heard nothing. Someone banged the wall inside the cabin and he jumped again. Feng hurried around the cabin to the old outhouse and quickly shut the door. Once inside, he propped his rifle in a corner along with his flashlight and unbuttoned his pants. The door rattled on its hinges like someone trying to push it in.

"You gotta wait, Damn it." He hollered.

He heard snuffling and scratching just beyond the door. The hair on the back of his head rose, and fear welled up in his throat as he smelled a rank odor that accompanied more bumps against the door and one side of the building. Feng pounded on the walls of the rickety structure and yelled.

"Hey! Go away! Hah!" His yells were loud but soaked in fear.

Feng grabbed his rifle and fired blindly through the sides and door of the outhouse, waking the men in the cabin. Fishman and the others were startled by the shots and the commotion. They could hear animal snarls in addition to Feng's yelling, followed by more rifle shots. Before they could grab their own weapons and get outside, there was a crash and the sound of splintering wood as the outhouse was pushed over.

Feng's yelling became screams as the Kodiak bear bit down on his shoulder and dragged him from the wreckage and started backing into the brush dragging the man with it.

The others rushed from the cabin with their flashlight beams searching the darkness surrounding the wrecked outhouse, trying to locate Feng.

In the darkness of the forest, limbs snapped. Each man fired randomly, unsure where to aim.

When they stopped shooting, the forest was silent. The beam of Fishman's flashlight flashed back and forth over the wall of trees and brush behind the cabin like a miniature searchlight while the men braced themselves for the bear to charge. Alex Cheng swore quietly as they listened for cries from Feng or any other sound. Minutes went by and no one ventured towards the brush. Slowly, they backed up to the cabin door.

Both the Kodiak and the young street fighter were gone.

CHAPTER 30

Chilkat Range, Alaska

With less than two hours before darkness enveloped them, Earl and his friends desperately searched for some type of shelter for the night. They had entered the main pass through the Chilkats, and it would be suicide for them to push on. They had been very lucky to find a number of cairns marking the trail, but they could easily miss one in the dark and slide off a cliff or fall into a crevasse. Pete spotted another cairn up ahead, and when the group reached it they discovered a rough board wedged into the rocks with an arrow pointing southward and the letters "S &W" carved on it.

"Does it mean we turn southwest?" asked Earl. "Or is it simply someone's initials?"

Pete put forth his own idea. "I think it means shelter and water. We can assume that someone trekking this route would need more than one day, including Old Mike. So it must mean there is some kind of shelter in that direction."

"What if the sign was supposed to point in the other direction?" asked Lewis. "It could have fallen down and someone just stuck it back up there."

"I don't think anyone would risk people seeing the marker and being misdirected," replied Pete. "That would be a cruel joke."

Leon examined the terrain both to their south and north. Then he pointed to the south—the same direction the marker indicated. "We need to check this out. It looks like there is a depression in the rock slope in the direction it is pointing. It cannot be more than a quarter mile, and none of us has much in the way of energy to continue on. Anyway, it is best we make whatever camp we can off the main trail." He turned and checked their back trail. He had been doing that since they left the safety of the alpine timber more than a mile behind them. "We are not being followed, at least not closely. What might the old miner have provided for us again?"

It took the group another twenty minutes to crunch through the snow on the south side of the pass. Leon was correct. It led them into a small canyon. A pair of ptarmigan fluttered across his path, nearly invisible with their all-white feathers, startling him for a second.

In the bottom of the canyon, a small stream of snowmelt flowed along, creating a series of small pools in solid rock depressions. They had found the old miner's water source. Pete once again had the eye to see something that was not natural. About a hundred feet from the stream, upslope against a rock overhang, stood two upright poles with a single cross piece on which a raven was perched.

Pete saw the raven and smiled. "Up there, guys. It looks like someone may have built a lean-to against that rock wall." The raven took flight and landed beside one of the water pools close to Pete. "Thank you, *Ye'il*, Brother Raven."

"Wait here," said Leon. "No need for all of us to traipse up there." Leon climbed up to the poles and looked around. He waved for the others to join him. While the others were on their way, Leon took a closer look around the makeshift campsite. Stored under the rock overhang, covered by an old canvas tarp, was some rope, a pile of firewood, a wooden box containing a jar of matches and, best of all, some canned food. There was also an old sleeping bag and a couple of blankets. Mice or some other rodent had chewed holes in both the bag and the blankets. No matter—compared to what they might have faced sleeping out in the open, what they found would be like a Hilton Hotel.

***

It had been over twenty-four hours since Bernie had been told to stay put at the motel in Juneau. Brooklyn and Johnny were not back from the rendezvous point with his dad and the others. Bernie was frustrated that he was excluded and now his frustration was turning into concern. For a while it was fun to use the bus to check out downtown Juneau, to watch the tourists from the cruise ships, and to explore the boat basins, looking at all kinds of watercraft. The large fishing vessels with the complex gear intrigued Bernie. By afternoon he was back at the hotel waiting impatiently, but Brooklyn had not called or returned. So he ventured out again.

With each hour, he became increasingly bored with the town and more and more worried about his dad. Maybe he could see them arrive if he remained close to the Auke Bay boat basin, which was the closest to the motel.

While wandering along the docks he noticed some men loading boxes of supplies onto a blue and white workboat. It had a Glacier World emblem on the side of the cabin. Curious, he walked down one of the floats where several large fishing boats were moored just across from the Glacier World boat. They provided some cover, as he feared one of men would recognize him from the disturbance he had been involved in at the park. The men left the boat and went back on shore.

Bernie continued around the entire set of docks, and as dusk settled, he doubled back and noticed that the boat was still there with no one around. Apparently, its crew had gone downtown to party or they were engaged in some other errands elsewhere in Juneau. He remembered the two men that Leon had prevented from fighting with his dad. Those men had been in Juneau to get supplies but had to return to Glacier World the same day. He went closer and peered through its side windows. The interior was stacked with the cardboard boxes that the men had loaded earlier. There were long bench seats on either side for eight or more passengers. There was a small pilothouse where two or three other people could sit. Steps led down into a forward cabin under the bow. Bernie heard some men talking and looked back towards the ramp to the shore to see the boat's crew returning with several other people, maybe eight or ten in all. Where he stood next to their boat on a finger pier, he was trapped. He would have to walk right past them.

Bernie made a quick decision. If he stowed away on the boat, maybe he could sneak into Glacier World and help gather evidence. He had his small camera and could take pictures, then get back on the patrol boat and hide in hopes it would make another trip back to Juneau in the morning. Bernie quickly climbed aboard and found the cabin door unlocked. He entered the cabin, slipped around the stack of supplies, and went down into the forward cabin. He saw a panel door to one side with a bunch of orange life jackets inside. He pushed them aside, climbed in, and pulled several of the jackets over him.

A few minutes later, Bernie could feel the boat shift as the men climbed aboard. One man told the others to see to the dock lines. Then one of them started the engine, and minutes later they were under way at high speed.

Bernie was asleep before the boat reached the Point Retreat lighthouse thirty minutes later.

***

Pete started a fire just outside the lean-to while Earl and Leon fixed up the camp the best they could. They sorted through the things in the cache for something to eat. Earl brushed off a one of blankets to sit on while Leon opened a couple of the cans of beef stew, setting them by the fire. Water from the stream of melting snow satisfied their thirst. With the hot food, even though they had to eat it with their fingers and sticks of wood, they began to feel a little better.

Earl remembered the raven Pete had seen. "You know, Pete," Earl said. "We have stories about Raven among the coastal tribes where Leon and I are from."

"That is right," added Leon. "Raven can be a friend or a trickster. Today he certainly was a friend by helping us find this place."

"You know the story about Raven and Crow's Potlach, Leon?" asked Earl.

"Yes, I have heard it many times," answered Leon. "Go ahead. I would like to hear your version."

"Okay," replied Earl. "I'm not really good with the legends, but I'll try. If someone falls asleep, there'll be more stew for me, kind of like Raven in this story." He drew a chuckle from the others. "Well, Raven was having a pleasant and relaxing summer, and one day he decided to visit Crow and some of the other animals. He found Squirrel first and teased him about working so hard to store up food for the winter. Then he found Bear who was busy catching salmon. Raven hopped from stump to tree and finally found Crow singing away, busy storing food as well. Crow scolded Raven for playing all the time and not working like the others. 'You'll be sorry when the cold winter months arrive.' And they soon did, and Raven discovered he was going to starve if he didn't do something. So off he went to visit his friends again. Surely they would share some food.

"Squirrel told him to go away and Bear was sleeping in his den. At Crow's home, he promptly asked why he wasn't busy preparing food for his Potlatch. This surprised Crow. Raven explained that all of the other creatures wanted to hear Crow sing songs, with his beautiful voice just like the Mountain Thrush, and by holding a Potlatch he could sing to them. Crow thought about that and said it was a wonderful idea and began immediately to prepare lots of food. Raven said he would take care of the invitations. 'Come to my Potlatch at Crow's place,' he told everyone. They all came, and Raven told Crow to sing while everyone else began to eat. Crow sang and sang and whenever he stopped to feed himself, Raven would reply, 'You can't sing on a full stomach.' When everyone left, Crow discovered all his food was gone, but that was okay as all of the other animals would invite him to their feasts. But no invitations came— the other animals thought it had been Raven's Potlatch, and he got invited instead of Crow. Crow was left to beg for food in the camps of men, and with his voice so hoarse from singing all he could do was 'Caw Caw.'"

Pete smiled. "That's a good legend, Earl, and it fits. The old miner left some food for us to share. I'm going to have to come back up here soon and restock the cache, maybe replace this old tarp over our heads. We eat, guys, while Earl sings or tells us another story."

Everyone laughed, including Earl.

CHAPTER 31

Chilkat Range, Alaska

Hayden took the lead as the three remaining pursuers followed the trail out onto the snowfields. They chose not to search for Feng Lee's body until their return to the park in hopes of catching Armstrong and his friends without cover. Fishman had talked to Rahman by cell phone and received blatant instructions to deal with the intruders harshly, even if that meant killing them. Rahman was pretty sure files had been downloaded from the GRI computers, and Fishman had orders to get the copies back at any cost. When Fishman told him about what happened the night before when Feng Lee was taken by the escaped Kodiak bear, Rahman seemed more concerned about recapturing the bear than retrieving Feng's body. He arranged to send out another team with rifles loaded with tranquilizer rounds to search for the bear.

Hayden was several hundred yards ahead of the others when he found the marker leading to the shelter. From the trail in the snow, he was pretty sure Armstrong and the others had returned to the main trail and continued on over the pass through the mountains, but he had to check it. Due to the low-hanging clouds creating foggy conditions, Hayden couldn't see very far up the side trail but took off anyway, not waiting for Fishman and Cheng to catch up. He found the shelter and the remains of a campfire. He could still feel some heat from the embers. Tossing aside the piece of canvas, he swore as he discovered the old blankets and the remainder of the food supply. He filled his water bottle at one of the snowmelt pools and hurried back down the trail to inform Fishman.

"They spent the night tucked up under them rocks with a fire, blankets, and plenty of food and water," said Hayden. He stopped to catch his breath where the other two men waited. "Had to be dumb luck to find a cache of supplies like that. Now they're fresh and going to be harder to catch up with. The remains of their campfire were still warm, so they can't be too far ahead."

Fishman turned to the man behind him. "Cheng, you hustle up the trail. Signal us when you catch sight of them."

Cheng nodded and set off slowly.

"Move it, damn it! I want those buggers cornered before they get into the trees on the other side of this mountain or wherever the hell they are going." Cheng started trotting, following the tracks eastward. Hayden adjusted the semi-automatic rifle that was slung over his shoulder and started walking again with Fishman just behind him. Fishman took out his cell phone to report in to Rahman.

***

Leon led, followed by Pete, Lewis, and Earl last as the four broke trail through the crusty snow leading down from the pass. Ahead of them in the early grey dawn light, they could see the bluish cast of a large ice field. It was not large, but looked nasty without any apparent way to go around. The trail markers appeared to lead directly to it. None of the four spoke much anymore. The light chitchat that had accompanied their hike the previous afternoon and evening turned to silence as they toiled to push through the snow. The respite at the old campsite in the canyon had helped, but their clothes and shoes that had dried out only slightly were again soaked through, and no help against a cold wind coming off the ice field.

As they approached the edge of the ice field, the snow along the trail dissipated but the trail was steeper. The bare soil was water-saturated and slippery under foot. There was a yell behind, and Leon turned quickly with the expectation that someone had seen their pursuers. Lewis had fallen.

"Dang it," said Lewis. "I swear I'm spending more time sliding on my backside than on my two feet." Earl helped Lewis to stand up, barely able to stand himself.

"I don't know which is worse—breaking through frozen snow banks or trying to walk on this stuff. The soil is frozen and covered in maybe an inch of thawed mud. It's slicker than you-know-what." Lewis took another two steps and went down again.

"Hey, guys," shouted Leon. "I think we better take the ropes we brought and tie ourselves together. Our trail looks to be a bit worse up ahead."

"How could it be worse than this?" asked Lewis.

"It gets real steep and slopes off to the edge of an ice field. If one of us was to slide down there, we would have a pretty tough time doing a rescue." The north- and east-facing slopes of the mountainside were still buried in snow drifts, the surface a thick crust of ice. There was no way they could cross it without each of them using mountaineering equipment.

Leon motioned for the others to gather around the spot where he had stopped to check out where the trail headed. It continued across more of the muddy, half-frozen ground and then down out of sight below the crest of the ridge. They had been steadily following the trail east and slightly north, but Leon had discovered that the trail turned southward into a canyon. Earl and Lewis each unwrapped the ropes they had carried since leaving the cabin and started tying themselves together like Leon and Earl had done during their trek in the Olympic Mountains. When they were done, Leon started off again.

"Okay, watch your footing," said Leon. "The trail is going to be steep up ahead, and it is downhill with nothing to hold on to but each other, so be careful."

In another hundred yards, the trail reached a large stretch of rocky scree. While they were out of the mud-covered frozen ground, the scree was unstable and they had to be careful to remain on the trail.

"Looks like the trail doesn't cross the ice field," commented Pete. "That's a good thing, because I can see some crevasses with snow bridges over them. They don't look good from here."

"That's fine with me," said Lewis. "All of a sudden this trail looks like a superhighway. I dislike crevasses more than a forest full of bears. With my weight, I'd get wedged in so tight, ten men couldn't pull me out."

As they descended, the trail did get better. While it wasn't Lewis's superhighway, they made good progress, and after another few minutes of walking roped together, they were back in the alpine zone and the only snow was an occasional drift that hadn't melted. Below them, the terrain steepened until it became a cliff.

This concerned Leon as they followed along the narrow trail. They didn't have enough rope to deal with a repelling situation. Rounding another corner, he discovered something else: across the canyon was another trail—actually, the same trail—and connecting the two sections was a wire cable suspension bridge. Just upstream from the bridge was a high waterfall.

**

Bernie woke with a start, not remembering where he was. His legs were cramped, and for a few seconds he panicked, not able to straighten them out. The air around him was stale, and breathing was difficult. The smell of the life jackets piled on top of him helped him to remember where he was—hiding in a storage locker aboard one of Glacier World's boats. His first thought was to push open the door to the locker, but reason struck him, and instead he rubbed his legs and listened. The boat's engine was no longer running and he couldn't hear any voices. Bernie cracked the door, hoping there was some light, and looked at his watch. It was nearly 4:00 a.m. He had to make his move now, before there was activity on the docks and someone would spot him.

Slipping out of the locker, Bernie risked a look out at the dock. In the dull grey early morning light, no one was on the dock. On the back deck of the boat he hesitated, wanting to run for the ramp up to the dock, yet afraid of being seen. Something moved near the bottom of the ramp. He squinted, trying to make out what was there. It moved again and he smiled. It was an otter. Bernie climbed over the rail and ran for the ramp as the otter slid off the float and disappeared in the cold water of the inlet.

Each step he took on the ramp caused a metallic clunk, clunk sound, and so he ran faster, reaching the dock and dashing for the shadows of the buildings along the waterfront.

He dropped down behind a trash barrel to catch his breath and pulled out his map to check where he was. He was close to the assay office, and the Marine Mammal Amphitheater was off to his right. To get to the warehouses where Leon and his dad said there were some really weird goings on, he needed to walk nearly a half mile to his right along the promenade. It was too exposed to attempt it. There was an entrance to a people mover tunnel close by, and fear of getting turned around made that an impossible route. That left the paths through the animal enclosures. The bears were the farthest and close to the warehouses. So, tucking away his map, he walked quickly to an alley between the buildings and looked for a sign leading in their direction.

It almost worked.

***

According to Pete, the cable suspension bridge was a typical forest service design. There were two lower cables with wood plank decking fastened between them and two upper cables about chest high to use as handrails. Diagonal wires were laced between the handrail cables to the deck cables every three feet wire netting to prevent people from falling. Pete told the others there was a similar one over Indian River near the small town of Tenakee, but he had never encountered one as long or as high as the one in front of them. It had to be over one hundred feet to the bottom of the canyon and twice that distance across. At the end of the bridge there was a forest service sign that read, "Mike Sloan Memorial Bridge."

"Huh," said Lewis. "If Mike Sloan was the old miner that used this trail, maybe this is where he met his demise."

Lewis's lighthearted remark was his second of the day, and it raised spirits a little. One encouraging thing that everyone noticed was the trail on the other side of the canyon. It was in considerably better shape than the last several miles they had covered.

"Okay, we get across quickly," Leon said. "Nobody has caught up with us yet but we still have to be careful. We will be very exposed while on the bridge and for a short distance on the other side of the canyon. There is cover when we reach those rocks and trees a couple hundred yards farther down the trail."

Leon pointed at Lewis and Earl, who had been watching their back trail. "Lewis, you and Earl will cross together first. Go all the way to the trees. Earl, you have to cover us with the rifle. And, damn it, do not hesitate to shoot. I do not want this bridge to be a memorial to one of us."

Lewis untied the rope between himself and Pete and approached the end of the bridge, hesitating before taking his first step onto the wood planks. He looked around like he was searching for something. "You sure they don't store parachutes somewhere around here in case we have to jump?"

"I think they're on the other side," quipped Earl. "Anyway, you and I are still roped together."

"That's not a lot of comfort, Earl," replied Lewis as he pulled his leather flight helmet tighter on his head and started across.

The suspension bridge began to sway heavily once Earl and Lewis were maybe thirty feet out. Lewis had difficulty using the cables to maintain his balance. The two stopped for a minute. The sway stopped and they started walking again. Earl changed his stride to be opposite Lewis's to reduce the swaying. They were across in a few minutes and hustled down the trail to the tree line and rock outcrop where Leon had said to wait. Earl unslung the rifle and jacked a round into the chamber. He waved across to Leon and Pete, who saw Earl's ready signal and started across.

Earl was watching them on the bridge, and as they neared the center, a burst of semi-automatic weapon fire shattered the stillness of the canyon and echoed off the canyon walls. He and Lewis ducked down subconsciously. "Damn, I should have been watching our back trail." Taking a look, Earl saw three men near the ice field.

The rounds buzzed just above Leon's head and ricocheted off the canyon wall well in front of him. He started to run, then slowed for Pete who was hampered by his injured leg.

Earl managed to get off several shots with the old .30-30 and saw the three men turn and scramble for cover. They were pretty far away and his rifle had open sights, plus he was aiming uphill. Still, one of them did fall down before they disappeared over the crest of the ridge.

Earl risked seeing how Leon and Pete were doing. They were now at the end of the bridge. Pete stopped and crouched down, but Leon was walking back out onto the suspension bridge. Earl watched as Leon pulled the pistol and aimed at the deck planks. He fired two shots, then two more rounds into the adjoining plank and another two rounds in the next plank. Leon had sabotaged the bridge.

Earl looked back at the ridge. The men were picking their way down the muddy part of the trail and would soon be to the scree where they could move faster. He fired two more rounds, and rock chips flew up well short of the men. Then they were out of sight behind a small ridge. He could hear one of the men hollering, but it was too far to make out much of what he was saying. It sounded like he was ordering the others to keep going.

Leon and Pete reached Earl's position. Pete was laboring to keep up. Leon motioned for Earl and Lewis to move on down the trail, then took a second to check on their pursuers. A big man was in the lead and would reach the far end of the suspension bridge in a few minutes.

"Might have known. It is the guy I took out at the warehouse." Leon said. "Hope he does not notice the trap."

Earl held back with Leon while the others moved down the trail. "Yeah, that's Hayden alright. He looks determined to catch us."

"More like blind rage. Seen it before. Leads to making mistakes. In this case, maybe his last. If he makes it across, I will try to take him out once more. You will have to get the others to the beach, Earl."

"You're wrong. I'm staying. I made a promise. We'll take him out together." He patted his friend's shoulder. Leon just shook his head and grinned at Earl.

Hayden reached the bridge and charged across. He had his rifle in one hand and grabbed for the cables with the other. The bridge swayed and bounced as he ran. He was ten feet from the end of the span when his left foot landed in the middle of the three planks that Leon had weakened with shots from the pistol. The wood splintered, giving way under his weight, and Hayden found himself falling through the deck. He yelled and, letting go of his rifle, tried to grab the wire mesh. He missed. Earl and Leon watched as Hayden fell through the deck and hit the rock wall just below the bridge. His body flipped several times before landing in the stream at the bottom of the canyon.

The other two pursuers saw Hayden fall through the bridge deck. They moved cautiously forward to the start of the bridge but didn't attempt to cross. One of them looked down at Hayden's body. Then he took out a cell phone and was trying to make a call as Earl and Leon charged after Pete and Lewis.

CHAPTER 32

Glacier World

The pedestrian pathways behind the gold rush storefronts were vacant when Bernie peered around another corner. Even the animal enclosures at Glacier World were quiet. There was a sign pointing in the direction of Musk Ox Meadows and Bear River Loop. Bernie kept to the shadows along the rear of the buildings as he went in the direction of the warehouses.

On the day of the open house, people strolled along these same paths gazing at moose, caribou, wolves, and other wild game. The Sky Ride zoomed overhead with more gawkers. Now, nothing moved. At Musk Ox Meadows none of the animals were visible, and he didn't want to get closer even though he would love to see them. He chose a smaller path to his left and kept moving. He passed the River Otter Rapids area and then the Wolverine Ridge exhibit.

Bernie walked faster. Even in the shadow of the officer tower it was getting lighter, and he could now see the tops of some buildings that looked like warehouses up ahead. He reached a path intersection and saw two men coming from the Bear River Loop.

They were talking loudly, with one complaining about having to conduct another search that had taken all night. He ducked to his right, back toward Gold Rush Town along the side of Wolf Valley. The two men took another path and were now headed directly for him. He stopped and looked to his left and right, considering his situation. There was no place to hide next to the buildings. The only other hiding spot was over the wall of one of the enclosures, which he assumed was still Musk Ox Meadows. Bernie ran to the wall, slipped over, hung onto the edge, and then dropped. It was eight or nine feet to the ground, but it was a soft landing on grass. In seconds he was up and scrunched against the wall, hoping the men had not heard him and would not look over the wall. The voices faded but were replaced with another sound much closer—a low growl. Bernie, in his quick decision to hide, had jumped over the wall into Wolf Valley.

There was a large cedar tree about fifty feet from where he had landed. He ran to the tree and climbed up among the branches. The wolf chased him and put its front paws on a low limb. Though Bernie was safe in the tree, he climbed higher. The wolf was making quite a commotion and dancing around the base of the tree which attracted several more that loped towards the tree. His plan to help his dad was finished.

Looking over towards the wall, he saw one of the park employees looking his way—attracted by the wolves' commotion. The man pointed at him and spoke into a portable radio. He would be free of the wolves soon enough but then what—a captive again.

An hour later, Bernie was sitting in the Glacier World security office. Both his hands and his feet were bound. He had been relieved of his camera, cell phone, and a half-eaten candy bar he had forgotten was in a jacket pocket. They also had his wallet and identification card.

A dark-skinned man with a mustache and sunglasses spoke to the two men who had removed Bernie from the wolf enclosure. When the man glanced at Bernie, he clearly was not happy. Then the man's cell phone rang and he began talking to someone. Bernie couldn't understand much of the conversation and was confused when the man said to leave the body and find their way back to the park. Mostly the man listened and nodded. When he put away the phone, he turned towards Bernie, crossed his arms, and smiled. Then his expression changed, like he had a satisfactory thought, and Bernie was a part of it.

Bernie hopes of being a hero and getting some photographic evidence were dashed. He had done something stupid and allowed himself to get caught. Looking at the man, he was afraid.

CHAPTER 33

Sisters Cove, Lynn Canal, Alaska

Brooklyn stood on the top deck of the *Huna Spirit,* scanning the beach in the small cove next to the Sisters Rocks. This was the backdoor pickup point that Leon had agreed to, and there was no sign of her friends.

A bald eagle was perched like a forward sentinel on a USFS trailhead sign just above the pebble beach. The sign marked the start of a primitive trail that wound up a long valley to several waterfalls and on up to a pass through the Chilkat Range. The trail was little used and not maintained beyond the waterfalls. Leon had told her that he and Pete would try to find the trail and lead everyone out using that route. He didn't know how long it would take them, and during their last brief communication he had guessed maybe two days at the most. Forty-eight hours had come and gone.

She knew it would be a very difficult trip. There was still plenty of snow, and she could not imagine how they could remain on the trail and not get lost. It was now early afternoon and there was no sign of them. Low-hanging clouds obscured the top of the mountains. It looked like rain could start to fall any time.

Johnny and Brooklyn had arrived at the cove earlier that morning, and the boat was anchored as close to the shore as possible while allowing for the tidal change. They launched an inflatable to have it ready for trips into the beach. The small rubber raft drifted back and forth in a breeze where it was tied to the stern of the boat.

Brooklyn was worried, and not just about Leon and the others. She was also concerned with not being able to contact Bernie in Juneau on the cell phone he was supposed to be carrying. Bernie must have turned it off and forgotten to turn it back on or had let its battery become exhausted. She tried calling him again, and again no answer.

"I can't reach Bernie at the motel," Brooklyn said to Johnny as he climbed up the ladder to the open deck and sat down on one of the long plastic benches.

"Did you try the motel front desk?" asked Johnny. "Maybe they can check his room, or they might have seen him leave to get something to eat."

"Okay." Brooklyn searched the directory on her phone and found the number. "Hi, I'm trying to reach Bernie Armstrong. I think the room is registered to his father, Earl Armstrong? Can you connect me?" The desk clerk tried the number and in a minute came back on the line. "Sorry, there's no answer. Do you want to leave a message?"

She watched the eagle lift off from its perch, flying higher to land on the top of a spruce tree. A brown bear ambled out from the trail, sniffed the salty air, and began to chomp on the tall sedge grass next to the sign. "Can you send someone to knock on the door to their room?"

"Let me check," the clerk said. "Can you call back in maybe fifteen minutes? I can have one of the housekeeping ladies see if anyone is in the room."

"Yeah, I'd appreciate that," answered Brooklyn. "I'll call you back. Better yet, have him call Brooklyn." She hung up.

The bear moved on down the beach in search of something else to eat—maybe to check out the stream in the corner of the cove to see if there were any early salmon arrivals. A raven took over the sign perch.

"Well, I'm going to make a fresh pot of coffee," said Johnny. "Those guys are going to want something hot to drink when they get here. I'll break out some blankets as well. You want a Coke?"

"Toss me up a bottle of water. I'm going to keep watching the trailhead."

***

After leaving the suspension bridge, the trail through the mountains was considerably easier. The four men no longer worried much about being followed, but they were tired, and each mile was a struggle. With frequent signs of brown bears along the trail, their principal concern was coming upon one. Pete took the possibility lightly and teased Lewis by saying, "Well here it comes," which reminded Lewis of an old Van Morrison tune. So every few minutes, Lewis would sing in a loud voice, "Well here it comes. Here comes the bear." To which Pete would respond, "Oh oh yeah!" Leon cringed each time Lewis and Pete sang their little ditty, but if he reacted to it, he figured a bear would too and run the other way.

Earl trudged on, following the others and spending his time thinking about his family. He thought about what Sally and Christine might be doing at home, that it had to be a lot more pleasant than enduring this mountain trek and being chased by bad guys. He was essentially asleep on his feet, and weakly slapping at the incessant mosquitos that buzzed around his face kept him awake. Every so often he would trip over a tree root or rock but managed to stay on his feet. As he daydreamed, Earl failed to notice he was falling farther behind the others.

Up ahead, Leon saw a side trail that, according to a sign, led to another waterfall. The trail went down the side of the mountain while the main trail climbed up at that point and into heavy timber. He stayed on the main trail, followed by everyone except for Earl.

When Earl reached the junction, he didn't see the others in his stupor. Instead of climbing, he plodded down the side trail towards the waterfall. He continued downward for five or ten minutes until he came to a clearing. Earl stopped and stared. The trail had disappeared, wiped out by a landslide. Earl was now fully awake, and his pulse rose rapidly. His anxiety and alarm over the condition of the trail increased. From faint imprints, it looked like someone or something may have ventured across, but there were no signs of Leon and the others on the other side.

"Leon? Lewis?" he hollered. "I need a little help here." No one appeared on the far side of the landslide. "Leon! Lewis!" Earl yelled a little louder.

Earl peered down the landslide. It extended downward several hundred feet, ending in a jumble of boulders, dirt, and debris. If he slipped, he would end up as part of the debris pile. Earl's fear was multiplied as he recalled his tumble in the Olympics. He had been saved by being roped to Bernie and Leon. He was carrying some rope, but it wasn't long enough to tie off before attempting to cross the slide. It had to be over one hundred feet to the other side of the landslide, and the rope was maybe fifty feet long. With no one appearing on the far side, Earl decided he had to try. He took one step and then another. His right foot slid and he froze. He was paralyzed with fear, afraid to take another step forward or back.

A hand grabbed his left arm. "I've got you, Earl," said Leon. "You took a wrong turn on the trail. You don't have to cross the slide."

***

Brooklyn kept her vigil on the top deck of the boat. There had been no word from the motel about Bernie's whereabouts, and no call from Leon. The bear was long gone after spending some time foraging for clams in the mud near the mouth of the stream. Johnny brought her a blanket to wrap around her shoulders. She adjusted it and scanned the beach for the umpteenth time. A movement at the trailhead caught her eye, and she stood up and waved as someone appeared on the shore and yelled to the boat.

"They're here, Johnny!" yelled Brooklyn. "They made it." She leapt onto one of the top-deck seats and waved back. She counted all four men on the beach. Lewis and Pete were already sitting on a drift log and waving back to her. She wiped several tears off her cheeks with the sleeve of her jacket as she watched Johnny climb into the inflatable to make the first of several trips to shore to pick the guys up.

A few minutes later, as Brooklyn watched the inflatable push off the beach and start back out to the boat, her cell phone rang to the sound of an old Madonna song. She fished it out of her pocket and saw it was Bernie.

"Hey, Bernie, it's Brooklyn. Where you been? I've been trying to reach you all day."

"Brooklyn?" said an unfamiliar voice on Bernie's phone. "You sound excited about something. Perhaps it's about a certain Glacier World trespasser by the name of Armstrong?"

Brooklyn didn't respond as her thoughts raced. Bernie wasn't in Juneau? He was at Glacier World? How? The phone felt like it was burning her hand but she couldn't let go.

"Brooklyn? Are you listening?" the man continued. "I seem to recall that you, too, visited Glacier World and were the start of a major problem for me. When you see Bernie's father, have him give me a call. When he and his friends left here, they took something that I would like to get back. Two of my men are dead because of him. Now I have your unfortunate friend Bernie, who decided to make another visit to Glacier World." The man disconnected. Brooklyn was in shock for the first time in her life as she watched the first of the joyful shore party climb aboard.

Within an hour Johnny had his boat speeding back towards Juneau. They had to restrain Earl when Brooklyn tearfully told him about the call. Earl was enraged and lashed out at whoever was closest to him when he heard that Bernie was being used as a hostage. He insisted the boat go straight there. Leon and Pete had to force him into a seat and finally calmed him down enough to listen to reason.

"This is a police matter, Earl," said Leon. "The Alaska State Troopers will know how to handle it."

Earl's body shook uncontrollably as he tried to convince Leon and the others that something had to be done immediately. "If I don't call, they'll kill him. If they don't get back what we took, they'll kill him. We've got to go back!"

"You cannot make that call, Earl," said Leon. "You just cannot—not yet. I know how you feel, but you and I have to think this through. We will get Bernie back, I promise you that. Listen to me, Earl. They will not hurt him as long as we cooperate."

"But if we go to the authorities, we'll have to show them what we have," replied Earl. "The damage will be done. They'll get rid of Bernie at the first opportunity. Oh my God, what am I going to tell Sally?" Earl lowered his head in his arms, rubbed the back of his neck, and moaned over and over.

Their escape over the mountains had taken a toll on all of them, but Earl's agony and worry about Bernie was unbearable. He tried to rise and reach Johnny at the controls one more time but all his strength was gone. He was exhausted physically and emotionally as Leon gently pushed him back into the seat again.

"Earl, they have not called back," said Leon. "We have some time. We can still nail them. There has to be a way."

"You heard what they told Brooklyn," hollered Earl, weakly struggling to push Leon's arm away. "They don't need to call. Give me the damned phone. I'm supposed to call them. You and I both know they want the data back."

"It is not that simple," replied Leon. "Think about it. Lewis knows things about their operations. You and Pete both saw things and took pictures. It will not be just the copies of the data they will want to eliminate. These guys are dangerous. They killed people to protect their secret operations. They came after us. We know one of them died at the bridge. They know that we have information about what they are up to."

Remembering the photos triggered something within Earl, and he began to think about what Leon was saying to him. "Yeah, I've got the pictures," said Earl. "I took some great digital photos inside the warehouse. I never did get the chance to tell you about them."

"Tell me about what you and Pete saw, Earl. What was in the warehouse that was so interesting?" Leon took the opportunity to lead Earl in a rational direction, and he could feel some of the tension in Earl's shoulders relax.

"There were pallets with box after box of silicon wafers and other high-tech products. There was even a pallet stacked with new Harleys. There had to be millions of dollars of stuff in that warehouse. I photographed everything, including the serial numbers on the bikes."

"Good, then we have evidence they might not know about and that the feds can use to build a case and get a warrant for a search," he said. Leon could see that Earl was listening to him now.

The tension in Earl's body lessened, and Earl grabbed a bottle of water and took a drink. Leon was trying to get him to stay focused on their mission, but Earl was working on another angle. Get the evidence to the authorities? No! That wasn't the most important thing any longer. It was Bernie. Earl's mind was filled with confusing facts, but one thing kept coming up: neither the police nor Leon would get Bernie back. He would have to get him myself and make a deal. He had to talk to the guy. He would go along with the others until he figured out what to do.

"Just what did you and Lewis get out of their computers that they want to protect?" said Earl.

"We got very lucky," Leon replied. "Lewis was able to access their whole computer database, including records of inventory from several of their piracy operations, as well as sales records indicating where the goods were being resold. I would not be surprised if what he grabbed even included data on those Harleys you saw."

"Do you think he tracked any of my premium lumber?"

"Probably. I think he went back several months. It could be there. We have to wait to see what the data-mining experts come up with. We need to let them work it over. Right now, we need help, and it is best if we talk to the state police. I want to call Dave Williams—he was the officer I talked to when we first arrived in Juneau. There will need to be a lot of resources mobilized if we are going back to Glacier World. You can count on me, Earl. We will get Bernie out of there."

Pete had been half dozing, half listening to their conversation. He lifted his head and looked at Earl. "You can count on me too, Earl. I'm now convinced they killed my brother because they thought he was snooping around, and I won't be satisfied until we get the lot of them behind bars. A hole in my leg isn't going to stop me from going back into Glacier World, if that's what Leon has in mind. Leon got us in and out the first time, and I'm counting on him doing it again."

"Right!" said Leon. "But like the first operation, we need a plan, and that means buying a little time. Earl, that means you are going to have to do a little deceptive bargaining. We do this fast and with surprise."

"Yeah, but Glacier World is a big place, and they could be holding Bernie anywhere," said Earl. "How are we going to pin down what building he's in?"

"When it is time to talk to this guy, you will insist on talking to Bernie. You take the time to give Bernie some fatherly encouragement without letting him know what is going to happen. This will let the feds get a GPS reading on his phone. I am guessing he will be in the same building as the computer center."

Earl assumed Bernie was being held somewhere in the office tower and there was a distinct possibility the rescuers might not find him before he was hurt or killed. The only way to get Bernie out of there was to get there first and make a deal.

Johnny had been pushing his boat to over twenty knots as they crossed Lynn Canal and turned south into Stephens Passage. They passed Shelter Island and were well into Auke Bay when he began to slow down around the sport fishermen and some kayakers. Leon remembered that his own phone had died somewhere on the mountain and asked to use Johnny's phone to call Dave Williams with the Alaska State Troopers. Williams was still in his office when he answered.

"Officer Williams? This is Leon Pence. I met with you a couple of weeks ago about the death of Eddie Jackson at Glacier World."

"Yeah," answered Williams. "You still in the area, or did you return to the Lower 48?"

"I have been hanging around and ah…been snooping around a bit too," replied Leon. "We learned that what is going on at Glacier World is not all that it appears to be. We think GRI is behind the piracy occurrences out in the gulf, as well as a couple of murders. Add kidnapping for ransom to that and the situation is pretty serious."

"You're accusing Glacier World of these things? Those are pretty astounding assumptions," said Williams. "You got any evidence to back up these accusations?"

"We have got plenty, and we want to hand it over to you when we reach Juneau in a few minutes. You are going to have one hell of a case to handle."

"Okay, where are you?"

"Just coming into the marina out at Auke Bay. We sure would like to meet up with you as soon as you can get there. We have a wounded man on board, too. He was shot in the leg. Can you arrange for an ambulance?"

"A shooting too? I'll be there, but you've got one hell of a lot of explaining to do. If you did what I think you did, I might have to arrest you."

"I know how this sounds bad, but before you do that, just give us a chance to explain," pleaded Leon. "This is big. Is there someone from the FBI you can bring along?"

"That crossed my mind," said Williams. "The bureau has been looking into the pirated cargo incidences. I've seen some memos their Anchorage office puts out to all law enforcement units, including the state fisheries guys. It's pretty mystifying to everyone, and there's not much to go on."

"It will all be clear when you see what we got," replied Leon.

"Okay, I'm going to call Ray Hanson. He's with the FBI's local agency office. I'll get him to join me. Watch out for him though, he's kind of a Bruce Willis-type character—doesn't care who he steps on or if he gets shot in the ass. I'm a bit more careful because I've still got kids in school. You better have a really good story because I still think I've got to arrest you for something, once I figure out what the hell for."

"Fine! Just get here," replied Leon as he glanced out the side windows of the boat. They had entered the harbor and slowed down to maneuver into the transient dock.

Williams had the last word. "Nobody gets off that boat until an officer gets there, okay? That ambulance is on the way."

Williams disconnected, and Leon peered out the side windows again. There were flashing lights from a state patrol car already driving into the parking area from the highway.

CHAPTER 34

Juneau, Alaska

Williams arrived at the Auke Bay Marina fifteen minutes later, followed by two more patrol cars and an ambulance. The small parking lot was a chaotic place. One officer was assigned to be on the dock next to Johnny's boat, and another diverted traffic up at the roundabout on the highway. Earl and Lewis stayed with Pete until the EMTs took over, who manhandled the stretcher up a steep boat ramp. Williams called for another officer to meet the ambulance at the hospital emergency room and then remain with Pete. He gave Leon and the others another warning to stay close, but allowed them a few minutes to get something to eat at a burger stand just across the parking lot.

Agent Ray Hanson arrived ten minutes after Williams, and they had a swift and rather pointed discussion in the parking lot as to who would direct the investigation. Williams nodded towards Leon, who was already wolfing down a burger with Earl and Lewis at the outside picnic table next to the Harbor Burger Bar. It was agreed that Williams would be in charge—at least until it was determined whether any crimes had been committed, what charges might be made, and against whom.

Hanson's primary interest was the Gulf of Alaska piracy. If what Williams had briefly told him over the phone was true, this could be a really big break for him to move up in the bureau. Hanson walked over to the picnic table.

"You're Pence?" said Hanson. "I'm Ray Hanson, FBI. We need a statement. There's a room in the harbormaster's office we can use. Bring your food. We want to hear your story from the beginning."

Despite what he had agreed with Williams, Hanson took the lead in asking questions and kept the interview focused on the theft of marine cargo rather than on the apparent missing juvenile. Williams resigned himself to be patient, and after a half hour and another ordered burger for Leon, he finally got to talk about Bernie being forcibly held at Glacier World.

Earl waited impatiently at the burger stand. He was still worrying about Bernie and what he could do about it. If Lewis had the data files, there must be more than one copy. Maybe one copy could be used in exchange for Bernie

Lewis had ordered a second basket of French fries and was on his third refill of Coke when Earl decided he needed Lewis' help.

"You were able to make two copies of the computer data?" asked Earl.

"Well, sort of," Lewis admitted. "I copied as much as I could onto two flash drives. Some of it was strictly accounting records. Those files were so big they are only on one of the flash drives. Other stuff on inventory and sales got copied twice. I wanted a copy for myself so I could have names and try hacking in to see where stuff leads. You know, like finding out who ultimately received your lumber shipment."

"They're going to want those flash drives as well as the photos I took. So, what I've been thinking about is whether you could lie a little and say you lost one of the flash drives on the trail—maybe when you and I took that tumble?"

"I've been thinking about that too," replied Lewis. "Like I said, I want one to play around with the data myself."

"Here's the problem. The FBI want the files, you want a copy, and the guy at Glacier World wants back whatever you have. I'm more worried about the last one. If I don't get the data back to him, he could kill Bernie. I just can't let that happen."

"Ah, I think I know where this might be leading, Earl, and I'm not sure I like it because of the risk you could be taking. So, how about if I get a chance, I upload the files to my cloud storage site, then the other flash drive becomes meaningless."

"Sounds good," said Earl. "Somehow Rahman is going to get another message to me, and when he does, I'm going to agree to meet with him.

Try to make the exchange. Bernie's life is more important than mine or the data. I couldn't live with myself if Bernie got killed because I brought him up here and allowing him to be involved in this."

"I like Bernie, and I want to help any way I can. After the state police and FBI finish with Leon, they are going to want to interview both of us. You need to cover for me while I use one of the computers in the harbormaster's office to upload files."

Hanson and Williams took an hour to interview Leon. His responses bordered on the unbelievable. Williams made a call and arranged for a marine patrol to be dispatched the next morning to hike up the USFS trail to the waterfall to look for the body of the Glacier World guy. They took possession of the pistol Leon had taken from the GRI security guard and put it in an evidence bag.

When Williams came to get Earl, Lewis asked to come along, complaining he needed to use the bathroom. Williams agreed and closed the door to the inner office he and Hanson were using for the interviews. Hanson again took over the questioning.

"We know about the pictures you were able to take in the warehouse. So, where is the camera?"

"Lost it during our escape, but I have the flash card."

"We'll take it," said Hanson. "So explain just what you saw."

"We started getting suspicious while we were observing the park and its dock from the opposite ridge. They were unloading what appeared to be full cargo containers, then moving them into a warehouse. Some of the containers were repainted in another building in the colors of other shippers, then the containers were refilled and placed back on the vessel. If it had been materials for the park, the containers would have been empty and handled differently, or maybe even stored somewhere. Instead, it was a steady operation of emptying them and filling them back up again. Sound confusing?"

"Yeah, but we already heard this from Mr. Pence. What about the warehouse you broke into?"

"When Pete and I got inside, we understood what was happening. There was pallet after pallet of cargo that didn't relate to the park—like a bunch of brand new Harley-Davidson motorcycles. So I photographed them."

"Motorcycles?' asked Hanson.

"Yeah, expensive ones, limited-edition models."

"I suppose your lumber that disappeared was there as well?"

"Couldn't locate it. My shipment was probably gone weeks ago. I'm telling you, they are organized. That's why we went for the computer records. It's all one big operation: steal expensive cargo, find a buyer, and resell it. Lewis calls it a black market eBay."

Williams finally got to say something. "Let me sum up what you and your friends did. You secretly spied on Glacier World. You trespassed. You stole computer records and took unauthorized photographs. Am I clear on that?"

"Yes," answered Earl. "But my son was—"

"I know. Your son was supposedly kidnapped. Maybe he just went looking for all of you and got lost or disoriented."

Earl's concern for Bernie and frustration at what Williams was saying showed. "But I got a call saying if I want to see Bernie alive, return the data."

"That's exactly what the guy said? Are you sure about that?"

"Well, pretty damned close to that," responded Earl. He was mad now.

Williams shook his head and turned to Hanson to express his skepticism. "I don't know, Ray. It's all pretty circumstantial, and a good bunch of lawyers could shoot huge holes in all of their testimony. If you want me to try to get a warrant to search for the kid, I will, but you're going to have to make the decision. I want to keep my job a few more years until I can retire on a full pension."

Earl stomped out of the makeshift interview room, and Lewis was brought in. Lewis gave him a high five and slipped him one of the flash drives as they passed each other. Lewis's interview had the same result, except they received the flash drive that supposedly had GRI file data on it. What was to be done with it was another matter—it had been obtained under illegal means. In the end, Williams agreed to let Hanson have it so it could also be forwarded to the FBI center in Seattle, and ultimately to Washington, DC, along with a memorandum bearing his signature and not Williams's.

Neither Lewis nor anyone else had revealed that there was a second flash drive containing GRI data. Lewis was informed that he and Brooklyn could fly back to Hoonah in the morning. So if his luck held, he might be able to do a little data mining of his own. Lewis was anxious to figure out just how GRI was pulling off their piracy operations and was pretty sure he could beat the FBI computer whiz kids at their own games. He was willing to do a little more clandestine hacking.

Williams, for lack of a formal complaint or maybe just a moment of better judgment, decided to hold off on arresting anyone. Whether it was an oversight or that Earl might receive another call from someone at Glacier World, Earl got to hang on to Brooklyn's cell phone. He was glad to have it, and expected the call about Bernie. He knew that as soon as a warrant was issued, the FBI would contact the telephone company and monitor any calls to the phone.

They didn't do it soon enough.

***

Earl kept the phone close and was asleep in a motel room near the airport when it started ringing. He struggled to wake up and answer it.

"Armstrong?" said the caller. "Your kid has a message for you."

"Dad, that you?" said Bernie. "I'm fine. I was worried when you didn't show up and I did a pretty stupid thing. They need you to return whatever it was that you took, Dad." That was all Bernie got to say.

"You have a fine boy," said the caller. "It would be a shame if there was an accident and he fell into the wolf or wolverine enclosure—maybe he could play with the otters."

"Okay, I'm willing to make the trade," replied Earl with signs of desperation in his voice. "What do you want me to do?"

"Be at the private seaplane area at the airport at daylight—just you. And bring the data files. You'll be told what to do after that."

"Are you bringing Bernie?" asked Earl. There was no answer. The call had ended.

CHAPTER 35

Juneau, Alaska

Judge Ronald A. Jenkins was saying goodbye to the last of the twelve guests who had attended his wife's birthday party when he got the telephone call from Lieutenant Dave Williams with the Alaska State Troopers. He didn't get many requests for search warrants after hours. Usually requests to conduct searches involved drugs or stolen property and were events planned weeks, or even months, in advance. There was plenty of evidence of probable cause.

Williams's request came as a total surprise, and he hustled the last remaining guest out the door to take the call in private. His wife, Maurine, started picking up wine glasses and plates of half-eaten birthday cake as he slumped into a leather easy chair and listened to Williams explain the circumstances and evidence.

"I know it sounds odd, judge, but there is some evidence that GRI is up to something and could be the source of the gulf piracy incidents. More importantly, we are pretty sure they are holding a young boy as a hostage. We've got to go in."

"This is pretty hard to believe, Dave," replied Jenkins. "GRI has made a huge investment in the economy of Southeast Alaska. Yes, the state legislature has granted them a lot of special privileges, but as a cover for high seas piracy? How could they do that? I was informed this afternoon that they have a cruise ship with over fifteen hundred passengers arriving at Glacier World within the next day or so. Why would they put such an operation in jeopardy?"

"I'm afraid we don't have all the answers right now. But the evidence turned over to the FBI sounded pretty plausible. GRI isn't what we have been led to believe."

At the mention of GRI, Maurine stopped what she was doing and listened to her husband's conversation at the door to the kitchen. She overheard him mention GRI and Glacier World and some talk about issuing a warrant. She wondered what was going on.

"Is the evidence admissible?" the judge asked Williams. "Have you discussed this with the district attorney?"

"No, I haven't. He's out fishing somewhere and doesn't answer his radio. I admit, what evidence we have is pretty weak, but the bureau is willing to take the risk. It will be their show."

"Alright," the judge finally said. "Send a copy to my email and I'll approve it, but I'm doing this more for the kid than anything else. I don't like threats to harm juveniles—no matter who's behind

them. So you better find him or find another job—
that is, if anyone will hire you after the press gets
through crucifying both of us for making false
accusations about Glacier World."

***

Before retiring for the night, Maurine Jenkins called
her sister, the wife of Senator William "Mac"
MacDonald. The Macdonald's had been unable to
attend the party, as they were in Anchorage for a
regional meeting with the Alaska Native Brotherhood,
which Senator MacDonald counted on for support
for his reelection. She chatted about a really pleasant
birthday party and then mentioned the call her
husband had received.

"You know, Monica," she said, "Ron got the
strangest call this evening. The state troopers wanted
a search warrant to enter Glacier World. It had
something to do with them holding a young boy
captive. Can you imagine that?"

"At Glacier World? There must be some
mistake, Maurine. Why would they do such a thing? I
bet the boy just snuck in there to see the animals. Mac
and I were there for the one-day open house, and it's
such an exciting and fabulous place. You and Ron
have to go out there. When you do, be sure to go on
the Sky Ride. You pass over all those predators. I was
so scared I wet my pants."

"Monica!"

"Just kidding, but it is a thrill. But really, the people that developed it just can't be kidnappers. They have been so nice to Mac."

"I know. It sounds so weird. Ron was informed that GRI might also be responsible for all those awful piracy operations we've been reading about."

"Stealing of cargo out in the gulf? That's a big leap from holding a trespassing kid. That's insane. Mac is going to have a fit when he hears about that. Anyway, I'm glad you had a nice birthday, sis. Sorry I couldn't be there. I've got a neat birthday present for you when we get back to Juneau. We'll have lunch at the Hanger. Think nugget."

"Ooh, that sounds golden. Goodnight, Monica."

CHAPTER 36

Juneau Airport, Alaska

It was a restless night for Earl. A nightmare woke him around midnight. He dreamed about being chased by a bear through an endless patch of muskeg, and he fell into one of the ponds and couldn't get out. The bedside alarm clock woke Earl up at five in the morning. Groggy and still tired, he dressed and quietly slipped out of his Super 8 motel room, using a back door to leave unnoticed. The Super 8 was only a few blocks from the airport, but the private hangers were at the far end, so he walked fast to be sure he was on time.

Despite being tired from the ordeal of climbing over the Chilkat Mountain range, he had slept lightly. Getting Bernie back was everything— even more than his own safety. Earl knew that arranging to meet with someone from GRI without informing the state troopers was foolhardy, to say the least. Leon, Williams and Hanson were busy planning to bust GRI's Glacier World in one big sweep. Bernie could be hurt, or worse, when this happened. Maybe, just maybe, his presence would give both of them a chance to survive and be rescued. Lewis was the only person who knew what Earl intended to do.

Earl had been told to find the office for Wrangell Ellis Flying Service. The gate to the airstrip behind the building would be unlocked. He was to wait by the building until he saw a plane land and taxi over to the building.

A Cessna Turbo 206 landed and taxied towards him. It spun around without cutting its engine, and a man next to the pilot motioned for Earl to board the plane.

As Earl approached the right side of the Cessna, the man who sat next to the pilot thrust a door open.

"Mr. Armstrong, I must insist you join us," said the man.

"Where is my son?" Earl asked, noticing that there were only two men in the plane.

"All in due time, Mr. Armstrong. Now do get in the plane."

"Where are you planning to take me? It had better be to Bernie."

"So many questions! My name is Fishman, and I will do the asking. Did you bring the data files?"

"I have them," replied Earl grudgingly.

"Good," said Fishman. "Did you think we would simply accept the data without being able to confirm it? We are going back to Glacier World to see if what you have is the copied data, and then we can see to the trade."

Earl reluctantly climbed through the door, and Fishman quickly closed and secured it. The pilot revved the motor and spun the plane around, heading to the main runway. He did not even taxi to the end, and instead turned and pushed forward on the throttle. Within four hundred feet the plane was in the air and climbing.

Earl glanced back towards the buildings and could not see anyone watching the plane. Without saying anything more, he fastened his seat belt and sat back, accepting the realization that he was not in control of the situation. He was going back to Glacier World after all. He managed a slight smile, knowing the law enforcement guys would be there soon. Hopefully, Leon would be with them.

He turned his attention to the interior of the plane. There were six seats of rich, soft leather. A large Garmin navigation display could be easily seen in front of the pilot. The cabin was also pressurized, and Earl could sense the change as they climbed. In a few minutes they were over the Point Retreat Lighthouse and crossing Lynn Canal. The flight would take less than forty-five minutes. After gaining a cruising altitude of twenty thousand feet, Fishman made a phone call, so Earl figured he was probably going to be expected.

The Cessna circled once over the small airstrip just south of the new park. The strip predated GRI's ownership and had been used seasonally by a fish-canning operator. GRI had made a few improvements, including extending the airstrip several hundred feet and adding some landing lights so it could handle corporate jets. As the plane made its turn, the view of the park was familiar to Earl after spending nearly a week on the opposite ridge studying its layout. The same small ship was at the dock near the warehouse, and he could see activity. They appeared to be involved in a loading operation—several containers were stacked up, ready to be swung aboard. The name on the stern of the vessel was easy to read—*Predator.*

"How appropriate." Earl mumbled to himself.

CHAPTER 37

Anchorage, Alaska

At breakfast, Monica told her husband about her sister's phone call, and Mac quickly excused himself to go make a call himself. He walked out of the hotel restaurant to a corner of the lobby where there was some privacy and called Rahman, who heard the panic in MacDonald's voice.

"It's quite all right, Mac," responded Rahman. "Your wife was pretty close to the truth. We had a couple of kids paddle into the park in kayaks and try to walk around to see some of the animals. I think one of them had been here for the open house. Their parents must have reported them missing. We'll have it all straightened out by noon today."

"But what about the other rumor about reports of stolen cargo ending up at Glacier World?"

"Again, they are quite false. If the state troopers would like to look in our warehouses while they are here to pick up the kids, they are welcome to do so. All they will find is materials and supplies for the park's construction and opening of the facility. We have had a huge amount of shipments in the last few months, what with furniture and equipment arriving. It would look strange if someone didn't notice the extraordinary amount of ship traffic coming into our dock. You saw some of the changes yourself this last visit you made out here."

"Yes, I did notice the changes," said Mac. "You've done an amazing transition from an old rundown cannery into a top-notch tourist destination here in Alaska. But they have a warrant—there must be some evidence for these accusations. This is going to be public news by this evening, and I'm damn worried about what it could do to my reelection. The newspapers will be all over this, and I've been pretty vocal about my support for GRI. I could drop ten or twenty points if the press makes much of this thing."

"Mac, listen to me," responded Rahman. "You know the newspaper editor. Wait until later today when you're back in Juneau. If there is any talk about a negative story, give him a call and set him straight on the facts about your relationship with GRI. I'm sure it will be okay. Now, I have urgent business meetings with my staff concerning our first cruise ship visit later this morning, which will be the really big story for the press. As a matter of fact, your newspaper should have a reporter here at the time. They have been invited. Thanks for the call, Mac."

***

Rahman was fuming after ending the call and snapped at the captain of the *Predator* and a warehouse supervisor who were sitting in his office. "I want every last bit of our inventory loaded into containers and put on the *Predator*. And I want it done now."

"You want everything on board?" the captain responded, not sure he heard Rahman correctly. "We're loading the silicon wafer shipment right now."

"We are about to have a visit by the state troopers, who received a warrant last night to conduct a search of our warehouses. The *Predator* sails as soon as she is loaded. Dump the containers overboard once out of sight of land and don't return until you hear from me."

"Dump everything? Including the silicon wafers?"

"Everything! It's too hot at the moment to have loose ends. And the entire warehouse crew goes on board as well. I don't want people hanging around who might talk and let something slip. We've got two hours, maybe three, before they get here."

The supervisor and ship captain nodded in agreement and started to leave, but the captain stopped and turned back to face Rahman. "What about the Armstrong kid?" he asked. "What are you going to do with him?"

"Put him on the *Predator*, too," said Rahman. "Fishman picked up the kid's father. I plan to get our files back one way or another. This isn't over yet."

***

Earl waited impatiently in the small locked room next to the security office. It had been several hours since the plane landed, and still no one appeared to talk to about Bernie's release. Fishman hadn't said anything more before leaving him. Earl was pretty sure he was in the office tower that housed the computer operations center. They arrived using the service tunnel and entered through an underground lobby where there was a manned security guard station.

The door opened and two men entered. Without a word, Earl was led over to an elevator and pushed inside. They got off on the fourth floor. From the elevator, they walked through a set of glass double doors and then into a side office. Earl didn't know it, but it was the same data center manager's office that Lewis had used.

Two men were already seated in the office. One was short, fairly young with close-cropped hair. He wore glasses and a light blue shirt—typical of staff Earl had observed previously. The identity of the other man was not hard to guess. He was tall and looked Asian. It was the pistol lying on the table that was the sure sign that this was the man who was in charge and was going to be asking the questions.

"Good morning, Mr. Armstrong," the man said politely. "I assume you had a pleasant trip. I will avoid the formalities of welcoming you to Glacier World, as we both know this is not your first visit. Let me just introduce myself and leave it at that. I am

Raul bin Rahman, the operations manager for Glacier World."

"Really, Mr. Rahman," replied Earl. "Don't you mean you run the piracy operations and steal cargo, like my valuable cedar lumber?"

"Hmm, that's a rather interesting question, Mr. Armstrong," said Rahman. "I didn't realize you had a personal interest as a reason for trespassing and breaking and entering on my property. I was thinking of pressing charges with the authorities. This presents me with something to think about regarding your near future. But first, we must address why you are here."

"Yes, we do," Earl said as he purposely glanced around the room and out into the larger room of the computer center. "Where is my son, Bernie? He should be here for this little business exchange."

"As Mr. Fishman no doubt already informed you, you will shortly be reunited with your son if you have kept your side of the arrangement. We would now like to see the file media you and your friends employed to break into a highly confidential corporate computer system."

Earl dug into one of his jacket pockets and removed a small flash drive. It may have been small, but it had a huge capacity. Lewis had used one-terabyte flash drives. "From what I have heard, it was not all that difficult to inspect your computer network. Your people leave a lot of holes. It was pretty easy to learn how you change the shipping records of international import and export companies."

The manager raised his head with a questioning look on his face. Rahman's face reddened slightly as he snatched the drive from Earl's hand and handed it to the supervisor.

"Take a look at what they copied," ordered Rahman.

The computer supervisor opened the folders on the flash drive one at a time and examined the file contents. He nodded several times while staring at his monitor and then looked at Rahman. "It's authentic, but they got away with quite a bit of information. I'm going to have to tighten up our encryption and firewalls."

Rahman, still not looking pleased, was satisfied as he replied. "Destroy the copy. Wipe it clean and get rid of it. A copy never existed, you understand?"

"Yes, sir," replied the supervisor as he began the process of deleting what was on the drive.

"Aren't you going to offer it to the state troopers when they arrive, as evidence to our illegal entry?" asked Earl with a smirk on his face.

"I'll consider that a bad joke, Mr. Armstrong. We have enough evidence and witnesses to bring charges against you and your friends. And yes, I know about the warrant and pending arrival of the state's law enforcement group. In fact, they should be here any time now. A cruise ship is about to arrive as well.

It will be interesting to watch them conduct a search with fifteen hundred tourists milling about."

"What about my presence?" asked Earl. "Isn't that going to be hard to explain?"

"Your presence? No one knows you are even here. It's my decision whether to get rid of you or let you live," replied Rahman.

"Okay, now that you have the data back, I would like to see Bernie," Earl said emphatically as he stood up.

"See your son? I guess I can allow that." Rahman rose and went over to a window that looked down the length of the park and dock towards the mouth of the inlet. "Please, Mr. Armstrong, come over here to the window. There is a fine view."

Earl was confused with the request but did as directed. Standing at the window next to Rahman, the only notable thing he could see was the departure of the *Predator*. It was maybe a half-mile away from the docks, steaming towards Icy Strait.

"I regret to inform you that Bernie Armstrong is, shall we say, enjoying a little sea voyage." Rahman enjoyed his little charade but did not show a smile.

"What? You put Bernie on that ship?" exclaimed Earl.

"Mr. Armstrong, did you think I was stupid enough to believe you gave me the only copy of the stolen computer files? They could have been copied. One of your friends may have examined them. Why, even the state troopers or FBI may have seen a copy of those files. I need to be sure nothing will be disclosed that reveals any form of irregular or illicit activity on the part of GRI. Of course, you and the others will be arrested on criminal charges. I do hope you have a lawyer who is up to matching our own. I might even have my lawyers come up with a civil suit against you and your friends for the damage to the reputation of Glacier World and the economic interests of GRI and its investors. We are not finished with this matter—far from it. I'm afraid the next move is yours, and the law enforcement guests are soon to arrive."

"But you kidnapped my son," protested Earl in desperation.

"The state troopers will be informed that Bernie Armstrong and another boy left here yesterday evening by kayak. The same way they arrived."

Fishman entered the room at that moment to escort Earl out of the building. Earl ignored his presence and lunged at Rahman, but Fishman hit Earl with a fist in the center of his back. Earl collapsed to the floor. As he was forcefully picked up and shoved towards the door he hollered at Rahman, "You're a monster, Rahman. I'll get you for this."

"Show Mr. Armstrong one of the predator enclosures. When the cruise ship departs, we'll deal with Mr. Armstrong like previous trespassers.

As Earl continued to struggle to free himself, he realized what Rahman had just said. "You killed Raz Hunt, didn't you? You probably killed Eddie

Jackson for the same reason. They saw what you are really doing here at Glacier World."

Rahman laughed as he answered Earl. "Mr. Hunt was a stubborn fool and served my purposes for maintaining secrecy. Mr. Jackson was also stupid, and stole evidence from me like you and your friends. None of which I take lightly."

Rahman turned to Fishman. "Lock him up someplace where he won't be found. When this is over, Mr. Armstrong can pay a visit to one of the predator enclosures. Only this time, he won't escape."

CHAPTER 38

Juneau, Alaska

By midmorning the next day, after some exhausting hours spent in planning and a call to the Alaska district judge for a warrant, everyone was ready to conduct the search of Glacier World. But not everything was going as Hanson wanted. First, none of them had ever set foot in Glacier World. Dave Williams and one other officer had been to the dock, but no farther, which meant they had to use Leon Pence and Earl Armstrong to guide them. The second problem was that they couldn't locate Earl. He had disappeared.

FBI Agent Hanson was upset and in Dave Williams's face more than Dave desired. He was that kind of a guy. Ray Hanson had been the team leader for rounding up a group of Philippine fishermen who were transporting illegal Asian immigrants into the United States to work in several fish canneries. He had gotten some pats on the back from his superiors, but no promotion. A raid on Glacier World was just what he needed to get his career on a fast track to a high civil service position in Seattle or one of the other major bureau offices.

Williams let Hanson help with the resources they needed from the other federal agencies, like the Coast Guard, customs, and border patrol. There were maybe eight state officers who were weapons qualified and fit for this kind of assignment. They needed at least another twenty people, so that meant Hanson had to bring in reinforcements from other agencies. They also needed to transport everyone by either boat or helicopter, which with that many people meant relying on boats.

It was nearly nine in the morning before everyone was ready to leave. The entry was set for noon, with two helicopters holding at the Juneau airport and landing at the airstrip at Glacier World just as everyone else went by boat. No one checked the cruise ship schedule, or they would have learned that a large cruise ship, the *Odyssey of the South Seas*, would be docked at Glacier World at the same time.

***

The *Odyssey of the South Seas* arrived exactly at 11:00 a.m., and within another hour the helicopter carrying Williams and Hanson touched down at GRI's airstrip. Fifteen hundred Asian tourists had already happily disembarked for their exciting tour of Glacier World and to take pictures of themselves in front of Alaska's predators. The vehicles that Leon Pence called people movers were technically known as ROTVs, or Remotely Operated Transportation Vehicles. They operated perfectly and delivered tourists to the predator viewing towers for the Bear River Loop, Wolf Valley, and Wolverine Ridge. The whale watching and salmon fishing tours were now operational, with six small boats zooming out on Excursion Inlet for various destinations. People were pouring into the Journey to the Arctic Aquarium and its amphitheater for an afternoon show with the orca whales and white-sided dolphins. There were long lines for the Moose and Caribou Tundra Sky Ride. Gold Rush Town was packed with people shopping for gold nugget jewelry, fur-lined hats and boots, and Eskimo Pie ice cream. The first cruise ship tourists to arrive loved the park, and so did the two TV stations and four newspaper reporters from Juneau and Anchorage.

CHAPTER 39

Gulf of Alaska

Locked in a small stateroom aboard the *Predator*, Bernie Armstrong was beyond being afraid. He was frantic. What had been a bad situation when he was caught sneaking into Glacier World now was worse by having been marched aboard a ship that was headed for the Gulf of Alaska.

Bernie was also worried about what his dad had to be going through because of his stupidity, and he didn't even want to think about his mom. Hopefully, his dad hadn't called her to report him missing and she didn't know anything about what was happening. What was supposed to be a casual trip to Alaska had turned into a disaster as far as Bernie was concerned. When he had had a few seconds to speak to his dad the night before, he had gained some hope that the whole thing would soon be over. His dad would somehow arrange to get him, but how would he know about this latest turn of events?

Bernie's thoughts turned to his new friends. His dad had not been able to tell him anything about their escape over the mountains. Since he was able to talk with him, he must be okay, and that could mean the others were, too. He wondered about Brooklyn. What was she doing and thinking about? He had acted wrongly in her eyes, not remaining at the hotel in Juneau. Her team's participation in the MATE competition was coming up, and she could end up not being involved. Would she ever forgive him for that, or for putting more than himself in danger? For one of the first times he could remember, Bernie cried—heart-wrenching, uncontrollable sobs.

CHAPTER 40

Glacier World

The timing of the raid on Glacier World was both perfect and a disaster. Three Coast Guard boats and two helicopters landed simultaneously. In all, twenty-nine officers, all armed and wearing bulletproof vests, had been transported to Glacier World. The boats charged up to the piers while one helicopter landed next to the warehouse area and the other at the airstrip. The helicopter carrying FBI agent Ray Hanson landed next to the warehouse where they waited for Raul bin Rahman, who arrived shortly via the tunnel from the office tower. Agent Hanson approached the vehicle with his warrant in hand, and Dave Williams was right behind him. As soon as Hanson served Rahman with the search warrant, Williams would signal the others by radio to begin their search.

"If you're Mr. Rahman, I have a search warrant to look for a missing boy whom you are allegedly holding, as well as for committing acts of terrorism on the high seas, threats to maritime security, and unlawful possession of contraband," said

Hanson, waving the piece of paper and holding up his FBI badge.

"I'd like a closer look at that warrant if I may and for the record, sir, I would like your name," replied Rahman in a calm voice. "And if I may say, welcome to the grand opening of Glacier World, on what looks to be a very nice day in Southeast Alaska."

"It's Hanson, Agent Ray Hanson. And I have to warn you that my men have the authority to use lethal force if provoked by any of your people."

While the two men were talking, Williams issued the search order using a radio mike attached to his vest.

"Look around you, Mr. Hanson," replied Rahman. "This is a destination resort. We have a cruise ship docked here today and over fifteen hundred visitors. Why do you think we would commit any acts of violence? In fact, we have nothing to hide whatsoever. This warrant is for a search for a missing juvenile. You may look wherever you like, but I would sincerely hope you do not disturb or upset any of our visitors. You should also be aware that the press is well represented here today. If your people should do anything to disrupt activities or, as you so mildly stated it, provoke my employees, it will be noted, and a lawsuit will be filed against the state of Alaska."

"Do I take that as a threat?" asked Hanson.

"Take it any way you want," replied Rahman. "I have made my point. Now if you wish to examine the inside of our warehouses, feel free. If you want to search our offices or quarters, I will provide transportation and escorts. If you would like to ride the Sky Ride, I can provide you with some free tickets."

Hanson ignored the last offer and realized that Williams had not been introduced. "Ah...Mr. Rahman, this is Lieutenant Dave Williams of the Alaska State Troopers. I think you have met before?"

"Yes, we have met, and I believe Lieutenant Williams will recall that my staff has always been helpful with any investigation they were handling. Isn't that right, Dave?"

"Yeah, although helpful might be overstating things a bit," replied Williams. "So where's the kid, Bernie Armstrong?"

"They paddled out of here in their kayaks late yesterday. We escorted them to the start of Icy Strait. They should have returned to Hoonah by now, I believe. Haven't you heard from his parents or his friends?"

"No, we have not," said Williams as he made some notes in a small notebook. "First time we've heard that story. We'll check it out, but I don't think your explanation will satisfy Agent Hanson." Williams looked around for Hanson, who had pulled out a radio and walked a few feet away to talk to several of the other group leaders who were waiting for instructions. He shook his head and went and got in

Hanson's face. "Hanson, can I have a word with you right now?"

Hanson waved a hand and nodded, acknowledging Williams's presence and finishing his instructions by saying, "Keep me informed. We just found out the kid isn't in the park anymore, that he went back to Hoonah. Until the place is searched, I won't believe it for a second."

Hanson looked at Williams and shrugged his shoulders. "So...what now?" he asked.

"So what?" said Williams, pissed but trying to show some restraint. "Do you realize what we just rode into with this organized swat team? We have a public relations nightmare. If I don't hear from the governor in the next fifteen minutes, I will be damned surprised. Your men better find something and be quick about it so we can justify having this warrant, or I'm going to put it somewhere that will be damned uncomfortable."

Hanson nodded, backed away, then turned and hurried towards the closest warehouse. Williams just shook his head and looked down the promenade. The area was full of tourists, including families with kids. A woman squeezed through the barricade separating the park from the warehouse area and hurried towards him. He knew the woman—Jenny Marks, a tenacious little homegrown reporter for the *Juneau Empire*. "Why me?" Williams groaned. "Jenny, I don't need this right now."

Jenny Marks walked quickly across the dock, straight for Williams. "Hello, Dave, are you and your people trying to protect us from all the predators?" asked Jenny. "Or is there more to this? Why all the macho guys with guns?"

"Now, Jenny, don't try to make too much of this. We have a warrant to conduct a search, that's all. It's not like we're about to make any arrests. We got a report that a kid was missing and Judge Jenkins issued a warrant. You know how he feels about missing juveniles."

"Huh, seems like a lot of trouble coming in here all stealth-like just to find a missing kid. Then you won't mind if I call Ron Jenkins?"

"You know I can't stop you, Jenny. He's your uncle. But I don't think he will have much to say about what we are doing. If you need some more facts for a story I know you're sure to write, you need to speak to Agent Hanson. He's pretty busy right now with the search, but I'll be sure to tell him you want to speak to him."

"Ray and the FBI are behind this crazy stunt?" said Jenny. "You're holding out on me, Dave. And that would be just like Ray. Always looking for a break that will get him promoted out of Juneau."

Williams mumbled a response to her words. "Yeah, like reassigned to Nome if this search blows up in his face."

"What was that you said, Dave?" asked Jenny.

"Nothing important for your story, Jenny," answered Williams more clearly. "Hanson is your man." With that, he turned and walked slowly towards the nearest warehouse.

Agent Hanson directed six heavily armed men, who had been standing at the edge of the dock doing nothing, signaling them to surround the warehouses and begin their search. Several of the men trotted toward the far end of the buildings with their rifles ready. Another man pushed open a large door on the end of the building just in front of Hanson, checked the interior, and waited for the others.

Pallets and shipping debris littered the inside of the warehouse, but on close inspection, everything was construction materials or furnishings such as park benches, restaurant tables and chairs, even pallets stacked with non-perishable food. There was no sign of any expensive, limited-edition Harley Davidson motorcycles, not even a bicycle.

The contents of the second warehouse were more interesting. It contained a large paint booth, and several flat file drawers filled with paint templates for names and logos of various corporate container companies. Pictures were taken, as well as samples of the paint and the templates, but as evidence they were going to be circumstantial, maybe even non-admissible, if there were charges filed.

***

Leon Pence arrived at Glacier World as part of one of the Coast Guard search parties, and as soon as his group received the order from Williams they headed for the office tower to begin a floor-by-floor, room-by-room search for Bernie Armstrong. He refused to believe Bernie was not there. Fifteen minutes later, they reassembled on the main floor, having found nothing. Leon suggested the search teams move to the tunnels and check the storage and maintenance rooms. It didn't take long to discover where a hostage was being held. Only to their surprise, it was Earl rather than Bernie.

"This is Petty Officer Crane with B Team. We've located a man in the Timber Wolf Den access room. Says his name is Earl Armstrong."

Williams heard the radio call along with everyone else and it took him totally by surprise. "Can you repeat that, Petty Officer Crane?" responded Williams. "You say you found the boy's father, Earl Armstrong?"

"That's right, sir," answered Crane. "Armstrong says the boy is not here, but he knows where he is. He's a bit shaken up, sir. What do you want me to do with him?"

Leon heard the communication with Williams and used a radio to respond. "Dave, this is Pence. I'm heading to the wolf enclosure access and can assist with bringing Earl to your location. Where are you?"

"I'm outside the warehouses at the south end of the park," said Williams. "I want you and

Armstrong here as quickly as you can." He released the mike key and shook his head. "What the hell is going on here? We're stopping this search right now." Williams didn't want to see pictures of federal or state officers searching a café full of tourists eating pizza and ice cream cones.

He didn't get his wish. Somehow the press got ahold of a picture of three Asian tourists being shaken down with their hands on a glass wall and several cute otters on the other side of the glass watching two federal officers search their backpacks. The picture got a headline of "Opening Day at Glacier World," and the governor called. At least he had the courtesy to wait several hours.

***

Dave Williams insisted that Earl Armstrong and Leon Pence ride back to Juneau in one of the helicopters. He didn't want them out of his sight until Earl could be questioned about his disappearance and his discovery at Glacier World, and whether there was any truth to the story about Bernie. Earl insisted that his son didn't paddle back to Hoonah in a kayak but had been placed on a ship that had left Glacier World earlier that morning. He had a lot to tell Leon Pence, but that could wait.

As to his own kidnapping, Earl remained vague about why he had been found locked in a supply room at Glacier World, other than he had been generously offered transportation to see for himself that Bernie was not there and had gotten lost wandering. Williams did not believe that story either. There were too many loose ends, and someone had to be lying.

CHAPTER 41

Hoonah, Alaska

Lewis and Brooklyn were able to catch a commercial flight back to Hoonah and went immediately to Lewis's office to begin examining the copy of GRI data he had stored in the cloud the night before. Lewis had not gotten very far when Earl called him.

"Lewis, I need your help. Bernie wasn't at Glacier World when I arrived there this morning to make the exchange. Rahman said they put him on a ship, which had already left. Then he gave the FBI and state troopers some crazy story about Bernie sneaking into Glacier World using a kayak and leaving the same way."

Lewis was about ask a question when Brooklyn motioned to him to use the speakerphone key on the phone. He nodded and switched it on. "I just put you on speakerphone, Earl. Brooklyn is here with me. Ah...so why didn't Rahman tell the truth? You talked to Bernie last night, right? Did he tell you how he got there?"

"Rahman didn't allow Bernie to explain anything. But remember, we left him in Juneau. He didn't have any money to buy airfare to Hoonah, plus he knew we were going to return to Juneau."

"Yes," Brooklyn injected into the conversation. "I told him to stay at the hotel, but he could walk around a bit if he got bored. I tried calling him several times but no answer until that call from someone, maybe Rahman?"

"It was Rahman," said Earl. "He told me Bernie snuck onto one of their boats while it was in Juneau. That's how he got to Glacier World."

"Alright, so he kept Bernie and got him out of sight," stated Lewis. "Why? What else did Rahman tell you, Earl?"

"It's not good news, Lewis," replied Earl. "He's convinced we have more data than I gave him. He knows you were the one who got into their computers. They found your notebook."

"Yeah, I figured sooner or later that would be a problem," said Lewis.

"Unless we figure out what to do, they're going to be coming for you. They murder people, Lewis. You could be next."

"Okay, then let's look at this differently," replied Lewis. "Right now Rahman is in control. He's making the demands, and we have to comply. Me dying is not on the table, so we need to turn this around. One way to do that is get Bernie back. That means we need to find that ship and convince the Coast Guard to board it. Tell me more, Earl. Tell me about the ship."

"Well, I saw it there this morning. It was moored at Glacier World. They were loading the ship with containers."

"That's interesting," said Lewis. "Probably removing evidence before the state troopers arrived. What time was that and do you know when it left?"

"I arrived just before seven a.m., and I think it must've left around ten a.m. It was almost out of sight when Rahman told me to take a look out a window of that office tower to where Bernie was. Damn that man!"

"What the ship's name? What does it look like?"

"If you have my earlier photos, you can see it. You're probably better at figuring out what kind of ship it is. But I think the name is the *Predator*."

"That's good, Earl," shouted Brooklyn. She was already at another computer and pulling up Earl's photo file. "With a name, we can look the ship up in the Coast Guard's documentation database."

"Yeah, but the ship left hours ago. No one is going to be able to find it."

"You can with today's technology," replied Lewis. "All ships have to be part of the Automatic Identification System, or AIS. It's a real-time vessel tracking system where vessels are registered and assigned a Maritime Mobile Service Identity number, or MMSI, that is continuously transmitted by their VHF radio."

"Really?" asked Earl.

Brooklyn added, "Yup! That's what we use for the NOAA grant. Every ship is required to transmit an AIS signal. That is, unless they went dark."

"And what does that mean, 'going dark?'" asked Earl.

"They turn off their AIS transponder," answered Lewis with a glum look on his face. "They're not supposed to do that, but unfortunately some boats do. Like a crab boat captain who doesn't want other boats knowing where he's setting his pots."

"Or maybe a vessel that is stealing cargo off another ship," added Brooklyn. She opened her browser and searched for the Coast Guard Documentation Center website. In a matter of seconds, she queried for the vessel name *Predator* and had its information. There were several ships with that name, and one was a 160-foot trawler/long liner. Its owner was GRI, with a home port of Seattle, Washington. Next, she queried the MMSI database at an FCC site for the *Predator* vessel name, along with its identification number. She copied down the MMSI number and ran over to Lewis's desk. Lewis started searching his NASA satellites for the signal.

"Earl, is that FBI guy still with you guys? If we're right, we need him to cry wolf to the Coast Guard one more time."

"We're at the state troopers' office. I think we can find Hanson. What are you going to try?"

"Try?" answered Lewis. "We have everything we need right here on our computers to get coordinates on the *Predator*. We're going to use our NASA nanosat system and find the exact coordinates of the location that is transmitting their MMSI signal. Brooklyn just looked it up. So keep your fingers crossed, here we go."

"You're going to use NASA satellites?" asked Earl.

"It would take too long to explain," replied Lewis as he rapidly searched through his live data streams. "Just trust me. We'll find them."

Lewis accessed the software application that he had developed for monitoring the location of fishing boats. All MMSI transmissions within a thousand square miles of the Gulf of Alaska were covered for the purposes of the University of Alaska study. He merged streaming data from all fifty of his project's nanosats, then narrowed the screen coverage to a fifty-mile radius from the west end of Icy Strait and studied the data points that showed up in sets of red numbers. He quickly searched the numbers for one matching what Brooklyn had found in the database. There it was—the *Predator*'s MMSI data showed the ship to be twenty-five miles northwest of Cape Fairweather, moving north at a speed of eight knots.

"Damn, we've got them, Earl," exclaimed Lewis, who was noticeably excited and breathing hard. "Get Williams on the line. We need to give him the whole story right now."

Brooklyn kept looking at Lewis's monitor. She focused on the other MMSI signals that were fairly close to the *Predator*. "Wow, look at this, Lewis," she yelled.

Lewis looked back at the screen. "At what?" he asked.

"There's a Coast Guard cutter within thirty miles of the *Predator*. I know their MMSI number. We see it all of the time when their patrols cross the fishing grounds. It's the USCG cutter *Nootka*. They're a long-range patrol ship used for fisheries law enforcement and catching drug smugglers. It has a speed of thirty knots. That means she can be on the scene in less than an hour."

CHAPTER 42

Glacier World

The mood at Glacier World should have been good. Initial reports about the tourists' reactions to the park opening were encouraging. The press representatives who covered the arrival of the first cruise ship were enthusiastic, and the newspaper articles that would run the next day were positive in reporting about the newly opened Alaskan theme park. The stories would immediately become syndicated throughout the United States, Canada, and Asia. The expectation was for a big boost in cruise ship bookings that would aid Alaska's economy.

But the FBI raid on the warehouses left a sour note with the park's employees. Rumors were flying. Those who worked in the park knew little or nothing about the activities conducted in the warehouses at the south end. GRI was a global organization that conducted its business through computerized international trade transactions involving nearly every Asian country. Management constantly reminded all employees that secrecy was important to competitiveness, and the Alaska operations center was important due to its isolation.

In his fifth-floor office, Rahman was making calls, trying to lay out steps to counter any negative publicity resulting from the FBI raid, and seeing how he could salvage his high seas piracy operations. If it had not been for the call from MacDonald giving a few hours warning, everything would have been exposed, and he would have been arrested. As things now stood, he might have to get rid of the *Predator* and find another vessel, maybe even relocate the warehouse operations. He had little or no concern for what GRI's investors would say or demand. They would remain in the safety of their high-rise condos in Singapore rather than risk another visit to Glacier World. He also had a priority: the computer data and whatever else Armstrong and his people had as evidence.

Fishman entered the office, returning from his unsuccessful attempt to capture the intruders. While he had cleaned himself up, the man looked exhausted.

"I've tightened up the park's security," said Fishman as he walked directly to the liquor cabinet and poured himself a glass of scotch. "There is very little to do until you make a decision concerning the warehouse operations and bringing back the *Predator*. In the meantime, we've got a lot of rumors floating around amongst the staff. Any ideas?"

Raul Rahman had been tight-lipped about the reason for the FBI raid. "Spread the story about the boy. After all, it was two park employees that discovered him. There is another cruise ship due in three days. That arrival should keep the park employees busy."

"And the *Predator*, what about the ship?" repeated Fishman.

"For the moment I haven't decided," replied Rahman

"What news do you have from them?"

Rahman checked his watch. "I received a call about twenty minutes ago that the ship would be safely outside territorial waters about now."

"Will they be able to dump the cargo as you requested?"

"The captain assured me that when they were clear of any other vessels, the process would begin. The idiot said it would take nearly a half day to finish the job. The process is slow because they have to attach ballast to weigh each one down and cut holes in the sides of the containers."

"I heard the FBI spent quite a bit of time looking at the container paint facility," said Fishman. "I've got an idea to explain its presence. It's rather clever actually." Fishman finished his drink and went back to the bar to pour another. He dropped in some ice cubes and filled his glass two-thirds full with one of Rahman's most expensive scotch whiskies.

"Are you going to share this brilliant idea?" asked Rahman.

"The fence at the end of the promenade doesn't provide any screening, and therefore limits times of activity around the warehouses. My suggestion is to paint up a bunch of the empty containers using a lot of attractive colors and stack them along the fence. We can tell the law enforcement people this is what we have been planning to do."

"That's a good idea," said Rahman. "See to it."

"What about the contents of the main warehouse?" Fishman asked. "Did they find anything?"

"They found nothing. Not even a scrap of paper that would suggest to them that anything reported stolen might have passed through our warehouses." Rahman turned and stared out the huge window that looked down Excursion Inlet and out towards Icy Strait. "I've got two more things for you to handle."

"Yes, what's that?" asked Fishman.

"I want another team out searching for that bear. Tranquilize it and get it back into the enclosure. Be sure the men are careful. When I purchased it, I was told it was a man-eater, and we know now it is for sure."

"And the second thing?" asked Fishman.

"We've got some loose ends over in Hoonah. Find these people and take them to my lodge. We'll figure out how to dispose of them when I arrive. When the job is done, we'll take the corporate jet and fly to Singapore. I'm going to take a vacation to let things settle down and see what the fallout looks like."

He pulled out Lewis's notebook and threw it on the conference table. "This guy Lewis Teeburt, or whatever his name is, knows too much. And I want this other guy, Earl Armstrong. He nearly brought down our whole operation. I want the satisfaction of seeing him die before we leave."

CHAPTER 43

Gulf of Alaska west of Cape Fairweather

Captain Samuel J. Borah finished his second cup of coffee in the officer's lounge and ascended two ladders to the bridge of the USCGC *Nootka* to take his shift as watch officer, a responsibility he enjoyed sharing with his other officers. He had commanded the *Nootka* for nearly four years and had distinguished himself and the ship with several missions to successfully interdict and make two arrests for illegal bottom fishing operations in the Gulf of Alaska, and one major cocaine seizure in the eastern Pacific near the mouth of the Columbia River. He had a reputation of being a tough commanding officer, insisting on strict discipline and a high level of training. However, his successes had brought kudos from the district admiral, leading to respect for his command and high morale among the 110 men and women on board the *Nootka*.

The officer in charge and four other crewmen on duty snapped to attention as he entered the bridge. He immediately put them at ease and asked for a status report from his OIC, his executive officer, Lt. Commander Shoemaker.

"Bill, what have we got?" asked Borah.

"Sector Juneau has had a couple of small-vessel distress calls—all inside waters. Outside, it's been pretty quiet, sir. There's not much vessel activity close by. We've got a cruise ship that just turned south out of Cross Sound, headed for Sitka. It's the *Odyssey of the South Seas*. There's a big longliner headed north about thirty miles to our starboard. There's some small-vessel traffic around the entrance to Lituya Bay and more down around Elfin Cove. Farther outside of us, we detected a freighter south bound, probably out of Kodiak, and an ocean tug with a tow in the sea lane for Valdez."

"Any radio communications?" asked the CO.

"Latest weather report is good and should hold for the next twenty-four hours. We got pinged regarding an alert from the FBI office in Juneau. They were going to conduct a raid on a possible source of these piracies over the last couple of months, but that message was followed by another one four hours later canceling the alert—false alarm, I guess."

"Hmm, that's interesting," replied Borah. "Have the radio operator monitor for additional FBI communications. We've got to get a break somewhere if we're ever going to catch these guys."

"Will do, sir," responded Shoemaker. "Sure would like to know how they get their information about what ships to hit. They seem to know exactly what kind of cargo is on board— right down to what containers to grab. Then there are the MATTS units that we require on every container. These pirates have got to have some pretty sophisticated technology to alter them so the containers can't be tracked."

"Yeah, it's taken a while for our intelligence guys at the district office to learn that much. The first couple of hits they made didn't make any sense. It just seemed like a rather preposterous operation to randomly steal cargo. Now we know they must be carefully planning their operations. And then there is the radio and radar jamming they employ. They're using some pretty sophisticated military technology there too."

"Going to make them hard to catch," said Shoemaker.

"Well, let's hope we're better trained at what we do than they are. Maybe they will make a mistake. I just hope one of their hits doesn't get deadly and someone is killed. Stealing cargo is bad enough, but if these guys make a mistake and get desperate, they could create an international scene just like what happened with the Somali pirates—killing a crew member, or an entire crew being kidnapped."

Captain Borah and his executive officer spent the next two hours discussing their patrol route for the next several days. They planned to run northwest and then crisscross two of the major sea-lanes to the Alaska ports near Anchorage. These sea-lanes were about 125 miles west of Cape Fairweather. From there, the *Nootka* would turn south for another 125 miles to pick up the major sea-lane to Japan and

Korea before returning to her home port in Seattle to resupply and then follow the route again. They had to put a stop to the piracy operations.

Shoemaker had just gone off duty when the radio operations specialist on duty rushed over to Captain Borah with a sheet of paper in her hand. "Excuse me, sir," said Radioman Johnson. "Sir, you need to read this communication we just received from Sector Juneau."

Captain Borah took the message and read it. The report in his hands amended the earlier report Bill Shoemaker had received. Apparently a vessel, called the *Predator*, had slipped out of port before the FBI raid took place, and they now had information that there could be contraband on board, as well as a hostage. The *Nootka* was to use whatever means it could to intercept and take possession of the vessel and to rescue the hostage.

"Damn, this is the break we've been waiting for. Good work, Johnson. There will be no radio contact with our target, the *Predator,* and no further communication on open channels until this mission is over, but keep me informed of any chatter."

"Yes, sir," replied Johnson. "Is this for real? I mean, are we intending to go after the pirates?"

"If this report is correct, we sure are!" said Borah as he turned to examine the navigation display. The target he was looking for was clearly visible as a dot on both the navigation display and radar at about thirty nautical miles to the northeast, just as

Shoemaker had reported. He gave an order to the man at the helm. "Go hard to starboard to a course of thirty degrees magnetic. Hold that course until further orders." He picked up his shipboard communication mike and contacted engineering. "Mac, we're changing course to close on a possible interdiction target. I want our speed increased to thirty knots." Finally, he hit the speaker horn button and his voice was heard throughout the ship. "All crew are to report to their stations immediately. This is not a drill. I repeat. This is not a drill. All coxswains are to report to the wardroom immediately for boarding orders. Three response boats and the MH-65 are to be fueled and ready to launch. Boarding teams will immediately report to the armory and draw small arms and ammunition. We are hunting for a trawler/long liner that is not what it appears to be. ETA to the target is sixty minutes."

There was a flurry of activity on the *Nootka*. The three boarding teams, each under the direction of a coxswain, were informed about their target before reporting to the aft launching ramp to prepare the twenty-five-foot Defenders they would deploy once the ship slowed. Each carried a crew of four men, plus the actual boarding team of six men. One of the crew was a gunner's mate who would man a .50 caliber machine gun. The helicopter on board the *Nootka* was an MH-65 Dolphin. The pilots were trained to be part of a HIT squadron to fly cover for the boarding teams in the response boats, which would surge toward their target at a speed of forty-five knots. Readied on board the *Nootka* were another four .50 caliber machine guns and a 76 mm cannon.

Fifteen minutes after the first announcement, an unusual thing happened on the bridge. The *Nootka*'s x-band and s-band radars both jammed. The AIS transmission of their target also disappeared off the navigation display. The helmsman made his report to the commanding officer, but everyone on the bridge saw it—including Shoemaker, who was back on duty, not wanting to miss being part of the mission.

"Looks like they've seen us coming," commented Borah. "They jammed our navigation systems just like the pirates do with the vessels they board. It must be them. Tell the HIT Squadron to launch, Bill. We need to get a visual."

Bill Shoemaker spoke directly to the pilot in the helicopter that was warmed up and ready on the flight deck, ordering him to lift off. Then he made a suggestion to the captain. "Sir, we can probably use our low-level tracking radar. They may not know about its 8-10 gigahertz frequency and be able to jam it. That will at least give us a target bearing once we are within twenty miles."

"You heard him," said Borah, speaking to the radar specialist at his station. "Bring our spook nine system up and running."

Seconds later, the specialist responded, "Target is locked in, sir. We've got them at eighteen nautical miles out. You should have a visual in about ten minutes."

Captain Borah and the rest of the crew on the bridge heard the Dolphin pass overhead and charge off towards the target. "Dolphin Zero Two Five to *Nootka*," radioed the helicopter pilot. "We have a visual on the target. It is underway."

"Roger, your observation is acknowledged. Swing wide to the south and maintain a distance of fifteen nautical miles from our target until ordered to close along with the boarding teams. Keep a close watch for anybody in the water. They are supposed to have a hostage on board. We're been maintaining open channel silence, but they've seen us on radar. In a few minutes, I am going to give them something to think seriously about." He turned and spoke to his CO. "Bill, I want three 76 mm rounds placed one hundred meters in front of their bow on my command when we get within ten nautical miles. I want that ship dead in the water when our board teams get there."

Borah directed the mission with the precision of a symphony conductor. This was what they spent day after day training for. He gave another order over his hands-free microphone. "Engineering, decrease our speed to twelve knots for ramp launching of the response boats."

With the decrease in speed, it was twelve minutes before they had their visual contact from the bridge. Shoemaker watched the chart plotter and his wristwatch. When they were ten nautical miles from the target, he received the order to fire the three rounds from the cannon. At eighty rounds per minute firing rate, the shots were hardly distinguishable from one another. The response boats and their accompanying HIT squadron were then ordered to close on the target. As soon as the pilot reported the splash and detonation of the rounds, Borah broke radio silence and ordered the *Predator* to stand to and prepare for boarding. The response boats had it surrounded in five minutes.

"*Nootka*, this is Dolphin Zero Two Five," the pilot radioed. "You're not going to believe this, captain. The *Predator* is dumping cargo containers overboard!"

CHAPTER 44

Hoonah, Alaska

A mood of apprehension hung in the Hoonah Community Center like a thick, early morning fog. Earl and Leon had chartered a flight to get them to Hoonah as quickly as possible. Along with their friends, they waited helplessly for word from the Coast Guard or Agent Hanson concerning the rescue of Bernie. Pete had been released from the hospital in Juneau and was able to fly back with them. He and Earl kept drinking cup after cup of coffee, giving Earl acid reflux.

Earlier in the day, Earl had reluctantly made a call to Sally to inform her about Bernie being held hostage. His ears burned from his wife's curt words and questions that he couldn't answer. He tried to ease Sally of her anxiety by describing all of the people and what they were doing to free him—that the matter was well in hand and it would only be a short time now. Earl agreed to call her back every fifteen minutes whether there was anything new to report or not. He took another sip of coffee and looked at his watch—five minutes and he had to call again.

Lewis and Brooklyn busied themselves on the computers to avoid thinking about Bernie's precarious situation and the possibility of saying something idiotic to Earl that they might regret later. Brooklyn quietly pointed to the monitor in front of Lewis, where she noticed the *Predator's* AIS transmission disappear. The ship had gone dark, as they assumed it might. They both knew what that probably meant. The *Predator* didn't want others to know where it was. Lewis glanced at Earl and saw that he was talking quietly to his wife on the phone. He shook his head—a sign Brooklyn took to mean that it was going to be difficult for the Coast Guard to locate the ship.

"I'm worried about something other than Bernie," Leon said to Earl. "You told me on the flight from Juneau that Raul Rahman killed Eddie Jackson and Raz Hunt to preserve the secrecy of his piracy operations. He is going to be a very desperate man when he learns about the *Predator* being taken by the Coast Guard, if he wasn't already. GRI is in trouble, and things are going to get worse. If the matter is simply left to fighting federal charges in the international courts with a team of highly paid GRI attorneys, that would be one thing, but desperate men are not rational."

"Yeah," answered Earl. "He probably knows where some of us are—like Pete and Lewis."

"There is my concern," said Leon. "Will he do anything about it?"

Before Earl could respond, a cell phone somewhere in the room started to buzz. Leon glanced across the room to where Lewis and Brooklyn were working. Lewis answered his phone. His face brightened immediately.

"He's safe!" shouted Lewis, not waiting to hear all of the details from the caller. Everyone else cheered. Brooklyn ran over to Earl and gave him a big hug. Pete had a big, big grin on his face. Leon smiled too, but something inside of him said this wasn't over yet.

***

Sally Armstrong couldn't concentrate on anything more than Bernie. She sat in the lounge at the South Bend hospital with a cold cup of tea in front of her that she hadn't touched. Earl's frequent calls were not reassuring because nothing had really changed. As far as she was concerned, Bernie was in danger, and she feared the worst—that he could be killed, if not already dead.

She moaned and swept the cup of tea off the table, sending it flying against the wall. She didn't even notice it as she pounded her right fist on the top of the table, breaking the nail on her index finger. She didn't notice that either. She had never felt so helpless in her life.

Her cell phone buzzed again. It was Earl.

"Bernie's safe!" hollered Earl into his phone. "The Coast Guard was able to rescue him from the ship."

Sally's eyes filled with tears. She couldn't speak and just held the phone tightly in her hand, not hearing Earl jabbering excitedly.

"Sally, are you all right?" said Earl. "Bernie is unhurt and the Coast Guard is transporting him to Hoonah. We're going to the airport now. Sally?"

"I....I'm all right, Earl," she said. "Thank God he's okay. You call me from the airport. I want to speak to Bernie as soon as he arrives."

Less than an hour later, everyone was waiting at the Hoonah airstrip. The word was that Bernie was getting a ride back on a Coast Guard helicopter. Sally did not wait for Earl's update, calling him back while he was standing on the tarmac, waiting with the others.

"Has he arrived yet?" asked Sally.

"Nope," he replied. "Soon though, we hope."

"Sorry I screamed at you earlier," she said. "I was quite upset. I let my emotions totally run away."

"You should have seen me yesterday. I am so sorry this happened, Sally. I thought he would be fine staying at the hotel in Juneau by himself."

"Well, you have a lot of explaining to do when the two of you get home," said Sally. "How could you have ever done what you did? It was so stupid. You should have let the police or the FBI or someone else do it."

"There wasn't enough evidence," Earl answered. "They would have laughed at us. Do you realize how powerful the company is that runs Glacier World? It's a global company and has plenty of political support."

"So, you let Leon Pence plan this thing like it was a military operation. He's a former Special Forces guy. You're just a forester, Earl. You—" Sally's phone indicating a second call. "Oh no," she said, displeased with the interruption.

"Go ahead and take the call, Sally. It might be someone there in the hospital. Call me right back."

Sally switched her phone to end the connection with Earl and took the second caller.

"Hi, Mom!"

"Bernie?"

"Yeah, I'm in a helicopter. It's pretty cool," replied Bernie, shouting into the phone over the noise of the helicopter. "One of the Coast Guard guys gave me his cell phone so I could call you."

"Are you all right, honey? I was so very worried about you."

"Ah, Mom! I'm fine, really. I was a little scared at times, but Dad said they would get me back safely and they did. It was fantastic seeing that big Coast Guard ship coming to rescue me. It fired this big gun at the boat I was on and everyone stopped what they were doing and surrendered. Then I got to ride in one of those orange inflatable boats back to their ship. Everyone had guns and bulletproof vests.

It was just like in the movies." Bernie looked out the side windows of the helicopter to see Hoonah below him. "I'm almost there, Mom. All my new friends are going to be waiting for me. Talk to you later tonight, okay?"

"Okay, but you and your father are to call me," said Sally.

"Mom, can Dad and I..." Bernie hesitated.

"Can you what?" asked Sally.

"Can Dad and I stay a few more days before coming home? One of my new friends and some other high school kids in Hoonah are going to be on a team in the MATE competition in Juneau. I'd like to be there with them. You could fly up and join us in Juneau, Mom. It's beautiful up here."

"We'll see," answered Sally. "I promise to talk to your father about it. I love you, Bernie."

"Love you too, Mom."

He kept peering out the window and grinned as he saw his dad and the others watching the helicopter gently touch down. Bernie thanked the Coast Guardsman for letting him use the phone. As soon as the door opened, Bernie jumped down and ran to his dad.

Everyone wanted to hug him. Lewis gave him a hearty bear hug, and even Brooklyn gave him a hug and a kiss on a cheek. Bernie was telling his story all over again when Pete finally got a word in and suggested they go back to town.

"Why don't we all meet at the café and order a couple of pizzas?" said Pete. "We all need to celebrate."

***

After Bernie Armstrong had been located and brought back to the *Nootka*, Captain Borah called Agent Hanson to report that the mission was successful. They had the vessel used for the gulf pirating in custody. With the boarding team providing security, he transferred another twenty men to the *Predator* to take full control of the ship. The first thing they dealt with was getting a half-submerged container back on board that had drifted well away from the ship.

They attached cables using one of the Defenders and slowly hoisted the container back aboard, the seawater draining out through the holes that had been cut in its sides. There were another nine containers still on board, and one of the crew confessed that another ten or eleven had already been pushed overboard and sunk.

The boarding team began to sort out and secure the crew of the *Predator*. They discovered dozens of dock and warehouse workers from Glacier World on board in addition to its normal crew. It took time, especially with the potential threat that someone might produce weapons and fight back.

Executive Officer Bill Shoemaker immediately took possession of the ship's bridge, and had an electronics specialist check the logs and navigation instruments for the ship's routes from the past several months. Tracking records for the *Predator* matched several of the locations where cargo piracy had been reported.

When everything was secure, Captain Borah put Shoemaker in command to take the *Predator* into Juneau. The *Nootka* would shadow the ship into port. On the way in, he had a lot more reports to make, another to Agent Hanson so he could prepare for their arrival and several to the Coast Guard commandant in Juneau and the district office in Seattle.

The crew of the *Nootka* was jubilant.

***

It was no more than a ten minute ride down the hill from the airport into Hoonah. Pete and Lewis had gone ahead to make arrangements for the celebration party at the café. Everyone else piled into the NYC taxi.

They turned left toward the town's waterfront and had traveled less than a mile when Brooklyn saw Lewis's car pulled over on the shoulder of the road. The right passenger door hung open. Leon, who was sitting next to the driver, bailed out as they pulled in behind Lewis's car. There was no one inside. He ran back to the taxi.

"Brooklyn, call Lewis's number, right now."

Brooklyn dialed. "There's no answer. Maybe they walked the rest of the way into town."

Leon shook his head. "I don't think so. Lewis's hat is lying on a seat. I think they've been taken by Rahman's men. Could not have been more than a few minutes ago. Maybe they are still at the harbor."

Leon urged the taxi driver to go as fast as the old cab would go. They reached the waterfront next to the harbor in three minutes. One small fishing boat was entering the port, and no boats were leaving. Lewis and Pete had disappeared.

CHAPTER 45

Pavlof Lake, Alaska

Thirty-two miles from Hoonah via a forest service gravel road was a small lake in a secluded valley. It was called Pavlof Lake, and the river that ran only a quarter of a mile from the lake to the western shore of Freshwater Bay was known as the Pavlof River.

In the early 1900s, a marginally profitable salmon cannery had operated at the mouth of the river owned by AAPCO, the Astoria & Alaska Packing Company. Now, the only remaining evidence of the AAPCO fish-processing facility was a diversion dam near the mouth of the river. The plant had closed after several seasons of disastrous salmon returns, and AAPCO sold the property to another cannery that operated just thirty miles to the north at Excursion Inlet. When Global Resorts International acquired the property at Excursion Inlet, the AAPCO property was included.

Shortly after arriving in Alaska, Raul bin Rahman became aware that his company owned this piece of land on Pavlof Lake. He decided to investigate and discovered a beautiful, pristine lake and stream. So as part of the Glacier World construction project, he built a private retreat for himself and called it Freshwater Lodge. It was a 10,000-square-foot home designed to look like a wilderness lodge, situated on the north shore right where the river drained out of the lake. It was set back from the lake and had a broad expanse of lawn down to a dock with a small motor launch and a floatplane ramp. Rahman could quickly travel by air between the retreat and Glacier World.

Pavlof Lake and its river were located on Chichagof Island, which, like Admiralty Island, was known for a very high concentration of Alaskan brown bears. With its prolific salmon run, the Pavlof River attracted quite a large number of returning salmon. Watching the bears catch and feed on salmon was one of the things that Rahman enjoyed, one of the reasons he had purchased a Kodiak for display at Glacier World. Guests at his lodge loved being entertained by his local bears, and Rahman added to their excitement by putting out bait to ensure the bears would appear. Guests could watch wildlife close up from a hide, a carefully camouflaged structure that viewers could approach without being seen from the forest behind it. There was a second hide farther along the shore of the lake for observing moose, beaver, and aquatic birds.

At this moment, Raul Rahman sat on the wide porch of the lodge with a glass of Dewar's Scotch and a cigar. Fishman sat across from him, cleaning and oiling a Nosler hunting rifle. Rahman wore his 9 mm Glock sidearm.

"How are our newly arrived guests doing?" asked Rahman with a smile. "Are they comfortable in their quarters?"

Fishman laughed. "I'm afraid they are slightly cramped and are going to be a bit hungry and chilled tonight. I've locked them in the pump house."

"That will do fine," said Rahman. "They won't be staying long."

"What's the plan for tomorrow?" asked Fishman.

"We're actually on a fairly tight schedule. A floatplane will fly in to pick us up and take us back to the airstrip at Glacier World. The company's Citation should arrive mid-afternoon, and we will be on our way to Shanghai."

Rahman paused, his thoughts already far away beyond his scheme for revenge. "I rather like Shanghai. It's an amazing feeling being swallowed up amongst millions of people—a perfect place to stay hidden from American eyes. Have you ever been there, Nigel?"

"It's been quite a few years. I assisted one of my employers who was acquiring a West African cocoa plantation and trying to persuade a group of Chinese to invest. Let's say they were glad to participate by the time we left them. I've heard that Shanghai has changed a lot, what with all the high rise construction."

"Yes, GRI owns a one-hundred-story building in the Pudong area."

Fishman checked the scope on the rifle by focusing on a loon that was swimming and feeding along the far shore of the lake. He dry fired the rifle just before it dove once more. Rahman had a fine collection of hunting rifles at the lodge, and Fishman appeared to be quite satisfied with the one he had selected for his assignment. He opened a box of 30 caliber, 180 grain bullets and began pushing several into the rifle's magazine. When he was finished, Fishman mentioned another thing that was on his mind.

"It's really too bad that a couple of people uncovered GRI's side business. That could have been a highly profitable venture. What will GRI do now? And what will happen with Glacier World?"

"GRI will turn the matter over to an international law firm who will keep things tied up for years. The US government will probably try to extradite some of the investors and myself if they have enough evidence. I am officially the manager of Glacier World and can confess no involvement in the business of stealing cargo. As to what happens with the park, it should remain a highly successful venture, although I suspect its ownership will be divested and maybe placed under a shell company."

"Okay, but what about Armstrong?" asked Fishman. "How do you plan to lure him out here?"

"I'll call Armstrong in a little while with an interesting clue as to where he can find his friends. If he doesn't figure it out and show up early tomorrow, I'll call with an easier clue. Making it a game is part of the enjoyment. They'll never find this place tonight. I want him to sweat a little and realize he's up against the clock, so to speak, to get to his friends. Now, that all depends on how soon the bears show up. It will be a matter of how long they can hold out before the bears chew them up a bit. It would be too bad if Armstrong arrives too late."

"So I should get those two down to the river at daylight?" asked Fishman.

"Yes, you'll want to bait the trap and get situated here on the front deck or use the hide down at the bear-viewing site. You know how to find it?"

"I checked it out late this afternoon, but with a rifle I rather prefer being here on the deck," responded Fishman. "The hide is frankly too close for what you have planned."

"Good. This should be rather interesting watching who gets to the bait first—Armstrong or that big brown bear that's been hanging around. Whichever way it goes, we kill Armstrong and the others, then tidy up the scene."

CHAPTER 46

Hoonah, Alaska

The day had been a roller coaster ride of emotions for Earl, with the long wait for Bernie's rescue, then being reunited, and now the disappearance of Pete and Lewis. They were going to need help to find them, and it had to be quick. Pete and Lewis were in big trouble and could be killed. At the harbor, Leon made a reluctant but necessary decision that they split up to keep the two teenagers safe.

"Brooklyn, you are to take Bernie to the café in Lewis's car and leave him with Flo. Then, find any of the community leaders you can and ask them to come to the café in an hour. We are going to need as many people as we can gather to help find Pete and Lewis."

"Okay," answered Brooklyn. She looked worried, glancing furtively at the boats in the harbor. Nothing looked out of the ordinary. There were half a dozen men unloading a fish net onto the dock from one of the larger boats. She could see two other guys cleaning equipment on a crab boat. The *Hoonah Spirit* was not at its slip. Johnny was probably out on a whale-watching trip. "Some of the men on the dock are friends of Pete. Maybe they have seen him or can help in the search. Everyone in town likes Lewis. If Lewis hasn't personally taught them some life skills, he's taught their kids. Ask anyone you see to join us at the café."

"Okay. Earl and I will check the harbor then work our way into town and grab anyone we pass." Earl and Leon piled out of the car and trotted towards the top of the ramp to the boat slips.

"We never asked Brooklyn if she knows how to drive," commented Earl. They heard a scrunching noise and turned to look back at the parking lot. The rear tires of Lewis's car were throwing gravel as Brooklyn stepped too hard on the gas pedal and the car slid sideways, then lurched onto the main road into town. "I guess she can," Earl added.

They chose to speak first to the bunch of guys working on the fish net.

"Anyone seen Pete Hunt or Lewis Teebottom in the last half hour?" asked Leon. "They might have been with some other guys."

Three of the men were standing on the dock and the others were on board the fishing boat. One of the men looked at his buddies. They all shook their heads. "Nope, we haven't noticed them come down here, but we've been pretty busy. The commercial season opens in Frederick Sound day after tomorrow."

"Well, if you do see them, get word to us at the café, okay? These guys may be in some trouble. We need to find them fast."

They got pretty much the same answer from the two men at the crab boat and a live-aboard couple that had an older Grand Banks yacht. Leon and Earl talked to a couple people at the market and several more at the liquor store. No one had seen Pete or Lewis. They asked everyone to spread the word that a search was being organized.

They met Brooklyn and Bernie at the café an hour later. There were several people from the community, including two teenagers who were friends of Brooklyn, and the old woodcarver, Frank. Lewis's elderly grandfather was there, as well as Pete's wife and Melvin George, one of the community leaders. Melvin used a cane and was assisted up the steps of the café by a grandson. The Woodcocks, the live-aboard couple from the harbor, showed up and immediately informed Leon that they were from Sitka but would try to help by checking out different places in Port Frederick.

Leon was disappointed with the turnout and hoped a few more would show up as he laid out the problem for those who were there. "Pete Hunt and Lewis Teebottom have disappeared and could have been taken hostage by some pretty bad people. We do not have any proof other than finding Lewis's abandoned car. It is a serious matter, folks. Pete and Lewis are good men and part of your community. We need help to find out if anyone saw them, saw anything suspicious, or might know where they are. They could get hurt, so it is important that we locate them as quickly as possible. Earl and I are outsiders. We do not know your community or the area around it." Leon looked at Liz, Pete's wife. She had been crying and hugged the baby to her bosom with a wadded handkerchief in one hand.

Melvin took a moment to stand, holding onto his chair. "I want to thank you for your words about two good people who are a part of our community. I heard someone say as I was coming to this place that it won't do no good. They won't find them because the Kushtaka took them. People say that when they are scared. How can we help? We cannot stand in the spirit of sadness and do nothing."

Earl tried to summarize what they knew. "We found Lewis's car abandoned on the road from the airport. One car door was open, but there wasn't any sign of violence or blood. We think they were forced into another vehicle. We were in the taxi not more than five or ten minutes behind them. If Pete and Lewis passed through town, somebody would have to have seen them. Maybe someone driving on the airport road saw something. So we have to keep asking. We're pretty sure they did not come back to the airport, as they would have passed us. We didn't see any other vehicles. So far, no one we talked to saw them leave in a boat, but I guess it's possible."

Leon raised his arms in a sign of frustration. "So, where are they? Is there another road out of this town?"

"There are several roads," said Lewis's grandfather. "One goes up to a mine, and there is a log haul road built by the forest service—could be a hundred miles of road, maybe more."

"Are there any other communities that can be reached by these roads?" asked Leon.

"There's a bunch of houses over on Freshwater Bay. Most of them are summer cabins for people from Juneau who like to come over here and fish, catch crab, and party."

"Good, we'll need to check that area," said Leon. "You said there is a mine outside of Hoonah?"

"Yeah, it's a pretty big operating gold mine. There's a gate with a security guard. Anyone going there has to stop, so that would be pretty easy to check. We can call them."

"Okay, I want to thank you all for coming here," said Leon, standing up and looking at a clock on the wall. "We have some places to check out. The Woodcocks will cruise around the bay tomorrow morning, right?" Mrs. Woodcock nodded in agreement. "Melvin, I would appreciate it if you would call the mine and ask whether Pete and Lewis came through there with anyone. Earl and I will check out the homes over on Freshwater Bay."

As people were leaving, Earl spoke quietly to Leon. "I think we should call Dave Williams and find out if he can put together a search party of Alaska State Troopers."

"That is probably wise," responded Leon as he watched everyone leave. "Let me speak to Liz, and then we can call Dave." Leon caught Liz as she was going out the door. "Liz, I am going to find Pete and bring him home. I mean it. Do not worry."

Liz's face was red from crying, but was now more angry than worried. "I wish you hadn't come here. Pete would have gotten through his brother's death. Now our baby is not going to have a father." Liz didn't wait for any response from Leon. There wasn't anything more she wanted to hear as she stomped down the steps and walked away.

"That didn't go well," said Earl as he overheard the conversation. "We might as well find out how the AST can assist us. A second call about someone getting kidnapped is not going to sit well with him." Earl took a cell phone out of his pocket and called Williams in Juneau. The man answered immediately, and Earl briefed him on what had happened.

"You sure do have a knack for finding trouble," replied Williams. "Damn it, my resources are tapped out assisting the FBI interviewing everyone from the *Predator*." Williams audibly sighed and took a moment to continue. "Okay, let me see what I can do. I'll see if some officers are available from Petersburg or Wrangell. Maybe they can free up three or four men, but it will be at least late morning before they can get to Hoonah."

Earl's frustration was evident in his voice as he continued to plead for help from Williams. "We're convinced Rahman is behind this but don't know where or why he took them. Do you have an officer over at Glacier World? Can he check to see if Rahman is there?"

"I already know he's not there," replied Williams. "I issued a warrant for his arrest maybe two hours ago and have an officer watching for him to show up. I don't think he will. In fact, I wouldn't be surprised if he's already left Alaska in one of GRI's corporate jets."

Earl looked at Leon and said, "He says Rahman's cleared out. They don't know where he is."

"He has got to know his operation is over," said Leon. "He has only got a little bit of time before he has to run. Tell Williams we would welcome any help he can send our way."

Earl relayed the request and thanked Williams. He was having difficulty sorting out what Rahman was doing. "If Rahman has to clear out to avoid arrest, why did he bother to take Pete and Lewis?"

"That question is really bugging me, too," replied Leon. "Rahman is no longer a rational person. So, I am thinking he wants revenge and he wants all of us—not just Lewis and Pete, but you and me."

"So, maybe he wants us to find them?" asked Earl. "That way he can kill all of us? Do you think he might be making a grim game of this—just like one of his Glacier World predators going after its prey?"

"If I am right, he is going to get in touch with us soon. Right now we need something to eat. All we can do is hope to hell he contacts us."

Earl and Leon didn't have to wait long at all. They had joined Brooklyn and Bernie inside the café, and no sooner had they ordered themselves a pizza than a text message appeared on Earl's phone. It read: "Looking for something? Check the deeds..." Earl repeated the message for the others. Like him, they were confused by the words. The first part was pretty clear—they were looking for Pete and Lewis—but what did Rahman mean by check the deeds?

"Did he misspell the last word?" asked Leon. "What does he mean by deeds? It could be a person's actions, but that doesn't make any sense either."

Brooklyn offered her thought. "The word deed is a noun. Another meaning is like a property record. You know, like a document filed with the government? Could that be what he's referring to?" She didn't wait for someone to speak and answered her own questions. "Maybe he's referring to the property records for Glacier World. Rahman knows we're smart. He knows we figured out his whole operation by hacking into computer records. He has given us another thing to research." Brooklyn jumped up and put on her old army jacket. "Come on! We've got to go use the computers at the center. We've got to locate any records for land ownership by GRI."

CHAPTER 47

Juneau, Alaska

With the arrival of the *Predator* and *Nootka* in Juneau, Agent Ray Hanson had a big problem and a little problem—what to do with over sixty people who were most likely felons and who needed to be vetted, fingerprinted, photographed, and held until a hearing could be arranged, and what to tell Jenny Marks from the *Juneau Empire*. The first problem was a resource issue. Between the FBI and Alaska State Troopers, he didn't have enough resources to handle the people the Coast Guard had taken into custody—let alone secure them. So he locked up most of them in the hold of the *Predator* and posted three off-duty police officers with the Juneau Police Department as sentries.

The second problem was what to tell Marks for the story she was certain to write. Jenny had cornered him during the search of Glacier World thanks to Williams telling her he was in charge. At the time, he wanted anyone but himself to take the blame for the fiasco, even if it was Williams's six-year-old daughter, Daisy. The whole thing had the marks of his career going south.

Now that it had flipped around and they had the pirates and their ship in custody, Ray Hanson was walking three feet off the floor. He couldn't believe how fast it had happened. Having to do damage control was over, but he had to carefully couch how much he told her as charges were still being determined. How many FBI agents got to charge people with committing acts of terrorism on the high seas and threats to maritime security? Hanson was going to play that for all he could. He could be famous within the bureau, and it could even result in a commendation from the director in Washington, DC. All he had to do was not make an ass of himself or blow it with this hometown reporter.

Jenny Marks had a deadline and had waited impatiently for twenty minutes while Agent Hanson made assignments for doing interviews and having two of his subordinates research what the hell was needed to charge someone with acts of terrorism on the high seas. Finally, Hanson invited her to take a seat in his office.

Jenny went right for Hanson's throat. "Ray, is this ship called the *Predator* really associated with Glacier World?"

The question caught him off guard. He hadn't looked into that yet. "Yes. Ah...we believe so."

"Well, I did some quick online research, and the ship's ownership and registry is fuzzy. The Coast Guard says the owner of the vessel is GRI, but on the Internet I discovered that the ship is really owned by a Bahamian company which is a subsidiary of a subsidiary of Global Resorts International, which is just a holding company."

"Ah, we...ah…are looking into the ownership of the vessel," admitted Hanson. "According to the captain, who has been only briefly interrogated at this point, he took orders from Raul bin Rahman, the manager of Glacier World. So there appears to be a relationship between the ship and GRI. At the moment, we have not spoken to Mr. Rahman about the ship or the alleged crimes. He apparently left for a business trip to California. You might speak to Lieutenant Dave Williams about his whereabouts. AST has issued a warrant for his arrest, I've been told."

"What about the three deaths that have occurred in the last several months at Glacier World?" Jenny asked. "Are they in any way connected with stealing cargo in the Gulf of Alaska using the *Predator*?"

"Three deaths? Ah...we thought there were two such incidences. There must—"

Jenny came right back pressing her question. "It's three if you include a contractor that was killed by wolves. I wrote about that several weeks ago. But what about the deaths of Hunt and Jackson?"

"We will be looking into those," replied Hanson. "I believe the AST will be reopening their investigations."

"If the deaths of these two men were a result of Glacier World wanting to maintain a high level of secrecy, that would appear to indicate they lobbied the state legislature under false pretenses by saying they needed an exclusive buffer zone just for the theme park operations. What do you—"

Hanson raised a hand and interrupted her. "Jenny, that's an interesting thought, but we are just beginning our investigation. I'd suggest that you ask Senator MacDonald about that. He certainly had a lot of influence with Glacier World being granted that right. Now, if you will excuse me, I have a lot to do and it has been a really long day."

***

Even before the arrival of the two ships in Juneau, Senator William MacDonald had heard the reports about the Coast Guard capturing the *Predator*. A rumor was being passed around on the marine radio by several fishing boats that it had apparently slipped out of Glacier World unnoticed with a bunch of containers filled with contraband. Radio silence had ceased, as the Coast Guard wanted clear passage for both ships all the way into port. Several cruise ships were requested to sail from Juneau earlier than planned. One of MacDonald's friends, who was fishing, heard the reports and called him.

MacDonald panicked. There were matters of his association with GRI that had to be considered.

Campaign contributions from Rahman and GRI would have to be returned even if it would be a big hit to his campaign fund. There would need to be a news release to lessen his involvement in legislation supporting Glacier World's development.

He called his campaign manager and then his banker, and was about to call one of his poker buddies, Tony Walsh, who was the editor of the *Juneau Empire*, when Jenny Marks called him first.

Mac tried to be courteous even though he was sweating so bad he had to wipe his forehead with a towel from the portable bar in his study. "Good evening, Jenny, to what do I owe hearing your sweet voice?"

"Stow it, Mac," said Jenny. "I will assume you have already heard about this ship the *Predator*. What it has been doing makes your friend Rahman a criminal of the highest order. I've got the lead story for tomorrow's special edition drafted. I just need to clarify a few things about your relationship with GRI."

"Jenny, I—" Mac tried to get a word in, but she continued.

"I have a copy of a bill of sale for a Beneteau 35 purchased by GRI from a dealer in Seattle. You have one, or should I say, *had* a Beneteau 35. What is strange is that according to the dealer's documentation and the Coast Guard's, both boats have the same hull serial numbers. Do you have anything to say about that?"

"I...ah...I bought the boat from Rahman. Apparently he couldn't find the time to sail and knew I was looking for one. I—"

"And would you care to comment on their campaign contributions for your re-election bid?" asked Jenny. "According to your last published report, they amounted to $75,000."

"Oh, we will certainly have to see that they are returned. I wouldn't want my supporters to think I accept campaign money from anyone who might be the slightest dishonest."

"Of course," replied Jenny. "Honesty is one of the foundations of political office, along with faith, charity, and integrity. You know what I mean? Have a pleasant evening, senator."

CHAPTER 48

Hoonah, Alaska

Brooklyn's suggestion that the property deed for Glacier World would reveal how to find Pete and Lewis sounded pretty good to the others, and they hustled after her up the street to the community center. It was dark and the door was locked.

"Wait here," said Brooklyn as she leapt off the covered porch and ran on up the street. "I'm going to find Melvin and get a key." She was back inside of ten minutes and was breathing hard as she inserted the key and pulled the door open. She switched on a bunch of lights and led them into Lewis's office. Most of the computers were already powered on.

"Earl, you work on that computer over there," said Brooklyn, pointing to a workstation to his left. She rolled Lewis's desk chair up to a double monitor workstation. "The password is Snowbird21. It works on all of them. You load Google Maps, and I'll find the Juneau district tax maps and deed records."

Bernie had traipsed along, and he and Leon watched as his dad and Brooklyn worked at the two computers. He was impressed by Brooklyn having discovered a possible lead and knowing how to use it. Leon wasn't all that familiar with computers, so he waited patiently for the two to come up with something—anything—that would lead them to Lewis and Pete. Meanwhile, he turned his thoughts to what they should do if and when they found the location.

"Okay, I've found the deed," exclaimed Brooklyn. "It's pretty long. I'm going to skim through it and see if there are any parcel maps." The document was over thirty pages and contained legal descriptions and a past history of owners, all of which were corporations. Near the end of the document she found a keyed map showing the property boundaries. There were eight or ten tax lots in all that were contiguous along the eastern shoreline of Excursion Inlet. They actually went up to the national park boundary on the north end. There was a small-scale location map in a lower corner, which showed some isolated parcels. She zoomed in on the map to see where these were. One was located on Pleasant Island just outside the inlet towards Glacier Bay. Another was a small parcel on Funter Bay across Chatham Strait to the east, and a third was on the west side of the strait near Freshwater Bay. The latter parcel caught her interest.

"Hey, guys, I think I found something that might be a possibility," she shouted. "Earl, find Freshwater Bay on the aerial-photo maps. Leon, come look at this. The document indicates that there are several isolated parcels that are part of the property acquired by Global Resorts International. Not all of the land holdings are in Excursion Inlet. I've got to read the legal mumbo jumbo to see if there is something more than this little map. Leon, can you help me?"

Leon stared at the monitor over Brooklyn's shoulder as she tried to find out more about Parcel 4, as the Freshwater Bay parcel was identified on the map. She found it under a heading labeled "Description of Parcels."

"This looks good," said Brooklyn. "Parcel 4 was originally owned by a company called AAPCO that operated a salmon cannery at Pavlof Harbor. It consists of eighty acres and includes a lake and tributary from the lake to Pavlof Harbor including rights to divert waters for the purposes of generation of electricity. Access rights include a right-of-way easement across federal lands to Forest Service Road C32 and the community of Hoonah.

"Hmm, it has road access," said Leon as he also read the description. "Maybe this property can be accessed from Hoonah. We need to look at the aerials." He and Brooklyn went over to stand by Earl.

Earl had found Freshwater Bay on the east side of Chichagof Island and zoomed in on Pavlof Harbor. "Here it is," he exclaimed. "There's a lake and a river down to the bay just like you said. And a road network all the way back to Hoonah."

Leon ignored the roads. He was focusing on what looked like a structure at the southeast corner of the lake. "Zoom in to the maximum scale, Earl. I want to see the buildings on the lake."

The aerial map had excellent detail when enlarged, and they could see a large building facing the lake with a dock. There was an access road coming down from a road marked on the photo as Forest Service Road 32C. Leon grinned as he said, "We know where they are. Now, we have to figure out how Earl and I can get them out of there."

"Whoa! You're not leaving me here," said Brooklyn. "I'm going with you. Besides, you'll never find the place without me showing you the roads. I've been to the lake before, but not since that lodge was built."

"What would your mom say? I have to ask Flo if..."

"You can't leave me. I'm going with you guys," Brooklyn insisted.

"Alright," answered Leon. "But on one condition—you stay with the vehicle."

Brooklyn reluctantly nodded as she added, "Ah...one more thing that you should be aware of—the Pavlof River is serious bear habitat."

"Let's hope that we won't have to deal with any bears," replied Earl. "It's early in the season, so maybe there won't be any salmon to draw them to the river."

"I am more worried about Rahman and whoever else he has at this lodge," said Leon. "He had to have help to snatch Pete and Lewis. So, we need to acknowledge the hard fact that he is trying to set us up to be killed. This is a serious rescue. Bernie stays here in Hoonah. Brooklyn can guide us as long as she remains with the vehicle. We meet at the café at 5:00 a.m. and grab a quick bite to eat before we leave. Earl, you and Bernie head back to the B&B. I will be along shortly, but for the moment I want to study the aerial photo and figure out if we can get close to Rahman's place without being seen."

When everyone left, Leon sat and studied the digital photomap. He adjusted the angle slightly and had a better view of the topography. The forest service road was on higher ground, possibly a ridge, north of the lake. Just to the east of the access drive, which took several turns as it dropped down to the lodge, there was a wide strip of cleared land. If this was an old logging road, he was pretty sure it was an area once used as a landing or storage for logs before loading them onto trucks. The spot was perfect for a staging point and might even offer a view of the areas around the lodge.

The slope below the road was thick with secondary-growth timber. He could make his way down to the lodge through the timber without being seen, but it could be tough if there was undergrowth. This was rainforest country, and undergrowth brush was likely. The timber extended right down to the river below the lodge, but the area around the lodge and its outbuildings appeared to be cleared. The river looked to be pretty wide, but there were riffles and rapids showing on the photo, so it probably could be crossed.

Leon wondered if there were any pictures of the lodge, and used Lewis's computer to Google the phrase Pavlof Lake Lodge. By luck, he found a couple of pictures that someone had taken on a hike up from the bay, referring to it in a photo caption as a beautiful lodge in the Alaskan wilderness. He examined the buildings carefully. There was a small house with a driveway on the north side, which he figured was the living quarters for whoever took care of the place when Rahman wasn't present. Just behind the lodge was a long building perpendicular to the main building, which probably was a garage, and maybe an equipment storage building. There was a smaller building next to it, with a boardwalk to the main lodge. He wondered if it was a separate guest cabin. Behind was a very small building, which he assumed was a well and pump house.

The main lodge had two decks. Facing the lake was a covered porch that ran the full length of the main part of the lodge. On the south end was an upper deck off of the second floor rooms. The upper deck also had an outside stairway, probably serving as a fire escape. Two areas further from the lodge, one near the river and one on a point north of the lodge, interested him. He compared the photos to the aerial.

They looked like camouflaged structures as he adjusted the vertical and perspective angles of the photo. Then his military mind figured out what they were—hides to observe wildlife. Studying the lawn and edge of the forest, he noticed there was a trail leading to each place. Leon stared at the photo for another fifteen minutes until he had memorized every detail. He considered using one or both of the observation points to determine how to approach the lodge. From there, it would be pure luck to avoid being shot. Once again, Leon might be leading his friends to their deaths.

***

The pump house at Freshwater Lodge was insulated against freezing and provided some degree of comfort to Pete and Lewis, who were tied up and confined in the small building. They were not given any food or water. Minimal floor space created cramped conditions when they tried to lie down, and it was actually more bearable if they sat because of the cold concrete floor.

Pete was accustomed to uncomfortable positions, having spent long days fishing in a small boat, but Lewis's bulk from spending every day in a soft office chair led to him constantly shifting his body around. As a result, Lewis slept almost not at all, while Pete did—although Lewis moving around frequently wakened him. They chatted some after being left alone, but then both men drew themselves inward. Pete worried about his wife and their new baby. Lewis worried about whether he would live to see another sunset. Both seemed rather improbable given how their captors had treated them.

Lewis shifted his position on the concrete again for the umpteenth time. "You awake?" he asked Pete.

"Yeah, my cold butt keeps waking me up," answered Pete. "Sorry for getting you into this mess."

"No more than me wanting you to be involved. We all recognized that what we did was pretty risky. At least we succeeded."

"Well, we can't give up hoping someone will find us," said Pete. "They kept us alive for a reason. The longer we live, the better chance we have of being found."

"Yeah, but not giving us any food or water, that sounds like whatever is going to happen is going to be real soon. Can you see my wristwatch? What time is it anyway?" Lewis twisted his body for Pete to see the watch face.

"Looks like a little after 4:00 a.m. It should be light in another hour."

What seemed to be only minutes later, they heard someone lift the padlock, rattle it, and then swing the door open. It was Fishman.

"It's going to be an interesting day for you two. Sorry to say, I didn't bring coffee or breakfast."

He undid the bicycle lock that had restrained them to a water pipe along the floor of the small room.

"Get up! You're getting a chance to stretch your legs while we take a short walk."

Pete and Lewis struggled to rise and had to help each other. Their hands were still tied, and they were also tied together. Fishman took a steel band off a hook on the wall and fastened it around Pete's waist, then took another one and put it around Lewis. They were puzzled as to the purpose of the bands as they stumbled outside and looked around. They could see the lodge with some lights on, a grass lawn extending down to a lake where morning mist rose off the water.

Fishman motioned with the barrel tip of his rifle. "That way—down towards the river."

Pete and Lewis shuffled across the lawn and down onto a spit of gravel that stretched into the river where it left the lake. A huge log, maybe thirty or forty feet long and three feet high, extended out into the river. Fishman picked up a piece of steel chain that went through a huge eyebolt on the log and threaded it through a small eye that protruded from the steel band around each of their waists. Then he pulled the ends of the chain together and snapped a padlock on them.

Lewis finally spoke. "Why are you doing this? What do you expect us to do?"

"Why, nothing of course," replied Fishman. "You two are the cheese." He turned and walked back toward the lodge, leaving the two of them to ponder his response.

Lewis looked around, totally unsure what they could do. Pete yanked on the chain. The eyebolt was unaffected. Lewis looked down the river and out at the lake.

"What do you suppose the guy meant with the cheese remark?" asked Pete.

Lewis ignored his question. "Hey, I know where we are. Do you recognize this place?"

"What?" asked Pete. "I—"

"This is the Pavlof River. My dad and my uncle brought me here as a kid to fish for trout. It's only a quarter of a mile down the river to the bay. If we can get loose, we might be able to get away that way."

"Not likely," replied Pete, having finished examining where the chain around their waists was secured to the log. "Without a bolt cutter or something, we're not going to get free." The two of them pulled on the chains together. The eyebolt in the log held fast.

Lewis shook his head and slumped down. He looked longingly at the river. The chain was not even long enough for them to satisfy their thirst.

They were not entirely alone on the bank of the river. A flash of something moving along the streambank not far from them caught Lewis's attention. He saw it move again. Something had dove into the water. It was an otter. Another memory of his childhood fishing trips to the river came to him. He remembered seeing an otter den. Lewis never admitted it to anyone, but otters scared him just as much as bears. He used to have nightmares about stories of otters and the place where they came from—the Bay of Death.

CHAPTER 49

Hoonah, Alaska

It was still dark when Earl left Bernie sleeping at the B&B and joined Leon at the café for a quick breakfast. Brooklyn avoided the café, as she didn't want her mom to be aware that she was going along, so she met them next to Lewis's car. Earl was designated as the driver, with Brooklyn navigating. It took them almost an hour to reach the point on the forest service road where there was a turnoff to the sparsely developed subdivision at Freshwater Bay. They ignored the area and turned south towards Pavlof Harbor. Just before the access road to the lodge, Leon spotted the old log storage area he had seen on the aerial photo.

"Pull over into the cleared area up ahead on your left," said Leon. "We're going to leave the car there and go the rest of the way on foot."

Earl pulled off the road onto a graveled area littered with tree bark. He turned off the engine and waited for Leon to tell him what to do next. Leon rolled down his window and listened. It was quiet except for the tick of the hot engine and a faint chuckle of a raven somewhere deep in the timber below the road. Leon looked at the forest beside the road. It was dense and there were deep shadows. The sky was overcast with low clouds. Maybe without bright sunlight it would be a little harder for them to be detected in the forest when they got close to the lodge.

"From here on," said Leon, "we talk in whispers or use hand signals, Earl. When you get out, shut the car doors as quietly as possible." Leon looked at Brooklyn with a very serious face. "As I said last night—you *remain* with the *car*. That is important, because if this goes wrong, you have to drive back to Hoonah to get the Alaska State Troopers. They should be there later today. Besides, I am already in enough trouble with Flo for allowing you to be part of the crazy operation." Brooklyn smiled, but nodded in agreement. Leon thought he recognized in her eyes a willingness to actually do what he asked.

Leon and Earl got out of the car and walked a couple hundred feet or so farther up the road, just beyond a gated driveway to the lodge. Leon figured from there they could cut through the timber, avoid the caretaker's house, and reach the bird watcher's hide on the edge of the lake. He wanted to use the higher elevation hide to get a closer look. From the road, they could see the roof of the main building and part of the lake, but the caretaker's house wasn't visible. Leon checked the old military .45 caliber semi-automatic pistol that Lewis's grandfather had brought to him late last night and stuck it in his belt behind his back. Earl did not have a weapon. His job would be to free Pete and Lewis and get them back to the car. Leon would go after Rahman and whoever was with him. They waited another couple of minutes, staring down through the timber. The echoing trill of a loon and an answer from its mate broke the silence farther down the lake.

"Do you think they know we're coming?" whispered Earl.

"They are planning on it. Do they know we are already here? I hope not," Leon whispered back as he slid down the bank.

Earl followed right behind, and seconds later they were in the brush. It was about three hundred yards to the shore of the lake—one of the most difficult bushwhacking hikes Earl had ever done. The woods in Southeast Alaska seemed to resist his presence. Cedar branches slapped him in the face. Moss-covered tree roots tried to trip him. At one point he grabbed the stem of a devil's club plant, and his hand came away with spines stuck in his palm. He winced as he tried to scrape them away while following Leon, who took his time and moved cautiously.

The ground was soft and damp, which made it easier to be quiet, but it still took them thirty minutes to cover the three hundred yards. They found the trail to the observation hut first. Leon checked for fresh tracks and was satisfied no one had been out the trail recently.

The observation hut was made of wood and covered in branches. It was intended to be a hide, a place where people could observe wildlife up close without scaring it. The view from the hide was excellent. Unfortunately, what they saw was worse than anything Leon and Earl could have imagined. They were able to see the front of the lodge and its broad front porch where two men stood at the far end, talking in low voices. One of them was Rahman. Leon did not know the other man's name but remembered him as Rahman's head of security. He was a big man—taller than Leon.

Earl recognized the man from the plane trip to Glacier World. "The guy with the rifle is Fishman," he whispered to Leon.

The two men were looking across the open area of lawn down towards the river. Where the river flowed out of the lake there was a gravel bar. A large log extended from the cut bank across the open area and into the river. Pete and Lewis were sitting on the log in full view with their backs to Leon and Earl, as well as to the men on the porch.

"Why are Pete and Lewis just sitting on top of that log?" whispered Earl, puzzled by the strange scene in front of them. Farther down the river where it flowed through the trees, Earl saw some movement. A brown bear was foraging in the grass along the far bank.

"There's a bear farther down river. See it?" he whispered.

"Yeah, I see it," replied Leon, who had been studying Pete and Lewis. "Take a closer look at the guys."

While they watched, Lewis tried to move slightly on the log. He seemed restless but did not get up and leave.

"Lewis just saw the bear," whispered Leon. "I think I can see a chain securing them to the log. They are stuck there." Leon turned his attention to the two men on the porch. "The guy with the rifle, Fishman, has no intention of protecting them from the bear."

"How are we going to approach Pete and Lewis?" asked Earl. "He can pick us off if we try to get to them. What do we do now?"

"There is another hide on the river just below the point where they are sitting. We work our way around through the forest to that point and figure out what to do." Before leaving the hide, Leon took a moment to see what the bear was up to. It had disappeared from view.

They took the trail back towards the lodge until they were close to the caretaker's house, then they detoured around it through the woods, crossed the driveway, and then moved around to the other outbuilding. Leon tried the door and discovered it was unlocked. Holding his pistol at the ready, he stepped inside and looked around. It appeared to be an equipment and storage room containing a riding lawn mower, garden tools, and a workbench. On a wall above the workbench, he noticed a hack saw, took it down, and handed it to Earl. They checked outside and then headed for the trees, using the building to screen themselves from the main house. It took them another fifteen minutes to reach the second hide. At this point, they were maybe fifty feet from the log where Pete and Lewis still sat and a hundred yards from the lodge. They could not see directly to the front of the lodge, but that also meant Rahman and Fishman probably could not see them.

Earl nudged Leon and pointed downriver. The bear had reappeared and was much closer. Leon looked at Pete and Lewis. They were watching the bear. It was going to be a problem if the bear kept moving up the riverbank. It lifted its head and sniffed the air. Leon glanced up at the trees across from the hide. From the movement of the branches, the breeze was upriver. As long as Pete and Lewis didn't make any quick moves, the bear might not see them.

"Earl, you are going to have to free them. You should be able to slide down to the riverbank in front of us and crawl real slow right up to the log. The bank is high enough that you should not be seen from the lodge. Do you think you can do that?"

"Yeah, shouldn't be too difficult. Can you distract the guys up at the house while I try to get the chain off them? I'll be exposed."

"I will take care of them. Just be ready."

"Okay, but don't take too long. I'm going to be exposed to the bear as well," said Earl. "How will I know when to leave the hide?"

"You will know," answered Leon as he backed out of the hide and started walking back into the forest, hunched over. The path back to the lodge kept well back in the trees and brush. When he got to the edge of the open area, he peeked out. He could see the end of the lodge and the upper deck but not the front porch. The guest cabin and outbuilding were off to his right. He decided to stay out of sight and work his way around the cabin to the end of the outbuilding.

Using the building for cover, he crept along the end to where he could see a black Suburban parked in the driveway in front of one of the garage doors. He looked in the driver's-side window and noticed Fishman's security equipment belt lying on the seat. One of the items was a net gun. Leon quietly opened the door and grabbed it.

***

Earl watched as the bear moved slowly to another swath of grass and took several bites. The bear was a big one. It still had not seen or smelled Pete and Lewis. He looked back at the two men, and from their slight movements could tell they were nervous. If the bear saw them and charged, they were essentially helpless with no chance of evading it. Earl could not believe the cruelty of what Rahman had planned. It would have been better to just shoot them. Instead, he was intending to have a bear kill them.

Earl was watching Pete and Lewis when suddenly Lewis moved. He must have gotten scared. He stood up on the log. It attracted the bear's attention, and it stood upright on its hind legs, sniffing the breeze and staring in the direction of the log. Something clicked in Earl's mind—the bear has been the subject of this cruel game before.

There had not been any signal from Leon, and Earl was getting very uneasy about the situation. He looked at the bear, then back at Pete and Lewis. Signal or no signal, there was no more time left before the scene he had pictured would play out and end in a horrible death for one or both of his friends.

Earl picked up the hacksaw, backed out of the hide, crawled around the side of the structure, and then slid down the bank and into the stream. He kept his head down and began crawling along the edge of the river. Earl was now in plain view of both his friends and the bear. Pete, who was still sitting on the log, glanced up at the lodge. Fishman sat with his rifle resting in the railing, using the scope to look directly at him. Pete made an obscene gesture and hunkered down pulling Lewis down with him. They were out of sight of Fishman but now were fully exposed to the bear.

"Sure glad you found us," said Pete as Earl reached them. "But you just put yourself in the same fix as us."

"Where's Leon?" asked Lewis. He kept staring downriver at the bear.

"He's around," replied Earl. "Don't look for him. He's got a job to do, too."

"We've got a problem, Earl," said Pete. "Fishman chained us to this log. He intends for a bear, like that one down there, to kill us."

"We know. I came prepared for that," answered Earl as he held up the hack saw.

Pete shook his head and tried to smile. "It might work if we had the time, but I think this chain is made of hardened steel."

Earl looked up to where the chain was fastened to the log and then at the steel belts fastened around the waists of Pete and Lewis. "Then we need to work together to get you guys loose by tackling it from both ends," replied Earl. "Turn around and hold your hands out." Earl quickly cut the ropes and then handed the hack saw to Pete. "Cut Lewis's hands loose, then see if you can saw the belts rather than the chain. I'm going to try to work loose the eyebolt holding the chain to the log. That might be quicker."

"It's on the top of the log, Earl, and Fishman's got a rifle trained on our location. You expose yourself and he'll shoot you."

"I've got to try," said Earl. "Start sawing on a belt. And Lewis, keep an eye on the bear. You start yelling if it decides one of us might make a good breakfast."

"You can sure count on that," answered Lewis.

Earl hunted around on the riverbank for a rock that would make a suitable hammer, found one, then reached on top of the log and took a big whack at the eyebolt. A bullet buried itself in the log inches from his elbow. The rifle shot reverberated off the forest across the lake. He quickly took another swipe at the eyebolt before the shooter could chamber another cartridge. Earl took a peek at the eyebolt. It was leaning over. He would have to hit it again in the other direction to work it loose, which meant the shooter would be expecting it and have time to fire at him again.

Lewis continued to keep his eyes on what the bear was doing. Both he and the bear flinched at the sound of the rifle fire, but the bear didn't turn and run. Instead it stood on its hind legs again, then dropped down and started walking at a faster pace directly towards where the three men huddled against the log.

"Guys, better speed it up," said Lewis. "I think it's going to charge us."

Earl got an idea. He slipped one arm out of his jacket, stuck a piece of wood in it, and raised it up over the top of the log. There was another shot immediately, and the bullet tore through the sleeve. He reached over and whacked at the eyebolt again, then quickly tried to pull it loose. It wouldn't pull out.

***

At the car up on the road, the sound of the three rifle
shots was too much for Brooklyn. She started running
as fast as she could, climbed over the gate, and ran
down the road down towards the lodge. Reaching the
parking area, she hesitated. Then she heard Lewis
shouting from somewhere to the left. She ran around
the outbuilding and stopped to see where he was. She
heard two people yelling this time.

"Yaw! Yaw!" Pete and Lewis were hollering as
loud as they could. To Brooklyn, who had been on
Alaskan rivers and trails many times, it meant one
thing—they were trying to scare away a bear. The
shouting seemed to come from down by the
riverbank. Farther down the river, she saw the bear
start to charge. Then just as suddenly it stopped and
stood on its hind legs, looking up river. It was a bluff
but another charge bringing it closer was highly likely.

Brooklyn remembered an old tactic to bluff a
brown bear. Leaning against the outbuilding was a
canoe. She tipped it over and saw two paddles inside,
which she grabbed and began running straight across
the lawn to the riverbank.

***

Fishman cursed, realizing he had been fooled by an
empty jacket sleeve. Whoever was there tried one
more time to free the chain. He ejected the spent

cartridge from the rifle, chambered another one, and watched for another sign of movement. Through his scope, he could see the bear drop, charge a short distance, and then stop to look. Either Armstrong or his friend must be there just out of sight. All he had to do was keep them pinned down until the bear decided to move in. Fishman glanced back at the porch, looking for Rahman. His boss had disappeared. Fishman didn't care whether the man observed what was about to happen, and chuckled at the thought.

Another movement caught his attention, and he looked away from the scope for a second. Someone was running across the grass straight towards the others. He swung the rifle in the direction of the running figure and followed it with the scope. He was about to pull the trigger when he heard a noise over his head. He started to look up and was slammed to the porch deck by a person hurtling off the balcony.

The rifle toppled over the railing. Fishman lost his vision for a few seconds from a blow to his head as Leon swung the stock of the net gun at him. Sensing where the person was, Fishman rolled quickly to his right and leapt into a crouched position, simultaneously drawing a knife from a sheath on his belt.

Leon ignored the pain that surged through his right foot after landing on Fishman and slamming into the deck himself. He spun around in a full circle and kicked out with the injured foot, landing a blow on Fishman's knife hand. The knife spun away and slid off the deck. Leon followed through on the kick with two punches to Fishman's stomach and face. The man fell back against the rail and tried to recoil against his attacker with a punch of his own. Leon dodged and hit Fishman two more times in the face.

Blood spewed from Fishman's nose, adding to the flow from the cut over his right eye caused by the first blow. Fishman wiped away the blood with his right sleeve and launched himself at Leon. The two hit the porch rail, which gave way, and they tumbled onto the lawn. Fishman saw his knife and got a hand on it, rolled to his left and tried to stick Leon in the side. Leon rolled the other direction and went for the pistol he had tucked into his belt. It was gone— dropped when he jumped off the upper deck. Fishman's rifle lay next to him. He grabbed it by the barrel and swung it in an arc, hitting Fishman above his left ear. The man collapsed.

Leon looked at the lodge for any sign of Rahman, then picked up the knife and threw it and the rifle across the yard. He limped up the steps to the porch and saw his pistol and the net gun lying near the broken rail. He grabbed both of them and slipped carefully through the front door of the lodge—quickly checking the huge great room. The room was empty.

He had started going from room to room looking for Rahman when he heard a door slam shut at the end of a long hallway to his left. He headed in that direction, using furniture and doorways for partial cover. At the last door he paused, then kicked it open. Leon went down on one knee and slid to his right with the pistol ready. The room was Rahman's office, standing empty with a door to the porch open. Outside, he heard a plane cut its engine and glide in over the lake for landing. Looking out the open door, he saw Rahman standing on the dock next to the ramp, waiting for the floatplane to land. The pilot reduced the speed of the single-engine plane as the floats touched the surface of the lake. The plane made a quick turn and headed for the ramp, where the pilot climbed down onto a pontoon. While Rahman got aboard, the pilot turned the plane around, then climbed back in and revved the engine. They began to move away from the dock into the center of the lake.

Leon noticed Rahman had a launch tied to the dock and decided there was a chance to stop the plane from taking off. He hobbled across the porch to the main stairs and down to the path to the dock. The plane was now taxiing down the middle of the lake where it would have to turn and come back into the wind to clear the trees. Leon leapt into the boat, tossing the pistol and the net gun on the dash. He pressed the electric start for the outboard motor and heard the motor start. Untying the dock line, he threw the throttle forward, almost falling backward over a seat as the boat surged away from the dock. He grabbed the wheel and swung the boat in the direction of the plane. It had already turned, revved its engine, and was roaring back towards him. Four hundred feet away, the plane's floats lifted off the water, and it was airborne and climbing. Leon fired several rounds with the pistol before realizing he wasn't going to be effective in stopping the plane. He grabbed the net gun, held it with both hands, aimed just above the nose of the plane, and pulled the trigger mechanism.

The pilot of the floatplane was surprised to see something hurtling into the air in front of him. In an instant, the propeller was wrapped in nylon mesh. The net was torn to shreds, but the lead weights on the corners did their damage. The pilot threw up his arms as two of the lead weights smashed through the windshield in front of him and hit him in the face. Rahman ducked, but hit the throttle control and put the engine into a stall. The plane careened over the launch, losing altitude as it headed for the trees along the river.

Leon turned to watch the plane swoop over the log at the mouth of the river, crash into the trees, and then erupt into flames.

***

Brooklyn did not bother to look at the lodge and heard the commotion behind her as she ran. Her focus was on the bear and getting to the guys before it did. Reaching the river, she leapt down the bank and thrust the canoe paddles into Earl's hands. Pete was still busy with the hacksaw, and Lewis was now free of the metal belt around his waist. Pete was cutting furiously and had nearly freed himself.

Taking off her army jacket, Brooklyn held it up facing Earl and yelled at him, "Stick the paddles up the sleeves!"

Earl had a questioning look but did what she said. The paddles extended well into each arm of the jacket, making it look like a big green scarecrow. Earl and the others looked up as they heard a loud growl from the bear. It dropped onto its huge paws and charged them again.

Brooklyn spoke as calmly as she could. "Now we hold the paddles high over our heads and everyone growl together. We're going to make like a bigger bear." Together she and Earl raised the paddles above their heads and shook them. The huddled mass of four people took on the appearance of a ten-foot tall creature shaking and screaming.

The bear stopped its charge no more than twenty feet away, lifted its head to sniff the air, then turned to its left and splashed across the river at a run, disappearing into the woods. Earl dropped his paddle and hugged Brooklyn, then Pete and Lewis. They did a little dance as they laughed and yelled with their arms wrapped around each other.

The sound of the floatplane taking off interrupted them, and they turned to stare up the lake. It was a strange sight, with the plane coming directly at them and Leon in the launch running directly at the plane. They saw the plane lift up over Leon and seem to hang in the air for a few seconds before starting to glide right at them. They threw themselves down behind the log as the sputtering plane flew less than fifty feet over their heads and crashed into the trees beside the river.

CHAPTER 50

Pavlof Lake, Alaska

After freeing Pete and Lewis, Earl and Brooklyn got them up to the main lodge. Brooklyn used the kitchen to prepare a meal using Rahman's amply stocked refrigerator and start a pot of coffee. Both the food and the coffee got everyone feeling a lot better.

Two hours after Earl made another call to Dave Williams, four AST officers arrived at the lodge. They taped off the front porch and lawn around Fishman's body and the plane crash site, which was still burning. There wasn't anything that could be done except let it burn out. It would be a while before the remains of Rahman and the pilot could be reached.

Williams informed Earl that he planned to take over the investigation and would use a state floatplane to fly directly to Pavlof Lake. He would leave Juneau as soon as he could hand off all the *Predator* paperwork that still needed to be completed.

Leon Pence had a few bruises and a sprained ankle, for which they found some bandages. There were some painkiller pills, which helped, but what satisfied him the most was just sitting on the deck, taking in the view of the lake. Earl joined him, carrying his third cup of coffee, leaving Pete and Lewis in the kitchen with Brooklyn. They were making calls to their families in Hoonah. Earl knew he needed to reach Bernie and call Sally at home, but first he needed to thank Leon.

"I sure hope this thing is over," said Earl as he dropped into a chair next to Leon.

"It is over. Rahman is dead. He wanted his revenge. It is too bad others had to die as well."

"What about GRI? Do you think they might try to get to us?"

"With the evidence FBI Agent Hanson and Dave Williams are pulling together, GRI will turn everything over to their lawyers. Who knows, they might even avoid prosecution."

"Piracy on the high seas is a pretty serious crime. It will be interesting to see where this all leads." Earl smiled to himself. "Hey, we might even get a trip to Belgium or somewhere to testify in an international trial someday."

"Yeah, like ten years from now at the speed those international tribunals work, or whatever they use to try people," replied Leon.

"You heading home now that you've done everything you can about the death of Eddie Jackson?" asked Earl.

"Maybe not just yet," said Leon. "With all that has been happening, I missed attending Eddie's memorial service back in La Push. So paying my respects can wait a bit longer. When I was in a sweat lodge with Frank, he told me I have to have closure, and honoring Eddie would be a good thing. You know what?"

"What?" responded Earl with a very confused look on his face.

"Frank is carving a totem for me to take home. Eddie is going to get his totem."

"That's great, Leon."

"So I get to hang around a while until he is finished." Leon was silent for a minute. "This is beautiful country. I might just charter a boat and explore it a bit. Do some fishing."

"I haven't had much time to think about Alaska myself, but Bernie sure has. He told Sally that he wants to attend a robotics competition in Juneau that Brooklyn and some other kids are entering. Like you just said, it might be fun to enjoy a few days up here before going back to work. Maybe Sally and Christine could fly up to Juneau and join Bernie and me."

"Nice plan—you should think about it," replied Leon as he watched two loons slowly swim along the shore of the lake. It was a peaceful scene, seeing the pair together living in a small paradise.

EPILOGUE

Juneau, Alaska

Sixteen high school teams from all over Alaska arrived in Juneau for the state MATE competition. The event was being held in the swimming pool and gymnasium of the Juneau-Douglas High School. Most of teams had to fly into Juneau. Several local teams, like the Hoonah Braves, arrived using the state ferry system. A few of the teams had competed the year before when the ranger class ROV competition was held in Anchorage. The South Anchorage High School team had won and gone on to compete in the nationals in Columbus, Ohio, where they placed tenth. Eight of the teams were newbies that had never competed before.

Bernie Armstrong arrived early with his mom and sister. They found seats in the stands around the edge of the floor, and Bernie wandered around the gymnasium where sixteen teams were setting up their ROVs and equipment. He found the Hoonah team near the middle of the floor and hurried over to say hello. Brooklyn had been officially made part of their six-person team when their software specialist came down with the flu. She was wearing a maroon T-shirt, and the usual red and orange streaks in her hair were now maroon.

"Hey, Brooklyn," said Bernie as he squeezed through the throng of people and came up to their table. "When's your presentation? Is everyone ready?"

"Hi, Bernie. We're number five to present to the judges. So, maybe pretty soon. I think we're ready. We've been practicing what each of us has to say for hours and hours. Smithy drew up our fluid flow diagrams, and we got our safety protocol all prepared. We wouldn't have gotten this far if it hadn't been for your mentoring, Bernie. I want to thank you for your help."

Bernie stumbled for what else to say or do. He knew once the team judging started he would have to leave the floor and rejoin his mom and sister in the stands, but he wanted to remain and talk with Brooklyn. I'm…ah…glad I could—"

Brooklyn realized that Bernie was searching for what to say. "Is your dad here?" she asked.

'Ah…no. Just my mom and sister. They flew up two days ago. Maybe you...ah… "

"Bernie, there's something I want to tell you. When you disappeared from the hotel, we were all worried, but your dad was devastated. He desperately wanted to find you, and took on a really big risk to his own life by letting himself be kidnapped. You've got a wonderful father, Bernie. I wish I had a father like him."

Bernie grinned and relaxed. "Yeah, he's pretty great." He glanced around the room at the other teams. "You know, you guys only have maybe thirteen teams to beat."

"Thirteen?" replied Brooklyn. "I thought there were..."

"A couple of teams didn't qualify," responded Bernie.

Brooklyn glanced over at the Wolverine team talking about their ROV with Jenny Marks from the *Juneau Empire*. Their ROV looked much more maneuverable than her team's. It had four thrusters attached to its frame. The Hoonah Braves' ROV only had two.

"Oh, but one of them is the Wolverines from South Anchorage. They're going to be tough," said Brooklyn.

The rest of the Hoonah Braves were now listening to their conversation with worried looks on their faces. "Try not to worry about the Wolverines, guys," said Bernie. "Don't let their reputation get to you mentally. Focus on everything you practiced. You know what the underwater tasks are going to be, have done them all, and your ROV handled them perfectly." He started to leave but hesitated. "Here's a little tip. For every minute under the allowable fifteen minutes, a team is awarded bonus points. Those bonus points could be important to winning or losing."

Bernie noticed something different with the Hoonah team's ROV. It had a name stenciled on the upper buoyancy tanks. They had named it STIKEEN.

Brooklyn caught him puzzling over the name. "When John Muir, an early explorer, traveled about Southeast Alaska, he had a little dog named Stikeen. Like Muir, we're going to go places with STIKEEN, our ROV."

"That's a great name," replied Bernie. "So, be careful and watch your time."

"Okay, we'll do our best," replied Brooklyn. One of the MATE volunteers approached their table and asked them to pack up and head for the hallway outside the presentation room.

"Ah...I see a lot of people wearing maroon," said Bernie as he started to leave. "Looks like your team has a bunch of fans here. Did Flo, I mean your mom, come over from Hoonah?"

Brooklyn giggled. "She's wearing a maroon shirt along with the other fans from Hoonah. She's having the time of her life."

"Ah...I better go. We'll be cheering for the Hoonah Braves. Good luck!"

"If we win, we will see each other at the regionals. We're gonna beat those South Bend Sea Lions," said Brooklyn.

Bernie smiled as he turned and started to walk away. "Don't count on that. The Wolverines are a cake walk compared to us."

"Hah! We'll see about that." She smiled and joined her team that was heading for the presentation room.

In the afternoon, the teams were escorted to the pool to compete in the underwater phase of the competition. Each team had five minutes to move into the Mission Station and manually launch their ROV. Then they had fifteen minutes to perform all of the tasks at different stations on the bottom of the pool. Three of the remaining teams were unable to get their ROVs to operate and received no score. The other newbie teams didn't score well. Most of them had not practiced with their ROVs, as Bernie had assumed would happen.

With the scores for the morning session posted, Bernie got super excited. Only two teams had perfect scores—the Wolverines and the Hoonah Braves. A couple of teams trailed by ten or fifteen points, but it looked like it was going to be a two-horse race. Just as his own competition had played out, the team to beat was up first. As expected, the superior ROV launched by the Wolverines performed beautifully. While the Wolverines completed all five required underwater tasks, they encountered a last-minute problem. Their ROV got hung up on a corner of one of the pipe boxes that represented a sunken vessel. They used up their fifteen minutes getting unstuck, and their ROV was still underwater when the clock started running on the five minutes allowed for demobilization. They were penalized one point for taking too long to clear the Mission Station. Bernie thought the Braves now had a chance to win.

The Braves moved to the Mission Station to the screams of their high school classmates and families from Hoonah. Brooklyn's mom was one of the louder screamers for the Braves. All of the hours working under Mr. Tee's mentoring paid off for the team. Their setup was flawless, and they had STIKEEN in the pool ready to lower ahead of time, waiting for the judges to determine that all safety rules had been met. A buzzer sounded and the Braves lowered their ROV. Fourteen minutes later they retrieved STIKEEN, and when their score was posted, they were given bonus points.

The Hoonah Braves had won and began jumping and hugging each other. Brooklyn broke away and waved to her mom. Then she looked for Bernie. He saw her searching the crowd and waved frantically. Brooklyn spotted him, waved, and blew him a kiss.

Bernie was ecstatic. He jumped up and down yelling with the rest of the Hoonah fans. Turning to Sally he said, "I sure wish Dad had been here to see them win."

"Oh, I think your dad is enjoying himself wherever he is at the moment."

***

Ten miles north of Juneau, Earl Armstrong and Leon Pence had just anchored their chartered thirty-two-foot boat. They had fishing poles all set and were sitting back, waiting for a halibut to take the bait. Leon relaxed, put his feet on the rail, and stared at an unbelievably beautiful view of the snow-covered Chilkat Range towering high above the calm waters of Lynn Canal. Two humpback whales were feeding about a mile from their boat.

"I now know why Eddie loved being here in Alaska," said Leon. "He was an artist, and there is an inspiration everywhere you look—the mountains, the water, the wildlife."

"Yeah, and Rahman squashed him like he was a mosquito—just a damn nuisance to his business," replied Earl. "Both Eddie and Raz Hunt got in his way and..." Earl's cell phone vibrated in his shirt pocket. The caller ID said Ron Pike. "Good morning, Ron," he said. "What's happening in the Lower 48? You should be up here. It's a gorgeous day." He listened for a few seconds and then replied. "That's great. My friend Leon will be glad to hear the insurance company agreed to pay on the claim. I'll talk to you when I get home, Ron—if I can convince myself and the family to leave Alaska. Bye."

Leon smiled. "Toss me one of those beers from the cooler, Earl."